*T*hat Time
of Year

*For Eve, with
warm wishes,*

That Time of Year

of Year

A Novel

Edward Engelberg

iUniverse, Inc.

New York Lincoln Shanghai

That Time of Year
A Novel

iUniverse books may be ordered through booksellers or by contacting:

iUniverse
2021 Pine Lake Road, Suite 100
Lincoln, NE 68512
www.iuniverse.com
1-800-Authors (1-800-288-4677)

This is a work of fiction. All of the characters, names, incidents, organizations, and dialogue in this novel are either the products of the author's imagination or are used fictitiously.

ISBN: 978-0-595-42299-9 (pbk)
ISBN: 978-0-595-86637-3 (ebk)

Printed in the United States of America

FOR ELAINE

AUTHOR'S NOTE

In view of certain recent events in the world of books, the author feels compelled to make the following statements:

This work is not a fictional autobiography, nor is it a disguised memoir. It is not an autobiographical piece of fiction.

The author was a professor of literature in a university near Boston. He is married and has three children.

He retired on his own terms, but without any doubts.

That is where the similarities between the author's life and this work end. As proclaimed in the official disclaimer: this is a work of fiction.

ACKNOWLEDGMENTS

Over the years, as this book took shape, many have encouraged me. I thank them all.

Others have read the evolving manuscript, sometimes several versions. To these I am much indebted, and I single them out by name:

First, family: my wife, Elaine, who always urged me forward; my son, Stephen, who has done so much; his wife, Gabrielle Glaser; my sister, Melly Resnicow. And dear friends: Fedor Kuritzkes and his wife, Théa; Philip Winsor; Joseph Ratner and his wife, Esther; Robert Szulkin; Alan Lelchuk; Paula Barker Duffy. Their collective wisdom made this a better book.

I am grateful to Nancy Rosenfeld for her advice, and to Robin Dutcher for her excellent initial editing.

My thanks to Kristin Oomen of iUniverse for her courtesy and patience; and to Brian Harrah of "The Oregonian" for his meticulous copy editing.

I wish to express my gratitude to three teachers who transformed my love of language into a passion: Bernard Malamud, Erasmus Hall Evening High School; Hy Lichtenstein and David Boroff, Brooklyn College, Evening Session. No one of them is responsible for any shortcomings.

That time of year thou mayst in me behold
When yellow leaves, or none, or few, do hang
Upon those boughs which shake against the cold,
Bare ruined choirs, where late the sweet birds sang ...

—Shakespeare, Sonnet 73

Fall

Prologue

She would be trouble. I knew the moment I saw her sitting against my office door, arms akimbo, her head bent toward me, its straight dark hair flowing; quizzical, imploring eyes, a faux Mona Lisa smile framed to seduce sympathy. You get to know all the signals after forty years of teaching. The crossed legs suggested serenity; the arms sent quite another message: not the peace of the Buddha, that's for sure.

"Hi? Professor Morris?"

"That's me."

She stood up, a tall girl in neat jeans and a flower-covered summer blouse. "Can I see you for a minute? I'm registered for your poetry course? I hope I'm not bothering—?"

"No, no. Sure. Let me open this door."

And I welcomed myself back to familiar surroundings. Maintenance had recently washed and waxed the floor. My shoes detected the stickiness, and I inhaled an acrid smell of detergent. Outsourced now, these professional cleaners left messages of intruders. Bookcases were moved an inch or two—I noticed black outlines where they had been—and my desk faced the wrong way; the computer wires were a tangled mess. This time they had broken my mug, for I spied only the white handle on top of a file cabinet.

I almost forgot my uninvited guest standing in the doorway.

"Sorry, bit of a mess. Come on in. Take a seat."

She sat on a chair I pulled over from a corner and then crossed her arms and smiled as if posing for a photograph. "I'm Milicent L. Jacobs, Milicent with one 'l' because I never had a middle initial, and I wanted one *soooo* much, so I took the second 'l' out and made it my initial." She looked at me like a child who had accomplished something very mighty and deserved praise.

"Nice," I said. "How can I help?"

"Well, I want to get started? I came for a book list? Can I have one?" Her inflection rose to a question every time.

"Gladly, except it's not ready. Have to check the bookstore and make sure everything's in. But I can write out some titles."

"Awesome, that's great?"

I wrote down the names of the volumes we would use on a note card and placed a star next to the first one. Custodians would need to move the desk; I sat down facing the window.

"You know, poetry—well, it's not the same as reading novels. I mean you're welcome to start, sure, and I've starred the first book, but I'm not sure how much it will help."

She looked glum but took the sheet. "Cool? Nothing like getting that first step, right? I so *absolutely* want to get going?"

I took her words to suit me. "Right," and I got up, because frankly it wasn't time for students yet, and I wanted her to get going. She had intruded too early; and besides she struck me as one of those not yet able to distinguish a poem from a novel. Good luck, Milicent with one "l"! She got the point, rose and smiled broadly again. I showed her the door and she said in a whisper as she left, "Bye?"

I had always returned to my office well before Labor Day, the weekend when the campus erupted into a circus of arrival and orientation. The roads around the university became almost impassable. SUVs and U-Hauls snaked uncertainly, stopping for directions; parents and incoming students zigzagged like a disturbed anthill; furniture, stereo equipment, computers and printers rose in perilously stacked piles everywhere; student guides directed operations with relished authority to the relief of hopelessly lost parents asking myriad questions. Anyone with sense knew to stay away.

Today the campus was quiet. Summer session had ended, and only a few early arrivals and staff strolled along the walkways. I had dropped a bundle of mail on the desk, and it had by now slid apart as if exhausted under its own weight. I glanced quickly at each piece as I worked my way through the pile, putting aside unwanted book catalogs and redundant notices.

Always I had treasured the surge of energy, the pleasurable anticipation flowing through me just before classes began each fall. Despite all the anxieties—Did the books arrive? Were there enough? Was the class list accurate? The room, was it posted correctly? Did they bring sufficient chairs?—the new smiling, shy faces would greet me with a beginning, a renewal, another year to do what I loved and had been doing for so long. But today—actually before today, maybe some months ago (was it longer?)—my pauses of doubt—how will it be?—accentuated melancholy. Looking at my syllabus now, I heard my stomach growl. Last year, to be honest (well, even the year before that) could hardly be counted a triumph. In the fall I had my encounters with that small class of twelve, only about half of whom ever managed to come. They turned sullen mid-semester, fought me on everything, made faces whenever I assigned a paper, turned in sloppy work. And in the spring I had walked into a large class that kept diminishing. Signing drop slips the first two weeks became a ritual. I had been bewildered, angry, embarrassed. But I also had been blessed with a really splendid group of seniors who came dutifully and produced fine papers and engaged me in weighty class discussions.

If I now felt a little lack of bounce, blame it on the weather, for a storm was rolling over the campus and the thunderclaps were very loud for so little rain. Should I leave or wait it out? Why drive in the rain? It wouldn't last long. Leaning back in my chair, I turned toward the window and gazed at one of the few trees on this part of the campus. To my surprise, some leaves here and there were actually beginning to turn. They looked dry and tired, despite the light drizzle.

I fumbled in the mail pile for a manila envelope. Every year I opened it, glanced at the capital letters identifying it clearly, and sent it unread into the trash. Today I opened it, removed the booklet, and began to read. Someday I would retire. Someday. When *I* chose to. After all I still had a few months to go till Medicare age. Now I glanced down the first page headed "Getting Started," which began cheerily: "Dear Colleague: Retirement? You never know when that thought might enter your mind, so this little primer has been prepared as a guide for when that moment arrives. But you might wish to read it at any time, at any age. It's just our present for the future." Punning? Indeed. For those interested, Retirement Seminars were available three times a year (in a bottom drawer I had actually saved some brochures), and experts would lead explanatory sessions on financial implications, etc. There was more, lots more. But now I placed my present back into the manila, made a forward pass toward my future but missed, and I had to get up, bend down, and slide the large envelope into the trashcan. A twinge in my back.

The rain, little as it was, had stopped. As I looked out the window, the glistening leaves were barely wet. On a branch nearby a small, bright yellow bird landed gracefully. We appeared to be staring at each other. There was no sound, and once alighted on the branch, the bird perched in unnatural silence. It did not move, and its beak was shut. Still, for whatever reason, its presence sent a happy message coursing through my body. This time the thought of beginning classes brought a joyful quiver. Yes, at it again. I did really love all this, another beginning. The many-colored coat of fall leaves and brisk October days were not far off—my favorite season. As I rose to leave, I saw the bird fly away. It had delivered its cheerful message, time for it to move on as well.

I heard a familiar voice at my door. Leon Adler, friend and colleague, was teasing me about being here so early, beating everyone to the punch. But I teased back, well, what about you, and he said he was picking up *David Copperfield* for his daughter. Sure, I bet! But he did not relent and wagged his finger at me, called out "compulsive Jack." Then we waved to each other. "See you in the salt mines on Tuesday," I said, just happy to hear Leon's voice. He guffawed and we walked in different directions. My step was lively, the air was cleared, and I smiled as I recalled Milicent L. Jacobs. When I told Julianna about the silent bird that had made me so happy, she was surprised that it did not make a sound. She thought it was a songbird, a yellow-rump warbler. Well, for me it had no song, only a dignified stare.

I spoke to Leon Adler once more. On Tuesday we lunched briefly, but later when our classes began he rushed past me, on the run as usual, his trim athlete's figure in a rhythmic trot. Wednesday I had no classes until late afternoon, and Thursday I was busy all day with students and teaching. That night the phone rang around eight. It was Leon's daughter, Rachel, and she was crying. "Mom said to call you," she said, "something terrible has happened to Dad."

Shortly after Leon had gone to his study after dinner, his wife, Natasha, heard a loud thump. She had rushed up to find her husband lying on the floor. By the time the ambulance arrived, Leon Adler was dead.

A hasty family-only burial was arranged on Long Island before sundown on Friday. Leon's parents, both killed in an auto accident, were buried there, and long before Leon was married they had bought two plots next to theirs. Natasha decided to honor their wishes. Our Hillel rabbi arranged for the memorial service on Sunday.

1

After a summer so hot, so humid, so dry that some of the dearly tended plants in our garden had fallen early victim to drought, my wife Julianna and I were preparing for Leon Adler's memorial service.

"Dark suit?" I asked, though I knew the answer.

"Think so. It's in the garment bag in the attic, the one on wheels. Better let it air out."

Julianna was Chair of the history department. She was not a "spousal hire." She arrived on her own merits, a degree in hand, only a few years behind me, and all that after raising three children to school age. And she was sought after, quickly tenured, promoted, and honored. Her first book won accolades crowned with a prestigious prize.

I opened the door to the attic and slowly climbed the wide, wooden steps. By the time I reached the top, I was taking deep breaths. In front of the garment bag on wheels was a stack of five or six liquor boxes filled with memorabilia (Julianna called it "junk"). I pulled over an old wooden rocker, slumped into it and opened a box filled with papers in manila envelopes: English 11, English 120. These dated from my first teaching job at a state university in the Midwest. As I lifted the folders, one came to view marked "Award." I opened it and there, enclosed in translucent plastic, was my teaching award. After my name, written in large calligraphy, it said simply "Excellence in Teaching, The John S. Hallmayer Award." Now the piece of paper brought back memories of my salad days, but one didn't use that expression anymore. Once I had said it in class, and the students wanted to know what it meant—had I been a vegetarian?

Freshmen (these days they were "first year students") had come from all the state high schools. Matriculation was a revolving door, and many did not make it past the first year. But the survivors were fresh as Midwest country air, eager, polite, anxious to succeed, many the first in their family to attend college. Pride of achievement glowed on their healthy faces, and though they were rarely sophisticated or knowledgeable when they began a course, by the end of the semester most were sated with discoveries of worlds hardly ever dreamt about. Even the city students were awed in class, confronting what they imagined to be their authoritative sages. Most of all I marveled at their curiosity, their generous ways. In those days, just as the sixties loomed, you still called them "Mr. Jones," or "Miss Smith," and the wealthier women hosted Sunday tea parties at their sororities, dressed in satin, shaking hands with white gloves, pearls around their necks; the men wore blazers and ties. I remembered with a certain fondness the football players, huge fellows with puzzled, sensitive eyes (the faculty dubbed them Teddy Bears), who never ceased trying and were grateful for a C-. It was a different time. Students were of another breed; but so was I.

I placed the teaching award back into the box, unzipped the garment bag, and removed the all-season blue serge suit. It smelled of pine. Julianna was right, it would need an airing.

I had last worn it to the memorial service for Sean O'Connell, acerbic art historian, respected but disliked. It was the first day of March last year, which had been blustery following a mild end of February. Julianna was off to one of her conferences in Vermont, where the sap was running. And when she returned later that afternoon she reported sightings of snowdrops and an aborted crocus or two. Even here, lining the highways, willows had, appropriately enough, wept yellow, and the rhododendron leaves extended horizontal, almost rigid. I had gone to the service as a colleague, out of respect for a man the priest had called a "perfect servant of God."

That night we had dinner with the Adlers in a small Mediterranean bistro near Harvard Square; good food, noisy ambience. But who cared? We had a playful argument over whether to order red or white wine since Leon was the only one who had ordered meat. Now Leon was gone. Just like that.

Julianna and I ate our meager lunch in silence and without appetite. In moments of crisis Julianna was quiet; her tall slender body rigid, her large dark eyes focused unnaturally on her plate, on the carpet, straight ahead. Holding herself together. She left the table and slipped into a dark dress, and I also changed into my dark suit. As I walked to fetch the paper from its tube, the first acorns crunched underfoot; two squirrels playfully crisscrossed the driveway in pursuit of each other; a lonely pinecone lay by the mailbox, still greenish. The air was cool for this early in September, but I knew it would warm up again, as far as into late October, our New England Indian summer.

We walked slowly to the car, which I had moved out of the garage to warm up. The abnormally cold night and the frostiness had momentarily silenced the black screams of the crows. Of course, they would be back. As I pulled out of the driveway, I noticed small mementos of light and dark brown at the edge of the house.

"Dog's been here," I grumbled. Julianna, looking straight ahead, seemed not to hear.

I now sat again near the back in the same lecture hall where O'Connell had been remembered. This time I was comforted to have Julianna sitting beside me. Leon Adler had been a good friend, not merely a colleague. An athlete who worked out devotedly, his handsome face tanned by the summer sun, he had few, if any, gray hairs. Everyone agreed that fifty-five was an "untimely" age to die. Recently I had been seduced to an earnest reading of W. B. Yeats, and some lines surfaced,

> Or what worse evil come—
>
> The death of friends ...

It was my project, not to replace T. S. Eliot, but to teach him extensively, so I had been preparing myself.

The doctors said it was an aneurysm, one that had most likely been hibernating in Leon's brain since birth, waiting for its moment to awake, attack, and accomplish its deed. As I sat in a narrow wooden chair, raincoat over my lap, I listened to every word, not because words helped me to understand anything but because I waited for them to help. They didn't.

Having flown back from Paris from his year abroad, Leon Adler's son, David, looking somnambulant with jet lag and white-faced with shock, read John Donne's "Death, Be Not Proud." Whispering without emotion, in a flat voice, he exhaled the words: "Death, be not proud, though some have called thee/Mighty, and dreadful, for thou art not so...." Oh, yes, I said silently, thou art mighty. And dreadful, too. I glanced toward the front where the family sat: Leon's wife, Natasha, and her two other children: Benjamin and his younger sister, Rachel, both still in high school. Natasha's parents sat stiffly; Leon's two sisters were next to the children; and other family I did not know sat in the row behind. Most of these faces were frozen.

Natasha sat upright, rather queenly, staring straight ahead. She was an Israeli born to a Yemenite mother (whose deep brown complexion she had inherited) and a Russian father (who was a physician). After living in Israel for years, her parents immigrated to the States. Natasha shone with a silently vivacious nature, and her slight accent sang sweetly without the harshness of some sabras. As yet I saw no one from my department, but I sighted others from the university and we nodded our heads slightly. It was a bit like being in an old silent film. Julianna quietly took my hand, and its warmth, its life, made me feel safer.

Aneurysm. I did not really understand aneurysm, but the thought that Leon had been walking through life with a "time bomb" since birth (that's what most people were calling it) was unsettling. In Leon, I had found a kindred spirit, a decent younger colleague, energetically bright. Our wives spent a good deal of time together. Natasha was an amateur painter, and when she settled in for a visit (that's the way she put it), she would be cloistered for weeks in the studio Leon had added to their house. At other times she stayed away from the studio for weeks. "The muse is capricious," she often said, shrugging or smiling impishly. Everyone liked Leon and Natasha.

Aside from extended family from both sides, many neighbors and friends outside the college community filled the chapel, and the university was well represented. Now and then my eyes now made contact with department colleagues, and quiet signs of recognition passed between us. Shock, sorrow, and genuine incomprehension projected a tactile presence. One heard it in the silence. Certainly no signs of acceptance.

What was I searching for? Confirmation of grief? Signs of reassurance? I found only tears, some quiet sobs broke through the silence; but mostly there was disbelief in staring eyes, closed lips, lined brows. How could such a thing happen? The rabbi read a homily and spoke warmly, anecdotally.

"Once when Leon and I played tennis, he hit one out. He was sure it was in and we argued mildly, but then Leon said, 'Rabbi Josh, I know better than to take you on. With your connections, I'd rather be wrong even when I'm right!' Then he smiled and hit a true winner."

A ripple of barely audible chuckles filled the chapel, and some heads nodded, almost imperceptibly. Well, yes, they seemed to say, that was Leon. *Was.* Julianna again squeezed my hand, just barely. She did not turn her head.

Maybe the ball *was* in, I bet it was.

Then I returned to listen and, at the same time, mouthed with closed lips the word "aneurysm" over and over. And from birth? Just like that? Aneurysm.

Today was Sunday. On Tuesday, first day of classes, we were both rushed, but during our quick lunch we had talked about children and the future. The Adlers were planning a mid-year trip to Aruba, their first such adventure, since the children were now older but still willing to travel with their parents. That, I had said, would stop soon, so yes, yes, do it! Leon had laughed out loud in anticipation. Even then that sneaky aneurysm had been preparing for the kill.

Leon's brother was delivering a eulogy, and through the low voice my mind wandered, guiltily and without reason, to Milicent L. Jacobs. I should not be thinking of this, I said to myself, it's unseemly. But I could not help it. How would this play out? Ms. Jacobs would struggle mightily with the course, and then, at the end, would she appear in the office with that half smile, her enlarged, perhaps even watery eyes, imploring me for a better grade?

I drifted back to the service. No, we don't grow old alone, I knew that. This brings pain, and I suppose also comfort, but I had not arrived at comfort. As I scanned the faces, I realized we grow old together, with our wives, children, friends. One day we notice we're visiting hospitals, homes of the ill or recovering, even the dying—or, as we soon would, the survivors of the dead. Recently Julianna sent me to buy a Sympathy card for a neighbor's wife who had died. As I walked in search of it, I passed the birthday section and my eyes caught a huge card decorated with a cake and scores of lit candles. But it had become a reverse celebration, one candle going out here, another there. Gone. Gone. Leon gone, and so much sooner than he should. How I ached!

Yes, you attend overcrowded and long memorials, like this one, where family and friends struggle to sum up the life of the departed in a paltry hour. Sometimes you drive to cemeteries, in any season a cold journey. I was selfishly glad we had been spared the burial, the hollow sound of shovel-fulls of dirt landing on the coffin, the sobs, the sounds of grief. We would drive back to the house, where people would pick joylessly but greedily from overloaded plates. We would leave with guilty relief and think, Who of us is next?

I had not thought that much about death before Leon's catastrophe. But this past summer an impersonal, capricious squatter took up residence on occasion, a vagrant, who disappeared for a week at a time and then returned sneering—so you thought I was gone, well I'm not. By late summer I slept fitfully at times, and some dreams were the usual anxiety scenarios before starting the semester: I could not find the room; I was late; I forgot my book and notes; I was in my pajamas or, worse, stark naked. But there were also darker dreams, some approaching nightmares. I recalled no details from those dreams except that they were discomforting, noiselessly dark. Then some physical newcomers made their visits, too.

After the service everyone was invited to the Adler home. At the exits men in black suits distributed maps (most of us did not need any). As we wedged into the car, Julianna's eyes were moist. "God," she said simply, clicking in her seat belt. "I was so very fond of him." She shook her head, she had loosened. "So very much!"

"I know. So was I. So was everyone. Is it dumb to repeat that cliché about good people dying young?"

"No … No." She blew her nose, energetically.

Writing of the death of even a younger man, Yeats had asked, "What made us dream he could comb grey hair?" What indeed?

The drive to the Adlers was not long and was completed in silence. Small groups gathered in various parts of the house, as if for some sort of party. I noticed Rachel standing by herself staring out of the window. Looking for someone? For her father? With all those people milling around, balancing paper plates and Styrofoam cups, we did not stay long. Later we would pay a private Shiva call. Natasha understood. I disliked the after-memorial receptions more than anything else in this ritual of death.

Fall semester had only just begun, I was thinking, and we would have to juggle courses, find someone temporary. My attention was repeatedly interrupted. Throughout the service I had tried to understand something, but I had understood nothing. Except that Leon was dead, had left a widow and three children, and had been slipped into the newly dug earth somewhere on Long Island, near parents who had been there for decades and had the foresight to make sure their son and some future wife had two plots. This aneurysm was perhaps a gift on the day he was born. A cruel way of thinking, but couldn't it have waited, say, another ten or twenty years? What had prompted it to blow itself up just now?

As we pulled into our driveway a light rain began to fall. It had turned mild. As I knew they would, the crows had returned and their shrillness was now especially unwelcome. Once we were inside the front door, Julianna hugged me tightly, and without saying a word we both understood. For the first time in our lives together (and that was now nearly forty years) a chill blew past us—no, not so much past as *through* us—and it had a peculiarly unfamiliar and unpleasant feel to it. It said something like, "You are not protected either." Julianna began to sob and I held her tightly and kissed her forehead and kept saying, "I know, I know." It was some time before she ceased to weep, and my own eyes were not exactly dry.

Leon Adler's sudden death had inflicted a deep wound, but in the days and weeks that followed I could not properly begin to mourn him. In time, yes. But not yet. A few days after the memorial service, one morning after class, I entered his office which was unlocked. Shutting the door, I made my way to his desk, but I did not sit down on his chair, which I felt was still occupied. His desk was not neatly organized, rather left by someone who certainly expected to return. Life interrupted. An open book, several closed ones stacked on top of one another, a yellow legal pad with half a page written, a pen. Even the computer had not been shut down, and its whirring sounds made the whole scene appear all too normal. Any moment now Leon would come back to his office. Man interrupted. The blinds were up, and since the office faced east, the sunlight filled it. I simply stood at first, then sat on the wooden chair next to the desk, where Leon talked to his students. Like mine, his office was lined with bookcases and their multi-colored spines, and the light and shade dancing their ballet almost made the otherwise dowdy office look festive. Leon had also put down an inexpensive patterned carpet, and its reds and yellows were a cheery counterpoint to the gray walls. I should have done so as well, wanted to, but somehow never got around to it. On the little wall space there was, he had hung a few posters and one of Natasha's drawings, a small but beautiful pastel of a seaside, ocean waves billowing against rocks. Familiar stuff, but it bore her mark, strong, assertive strokes, resembling Japanese prints to which she willingly acknowledged her debt.

Nothing seemed to suggest Leon's absence, except his corporal self was not present. His coffee mug was empty but the bottom rim was circled with residue. No time to have cleaned it? I was tempted as I held it in my hand: go to the water cooler and wash it out, but I dared not. Gingerly I placed it back on his desk. How long I stood there, I can't say, but longer than a few minutes. I was numbed, until the sunlight moved a little, and I was ready to leave.

The open book on the desk was irresistible. I took a step toward his desk chair and leaned over *David Copperfield.* Ha! I thought you were bringing it for Rachel that day in late August when you chided me for being compulsively early in my office! I realized I was almost saying it aloud, and I responded for Leon, in my mind: but I was! Oh, really? Probably reading it again so you can help her? Yes, that's right. Great book! Poor David, fatherless and then motherless, so young! Well, yes, but now you left three of yours fatherless—not so young maybe. No reply to that. But so began my conversations with Leon Adler.

As quietly as I had come I left, shut the door and told our secretary to silence the computer.

Absentmindedly almost, I understood that as Leon's friend I would be asked to speak on behalf of the department, to deliver the memorial minute (which was actually more like five minutes) at our first faculty meeting, only days away. I shuddered at the thought. Often I had listened to these, but I had never been the speaker. Mostly the audience was politely indifferent and inattentive. Some doodled, some read through materials, discreetly; some whispered; a few listened. How to do all this in five minutes, to talk about a man's life meaningfully, unsentimentally, but with feeling? Loss is perhaps better left to silence. Words can demean the occasion. But I would have to do it, there was no way not to. Natasha would be there, and perhaps the children. It was done at the start of the meeting, and after a few moments of silence we would move forward with the business of life—agendas, motions, announcements, discussions, arguments. University business was then followed by the introductions of new faculty members. Goodbye. Hello.

What an absurd juxtaposition, come to think of it.

2

Physical intrusions became more insistent after Leon's memorial, so the call to Dr. Julius Hoffman, who ordered endless tests. Julianna noticed some changes, remarked on my fatigue, but I simply said that the new semester already tired me, and Leon's death was still so close, and mostly I believed it. I made light of it all, not wanting to worry her or myself. She looked at me skeptically, but did not press. But I also missed sharing and the certain reassurance that would follow.

Sometimes, during the morning shave, I did not like the face in the mirror: it was paler, and some deeper furrows curved across the brows continuing down to lines beneath the eyes. I was aware of my thinning hair, the bald spot visible when I bent a little. Running my comb through my hair left silvery strands between its teeth, which scraped my scalp. For the first time I *noticed*: aging is for real.

And since Leon's sudden death, the abstract had become more personal. Occasionally now I really did begin to think of *my* death. Oh, it would come to me as well. But how? Sudden? An aneurysm? A hammer blow to the chest? A precipitous loss of balance? A car you barely saw coming? Or slow? Surgeries, tubes, long weeks and months of pain, a gradual withering away? On occasion my dreams woke me, and I was in a sweat. Recently I suffered from sudden, if transient, anxiety. In a few short months I had become vulnerable in ways totally new, and Leon's death had really speeded up what had been a more casual state of mind. Now I worried too much about everything. Like wealth, the acquisition of loved ones multiplies the risks of loss. I fretted about the children, Julianna, myself. What embraced me at unsuspecting moments was this sense of vague dispossession, lost time, nameless regrets and self-reproaches, disappointment, self-recriminations for not having loved enough, and sometimes—when melancholy—feelings of not having been loved enough. Once I recalled the first girl who kissed me on the lips and whispered, "I love you, I love you!" I was sixteen. Her lips had burned mine. It was unsettling, this remembering of things past while looking ahead to a shrinking life. I shuddered. Not yet! But at times I almost lost my bearings, felt trapped, fixed, nailed to the present where the future seemed too short. Then I'd recover, get busy, push away those uninvited brooding battalions. But it was an effort. There were moments when it seemed as if I were holding a door shut with both hands against an onrushing wave.

So I could hardly believe that a mere month after Leon Adler had collapsed into death, I was sitting on a round swivel stool in my doctor's office, waiting. Waiting for a verdict. All tests had been completed, now the grade. I had been Dr. Julius Hoffman's patient for almost twenty years. We had a polite relationship that ventured slightly beyond professional: the doctor called me "Jack," but I never got up the courage to say "Julius," just things like "Hi." A few minutes of chitchat about children, travel, and politics were the norm during checkups, when the doctor was unhurried. But this was a special visit prompted by those strange symptoms, followed by tests with needles, scans with magnets, probings with ultrasound, invasions of orifices by fingers and instruments. I held a *Field & Stream* in my hands (actually it rested on my almost bare forelegs), feeling chilled. After all, I was clad only in one of those scanty short polka dot straight jackets which one can never reach behind to tie, so that the strings dangle and you scrunch your body to keep yourself reasonably covered. Dolefully I took at the bare examining room, with peeling paint on the corners of ceiling and wall. Hissing sounds of steam escaped from a small, rusty radiator, but at the same time the warmth of a sunny early October day penetrated the clouded windows.

There was a knock on the door, and Dr. Hoffman, a nearly bald man in his fifties, entered, nodded a greeting with a smile. "Hi, Jack," and then he bent over his chart, noiselessly and expressionless. Of this I immediately made something: he is hiding the bad news by pretending to look at the file. Or is he rereading the results to be absolutely certain before pronouncing sentence? In fact, I mused, he looked a little like a television drama judge, glasses halfway down the nose, intent, hesitant, ominously silent. In a gesture of feigned indifference, I pretended to be reading *Field & Stream* and waited.

Under Dr. Hoffman's arm was a large envelope from which he removed white-on-black plastic sheets. He slid a few of these x-rays into illuminated background panels, and I listened to the rustle of the sheets and then heard the sharp click-click-click as each picture was secured for the expert's eye. Julius Hoffman cleared his throat. Bad sign. Bad news. I stared at these incomprehensible images of my body. Click.

"Jack," came the voice, steady, non-committal (another bad sign?), "we just can't find anything dramatic here. I'm not overly worried." I took note of the word: "overly."

But the remaining conversation was an anti-climax. Just wait, observe, report back—in a month, or earlier if I needed. No, there were no more tests right now. He had been careful and screened everything out. Oh, it might get better on its own; yes, it might get worse, too. No it wasn't all in my head, but anxiety is bad. He wrote a prescription for a mild tranquilizer, which I stuck into the back pocket of my pants hanging from a hook. I shouldn't be concerned. He wasn't, he repeated. "Meanwhile, get on with your life," he said cheerily. How was my youngest? Settled in New York? He was obviously done with me. Yes, in computers. "Glad to hear that," he said and smiled. "See you in a month!"

I transferred the prescription into my wallet and headed for Hazel, the office manager, to make my appointment. She was a Rubenesque woman in her forties, whom I liked. A month exactly, November 9th. "Kristallnacht," I heard myself saying, the night of broken glass, of which I had scarcely any memory.

She smiled a friendly good-bye. I was out the door and, as if waiting for me, the elevator was standing there wide open. Three floors down I stepped out into the balmy, bright sunshine. I did not immediately walk to my car a block or so away, with a meter probably expired and no doubt a ticket under the wipers. Instead I leaned against a lamppost and turned my face toward the blinding October sun, closed my eyes and surrendered to the deceptive warmth, thrilled at the prospect that fall was holding on.

Get on with my life, I'd been told, but then what was this life I was supposed to be getting on with? I was happily married to a fine woman and an outstanding scholar who was awaiting proofs of her second book, a massive manuscript. She was unhappy with the prospect of a colon in her title, but I reassured her that a trade publisher would be on her side. And I turned out to be right.

We met at a graduate student party hosted by one of the young assistant professors; Julianna was among a handful of undergraduates invited, and I was a third year teaching assistant. Our romance blossomed after she graduated; before that it had been a friendship. Marriage was postponed until I landed my first job. I was a careful man. After years of laboring through that grueling climb toward tenure, we began bringing children to life, two boys and two girls.

Miranda was the first, now teaching English in a public high school in Washington, D. C., a challenge she was born to meet, her brave new world. During a recent phone call she hinted that she was thinking of marrying her live-in lawyer friend, Robert, but she had hinted before. Several times. When Miranda first met him she referred to him as Bob, but then told family and friends that he would prefer to be called Robert. Well, why not? Some Dicks, her younger sister had said with a straight face, insist on being called Richard. Besides Robert suited him better. They had been living together for three years, known each other for four. Miranda was thirty.

Helen, the second daughter, after two years of Peace Corps in Guatemala, was a senior at Berkeley, too far from home but a marvelous excuse for travel to San Francisco, which we so much loved. Every semester, it seemed, Helen had a different boyfriend. And every Thanksgiving she was likely to bring one home. Who would it be this year?

We had wanted a son, and so two years after Helen, Nathan arrived. But Nathan had not survived. Born prematurely, his tiny, frail body was burdened with a compromised immune system, and he died before we could count out two months of his life. But we had given him a name, taken him home after four weeks, attended him around the clock, and then buried him. I was so grief-stricken I needed counseling. It helped, but when I now summoned up Nathan (admittedly on rare occasions), the dark pain returned and hung around like a mist, longer than it should have. Almost immediately, we tried for another child, and to our great joy Seth arrived, on time and healthy—Seth the wanderer. He was taking a "time out" as he called it between high school and college. Actually he first called it a "rest" and was now settled in New York. Anyway this "time out," or whatever you call it, was becoming a little more permanent. A year passed; then a second. Now it was nearly three. Slowly we began to accept that Seth was not college-bound. We thought it was foolish and told him so but shed no tears. "Not everyone is cut out for college," Julianna said, "we more than anybody know that." I had nodded, ruefully.

After being tenured in the Midwest state university, we moved East. For these past thirty years I had settled into the English department where I had moved up rapidly. In a sentence: I was a decent teacher and had gained some recognition as a scholar, having published a fair number of books. Respected as a steady member of my university community, appointed to countless committees, a fraternal brother of a casual posse of luncheon friends, I reassured myself that my life was, in fact, something rather pleasant to get back to. Except now it would be without Leon.

Of course, there was all that peculiar business that had sent me to the doctor. And something else was nagging me. Someone at lunch had mentioned retirement, and I recalled that late day in August when I read the first paragraphs of the "Retirement Procedures," the day when Milicent L. Jacobs sat in front of my office door. I had thrown the envelope into the basket because the very word fought me. Not I? There were years ahead. By law I could stay on forever, and some of my colleagues took that seriously. "They'll drag me out in a pine box," they said. That's not the way I would go, if I had any say about it, but my time would come, and I was certain I would know when it did. Just thinking about it brought me to a place I didn't like, an unfamiliar acreage where I felt a stranger to myself.

I had begun to read obituaries age-first. I ignored the older ages (you have to die sometime) but took note of the disturbing numbers, 46, 57, 63, 68. In the *Chronicle of Higher Education*, to which I faithfully subscribed, the ages were, to be honest, mostly reassuring. Each week it listed a good many 80s and 90s, those leisurely academics of another generation, whose exercise had probably consisted of snail-paced walks on level campus walkways, who just saved their hearts and each afternoon drank sherry, which may have been the elixir that pushed them into old age. Occasionally, when my eyes scrolled down the names, I would find an old teacher, or a former colleague, a fellow student from graduate school, once even someone who, I learned later, had died of AIDS.

Heading for sixty-five, once the traditional and mandated retirement age, I began to pay some attention to certain realities even while dismissing them. Was it Leon's death? My symptoms? Something had awakened an awareness of some finality, some ending.

One evening I casually broached the general subject of retirement with Julianna. Someone in the French department we knew had just announced his intention to call it quits. We guessed he was in his mid-sixties. I had never before thought about the five-year age difference with Julianna, but now I realized it would count. Perhaps half-consciously I had wanted to test her reaction. She had looked at me with wide eyes and arched eyebrows.

"Well," she had said, "academics don't retire. I mean teaching, yes. But our work—"

"Yes, yes," I agreed, "our work," but I didn't volunteer that I was beginning to feel a little weary of "work," and the realization of that came over me so unexpectedly that I almost surprised myself. No more was said, but I knew I had planted an unthinkable thought and it would not quickly wilt. I changed the subject to our possible mid-spring trip to New Mexico, a part of the country we both wanted to see. Julianna's eyes brightened.

By this time I had reached the car (no ticket, small victory), adjusted my sun shields, fastened my seat belt, and felt pleased. Switching on NPR, I found myself in the middle of a discussion on health care for the elderly. Not now, thanks. I quickly slipped Mozart's *Elvira Madigan* into the CD deck and started driving toward campus.

Rolling down Commonwealth Avenue, that perverse road with its service side, its ins and outs, my eyes squinted despite the glasses. But Mozart was joyous, my body collapsed into wellness. I began rehearsing my one o'clock class, "Modern Poets, Ancient Themes," not as catchy as some titles my colleagues had invented, but at least honest.

Today I would continue with T. S. Eliot's *Four Quartets*, with its painfully piercing words everywhere—Between melting and freezing

The soul's sap quivers. The lines surfaced from mind to lips, like a swimmer breaking through the water after a deep dive. I heard myself saying them, whispering them, and then the sun faded a little. Something in *my* soul quivered.

Driving through the open steel-spiked gates of the university, I felt at home. With a late nineteenth-century look (though it was actually built in the nineteen-twenties), the campus was shaped like a large quadrangle, and my four story home was to the left. Buildings crowded against one another, most of them red brick, though a few new ones sported chalk gray. In the middle of the quadrangle rose an island of older structures, including the library and the administration building. Trees were far and few between, except in that middle oasis, where they blossomed in spring and were now dying in brilliant fall colors. Generally the campus was a pretty flat and unimpressive place, though the middle was raised on a slight hill, "the City of God," some mockingly christened it since, after all, that is where the power lived. When you visited the deans, you had to climb your way. Often I had wondered whether a descent would have been more appropriate, but hadn't Heraclitus said that the way up and the way down are the same? It was the very epigraph to the *Quartets* I had discussed the first day of class. It had been a difficult class hour; paradox was not exactly their thing.

The parking lot looked full, but next to an oversized SUV, I was sure I spotted a space. As I began my turn I heard the screeching of tires and saw a sleek black BMW convertible cutting me off and slipping into the open space like a laser. I acted without thought. Swinging open my door after putting my car into park, I approached the BMW from which a tall young man emerged, well over six feet, a green book bag slung over his shoulder.

"You have a faculty or staff sticker?" Very close to him, I looked up through the bottom of my bifocals, raising my head. I could feel my neck pounding. Usually I would have let this sort of incident pass with some choice words under my breath. Not today. The young man glared at me. "I got business," he said and began to walk, but I sidestepped, as if guarding a basketball player (which I guessed this fellow was) and blocked him. I now saw clearly his car was marked with a black student sticker that carried no privilege to park here.

"You're not allowed to park here."

"Says who?"

"Says I." I kept looking up at my opponent, who was now raising his arm as if to push me out of the way. Not a violent man, I knew I would resist and, astonished at myself, I raised my arm, hand spread.

With a thin smile he said," Get outta my way old man."

I snapped and grabbed the giant's arm and would have pushed myself into him if Shaunessy, the old-timer security cop, had not shouted, "Hey professor, any trouble?" Shaunessy now stood beside us and I lowered my arm. I was chagrined. "This youngster," I said, knowing at once that, though deliberate, my choice of word was silly, "cut me off and is parked illegally. That's his BMW, right there," and I pointed toward the black convertible. I sounded like a whining snitch. Shaunessy, who knew me well, looked at the car's sticker and shook his head. He was a burly fellow with a large belly hiding his belt buckle.

"Hey kid, move it outta here, okay?"

He turned to me. "Sorry professor." I nodded. For a split second the young man did not move and then he showed a game face and walked very slowly to his car, staring at me over his shoulder with a hatred so intense it made me feel sorry for him—briefly. Shaunessy saluted with a wave of the hand and left, shaking his balding head as the convertible pulled out as slowly as possible. When it reached straight pavement, I heard the tires screech again. I pulled my car into the spot with the final perky strains of the *Elvira Madigan* in my ears, as if they were summons to becalm me. Of course, I knew it was not the illegal parking that had almost driven me to blows, it was the *"old man"* that had struck like a hammer.

A sour taste rose in my mouth. Shutting off the motor I opened the window, and a light warm breeze caressed my face. The acidic intrusion vanished. By the time I walked into my office I was calm, wondering at my bravado. Really! I might have come to blows with this giant! Still, I was pleased with myself but in no mood to teach. Not even the *Quartets*.

> The salt is on the briar rose,
>
> The fog is in the fir trees.

"Down to 210—nearly normal," Stanley Habers said, grinning cheerfully, closing his thumb and forefinger in a circle. He was standing at the now open door, for as usual, Stanley, always knocking hard, without a second's interval had marched in. Dressed in his trademark corduroys and leather boots, he wore his blue and gold "Michigan" T-shirt under a bluish tweed jacket. One of his children had graduated from Michigan, probably ten years ago, and Stanley was a man of loyalties. I had been deep and far, somewhere else, with the briar rose and the fir trees—*had* was the word, for Stanley's invasion startled me. I swiveled my chair in the tiny office I had occupied—Grover Hall 202—since coming to the university, and it had become smaller as I had added bookcases, filing cabinets, computer, and the accumulation of papers and other academic waste that professors collect.

I eyed my intruder quizzically. About 5'8", black bushy hair and sinister thick eyebrows that guarded his charming, wide brown eyes, Stanley Habers had a weight problem, and he had fought it as long as I had known him. To his credit he truly tried, and of late had actually succeeded in losing a few pounds. Hating sports and all exercise, he finally succumbed to the entreaties of his children and pedaled away unhappily on an exercycle, until a famous Boston urologist published a paper, picked up by the media, that the strain of having certain nerves pushing against the bike seat can make you impotent. Habers immediately sold his cycle and purchased an expensive treadmill, which he obviously must have been taking seriously. For a man barely sixty, he was unusually healthy and hated the doctors he was sometimes obliged to see because of weight and cholesterol problems. In any case he certainly didn't look 210 pounds. But, though he avoided the medicine men, as he called them, he was always fearful of major disasters. He seldom flew, and installed so many smoke detectors, so many fire extinguishers in his house, one might have thought he was selling them. Once, when we chatted, I said, "But Stan, disasters are unforeseeable. They generally pounce when least expected. So why dwell on them?" To which Habers had replied, "Precisely because of that. If you let go and stop dwelling on them—you said yourself, 'when least expected,' right?" I had stared at Habers. The logic of preemption was impeccable. There could be no reply.

"Nice going, Stan, but I must have heard you wrong. You're getting to look better every day, no 210!" What did it cost to try a compliment? Besides it was true.

"What the hell, you think I'm talking about my *weight?*"

A little embarrassed, I went over it in my mind: if not weight, blood pressure? That had *two* numbers. I must have looked uncomfortable.

"Cholesterol, schmuck," Stanley came to the rescue. "What's yours?"

Relieved, but I actually did not know. Right now I was concerned about more serious matters that might be going on in my body than cholesterol, but it had always been near normal, and I had forgotten Stanley's. But I should be forgiven, for it might well have been weight or blood pressure. Stanley was a man who talked numbers—two kinds of numbers: those that concerned his (or others') health, and prices. "Seventy-five," he was likely to say, and you had to figure out that it might refer to the cost of some object in his hand, or on his body, or anything in the world really, because the number always preceded whatever it referred to. Today it was cholesterol; tomorrow it could be a stock, just a number hanging out there. Once he had come in looking flushed, hitting his forehead, "Up to 103." To which I replied, "For God's sake Stanley, for an adult that's high fever, get the hell home." And Habers had shot back, "Germtech stock! What fever?" So it went.

"I don't really know," I said with some annoyance, "but I'm glad it's down—yours, I mean." Stanley might tell you exactly how long it took him to drive to Westchester ("one piss and a knee stretch, three hours and twelve minutes!"), or he might discuss the cost of a dinner and then add it up, "Cost to the sonofabitch under ten bucks per person tops, some profit, but it was good, Jack, good. For the three of us, including wine and tip, under $150!" Yes, Stanley was a man of numbers, and despite his own skepticism about doctors, he commented on everyone else's health.

Since his divorce twenty years ago he was playing the field. He never remarried, but was fiercely generous to his two children. Undergraduates were strictly off limits, but he dated and flattered older graduate students. You had to admit he never talked details, kept it all low-key. Sometimes, when he slept with a colleague (none in his own department that I knew about) I would hear of it, but always indirectly. Whatever Habers shared was with a select few, and I had never been among them.

Habers had been a teetotaler until it became public knowledge that wine, especially red, was good for the heart. Then he began to drink it, a bit like starting a baby aspirin regimen, one glass at dinner. But after a while he took a liking to red wine. "If you pay a little more," he once told me, "it's not bad stuff."

By any measure Stanley Habers was the most prolific scholar in the department. His field? Hard to say, since he was always shifting. Like his personality his work was, to say the least, challenging. The first book was arrogantly entitled *The Real Shakespeare*, and it threw down the gauntlet to Shakespeare criticism through the ages. Still it received bouquets for its boldness and defiant originality, and after that books and articles kept coming—but not on Shakespeare. Habers decided he would take on the Romantics next, and then he paid a brief visit to the eighteenth century. Lately he had been much preoccupied with postmodern theater. Provocative, argumentative, but always well documented, his work had gained an international reputation, and as might be expected he wore his fame indifferently, saving his passion for departmental politics, his love life, and campus gossip. Since he was all over the map he could—and did—teach everything, a department's dream. Students loved him—mostly.

When he changed to another area he would organize a flea market for books (he bought everything on the area he was writing about) since there was no more room in his modest house. Most books he generously almost gave away. I treasured the beautiful *Hamlet*, bound in slightly peeling leather, that I had picked out years ago for a few dollars. Profits, said Habers, went for "reinvestment."

"It's not just that it's down. What's important is that the ratio's good. You probably don't even know what it's all about," he said with paternalistic anger. "Don't you take care at all? Your wife should at least get some consideration. It's not fair to her, you know. People die, you know." And I was sure I would now get a long obituary and with all the clinical details. Stanley Habers, standing in the doorway, glared at me through the open door as if a great insult had passed between us. Truth was, at that moment, he genuinely cared what my cholesterol might be.

Of course I *did* know all about cholesterol and ratios (who today didn't?), I just hadn't memorized my exact numbers, or the "ratio," except that it had never been an issue. My wife was none of Stanley's goddamned business! Some of the old impatience surged up briefly. We had never been able to sustain a close friendship, too different in temperament. But, though not buddies, we were campus friends, and when serious, personal matters came up, we had in times past always been able to connect and care. When Habers' son fell ill with bacterial meningitis as a college junior, Julianna and I were there to hold his hand, offer dinner, drive him to the hospital and watch over him a little until the crisis passed. And when I was put to bed with pneumonia, Habers brought food and books, sat by the bed and joked. We seldom really quarreled, and Habers was quick to forget minor squabbles, so our differences never came to anything. Now we were inevitably growing old together, though Habers was in fact nearly five years younger, Julianna's age. Without saying anything to each other, we had gradually arrived at an unspoken and more or less permanent, comfortable flying level where you sometimes end up after intermittent turbulence. Though not intimate we would still talk about personal matters, though less frequently and more discreetly. Care was taken not to offend, yet Habers would still worry what my cholesterol count was. Sometimes even that could be a pain in the ass.

"You're right, Stan, I should know. But it's never been high. So I guess it's not on my mind."

"I can't believe you could have low cholesterol eating all that sweet crap and doing no exercise in your damned lazy life. At least I run the treadmill, though I hate it."

Dangerous weather, and I decided to duck it. For right now I could not cope with Stanley Habers and his cholesterol hysteria. In fact I was waiting for a call from Julianna. With a wave of the hand, Habers left as abruptly as he had appeared, leaving the distinct thump of his tell-tale boots in my ears. It was nearly one o'clock, and I had no time to look over my cards. It's all right, I reassured myself, it would all come right. So far this was a pleasant class, not altogether as bright as one might wish but eager and decent kids. They tried so very hard to listen and follow my journey through each poem, but were obviously—most of the time—at sea. And some were drowning. Julianna had not called. I tried her at home; today was not one of her teaching days. Busy. No call waiting at the university.

Habers and Mozart still in my ears, in that order, I was again startled by a deliberate knock at my door.

"Come in." The door opened and she stood in front of me, this familiar young woman, perhaps a sophomore, since she moved with a certain acclimatized certainty. She wore a long denim skirt and a black turtleneck sweater, the collar floppy and high up nearly touching her deep black hair.

"Hi, Professor Morris? I'm Milicent L. Jacobs? I'm in your class? We met before the semester, you probably forgot—"

Of course I hadn't. She sat in the first row, pretty nearly in front of me, and always had her face bent forward a little, simultaneously clueless and attentive: What does it mean? I'm listening *so* hard!

"Yes, of course. Sit down Milicent. What's on your mind?"

She sat down and immediately pulled her long skirt even further over her closed legs, knees touching. Looking prim and proper, she eyed me with a smile I had seen before.

"Well, professor, I'm in need of help with this poetry? I like novels better? They have plots and characters?"

"Oh, I agree. Poetry *is* harder in lots of ways, as I told you when you first came to see me. Remember? In some ways easier. No plots and characters to remember, except in the really long ones." I was trying to be cheery, but her smile had frozen and stayed the same. "But if you bring me specific questions, I'll try to help."

"Specific—? Well, like I'd like some general—some advice on how—like, like how to read poetry? You know, a way of getting at this stuff?"

I hesitated. "Well, Milicent, there is no general advice on how to read poetry. Just listen in class; read it aloud at home. But if you bring some specific examples—" I repeated and stood up, the signal that the conversation was over. She looked at me for a split second with what I perceived was almost a glare, but her smile was soon back. Now she was standing as well, book bag hanging from her hand. "Okay, see you in class?"

"See you in class. And Milicent—don't worry so much."

She nodded nicely and left.

I looked out of the window at the cornucopia of colors still in the trees and was thinking, she's lonely isn't she? She wants company. Oh, she's having problems with poetry. But she wants to come here and talk. I had seen them before. Often. But lately, I welcomed student visits. I was a little lonely myself, and a visit reassured me.

I tried Julianna again. "Hi."

"Hi! I just got off the phone with Clara over in Anthro, and she's pissed, as am I, about the dean rumors." Clara was one of Julianna's close campus friends whose opinionated ways I disliked.

"Well, Clara would be upset with *any* new dean. We don't even know for sure whether his royal highness is leaving. Just rumors."

"I know. But reliable."

"Oh, well." I couldn't take it seriously any more. "What can happen? Aren't we too old to worry about the new dean?" There was a moment's silence.

"Nooo," she replied slowly and with a trace of surprise, "I don't feel that—"

"Have to run," I said. One o'clock class. See you later. Oh, department meeting, so probably sixish?"

"Okay." The tone was distant, as if Julianna was thinking—perhaps thinking about why her husband no longer cared about who would be dean. I was thinking, too. As I shut my office door and walked toward the classroom, I wondered almost aloud that there was a time I would have cared. Why not now? Truly I could care less who the next dean was. It was becoming clear that I was already, as they say in academe, beginning to emigrate. And that thought made my heart register a couple of hard thumps as I strode toward the classroom.

On my way I looked out the window and beheld groups of students sitting in circles on the grass, their instructors somewhere in the middle, everybody looking happy. This was the kind of day (a sudden burst of unusual sunny warmth) when students would always plead, "Professor Morris, can we have class outside?" And invariably I had to reply, "No, I don't think so. Last time I did that I had ants crawling up my legs." They would guffaw and sigh with resignation, and I always looked a little guilty. The truth was, I disliked teaching outside, for I knew I would compete with nature, animal and human: birds and squirrels and, yes, ants; voices from other nearby collections of students; and the roving eyes of women toward passing men and, of course, of men toward passing women. All this in addition to the noisy cleanup machinery. No thanks. And besides, it would kill my back to squat in the grass without support.

It was stiflingly warm. Students had not yet abandoned their summer wardrobe, if that's what you called it: T-shirts, everything short-sleeved, an occasional light sweater tied around the waist, even some shorts. The lingering summer weather and some other distractions made real teaching almost impossible. Lately I had noticed that mostly women would begin to file out and come back in a steady flow, and eventually I realized what was up. They came to class with water bottles and took swigs every two minutes. One might as well teach in the bathroom! Often I was on the verge of saying something, but how could I put it? Hey guys, your flow disrupts my flow? Drink and pee all you want, but don't do it in my class? So I merely took to staring down some of the students when they left or returned and let it go at that.

Then came the cell phones. Last year in one of my classes, two students, sitting in the back, emitted phone rings, one of them a merry "Mary had a little lamb." I watched in disbelief as students dug out cell phones and whispered into them. I tried staring them down, but a few days later it happened again. So I had made this announcement: "There will be no cell phones in my class! Shut them off and save the batteries. If you need to talk, stay away!" The line was drawn. The two students had glowered at me. One immediately dropped the course. But there were no more ditty rings. But when the laptops appeared, with their incessant click-clacks, I surrendered and said nothing.

The class had not jelled. Though the official shopping period had expired, students were still adding and dropping, and each day brought new faces. Others recounted identical experiences. Changing times. Indeed.

Today we would launch into the first poem of Eliot's *Four Quartets*, "Burnt Norton." As I waited for the buzz of conversation and distant giggle to quiet down (there were some twenty-two registered, and on most days four or five would be absent), I looked at my watch and decided to give them another minute. Usually they would stop on their own, like an audience at a concert hall anticipating the conductor. I sat on top of the desk, and a smiling student's eyes met mine. She was saying "Hello?" with her coded smile: "I am really trying, I don't get it all, but I *am* trying ...?" Reassuringly I smiled back. It was, of course, Milicent L. Jacobs, spelled with one "l." Now I was ready to begin.

"Last time we talked about the title of the whole poem, its musical analogy, why the word 'quartet' ..."

Milicent L. Jacobs was writing all this down while furtively looking up with a slightly furrowed brow. Oh, yes, she *was* trying. Then she leaned over and wrote something on the open page of her neighbor's spiral notebook and took her time. The student seemed annoyed.

"Now in 'Burnt Norton,' Eliot revisits his ancestral past in his adopted England ..."

I listened to myself and knew that I was already beginning to lose some students. My words had a hollow echo boomeranging in my ears. This distant sound of my own voice began some time ago—was it years? Perhaps. Such moments do not signal their appearance. That guest, too, like aging and death, arrives with the sudden arrogant confidence of a devil: "I am here and here to stay!" Well, so be it, so it is. But how had I lost my students? (Could I still say *my*?) Was it my aging or their perpetual youth? A chasm had grown between us, that much I knew. How did I know it? They were still friendly, making an effort to be alert. If anything, they had become more polite and diffident. Was this part of the game—give the poor guy some respect, make believe, and then behind his back talk of the old fart who should retire soon? Oh, he was a *nice* man, all right, but we took the course because—well, because we had to, my boy (or girl) friend is taking it, the hour is right, the poetry looks interesting, the room is close to the dorm, whatever. My student evaluations, once pretty enthusiastic, were lately more polite, discreet, with only the occasional rave and quite a few insults. I tried clutching the memory of my earlier teaching years, but they seemed so long ago that it did not help me to get over the hurt, which thankfully never lasted very long.

My discipline had long ago abandoned me (or had I abandoned it?): I was a casualty of the culture wars and beginning to sound like a curmudgeon who talked about the "good old days" when I could teach difficult texts to eager students and offer a B-without a hysterical onslaught.

I had reached that part of the poem where the poet takes the reader into the poem, and now I was trying to get my students to follow. The professor intercessor; the holy priest facing his congregants; the pied piper. This was the most difficult part of the fifty minute hour: asking them questions, hoping, praying for an answer close enough to allow me to move on with, "Yes, that's to the point. Good. But beyond that ...," and beyond that one prayed there might lie another answer just good enough to get eventually back to what I hoped for. At least I had achieved the obligatory "discussion," which rated high among the questions asked on the student evaluation report, *How to Choose a Professor*.

"'The detail of the pattern is movement,'" I read aloud, "How can that be? How can the detail be movement? Is the pattern moving?" It was not an easy question, it had no one right answer (of course, they were always sure there was one), but I hoped to get something started. Silence. ("Words, after speech, reach/ Into the silence.") As I spoke I scanned the class, made some eye contact, and realized that while Milicent L. Jacobs certainly could claim a smile unique to her-self, others were smiling too. What did those smiles say? A smile of vacancy, a sign, a plea, a protective preemption, a confession of utter incomprehension?

I tried again. "Think of it this way: can a pattern, once you look into a detail of that pattern, move your sight so that it follows that detail in the pattern from its source to its end?" Too twisted and complex, but I had provided a partial answer. Still there was silence, when a hand in the back slowly raised itself sky-ward. It belonged, I was pretty sure, to Sally Jenkins. "Yes, Sally?"

"Uh, what I want to say, is that like—I mean what kind of pattern are we thinking about here? A rug or something?"

Well, that was a good example, but the poet doesn't seem to have *a* particular object in mind. A rug? Well, why not? Let's call it a carpet. Sounds better. (For some reason Leon's office carpet came to mind.) Could be a painting on a vase? Or just a pattern of anything, really. All patterns have details. Sally made furrows on her brow.

"Yeah, but I mean, if it's moving—," and now she was lost. "I guess so," she said unconvincingly (and unconvinced), her words dropping into inaudibility, and I was glad to escape from this messy question. I might have asked a better one. Oh, well. Not a good ending to the hour.

We were not done with "Burnt Norton," but the shuffle of papers, the noise of scraping chair legs—these were the signs that they were done with time, "Ridiculous the waste sad time/Stretching before and after." Milicent L. Jacobs smiled again. Private pact: I have done my best again professor, think well of me, please! Okay, I will, I promise. I will. By the end of term you will have impressed me enough to give you that benefit of the doubt you so fearfully and guilelessly are asking for. Who can resist your terrified smile? Not I, Mona Lisa!

As I walked past the hallway window, I noticed clouds had thinned out the sunlight, and I shivered, touched by a chilly draft. It was the beginning of fall in New England. One day might be summer, the next frost.

Soon I would visit Seth on my trip to New Haven, where my eighty-nine year old father, retired now from Yale for decades, was resident in what was euphemistically called "assisted living." This was a journey always fraught with tension, especially the New Haven part of it, though Seth, if we both worked at it, might be fun. Julianna was not coming, off to a conference in Indiana.

The department meeting was at four. I had scheduled office hours until three, but there were fewer and fewer students dropping in, and for some time now I made them "open" hours. Still, I had to be there and lately had begun to resent this voluntary bondage to emptiness. Yet when students came, I tended to keep them longer than was necessary and then feel guilty for exploiting their time to comfort my loneliness. On occasion students appreciated the attention. At least that's what they said.

As I stared out at the golden and deep red colors of full peak October leaves, I found myself in the neutral zone, that place of reverie where the mind empties itself, becomes vacant of memory, when one simply slumps, tired to the bone, not unlike that filigreed moment before falling into sleep. Dejection? Had I looked into a mirror just now I would have seen a worn face with little color, weary eyelids, unsmiling. What had once worked almost automatically now came, if at all, with great effort. Had I bombed today? Failed again? If there was fault to find where was it? What jury could decide that? What judge could render a sentence? I could sense myself, open-eyed, slowly fading when I heard a noise. Startled I shook my head once, turned my chair toward the door, and saw Milicent L. Jacobs standing in my half open doorway. She was smiling, though not quite the same way she had been a little over an hour ago in class. This was our third encounter today.

"Come in, come in."

She was tentative, hesitated, but then walked in briskly to the chair and sat down. She carried only her notebook, the Eliot, and a little handbag, so as she sat she spread her legs and made a little crater on her denim skirt where she dropped the lot. Looking at her now a second time, close up, I realized that I was seeing her better. Her smile was intact but had closed a little while her dark eyes communicated a nervousness that made me uncomfortable.

"So, Milicent, what brings you back?"

Before I could realize any sequence of events she was in tears, sobbing. I quickly handed her the tissue box I always kept at the ready. Yes, I would need to close the door, which these past few years I never did anymore, whether students were male or female. But this was an emergency.

"Whatever is the matter? 'Burnt Norton'? Or something else?"

"Sorry? I'm really sorry, Professor Morris? I don't usually do this?" She daintily padded her eyes with the tissues she had taken from the box and then blew her nose, rather thoroughly.

I was treading where I shouldn't, since for some time I had made it a rule not to invest in students' private lives. It had simply become a dangerous place to go.

"Not exactly?" She hesitated. "No, not the course?"

"Health?" I said, and then realized at once it was a silly question.

She opened her eyes wide and looked me earnestly in the face. Appearing transformed, looking older than the nineteen or twenty, which was her probable age, she said, "Do you know Mike Schell, he sits next to me?"

I hesitated and tried to connect this name with a face, but I couldn't.

"A friend?"

"A *boy*friend," she said, now dryly, her voice steady.

Ah, I thought, I'm definitely where I don't want to be.

"Well, he and I—he dumped me? After class? Just like that? Said we needed to 'cool it' for a while?" Her lips had tightened.

"I'm sorry, of course." What else could I offer? She needed no more tissues. The box was back on my desk. Why come to me? But I said it a little more tactfully.

"How can I help—?"

"Well, I just *love* your class, but I need to drop it? I have the forms for you to sign?"

I failed to see the logic. Can't you act like adults? Sit apart? Be civilized? All of that went through my mind but not my lips. Instead I tried my best to look compassionate and puzzled.

"Isn't that a bit drastic? Maybe tomorrow …" But she stopped me with a tone that was sharp and a touch resentful.

"Look, it's my private life, professor. I didn't come for counseling. I came to drop the course." And she pushed the drop slip toward me, emphatically. Now there was no smile, and I noticed for the first time that she had dropped the upward rise of her voice. These were not questions; they were commands.

Frankly I was taken aback. I signed the slip and handed it to her without saying a word. She took it, slipped it into her notebook, and rose.

Again she smiled a little. "Thanks. And you're a great teacher? I'll miss 'Burn Norton' and all the rest, but that's life?"

Oh, yes, she would certainly miss burning Norton—and "all the rest." I opened the door.

"Good luck."

"Sure?" And she was gone.

Well, next class I would know who Mike Schell is. But it did not take that long, since fifteen minutes later a young familiar face appeared at the door. I pointed to the chair so recently occupied by Milicent L. Jacobs. He remained standing.

"Mike Schell?"

"Yup. Private stuff. Got to drop the course. Sorry." The last word was an afterthought.

"She dropped the course already. Fifteen minutes ago."

"Yeah. Got to drop it too."

"Whatever for?"

"Private stuff."

"She told me." How unwise to talk so much I thought, but too late.

Silence. The drop card was between thumb and forefinger, offered like a summons.

"Okay, I'll sign it." And I did. "There you are. Anything else?"

"Nope." And Mike Schell shook his head, a little vigorously, and was gone.

I sat back and tried to figure it out. Was it all a ruse? Just a little play? A deception? Go to all that trouble to drop? Did they hate the course that much? Were they laughing and kissing down the hallway somewhere? Shame and anger rose to my cheeks. "To hell with them," I blurted out loud, and then to myself, two papers I don't have to grade!

It was time for the department meeting.

3

The sole agenda item for the meeting was to decide on someone to take over reshuffled courses since Leon Adler's death. Of course, whoever was hired would not "take over" Adler's courses—that was left to me—but a body was needed. The cruel irony did not escape me: I had been charged with finding such a person and would myself be teaching some of the courses of my dead friend. In his generosity, the dean had permitted us to hire someone for the second semester, and if everything worked out we could offer another year. Though the dean mentioned no rank limitation, his salary cap limited the field. The Search Committee of three (Stan Habers, Hal Muzzey and I) had whittled down the list to four, placing at the top a young man, recently anointed with the degree from Penn. The others were risky.

That's not the way everyone would see it. One could expect to hear the usual complaints about age discrimination, the "You never know" voices, and those who sat stony-faced: whatever you want we'll oppose. In particular there were the two oldest members in the department, measured in time of service, Robinson and Bentwick, a medievalist and a scholar of the Renaissance.

Long ago they had forged an alliance, merged as it were into "a single bulwark representing at least four centuries of Western civilization," as some, mimicking their description of themselves, had mischievously described their seamless union. They found their strength in that, and their relationship was as firm as the loyalties of kin. Living only a few blocks apart they drove in and out of the university together in Robinson's car. Apparently Bentwick had never learned to drive. Both had taught at Ivy schools as young men, but neither had made tenure. Some attributed their dour disposition to those disappointments, and there were also whispers about alcohol (and, in earlier times, other stories intended to scandalize), but I was certain the bitterness of rejection decades ago was the real source of their curmudgeonly behavior. In any case, together they faced us in defiance, though their expressions of discontent were always precise and polite. No one could recall when they last voted for a new hire. In their three-piece suits and white starched shirts with subdued ties, they always sat together at meetings. Bentwick displayed a large Phi Beta Kappa key on the middle of his vest, hanging on a disproportionately modest chain. It was rumored that when he was young he pinned it onto his shorts when mowing the lawn. Someone swore he had once seen Bentwick with the key dangling from his swimming trunks. (Everybody dismissed that because we couldn't imagine him in swimming trunks.) At meetings they were mostly silent, but when they spoke it was brief and cutting. They simply voted "no" in causes they knew were lost. And the funny thing was almost everyone respected them; few showed any hostility. (Stanley Habers did.) They were just accepted as confirming and reassuring negatives. The absoluteness of negation was somehow comforting, knowing what was coming, depending on it. But in the end I was certain of a majority, and a young man would be happy—for a year and a half, since what the dean might do after that was predictable. Put it on hold. Of course, the new dean might throw it all out. Do without. You have enough staff to field a football team!

Until recently my department got by and we tolerated one another. Yet the loss of one of our own loosened rather than tightened our bonds. In the last few weeks an unmistakable gloom had set in, irritability was not uncommon, tempers flared, insignificant matters became magnified into major issues, members were insulted by totally unintended words. When the toilet was not working we blamed the secretary, and then the Chair, instead of calling down to maintenance. At first everybody thought it was grief and confusion, but clearly that was an insufficient explanation. We were just letting ourselves be defeated, and if that continued we would end up losers with the dean, who was certainly not fond of us, putting it mildly. Some of us self-consciously validated the familiar adage: academic strife is so petty and intense because the stakes are so low.

I picked up all the folders from the department secretary. Actually the university had changed the designation from secretary to Department Coordinator, but the pay stayed the same. Most of the hot shots had left after a brief stint, but Angelica Pastini-Schwartz had hung on for almost twenty years. Although she was no angel, "Angel" became her name, and at times she could act the part. A divorced single mother of two daughters about the age of my own, she was sharp, steady, and generous—if you were on her right side. If you were not, she could ruin more than your day: she could ruin your life. Her divorce from "Mr. Schwartz" (as she always referred to him) was bitter, but then aren't they all? Their marriage cracked when the children were still in grade school, so she had raised them pretty much by herself. A bit too short for her weight, she was sometimes tagged as looking "strictly Kmart," but she was always neatly dressed and well-groomed. When she had to she took to the computer like fish to water, and often berated me in a friendly way about my outdated "piece of junk," though in time that piece of junk would do me great service. We got along well, and even when I stepped down as Chair, I continued to make her happy with her beloved Belgian chocolates—on Valentine's day, Christmas, Secretary's Week, end of the year, any opportunity. They were not good for her weight, but she would eat them anyhow, so I might as well, on occasion, be the source of her pleasure. What had begun as the smart politics of petty bribery had turned into a genuine habit of affection.

Stanley Habers met me at the door, placed his arm around my shoulder and whispered, "I don't want these two jerks to screw us. If they do I'm not letting it go this time!" I whispered back. "Not to worry I'm a good counter." Stanley was not satisfied. "Well, I counted too, and it's going to be close." I sighed. "No, it won't. Sit down, Stanley. Take a deep breath."

We sat around an oval table in a comfortable lounge. The windows' tan drapes were drawn against the descending sun, but still thin enough to allow considerable light to filter through. Brass tea and coffee urns were at a side table also stacked with paper plates laden with chocolate chip cookies.

Edith Sellers, the department Chair, was a pleasant woman in her forties, hired only six or seven years ago. A specialist in drama, she was remarkably straightforward, but not dramatic herself. Before meetings she tended to be nervous, removing her glasses from her rather small nose and cleaning them repeatedly with tissues. When she was very stressed, and when she thought no one was looking, she would stick her forefinger up her right nostril several times, dart-like, much like a lizard's tongue, as if she were ridding herself of an unbearable itch.

In her second year as Chair she was slowly easing into the mix of personalities. With the death of Leon Adler, the department offered nine voting members and two adjuncts, who were never invited to these meetings.

Edith Sellers' Styrofoam cup was full of coffee and two chocolate chip cookies lay neatly on a napkin, but neither coffee nor cookies would be touched until the end of the meeting. Then she would usually devour the cookies and take a few sips of what was by then surely cold coffee. Her relief was always literally audible. She was happy enough to hand over the meeting to the Chair of the Search Committee "for the replacement of our late colleague, Leon Adler. Jack?"

Having chaired the department twice, I was relaxed. After all, I knew the play and the players and anticipated the plot. In measured words, I presented the case for all four candidates, then singled out the young man from Penn. He looked to us to be the most promising for a temporary replacement.

Then everything went almost as expected, everyone behaved predictably. Hal Muzzey, always looking a bit disheveled, pushed his fingers through his dirty blond hair, and stroking his ample mustache with a little comb (a signal he was about to speak) agreed this was the best candidate. Stanley Habers enumerated three reasons why the committee had chosen this "young fella," and each reason was prefaced with a number—"number one" and so on.

But the department's resident feminist, untenured Carol Gunderson, wondered why there were three male members of the committee selecting a male candidate? She was agitated, and I had not expected that. I tried to explain, but Gunderson, being from Minnesota farm country, liked animal metaphors and said, "horse out of the barn, no?" Actually she had an earthy sense of humor and seemed always to pace her stridency so that she seldom offended. Habers said with some annoyance, "Gunderson, let's not fuss today." That stiffened her back.

"Well, patriarchy lives on! The tyranny of testosterone!"

"I'm no patriarchal tyrant!" he moaned, but she just shrugged and said, "If the shoe fits...."

Habers looked quickly at his boots. "This kind of nonsense is really out of place. For a part-time appointment, Jesus, Carol!"

"It's the principle, but you just can't see that!"

They were shouting now, and before it went further someone had to step in. A soft-spoken Ann Rosenthal, a woman in her fifties, saved us. "May I say something, to move on?" She raised the fairness issue, tugging on the ends of one of her patented shawls (this one was blue and fuzzy) draped around her neck. Never married, I often wondered why. She was handsome, charming, smart, and sensuous—something of a middle-aged pre-Raphaelite (taught Victorian poetry, but not the 90s, "too dirty"). Good people in these folders were being rejected solely on the basis of age. "That's illegal, isn't it?" Again I explained. Habers was exasperated. Edith Sellers spoke quietly. And Ann Rosenthal just nodded with a resigned sigh. Robinson, however, sided with her and said they should not play God. If a fifty-year-old consents to accept an entry level position, that was his business, not ours. As usual Bentwick followed his colleague, brief, quiet voice, uncomfortable. How could we think a young man newly crowned with his Ph. D. could substitute for a full professor? Whatever the rank offered, we need maturity. Habers lost it a bit. He had taken to naming people from the characters of Shakespeare's plays, and was wont to pair them—Othello and Iago, Romeo and Juliet, Rosencrantz and Guildenstern. Mostly he was discreet and did this out of earshot, but now he blurted out, "The two gentlemen from Verona want maturity?" But it went no further since he laughed and said he was only kidding.

As I was just about to close the proceedings, Marvin Golden bestirred himself from his slouched position. Recently tenured, he had almost immediately distanced himself and shown disdain for his colleagues, become aloof and arrogant. It was his opinion that we should get the best in the country even for a brief stint such as this. He assumed we had searched thoroughly? There was a reputation to keep up. But, well, the man from Penn, he allowed, "would do."

So when we voted on paper slips, and the final tally was five in favor (Gunderson obviously voted to approve), two against, and two abstentions—the Chair abstaining by departmental rule. I guessed that Ann was the second abstention. Edith Sellers savored her cookies in large bites, leaving the cold cup of coffee untouched. She thanked everybody and said it was sad to have to make this decision altogether, and reminded of my friend, I thought that was a nice touch. As they walked out of the room Habers and Gunderson chatted amiably, probably apologizing to each other.

Job done, I returned the stack of folders to Angel, bid her good night, and walked to the parking lot.

Almost five-thirty, but the lowering sun still offered plenty of light to see the trees, in shadows now but resplendent in their darkening October colors. Soon the clocks would be turned back, and the dark would come in late afternoon. Alone, strolling toward the car, I found myself, as lately I was wont to, speaking aloud, this time from Yeats:

> The trees are in their autumn beauty,
>
> The woodland paths are dry,
>
> Under the October twilight the water
>
> Mirrors a still sky …

I lingered and, closing my eyes, summoned up—or tried to—Leon Adler. Funny how we cannot retrieve the precise image of someone recently dead, as if something had been ripped from us, there was an open wound there; it would take a while for the image to be reconstituted. Light was failing fast, and the colors of the trees disappeared into a monotone. It was fugitive light now, and I might have to turn on my headlights.

Julianna had broiled a piece of salmon and opened a cheap but decent bottle of Chardonnay. Over dinner I repeated the events of the meeting, and Julianna offered that, in her opinion, Carol Gunderson was right. I said it had been a long day and she backed off, but not without having a last word. "Well, fine, I know Carol can be a pain, but we must be sensitive." Closing my eyes, I thought I felt my eyelids flutter; I was weary.

In my study, I felt the wine had done some good. It had a nice honey color, and though I knew I had drunk more than usual, and that this would tire me more, I had needed it. Besides it was good for the heart, right? Sitting in my study, my mind wandered. Well, wandered was not the right word. Drifted? That was better. Separated from whatever part of the brain that focuses. I was determined to prepare for classes, but couldn't. Taking a few steps to my bookcases, I scanned the titles without aim. Like shoes or shirts my books had become familiar possessions, and not unlike habitual clothes these books had taken on some reassuring power, and many I was able to recognize by shape and color. Sometimes I played games, testing myself. When I missed, as lately I sometimes did, it made me irritable, reacting like an athlete who suspects he has lost a step or two.

Now I sat down and noticed the Yeats volume and opened it to one of the many places I had marked with a card with an inch or so peeking out. I had underlined a familiar line but couldn't even remember doing so: "An aged man is but a paltry thing …" Yeats was just about my age when he wrote that, a little younger, but then that was a time when a man of sixty was "aged." Why did I feel so aged lately? Was it the symptoms that had sent me to Dr. Hoffman and had prompted the ordering of all those tests? The detail was moving in my pattern? But what was that pattern? Not a rug. Was I becoming a "paltry thing"? All I knew was that my reflection, even in the morning shaving mirror, looked a little odd, a little like someone else. The wine must have settled in my head for I jerked it and drew a quick, startled breath. I had nearly dozed off.

By the time we got to bed and shut the light we were both exhausted. Long ago, we had arrived at that comfortable place where we knew each other's instincts, the place of reassuring habit. Lovemaking was less spontaneous and during the week hardly ever. But occasionally Julianna would ask for a quick massage and what she called "a close hold," as she did now, and for her it was an unfailing sleeping potion. I relished these routines, the small habitual rituals that make you feel all is well.

"You know, these two kids dropped my course this morning, nothing remarkable, but I was—still am—so bothered by it."

Julianna, sleepy voice, turned toward me and made a funny face. "Jack, you know how it goes, shopping period and all?"

"It's way past that, you know; it's been a month into the semester. Anyway it was weird."

"Well, true, past official shopping. But they do drop until they can't anymore, and that goes on forever. Shop and drop, you know? Want to talk about it?" She yawned.

I hesitated. "No, not now. I'm bushed! I'll tell you sometime. No big deal, you're right." Of course, it wasn't that she dropped, Milicent L. (*and* her nearly mute boyfriend), it was the way she told me in so many words to mind my own business, dismissive. Ah, forget it. But Milicent L. Jacobs could not be so easily ousted; she sat on my brain and pressed, so much so I was beginning to feel the onset of a genuine headache. So I had trouble falling off, wondering more and more lately how one could time precisely how long it took to fall asleep.

When I saw Milicent L. Jacobs I laughed. She was dressed in a long black robe. Or was it a shiny raincoat? She was smiling, grinning, really. What was she doing here? How did she get in? Stanley Habers, the old heavy Stanley Habers of years ago, wore a buttoned, deep black leather biker's jacket with wide lapels (clearly too tight) girdling white Bermuda shorts. He, too, was grinning. Next to him stood Mike Schell, Milicent's co-conspirator, in torn jeans, and he was shoving a naked, hairless chest at me. Then Stanley Habers stopped grinning and pointed an extraordinarily long silver revolver at my head. In the other hand was a drop slip.

"Listen, you bastard, sign it! I'm dropping your goddamned course because you're a colossal bore! Sign it!" and he waved the gun menacingly. Then all three began to laugh, and Stanley kept shoving his gun toward my head and the drop slip toward my hand in alternating motions.

I awoke with a start and sat against the headboard, fingering the wet pajama collar against my neck. I must have said something because Julianna vaguely brushed her hand over my back.

"Jack? You're in a sweat."

"I'm fine. Go back to sleep, dear."

"Bad dream?"

"Think so."

She was breathing her deep sleep breaths again in no time, but I lay on my back. In recent months falling back to sleep had become harder. A kind of whirling of images, like a rapid slide show, kept me awake for a long time. But, of course, the next morning I could not have said for how long.

4

Has there ever been a son who did not quiver to please his father? Long before Freud, the Russian in his long novel insisted that there was that dreadful pause when all sons want to kill their fathers. In happier times, when students appeared to have more patience, and before the Russian department protested, I had occasionally taught *The Brothers Karamazov*. I wondered whether now I could be objective about what I was beginning to see more personally. "Even fratricidal urges are driven by the hopeless wish to please, to be anointed, not to suffer the fate of Esau; bless me father—for have I sinned?" That was the drift of what I used to tell my students. And do sons know how passionately fathers yearn for *their* acceptance? And, like Abraham, do they also harbor homicidal thoughts? Each time I tunneled into that novel, its mysteries became more transparent. Anyway, you spend half your life craving the love and approval of your parents and the other half craving the love and approval of your children. But that's another story.

Early Friday morning, and I am preparing to visit both father and son, packing for my weekend trip. Julianna is doing the same for her conference. We stand on either side of the king-sized bed, Julianna calm and methodical, I nervous and disorganized.

"It's only a weekend. What on earth are you taking all that stuff for? You'll do yourself in with your back again." She sounds preachy.

"Late October is changeable. It could get cold." I'm defensive.

"Did the forecasts say anything about cold?" She doesn't wait for an answer. She advises me not to pack the thick tan cabled turtleneck, which I'm unsuccessfully attempting to subdue, and suggests I take the blue V-neck instead. I address the thick turtleneck sweater with a hangdog face, then put it aside and lift the blue V-neck out of the drawer. I am edgy, but then she doesn't have to be so lording it. Scowling, I look into space when, startled, I feel her arms around my waist. She has snuck up on me from behind.

"What's the matter?"

As my body relaxes a little, I fold my hands over hers. "Oh, you know. This is always hard."

"New Haven?"

"Yes. And New York."

"But the last visit with your father went fine. You said so yourself. And Seth will be fun. You're so tight. Massage? Quick one?"

"No, thanks. I need to get this finished." She has come around to face me, and I hug her tightly and kiss her forehead.

"I'm sorry I can't come to see Seth."

"I know. Seth *will* be fun," and I'm mentally crossing my fingers.

"You two have been fine lately. More than fine. He loves you so much. Don't crowd him. He wants so much to please—"

Yes, and for once, I want to really please *my* father. She is right; my body was tensing. "Flights okay? I meant to ask, did you get that return time changed?"

"No, but it's okay. I'll be back by about eleven. And you?"

"Oh, you know I don't like night driving, especially alone. I'll shoot for six, or earlier."

"Don't forget Natasha, dinner?"

"You've been talking to her. How is she?"

Julianna hesitates, lifting her head toward the ceiling. "I'm not sure. Much too calm, too accepting. It's going to hit her eventually. It's only been—what? Not even two months? It often happens that way."

"Yes. Well, if I come back before six."

"You will. Call her at the Welcome Center before you hit the Pike, just to confirm. You really should get a cell phone."

"Right. I'll call her from the rest area."

Without understanding why, I was now able to form an image of Leon Adler very clearly. Yes, it would take me time to grieve for my friend. Aneurysm … aneurysm … The word had taken on some chant-like magical qualities. Often I found myself mentally repeating it, until it sounded like a foreign-tongued word, an invocation uttered by some shaman in a distant land, a mantra—but threatening. I had become so obsessed with the word, that one day recently, sitting in my study, I did what scholars do: I looked it up. First I glanced in Webster's unabridged. From the Greeks. No surprise there. "A soft pulsating tumor formed by the unnatural dilation or rupture of an artery." A mixture of poetry and science, what with "soft" and "pulsating" linked to "dilation" (but "unnatural") and "rupture." Clear enough. But I decided to remove my A-O volume of the *Oxford English Dictionary* from its cardboard case and placed it on the stand. Squinting through the magnifying glass, I read, "A morbid dilation of an artery …"; 1656 was apparently its first medical usage. Except for "morbid" I liked the Webster better. Except for "rupture" and "tumor" the word did not sound like a killer. A morbid, soft, pulsating dilation. But it could, it did, kill. Funny how some words that kill you have such musical sounds. Aneurysm did. Cancer didn't. Occlusion sang; blockage not. Lesion was more sonorous than growth, suture bested scar. Researching aneurysm gave me some comfort, and in time the word began to unclaw itself from my mind.

I am brought up short as I hear Julianna snapping her overnight shut. She carries it downstairs. I survey the bed littered with my socks and underwear and four shirts. Four? For two days? By the time I have finally reduced my choices and zipped my hanging bag shut, Julianna has long since come up to kiss me goodbye and sped away in a cab, for Logan.

It had begun a cloudy, mild day, and some fog lingered until I turned south from the Pike onto Route 84 into Connecticut when the sun began to fight its way through. Now I needed the sun-shields, and I fumbled for them in the bin next to the steering column. All the Boston stations were fading, and I shut the radio. Sometimes on long trips I was so intent on driving that silence was welcomed. It also gave me time to concentrate on whatever crowded my mind, a reverie that words or music might break. There was very little traffic on this stretch, and I was driving faster than I realized because suddenly in the rear view mirror I saw flashing lights. My heart skipped a beat. Generally I had no fear of authority, but the police were something else. Looking at my speedometer I read 78, so I immediately released my foot from the accelerator. Some of these Japanese cars glided so smoothly you couldn't feel speed, especially on the open road. To my great relief the flashing lights passed me and sped ahead, but I kept it at seventy. Of course, I might have engaged the cruise control, but I found it too robotic, too out of my hands. I decided to calm myself by putting on a Sinatra disc, my dirty little secret. Saturday night and Seth. I skipped to *Saturday night is the loneliest night of the week ... You could understand this man's words. 'Cause that's the night my sweetie and I used to dance, cheek to cheek ...* I passed the police car, lights flashing, which had pulled behind a sporty red roadster in the breakdown lane. Loosening the gas pedal again, I slowed to sixty-five. Authority. *I sing the song that I used to sing of the memories ...* Yes, I was driving to see my father, and perhaps my heart had thumped a bit more vigorously with authority at my back and authority ahead. Images of Father so crowded my head my temples were throbbing.

Samuel Morissohn (he had almost immediately shortened the name to Morris, added the extra "r," and eliminated the second "s" because the pronunciation would be more English and dropped "ohn" altogether), was a German European, not merely in birth but in spirit. Jacob Morris became Jack. My brother Paul's name needed no alteration. Family lore was that the Morissohns counted themselves among the oldest of German families, originating in Frankfurt some time in the seventeenth century. That segment of the genealogy was accurate, but not until I was writing a high school term paper on my "roots" and talked to my mother did I discover that she had come from a humble family of shop owners in Galicia. As a young girl an aunt had brought her to Germany. Why, I had asked, was this so hush-hush? Well Father did not want that part of the family to interfere with his own lineage; German Jewry was not always welcoming to Jews from the East. Would I please not raise the issue with Father? I promised not to and never have to this day, but I did tell Paul, who sneered, "Snob!"

Before the war Samuel was already making his reputation in Europe as a young, precociously brilliant sociologist, someone sought out. But it was after he came to Yale that he earned his true fame. Some years after the war ended, he and my mother returned every year to vacation overseas, often in Switzerland or Austria. And Samuel Morris had also been invited back to German universities, delivered lectures, received honors and medals, and accepted these as natural consequences of his contributions to knowledge. He was always gracious but never gave anyone the idea that these honors were anything less than deserved, if not expected. (His Jewishness appeared not to trouble him during these return visits to the country that nearly killed him; it was a subject seldom raised.) In looks and manner he began to remind me of Thomas Mann. Though he had lived in America much longer than he had in Europe, he had never been able to adapt. His accent refused to soften, although his English was impeccable; his last books had been written in English, with some help from me—the "expert" as he called me, with slight mockery. There was no acknowledgment of this in the book.

Though he had escaped the worst of the Holocaust, he had been through its beginnings, and our departure was on one of the last ships out, December 1939, more than a year after Kristallnacht. Dismissal from his university post in 1937 had left him desolate, but he wrote with an ardent passion. After that first night of broken glass and fire, he spent a few weeks in Dachau, but that remained a taboo topic. Still, accumulating humiliations had left their mark. My mother was ten years younger but frail. Twelve years ago, without warning, she had died of heart failure. By then they were sleeping in separate bedrooms (her sleeplessness had kept him awake), and one morning my father found her, still fully dressed, slumped on the floor of the tiny sewing room that had been converted into her bedroom.

I was heartbroken. My mother had been the only solid link to family, and her stoicism inspired and at the same time saddened me. And sometimes it angered me against my father. Of my years in Germany, I recalled little; snatches of splintered memories—fragments I had shored against my ruins. Well, there were no ruins to speak of. I had been three.

At the urging of senior colleagues in all the right American universities, my father was finally granted an exit visa to leave with his wife and two sons. (My younger brother, Paul, after wandering around the country, studied engineering, remained single, and has recently more or less retired to live in Santa Fe.)

Our Jewishness was casual, not atypical of German upper class Jewish professionals. In Germany, Samuel Morissohn had taken assimilation for granted, and he had buried my mother's eastern origins. In the world of German academia that was a necessity. He shrugged off the occasional accusations of being a "Jecke" that came his way from his wife's family still living in Poland. Relations were strained. Eventually most of both families would perish in the fires. My father never spoke of this, but something had been ripped from the geography of his body, something slowly was devouring his spirit.

The harsh events of 1938-1939 had contributed to making my father, shortened name not withstanding, an even more distant, almost bitter exile. Gradually he sank into moroseness and depression. At sixty-five, as obliged, he retired from the Yale faculty to universal accolades. Yale had offered to make some "arrangements" to keep him on as an adjunct, but he had refused.

His retirement was a staged extravaganza with dignitaries from the world over delivering long speeches. Neither Paul nor I spoke; we weren't even asked. What could we say? I loved my father, of course, but it was a love that asked desperately for a sign of recognition. Paul sat like a stone statue, and that injured relationship of son to father had a history.

As I passed the long stretch of road toward Hartford I was overcome with a sense of helplessness. How these visits to my father reduced me to nameless terror! I could always feel my body tighten, rebellious signals, old and familiar companions since childhood whenever I was near Father. Of course, matters had worsened since he had moved to "assisted living," where he was just another resident (one dared not say patient), where no one, he claimed, knew him or spoke to him, though in fact he was increasingly becoming deaf and simply could not hear anyone's greetings. A hearing aid was out of the question: he had eyes hadn't he? The increasing signs of old age are seldom a pretty sight, but with Samuel Morris it was truly a slide show of dissolution, though curiously, despite his depression, he never talked of death. What he complained about was his isolation, not his aches and pains. And there was simply no medication for that malady.

I did not look forward to eating in the "dining facility" in this large assisted living compound (it was actually closer to being a fancy nursing home), but if I came and said I had already eaten, my father would simply stare at me accusingly, and I had to watch him eat lustily, for despite his obvious depressive state, he had never lost his appetite. In a flash of sudden defiance, I wondered whether I should pull off the road at the Long Wharf and drive toward New Haven center. Occasionally Julianna and I had stopped at a nice Italian place. I rationalized, Well, I *am* hungry now. There had been no promise to meet for lunch, and in any case my father would not remember. But then, had he ever internalized a memory about his sons? Perhaps, after all, it would give him pleasure to share a meal with me. I drove on.

As I approached Birch Manor. Dozens of tall, lanky white-trunked birches lined both sides of the white-pebbled driveway to the entrance, their leaves rather dry and ready to make their descent with the next wind. A gust shook the bright yellow oval sign BIRCH MANOR. The main building was a melding of Victorian Gingerbread and Colonial, clean and stately, even seductive. Residents were divided into three floors. The top floor housed the most infirm, the moribund, the bed-ridden; the main floor was for the still reasonably robust, those who had decided that "assisted living" with tennis courts, billiards, a gymnasium with all the new machines, and hot tubs was preferable to living in the suburbs, where one had to be at war with snow and leaves, alert to all the challenges of changing seasons and house repairs.

The center floor, where my father lived, housed those in the middle state who had graduated from the first story and, if they lived long enough, would eventually ascend to the third. An inverted Divine Comedy, I commented the first time I saw the layout, where Paradiso occupied the bottom and Hell was where the celestial was supposed to be, where one ascended to suffering and death.

Greetings from the staff were always cheery. "Hi, Professor Morris. How are you? Lost the sun for a while, eh? Had a nice drive? Your father's sitting in the Aquarium Chamber," a room with a large glass enclosure behind which schools of multi-colored fish swam back and forth as if on some exercise regimen, swimming laps. But no matter how clean everything appeared, how spotless and polished, I never failed to detect a faint odor of urine. When I mentioned it to the staff in the early days, I was told politely that I was probably sensitive to the smell of disinfectant.

My father was sitting alone on a leather armchair reading a book. Oh, yes, he still read, but often the same book. Sometimes he was precise as he was wont to be in his days of absolute intellectual rigor. I stood a few feet away from my father and readied myself as if I were meeting a very important stranger on whom much would depend. Like an interview, which each time we met it really was, for I would be judged. I studied his face: a little thinner, a little paler; gray hair still abounding and combed back, no part; a small goatee curling upwards. He was wearing gray flannel slacks, and a navy blazer hung a little loosely over a white shirt graced by a rather red tie. This was teaching dress.

"Hello, Father." "Father" had been the only form of address we had ever known.

"Hello." He had turned up his face.

"What are you reading?"

"My first book. Not bad, actually. I had forgotten I wrote all that."

I nearly laughed but checked myself. "Good! Nice to re-visit old friends."

"Ever read yours? You have, I believe, published a book?"

"Five."

"Oh, yes. Five?" He lifted his eyes.

"Yes, sometimes I browse in my own. It always gives me a strange feeling."

"How so?"

"Well, hard to say. As you said, 'Did I write all that?'"

My father had obviously wandered from the point. "Let's have lunch. I've waited."

"Sure, I'm sorry. Traffic was heavy, and I'm hungry." And we strolled slowly into the adjacent dining room. Of course, he was told to use a walker, but he wouldn't hear of it. So he walked slowly, upright if a little unsteady, using a black walking stick with a faux silver handle. (Early on I had learned never to call it a "cane.")

We sat down at a table for two. Incongruously, the walls were covered with chestnut wood panels, but where the wood ended, friendly pastels (deep rose and yellow), and many lights from the ceiling offered a luminescent cheeriness. One had the feeling that a day care center was being built on the premises of an old English country club. Somehow the contrast was too stark, until in time one got used to it—almost. Sunshine would have helped, but it remained cloudy and gray. Large potted plants stood in the corners. Julianna had once tested the leaves between her thumb and forefinger and proclaimed them as wax.

"So, how are you?"

"How am I? No one knows me here."

"Why not get a hearing aid?" I bit my lips.

"Don't need to. Think I'm deaf?"

"No, but sometimes it could help."

"I hear you fine. They just don't know me. I am no snob, but this isn't Yale, you know."

"No, of course not. But there are some Yale folks here, no?"

"None that I know. Or none that know *me*."

I ordered a tuna salad and an iced tea; my father asked for the steak sandwich with mashed potatoes and black coffee. Watching him, I marveled at how sensitive my father had become to lack of company. In his former life solitude was his haven. Age changes things. Long ago my father had sometimes joked that New Haven was a prophetic and preordained place for him, a new haven of peace and quiet.

"How's your wife?"

"Well, thanks. She sends regrets. Off to a conference. Chairing the department now."

"Hmm."

I observed him eating with relish, wiping his mouth often. Jacket, shirt and tie remained spotless. Cleanly shaven except for his white goatee, sticking out beneath his chin, he looked content and dapper. But I knew this would not last the visit. He had asked about Julianna, even if not by name, but the children had long ago ceased to exist. It was almost as if he had forgotten them, even though they did on occasion visit their grandfather—less and less. For myself, I had scarcely touched my food, but he would take no notice. He had just asked for a refill of the rice pudding dessert and more coffee.

"Why is mother not here? Where is she?" His face had in an instant turned angry. Well, here we are again, I could feel it in my chest, here we are. Sometimes I could change the subject, make him forget.

"Father, I meant to ask you, did you know that Harry Wentworth's son is now a member of our faculty?" The older Wentworth had been a friend and colleague at Yale.

"I asked about mother."

"She couldn't come."

"Why not?"

"She's dead, Father." There was no other way.

"And why is that? When did that happen?"

"A long time ago, Father." I could feel a tingling in my finger tips.

Silence. Father did not look confused or perturbed. In fact he seemed to be tunneling deeply into a long thought about it all.

"Did you see the fish?"

"In the tank where we met? Yes. They're running a race."

A trace of a grin. "Yes, well, that's what living is, eh?"

"Yes. Yes, of course." Then, surprising myself I said "Father, I'll be sixty-five soon. If you didn't have to would you have retired at sixty-five?"

"Retired? Yes, of course." Samuel Morris had swum back into clarity of mind. "Why do you ask? How old are you now?"

Perhaps, I wondered, if you hadn't retired you wouldn't be here? You were forcibly warehoused by law, not by us. Well, an exaggeration, perhaps. Still.

"As I said, I'll be sixty-five come December."

"Really? Why then it's time for you to retire!" It was not a question.

"Laws have changed. I don't have to."

"It's not a question of law. It's the decent thing to do."

"Why ever so?"

"Don't argue," Father said irritably. "It's what's done. Then you can come and stay here. At least I'll know someone."

I seized my father's eyes with my own and wondered if he had slipped back again, that this was not said with any irony but perhaps with genuine child-like desire. I couldn't be sure. But the conversation about retirement had put him into an angry mood. Finally he gave me one of his own looks, not angry, perhaps ironical might be a word, something between a slight sneer and self-satisfied contempt?

"No, Father," I said with rising voice. "I'm not retiring. And please don't lecture me on the right thing to do! Too old for that!" I was almost shouting.

This time my father looked at his son in astonishment, as if he had been struck. The eyes stared into space, unblinking, in disbelief. Something sank inside me. How stupid! But just as quickly my father's face formed the hint of a smile. "Did you enjoy lunch?"

"Yes, Father. Very much." And I said no more about retirement. Why had I brought it up in the first place? Luckily (or was it sadly?), Father would forget it all.

The remaining time we spent in and out of the here and now and the past, but thankfully there were no more queries about lost ones. Some of the time my father would suddenly slide into German, and I listened carefully and nodded. In truth I understood only some of what was said. Complaints. Even the fish were castigated. "Why are they swimming as if they were in a race!" he repeated. "Stupid animals."

After two hours it was time to leave, and parting was sorrow, not sweet, but sorrow.

By the time I was on the road again, I had put a disc in and was relaxing with Schubert's Octet which, depending on traffic, would almost last me to the city. The sun was still under clouds; it would be that way until I reached the Whitestone bridge at dusk. It was good to have some peace again. Only peace is what I did not have, because out of nowhere she stepped forward, Milicent L. Jacobs, who had so abruptly and oddly dropped out of my course. Why that still bothered me I couldn't say, except I disliked her phoniness, I guess, and those dark, angry clouds that shot across her face when I hesitated signing her slip. Oh, well, let it go.

And I did, turning my focus on Seth, of all the children the most mysterious, perhaps complicated is a better word. When he graduated high school, he had no plans for going on. After sixteen years of school ("not counting Kindergarten!"), he pleaded, he needed to be out of school for a while, and though coming from someone who had not worked that hard it seemed an odd thing to say. Julianna and I began calling Seth the "wanderer." First he moved to Seattle, then to Houston, now to New York. Recently there had occasionally been raised voices followed by sullenness on all sides; that was the extent of it. There was never anything to say "sorry" about, nothing to "compromise," nothing to mend. With Seth the only way was to wait, and eventually all would go away. Seth would not exactly laugh and hug (as the other children did), but you knew it was over, you just knew.

We had planned to meet for dinner at an uptown East side Italian place. Seth had suggested it was easier for me to swing down the FDR Drive for a couple of exits, and this was certainly true. Actually Seth had a fairly nice two room apartment close to the old Village, and I planned to stay there overnight. Seth would sleep on the couch. He was making good money and had not borrowed a cent, having always been frugal and insisting he had enough. And apparently he did.

We sat at a corner table covered with a white tablecloth, and clearly the place was run by an Italian family. In fact the waiter's tentative English unmistakably identified him as a recent immigrant. It all reminded me of a little place Julianna and I retreated to back home. Seth convinced me to try the veal marsala. A basket of garlic bread arrived, and Seth ordered a bottle of Chianti Classico. Seth was known here, and the owner, whom he called Fredo, came over and Seth introduced me. "Nice boy," Fredo said, and I nodded. Soon a plate of antipasto arrived, "Compliments, the boss," said the waiter. Seth and I nodded bowed slightly, offering thanks.

We ate and drank the splendid Chianti, and this was going so well, I promised myself I would do nothing to break the spell. Seth was not one to ask much about the family, or to talk about how things were at the university. It wasn't that he didn't care, but these areas seemed to make him feel awkward, because he had no way of weaving a conversation out of it. Besides, any mention of "university" might bring on some pressure about going to one. So we talked a lot about New York—Seth did: all the musicals he had seen, the bustle and life of the city, the great food and all the ethnic restaurants he had eaten in, even in Brooklyn's Brighton Beach, where he and some friends had a great time with Russian fare and the nightspots. Dessert came, sinfully rich.

To Seth's delight, I complimented the delicious meal, and said the wine had gone to my head. I couldn't drink the way I used to. "Once upon a time mother and I could kill a bottle, not any more." Seth laughed. Well, he wouldn't let me drive, he'd take the wheel, he was just fine. I happily agreed, I wouldn't dare drive. Besides it had been a long trip and Seth knew the way. When the check came Seth grabbed it so quickly I was astonished. It seemed prearranged since the waiter practically handed it to him. I protested, but Seth insisted that I was *his* guest.

I was so pleased, I could have purred. Sitting in the car and driving downtown on Second Avenue, on a moonlit night, silence. A soothingly drowsy heaviness descended.

Seth's apartment was on the ground floor, sparsely furnished but immaculate. We sat on the couch and Seth took the remote in his hand. By chance, the Celtics were nearby playing the Nets. Did I want to watch? Sure, if I could keep awake. For a while anyway. I wished Julianna was here; I suddenly felt defenseless. Why? My mind was being colonized by strangers who seemed to dictate my feelings, and I resented it.

Seth clicked the remote. He had changed into a white terry robe and slippers. The game was in progress, Celts down by 12 in the second quarter. I don't know why, but something inside began to grumble. Yes, I knew his limitations in talking about family, but Seth had not asked a word about his grandfather, as if I hadn't even stopped there on the way.

"Seth, you know I saw grandfather."

"Yup."

"Well, you didn't ask me anything about him. He *is* your grandfather!" Silence. "You haven't been there for ages."

Seth looked at me, his dark eyes narrowing. "I know, Dad."

"Well?"

"Well *what?* I'm his grandson."

"Exactly. As I said. What do you mean, 'well what?'—"

He interrupted, his voice rising. "Well what? He didn't even know my name last time! It's as if I'm some intruder! He kept reading. His own book!"

"I know. Look, he's old, and sometimes he's lost."

"Oh? No, that's not it. He's not really lost. He just lost interest in his grandchildren a long, long time ago. And you know it."

I knew Seth was right about that, but his tone was nasty. It provoked me. "You have no right saying that! Now he *is* old and often lost, and you might cheer him up. I mean New Haven? It's a couple of hours by train. Couldn't you do it for me?"

Seth looked incredulous. "For *you?* Sorry, no comprende."

The game was going on, but neither of us was watching.

"Well, comprende please. You're not an adolescent any more. Show some feeling. He's family. No, he can't give back, I know. But really, Seth, it behooves you to respect him. He's not dead yet!" My voice was rising, and Seth noted it, raising his voice to match.

"Hey, you know what Dad? I'm not getting into a shouting match with you about Grandfather. And I'm not taking any orders to see him, either, okay? So if you want to fight, fight alone, 'cause I'm going to the couch. And I don't want any lectures this time of night either! Bed's made. See you in the morning." And with that he made it clear I needed to leave since we were both on the couch.

For a few seconds I sat there and said nothing, looking absently at the screen, but then I grabbed the remote and shut it, mumbled a good night and walked to Seth's bedroom. It had been such a good evening, and I had spoiled it. Or Father had. Seth was not wrong. My father had *never* been interested in his grandchildren, not really. But then wasn't I right, too? Shouldn't an adult grandson overcome all that now? Then I remembered how loath I myself was to visit, and how hard it was, and I wanted to say something conciliatory to Seth, but I just kept sitting on the bed until my eyelids crawled down. I undressed, and once I lay in bed I was full of sorrow and regret. Failed my father, failed my son.

We said our goodbyes after breakfast. About eleven I was pushing my overnight into the trunk.

"Had a good time, Seth. Thanks for dinner. And bed and breakfast!" Father and son eyed each other: each of us was feeling both righteousness and regret. Seth's voice was flat.

"Bye. Have a safe drive."

I wanted to embrace him, but his eyes held me back.

"Next time bring Mom. Bed holds two, in a pinch."

I smiled wanly. Oh, yes, he needed protection. "I will," I said and waved my hand.

Crossing the bridge out of Manhattan, I almost wanted to turn around and give Seth that embrace, but I realized that was folly. There would be another time. Soon, I hoped.

Leaving this early, I would be home with time to spare to have dinner with Natasha. I'd call from the Welcome Center before turning into the Pike. Then a shower, rest up a bit, and drive over. It was all of eight blocks. Once out of New Haven, the traffic thinned, and I always sighed with relief when I swung into 84 toward Hartford. There was just more space, more air, more—well, also knowing I was about halfway home. No CD playing, the radio stations from Boston not yet in range, in silence, I began to shiver. My blue V-neck and thin zippered Windbreaker were not enough, but I disliked running the car heater. Glumly I justified my wanting to take the turtleneck and was angry with Julianna, more angry with myself for not standing my ground. When I neared the rest area beyond the Middletown exit, I pulled in to stretch my legs, visit the urinal, and steady my nerves. Stepping out of the car into a sunny and warm midday, I was now so overheated that sweat trickled down my flushed face. A breeze gently soothed. Julianna had been right about the sweater after all.

Standing over one of the countless sinks in the rest room, I cupped my hands and spilled cold water first over my cheeks, then letting it run on the pulse side of my wrists, something I used to see my mother do on hot days. I was just not feeling myself, as if I were being metamorphosed. Am I, I pondered, becoming a victim of identity theft? And what identity was I left with?

Then I called Natasha from the public phone; she was pleased and happy. "Absolutely, do come, Jack. I so look forward to it." Once in the car, feeling calm and refreshed, I was so warm I shed the Windbreaker. First I'm cold; then hot. I decided the whole episode was not worth any more attention, so I opened a Kit Kat I had bought. Recalling Habers' remarks about my chocolate habit, I curled my lips and prolonged the sweet taste with relish. It would do until Boston. My watch showed one o'clock; I had made good time. By two I would be at my door-step.

And I was, just about that time. The empty house was a tonic. These turn around trips were getting harder. Weary, my back ached, my eyes burned; I didn't bother to park the car in the garage but left it at the end of the driveway, where I bent down to pick up a thick *Globe* and the Sunday *Times* in their white and blue plastic wrappers from the leafy lawn. As I walked toward the house I stepped on a mine field of acorns, feeling and hearing them crack underfoot. The path to the front door was littered with crusty dark pine cones and carpeted with slippery pine needles that inevitably found their way into the house and onto the carpets. It had rained a little and some brown and even red leaves were matted down to the ground forming a multicolored mosaic. A slight gust lifted and twirled a few lost leaves upwards ("The detail in the pattern is movement"), and a few fell onto my shoulders from above. Close to the door I saw evidence of the neighbor's dog again. Indifferent to dogs, this mud-colored mutt I hated. Its name was "Betsy," which I always thought odd, and it belonged to neighbors two doors down, the dentist Dr. Archibald Munken. But his wife, whose name I didn't even know for sure, was the major dog walker, and at all hours she would scream at it, "Betsy! Betsy!" Long ago I had wanted to complain about the dog's deposits all over our property, but Julianna cherished peace and said, "It's good for the plants. Just think of it as fertilizer."

Before entering through the front door I shook the leaves off my shoulders, my hands full of papers, which I deposited on the coffee table. I fetched the over-night bag, and before settling down I made myself a glass of tea and pulled out some pretzels, which were a little stale. Better save the appetite for later. Natasha had said about seven. Fine, that gave me plenty of time. Then I literally collapsed into the living room easy chair and began to read, though very quickly I was fast asleep.

When I woke it was almost dark. It was not a good nap, more like a restless half-sleep. My head ached and I swallowed a couple of aspirins that left a bitter taste in my mouth. It was dusk, and I had just enough time to freshen up with a shower and change of clothes. Once done, I realized I had nothing to bring Natasha, who was not a big wine drinker, so on the way to her house I stopped at the local supermarket and picked out two bunches of chrysanthemums. Like Julianna, Natasha loved flowers.

Without Leon, the Adler house had an altogether different look. Empty. Which it was, since the children were with Natasha's parents in Grosse Point for a long weekend. They would come back Monday and miss a day of school; Natasha thought they needed to be away, and she wanted her own space, a breather to be alone. So she was the sole occupant, except for the old and docile retriever, who sat curled up against an empty lounge chair in the living room, unnaturally listless. Natasha offered me a glass of wine and took one herself.

"Don't drink on my account. I know you don't usually."

"I do now. The feeling of being a little out of it, which I never liked, is now welcome," she said. She was wearing black slacks, a white blouse, and a sea blue cardigan decorated with a subtle gold design in front. She looked very forlorn. I drew a deep breath as it blazed through my mind, What would Julianna do if I left this world before her? Look lost like Natasha in an empty house? Our children were almost permanently secured out-of-home. As I gazed at Natasha I was struck how petite she was, small-boned, but not unnaturally thin, her face not precisely oval with high cheekbones, an elegant nose, large eyes with moderately long lashes, thin lips—all of which I had known, of course. Perhaps I was looking more attentively now.

Awkwardly I stood facing the off-white wall where I was used to seeing Leon's portrait. It still hung there, modest in size, slightly abstract. She had caught Leon in a pensive mood, a barely discernible smile on his lips, in a dark bluish turtleneck sweater, hands folded, hair tousled. It was certainly a likeness, but not meant to be photographic. Ambiguities and ironies were painted into the face, eyebrows raised in question. What was he asking? One of Natasha's best, and it was her only painting she displayed on her walls, except for some funny and colorful silkscreens she had made for the rooms of the children when they were young. Conquered by a feeling of vacancy, unable to come up with anything more original, I asked "How are you doing?"

"'Hanging in there.' Isn't that what people say?" She sipped her wine. "It's not hit yet, I guess. Isn't that another thing they say? Well, to tell the truth, I'm doing lousy, I'm not hanging in there, and it *has* hit—very, very hard. Yes, there is the usual resentment, Why did you do this to me, and all of that, but mainly I cannot, Jack, cannot see any future. I am just past fifty, and the children will be gone soon—David already is, in a way—and then what?"

I guarded against saying something stupid. Anything like "I understand" would have been hollow, and even "I can imagine" was technically a lie, since I couldn't. "You'll find someone else" was out of the question. A man of words I had none to speak. Instead I moved closer, took her hand between mine and squeezed it. She looked at me teary-eyed. This was the time when I ought to be saying wise words expressing deep feelings, I ought to be reassuring and comforting, reminiscing about Leon but without touching the wounds. I ought, I ought. If only I could talk to Natasha as they do in a good old Russian novel, and we would end up both weeping and hugging each other. But none of that happened. Instead Natasha, eyes wide, looked at me intently.

"Thanks, Jack. For not saying anything dumb. That touch of the hand was the best response I could have dreamt of just now. I'm grateful, really. Come, let's eat."

The weekend had been so rough, I was grateful I had not blundered. We moved into the rather spacious dining room where the large table had been shrunk, all the extensions removed. It was already set, and Natasha brought dinner. Of course, I offered to help but she refused, so I sat guiltily while she served.

"Nothing fancy, Jack, just a roast chicken that I bought at the Gourmet Station," she laughed. "Even the potatoes are from there. But I did make the salad." She allowed herself a short laugh.

Mostly we ate in silence, a shared silence, not awkward. She asked about Seth and the other children, we talked about the wonderful Italian restaurant where Seth had taken me (though I omitted our quarrel), about the drive back, the changeable weekend weather. I noticed that she poured a second glass of red wine and was about to tease her, but checked myself. She's hardly going to become an alcoholic, and this new taste for temporary euphoria was better than lots of tranquilizers, and I realized I had never filled Hoffman's prescription: it was neatly folded in my wallet. She broached the subject about Leon's replacement, she had heard some things.

"Well," I said matter-of-factly, "we're looking at a very nice young man. In fact he's coming to campus next week. From Penn. Inexperienced, but at least on paper a better than decent record. Of course, everyone realizes this is not a 'replacement'—I mean—"

"I know. I suppose we're about to say, 'Leon can't be replaced'?" And she actually smiled.

"Well," I offered, "it wouldn't be a lie, but this life is full of ready-made clichés, isn't it?"

"I know. I know. You're so right; we live by offering homilies. But you know it would be a lie. You and I know everyone is replaceable. I don't mean to sound cynical or bitchy, but you have no idea what people write in their notes! 'You're still young, you'll find someone someday …', 'I know how you feel …', 'Our thoughts are with you …'. The hell they are!" she said in a voice unlike her, shrill. "Do you know that one of my neighbors actually hinted that they were interested in this 'big beautiful house' I was surely not going to be living in all alone? Oh, it wasn't direct, but I happen to know they're looking around, and believe me, that's what she was saying."

"Gross!"

"Yes, gross. But then, you know what kills me is that everything does go on, doesn't it? I mean it has to. There's nothing for it, is there? You know, there are times when *I* just go on, sort of mechanically. I shop, I clean, I pay the bills, I even watch dumb TV shows!"

Again I was at a loss. But she rescued me. "Jack, I do so much thank you for coming over after a wicked weekend of driving back and forth." She took my hand quickly, squeezed it, and I got the distinct impression that it was a sign for me to leave now, because she would probably sit down and have a good cry. So I made the obligatory offer to help clean up, which she politely refused. We were standing at the door.

"Thanks for the flowers, Jack. I love chrysanthemums. They are the first confirmation of fall, aren't they? Love to Julianna," and she raised herself up a little on her toes and planted a soft kiss on my cheek. She appeared smaller.

Driving back I shed a tear or two of my own. Whom were they for? For Natasha, of course, and for Leon. And for myself? Entering the garage, I noticed lights in the living room and upstairs. Certain I had turned off everything except the safety-timed lamp in the foyer, I was momentarily confused, even wondering for an instant whether I was in the right house, and then it struck me that perhaps Julianna had caught an early flight after all. As I opened the door I called out, a little anxiously, "Hi!"

"Hi!" Julianna's voice came back from upstairs.

"How come you're home so early?"

"You sound disappointed? Managed the early flight." She stood before me, having changed into her satin blue robe. We embraced and I kissed her cheeks.

"Disappointed?" I chided.

"Just kidding. At Natasha's?"

"Yes. She's not in good shape. Not falling apart or anything but—"

"What did you expect?"

"No—well. You're right. Still. I'm glad I went. We talked. It helped. I think?"

"I'm sure. She's very fond of you. How was the trip back?"

"Long. I can't do this anymore. And I really don't like driving alone, tedious! Seth missed you."

"Next time we'll drive down together. I'm also bushed, falling asleep on my feet. How did it go?"

"Seth?"

"No, your father."

"Oh, all right. You know there's always something. I asked him whether he would have retired if he weren't forced to, and he said of course! He wanted to know how old I was. When I said I was nearing sixty-five he sort of commanded me to retire, too. Right thing to do, he said. And come to live with him."

Julianna stared at me quizzically and couldn't hold back a smile. "But Jack, you know he's not really there. And what did you say?"

"I said absolutely no way would I retire. Law's on my side. I'm afraid I lost it a little. My voice was shrill. I told him not to lecture me. He truly looked—well, hurt or angry or both. But soon he took no notice."

"Good. Well, then, and Seth?"

I hesitated. "Oh that went fine. He paid for dinner. Insisted! He's found himself, I think. But after dinner we had a little spat over his not visiting his grandfather."

Julianna, I thought, was going to give me that "Not again!" look, but she just stared blankly.

Then, at a very slow pace, very quietly, sadly, she said, "I don't want to hear any details tonight, okay?"

I was relieved. "Of course not. How was the conference?"

"Tedious, like your driving alone."

"Barely touched the papers," I said.

"Well, they'll keep. Anyway, I'm going to take up whatever you've read and rest my poor body. Those plane seats are for midgets. I feel crumpled."

"I'll give you a massage."

"Deal."

She was lying on her side reading, her nightgown lowered so that her top was bare. I massaged her back softly and felt my fingertips traveling over some familiar raised birth marks, which I had charted long ago. It was all recognizable geography. My hands passing over a methodically heaving back, I knew she was asleep. So I removed her reading glasses and gathered up the newspapers. On a hunch, I decided to leave her nightgown down so as not to wake her and covered her snugly with the sheet and blanket. Then I quietly dressed myself for bed. Lying on my back and wide awake, I was paying a price for the afternoon nap. Everything roller coasted through my head like tumbleweed. Just before I fell off, I listened to her even breathing with a touch of envy. Wished she were awake.

Why? For reassurance? Inexplicably, a sensation of aloneness swept over me. Failed my father, failed my son, failed my wife.

As soon as I came into the kitchen after shaving and dressing, I knew Julianna, rested, was now ready for "details" about my quarrel with Seth. Her eyes gave her away, open wide and a little piercing.

We sat down to eat breakfast and I told her. It was, after all, not so complicated. I just thought he should visit his grandfather once in a while. Wasn't he old enough to deal with an old man's indifference?

"Twenty-three?" she said. "Well, not really, I think, but that's beside the point. He's hurt by it. As a son aren't you? The issue is that you make Seth feel guilty, you throw recriminations at him!"

"That's a bit strong, don't you think?"

"No, I do not. The thing between you has always been the same. You find fault, you accuse him, you make him feel lousy. He's only a tiny bit older than your students!"

"What the hell have my students to do with any of this?" I was angry now.

"Well, Jack, you do complain about feeling that distance from them. You didn't used to. Maybe you have to think harder now about how to connect with that age. They're young. And Seth is your son and wants approval. After taking you out to dinner? I think it's all very sad."

"And breakfast. Cereal and coffee. You know he doesn't keep bread around." I sounded spiteful, but I was stung at what she had flung at me. "So you think I'm too old to understand the young any more? I can't relate to this 'age' any more? Well, who knows," I finished sarcastically, "you're probably right. Seth, my students, just an old man who can't understand—"

She walked over to me and placed her hand on my shoulder. "Look, that was not nice of me. It kind of slipped out. I really didn't mean it that way. Sorry. I'm just concerned about Seth. This much I meant, you two will both have to deal with each other like adults."

"Oh? I thought you just got through telling me how young he is. Make up your mind?"

"Let's not blow this up. My only wish is peace—at any price! I said I was sorry."

"Well, yes, so you did. How about dropping it? I have a busy day ahead."

And I got up from the table without having touched my breakfast. By evening we will pretend to have forgotten this, but Julianna's comparison of my "distance" from my students to my problems with Seth had truly wounded me, and it would stay that way for more than a day. Mostly because I kept wondering whether she was right.

5

Martin Relling arrived from Logan by cab, and he made a good first impression. Given the casual dress code of the day, he was well but not overdressed: gray slacks and muted blue-patterned sport coat, shirt and paisley tie, and black shoes (*real* shoes, with laces) clean, even polished. Tall and rangy, he sported blond hair neatly parted on the right and a barely visible pencil mustache under his nose.

"Hi, Jack Morris." I stretched out my hand which was firmly grasped by Martin Relling, from Penn. "Good trip up?"

"Thanks. Philly is a short flight. I used to visit someone at Radcliffe."

"Oh, so you know the area?"

Smile. "A little. I used to date this Radcliffe girl."

"Good. Take a seat," and I pointed to the chair of consolation on which Milicent L. Jacobs had briefly sat but which her boyfriend had so unceremoniously declined.

"Let's see, it's eleven. You must have questions before lunch?"

And Martin Relling had a ton of questions. He pulled out a spiral notebook and began in no patterned order: office space, what kind of computer (and its memory capacity), benefits, housing, loans, availability of film and videos, payment for conferences, teaching schedule, salary, chances of reappointment, class size ... The list went on. By the time we got to class size it was time for lunch.

Lunch was at the Faculty Lounge. I had invited Hal Muzzey and Stanley Habers and, of course, Edith Sellers, who as usual was early, sitting rather forlornly at the table set for five. Her non-specific clothes made her look a bit dowdy; around her neck hung what appeared to be an American-Indian bead necklace, decorating the front of a white sweater. She waved her arm. (I had also extended an invitation to Bentwick who, on department stationery, politely declined.)

Edith jumped up from her chair and extended her hand. Just then Stanley Habers and Hal Muzzey walked in, and there were more introductions. Finally we all looked down at our menus, and Habers explained and evaluated the options: "The Reuben is terrific, the chicken Caesar salad is the best, and—"

Martin Relling seemed very much at ease. After the food arrived (he had ordered the chicken Caesar salad), the questioning began haphazardly. I intervened at one point by softly admonishing, "Let the poor man eat!" But actually

Martin Relling had no problem eating and talking between swallows. He seemed eager and prepared. Even when Stanley Habers threw a curve. Why would an Ivy apply here for a one year fill-in? No other offers? Edith stopped her fork in mid-flight and looked at her plate. Relling, however, was unfazed. At least so it appeared. Oh, yes, some offers. But as he told Professor Morris, he used to have a friend at Radcliffe, and he just *loved* this area. Anything to get to Boston for a while. Habers asked what happened to the friend, and Relling said, well, oh, that sort of "fizzled." She had moved on to UCLA Medical School. Well, Habers said, there was no shortage of women here, but Edith decided to change the subject. Relling was turning out to be a perfectly acceptable one-year-plus appointment.

Hal Muzzey tended to be the quiet one; I liked him, had heard him affection-ately called "our minimalist." He was of a slightly younger generation and had joined the department about the time Leon had come. Homing in on the talk, he wondered how Relling would deal with photography *and* cinema in both Ameri-can and British poetry, and for the first time Relling looked a little lost. He spent a few moments gathering himself and was absent-mindedly stabbing at the remains of his salad on which his eyes seemed intently focused. Muzzey took a sip of black coffee and said we would all learn more at the talk. Relling nodded and declined dessert.

The remainder of this lovely October afternoon, almost the last, young Rel-ling spent with the Chair, who presumably showed him the campus. She would take him to the library, the Student Center, show him the gardens around the administration complex, and then deposit him at the Office of Human Support (once known as the Personnel Office) to gather up his booklets on Health Care options and forms about other benefits. No doubt she was also selling the univer-sity and department and, what always worked, the Boston area, which the young man seemed already to know pretty well. I sped off to my two hour seminar.

This seminar of nine, seven women and two men, was in fact the course on "The Fiction of Family" that Leon Adler had been scheduled to teach. I won-dered whether the title (which I kept) was an intentional double entendre? Leon liked to play with words. Actually I was happy to inherit the seminar though, of course, more than a little guilty about the way it had come my way.

At our first few meetings the students were in shock. They had met with Adler only once. At first a sense of disbelief and courtesy perhaps made them appear polite and welcoming, offering reassuring smiles and nodding heads of approval. But the young forget quickly, a month was a year, and as I walked slowly up a flight of stairs, I was mopping a brow that was bone dry. Would there be a mutiny? How many would drop out? Disappointment was sure to take a toll; after all, I was not Leon Adler.

Sitting down at the rectangular table I saw nothing unusual. Eight were present. One woman, who had sighed audibly last week during my presentation, was not in the room. Just as I was ready to begin a hand went up.

"Professor Morris," said a lanky young man with black hair down to his shoulders, "are we going to—well, is there going to be some kind of theoretical angle—I mean Professor Adler said—"

Well, here it was coming, the start of rebellion. I said simply that I was, unfortunately, not Professor Adler: we would start at the beginning, with me. The young man looked unhappy. Another hand went up, a woman who was older than the rest, perhaps a little past forty. She wondered whether discussions were going to permit them to explore—as the "late Professor Adler had committed to—the psychogenic deep structures in the assigned discourses"? Her voice was husky, faux British. Dressed smartly in a blue linen suit, her dark blond hair hanging short and straight, very red lips, she had raised her closed pen from an unopened notebook and held it vertically in her red fingernailed right hand, tapping it lightly. From its gold rings and its golden top, I was almost certain it was a Mont Blanc. I knew Leon would never have said "psychogenic deep structures," but I tried to formulate his response in my head, saying psychology was Professor Adler's special angle, not necessarily mine. I heard myself and knew my voice had been petulant. And I could tell that the woman was insulted by the way she looked away and stared into air. (She sat like that for the remainder of the class, occasionally sighing, or so it sounded to me. The pen had been laid to rest on the notebook.)

It was going badly: they were becoming agitated; I was impatient. In the past I would have handled this better. What was happening here? Something in me was rebelling as well. They were less interested in the works, more hung up on theoretical frameworks that were, just now, in the air.

I staggered on despite the smirk of the long-haired student and the exasperated look on the woman who was hoping for the "psychogenic deep structures." By the end I had won most of them over, and this might all end well? Yes, perhaps.

Sin is Behovely, but

All shall be well …

But my head hung carelessly, eyes down. Yes, it ended well enough, yet the start was an absurd scene, all their phoniness and insensitivity, and my own missteps. Yet I must not give in to bitterness. Please, God, I heard myself say with astonishment, don't make me into an angry sad old man. Not yet. But then, "Why should not old men be mad?" asked Yeats. But, I protested, I'm not yet an old man.

We assembled for Relling's talk in a small lounge. Edith Sellers had made certain that coffee urns, soft drinks, and her salvation chocolate chip cookies were in place, and she was now fussing to arrange them, pushing plates side by side, stacking and unstacking Styrofoam cup towers. A projector for slides and a small white screen stood in their proper places.

She asked me to introduce, so I glanced at some notes I'd made to refresh my memory. Nearly four o'clock and graduate students were still coming in, including three from my seminar. In the front row I noticed "psychogenic deep structures." Her spiral notebook was open, she played a little nervously with her Mont Blanc, and stared straight ahead. Relling looked over his notes, smoothed his blond hair with his palm, perhaps a little repetitively. Undergraduates usually stayed away from these occasions, though a few had come. Someone familiar emerged into my vision, her head hidden by a tall young man. When I bent down to get my folder I saw her clearly—Milicent L. Jacobs, smiling at what or whom who could tell, notebook on lap, pen in hand. Well, what do you know!

I walked over to the table and held on to the wooden lectern. Glancing around I saw that those one would expect from the department seemed to be there, though no Marvin Golden. Bentwick and Robinson were obvious no-shows. So was Ann Rosenthal. I cleared my throat. What to call this young man—Dr., Mr., Martin? I settled on "Dr." I offered the essentials of his young academic life, then added that there would be some opportunity to ask questions, refreshments were available. The title of this talk was "The Poet's Lens: Photography, Cinema, and British and American Poetry, 1920-1950." Relling moved to the lectern looking confident and relaxed. He thanked me. There was one correction—well, not a correction, just a change. Time is so short, he decided it better to focus on photography and British poetry. Maybe we could talk about cinema and American poetry during the question period? The last four words ascended, one higher than the next. Relling gazed almost imploringly at me, as if asking permission. I stole a glance toward Hal Muzzey and detected a faint but benign smirk below his mustache. Then I turned toward Relling and said simply, "Sure. Fine."

Relling spoke with a good voice, made eye contact, but was having a little trouble with his pages, having to skip, one supposed, over the American part of the talk probably crossed out between lunch and now. But all was going well, judging simply by what food critics call "presentation," though I was trying to follow the meaning and had some difficulties. Relling began with the invention of the camera, going back as far as the *camera obscura*. At this rate there wouldn't be enough time even for the abbreviated paper, and the young man would run over and I would then be obliged to step in and somehow bring it all to an end. Then I lost track of the words. Relling was now quoting from *The Waste Land* and its "montage image clusters" whilst clicking some "photographic montage nexuses" onto the white screen. I was certain one of the slides was upside down, but no one seemed to notice. And I was distracted by Leon Adler's voice and lowered my eyes to listen. (I was lately beginning to have these imaginary dialogues with Leon.) Jack, it seemed to be saying, this will do, but it's not vintage stuff. Replacement. Temporary. Okay. You have my vote. Adler's intelligence was clean and sharp. Always diffident about himself but endowed with certainty arrived at slowly and logically, his mind was among the best I had known. Our endless talks had been sustaining me for some time, and his mischievous sense of humor had made me laugh, often at myself. "You're too solemn," he would admonish, and I would nod and agree and chuckle. What would Adler really have said of this talk that I had now ceased to hear?

At this point I had no idea how it was going, though as I raised my eyes, browsing among the faces in the semi-darkened room, I became convinced that most listeners were eager and attentive. Then some stirring in the audience signaled restlessness, and since Relling was running well past the allotted half hour, I raised my hand, which he understood. I had already motioned for the lights to be put on and now stood at the lectern next to young Relling, who had stepped aside. I thanked him for an interesting talk, and called him "Martin."

Good applause. Edith had left her chair and was edging over to the cookies. "We can have a few questions now," I said, and immediately a student's hand went up.

"Yes. I was just wondering. Do you think that the 'lens' you have in your title might be taken—well, put it another way, that the perceiver's lens is bonded, if inverted, with the lens of the perceived?"

Relling did not hesitate. "Yeah, sure. I mean the old subject/object thing is no longer in force in the 1900s. There's a sort of cohabiting—a sort of interchangeability—yeah—"

The student nodded and, satisfied, sat down.

A few more innocent questions followed, all by students. I was about to end when I saw Stanley Habers' hand shoot up as if touched by an electric prod. I felt a twinge but had no choice. Habers *was* the expert on this subject these days, and I was surprised that, preoccupied with the menu, he had not asked anything at lunch.

"Sir, I wonder, going back to the first question, whether the 'subject/object thing,' as you referred to it, can ever be eliminated, even if you're a total solipsist. Who eliminated it? I mean, what the hell, lens or whatever, there's always some *one* who looks at *some* thing. Even if they look at each other—assuming that's what you meant—they don't cancel each other out?" Habers—clear, challenging, blunt. Relling looked pained. I decided to save him and, I justified to myself, everybody else.

"That's a terrific question. Maybe we should loosen up now and move to snacks and continue discussion there. Thanks again ..." Applause. Stirrings. And Habers.

"Not appreciated, Morris. I was asking a serious question!" Habers was in a sweat (the room was overly warm), and his anger showed not in his tone but in the way he stooped down, as his words were hissed into my ear. And he called me by my last name, a bad sign.

"I know, Stan. But we're running over—"

"Bullshit! You stopped me! Why?"

"Because, frankly, it's been a long day for the kid, and he still has to fly back to Philly."

"You're not suggesting I was bullying him?"

I put my arm around Habers' shoulders and said most earnestly, "No, no. Bullying? Last thing on my mind. I meant what I said. Now come on, calm down, go over and have a cookie, and join in," and I gestured to a cookie eating group with drinks in hand that had formed around Relling. From the corner of my eye I could see Edith devouring. And I also caught a brief glimpse of Milicent L. Jacobs. She was gathering some cookies into a paper napkin which she carefully folded and dropped into her book bag. Then she walked briskly off. Our eyes did not meet.

Habers pondered grim-faced and then, smiling a little, said, "Okay, boss, the thin mustachio from Penn will do. I don't eat cookies at five in the afternoon. And you shouldn't either. But the guy's talking garbage, and you know it! See you later." And he fled from the room so quickly I had no chance to reply. But I was unhappy with myself. Damn! How to handle Stanley Habers was again a problem. I shrugged and joined the crowd, removing a Very Fine apple juice from a dish of floating ice water.

Relling was surrounded by students and smiling, in lively conversation. The neatly combed hair had an undone look now, as his brushing it with his palm had obviously inflicted some damage. Shirt was loosened at the neck, tie was pulled down a couple of inches, and he looked like a survivor.

As those colleagues who had come began to drift away, they discreetly handed me their slips: yes or no. Earlier I had picked up some absentee votes. Two letters on department stationery in one envelope: Bentwick's, on a large sheet, said simply "No. B."; Robinson had written on a small sheet, "Sorry, as before: No. Robinson." Golden's note card read, "Okay? Golden." I ignored the question mark. As usual Ann Rosenthal's note was beautifully written and longish, but it ended with a convoluted assent: "Under the circumstances, Jack, I do not wish to make difficulties for you or the department. You have my blessings, reservations notwithstanding. Collegially, Ann." Carol Gunderson's paper was ripped from a spiral notebook. "No problem. Carol G." She did not stay for refreshments.

As agreed beforehand, the committee and the Chair would meet in my office after everyone was gone and Relling had been safely put into a taxi for Logan. That was about to happen. Goodbyes were in order, and a few students said, "Hope to see you," or "Good luck!" I shook Relling's hand. "We expect to get in touch as soon as possible. A few days, Okay? Have a safe flight, and thanks for your visit. Your talk obviously went over well with our students, and they're not an easy sell! A taxi's been called and will be waiting by the front door, and John here," a senior who had worked the slide machine, "will show you where." Relling said his thank you and turned to walk away when he hesitated and turned around. Oh, he'd forgotten to ask about access to the Harvard libraries, and I promised to feed that into our deliberations.

Relling gave a nod. Again he asked when he would hear? I pursed my lips pensively, and promised, "In a few days, a week at the outside." I knew it was pro forma, and I would visit the dean the next day, but you never know, so I gave myself a little extra time. He thanked me, shook my hand, and was off.

Only three of us were sitting in my cramped office. I fished out the slips from my pocket and began by saying I was confident this could be done with dispatch. Six said "Yes." Two against, guess who? And Stan had to leave but gave me the thumbs up. So, I asked Edith whether she had any comments. No, not really, he'll do fine. But she hadn't followed much of what Relling had said, it was jumbled, was she alone? We all shook our heads. Hal Muzzey said that the fellow would be fine. Actually nice, if a little overanxious to please while also pretty sure of himself. But, fine, fine. I agreed. Relling was in.

Almost absent-mindedly I said he had wanted to know what computer memory he would get. Hal Muzzey started to laugh. He was wearing a worn-out brown suede jacket which hung a little lopsided on him, and his shirt pocket had one of those plastic guards and there must have been four pens and three pencils stuck down. He was playing with a pencil now, tapping it on my desk. Its point looked as if it had been sharpened with a pocket knife. Let's face it, he said chuckling, we didn't have computer memories to negotiate in our day, and we all laughed. Done, I said. I would call Relling after seeing the dean. By the way, did they think he'd come? Edith nodded confidently, Hal shrugged.

It would have been over, but I had a question. Just for the record, I asked Hal—since he and Stan were people I trusted—did he feel the way Edith did? About the talk? We had indicated she was not alone in thinking the talk a bit confused? "It was nonsense," Hal said simply. "And it would have been nonsense even if he had not cut it, just more of it. But hey, garbage in, garbage out, no?" Pretty severe for Muzzey, but as always to the point. And I remembered that Habers had used the word "garbage." I could not help thinking what we all must have had on their minds: Had all of just voted for "garbage"? Oh, Leon!

Edith asked for a minute to chat privately.

"Sure," I said, not showing my annoyance; I wanted to go home. Hal walked out with a generic wave.

"What's up?" I looked at her earnest face and I noticed, as I had not at lunch, that she had put some makeup on and had obviously had her almost brunette hair done. Despite her indifferent clothes, she was looking younger, not older—and prettier.

"Oh, it's nothing, Jack." And she began to tell me how she had asked Habers for advice on how to handle Carol Gunderson, who kept pestering her about tenure-schedule, salary, course assignments. (She asked Habers, not me?) She was struggling, twisting a thick silver ring on the middle finger of her right hand. Drawing a deep breath she exhaled. Well, I suggested, Habers was a bit mischievous, was he of help? Yes, he was. He had taken her off campus, to an Indian place. Joked that there were no chocolate chip cookies, did she mind? It was a nice hour or so away from it all.

Well, what wisdom had he offered? He had told her to read Gunderson the riot act, tell her where to get off, she had to learn to be a little more political, more assertive, not so naive, so nice. He had been very sweet, not condescending.

And then what? Well, then he had invited her to dinner at home for the next week, great cook, offered wonderful wine, she drank too much, and then, he flirted … Yes, I understood, I said casually, although I didn't really know how far all this had gone. Edith held back tears as her face reddened.

I said nothing but pointed to myself with a shrug.

Because she thought I'd understand. After all I was the department's elder statesman, its *eminence grise*? She liked Stan, but he was—well, she was scared to start up with him. He was getting too close. She wanted out. Wasn't it a sort of a conflict of interest? With the Chair of the department? She's old-fashioned.

Yes, I saw the point. Actually I didn't, but then this was Edith. And she wanted my advice on how to get out of it? I didn't wait for a reply. With Stan it's more bark than bite. Just say, no thanks. He'll look wounded for a week or so and then he'll make out as if it never happened. It's that simple? She was astonished. But will he tell? That I doubt. I couldn't say, Edith you're not exactly in the category of a grand conquest, if there even had been a conquest. She was so grateful. Maybe I could even talk to him? I was such a good friend? Heavens, if I did that *she* would be the one to have told! Besides, yes, we're friends, but not perhaps the way she thought. In any case, she wouldn't want to be the one to kiss and tell? Of course, she readily agreed, embarrassed, and changed the subject. How was Julianna? Fine, worried about the next dean. So was she. Give her my best. Thanks again. She'd handle it all right, and she was out the door blowing me a kiss and looking very flushed.

Truly, I was thinking, she is a child, a good, a very good child, and she would not handle it all right, and months would pass, and she might be sleeping with Stanley Habers—that is, if what this was about. Should I interfere? "Elder statesman? *Eminence grise*"? That didn't sit well.

As I drove toward my house in the twilight, I saw the tall tree at the end of it, towering over the evergreens. While many other trees still had a little color, this one always stripped itself bare early. A few dried yellow leaves hung on, barely. Fall itself was over. I heard noises overhead and stopped, watching two V shaped formations of geese flying south. Was their screeching a lament or a joyous anticipation? The latter I thought. I envied them. I too wanted to migrate. Yes, that time of year, final days of fall, when you can almost smell winter.

6

The next morning I climbed the little hill to see Dean Walter Scott Livingston. Of English descent (he always told people that on first encounter), his American roots went back a bit in time, since his parents were both born New Yorkers and Walter (named, he claimed, after the novelist, whom he readily conceded he had never read) was born in Brooklyn, though he went to high school in Boston after his parents moved to that city where his father was in some kind of financial business. The dean's reputation, as they say, preceded him: almost everyone was in fear of his burly size and gruff demeanor. Tough, decisive, energetic, even ruthless, his pronouncements exuding finality, Walter Scott Livingston had made some order of what had been, to be candid, a mess.

Himself a computer scientist, he was wary of almost all other disciplines and seemed to have a special contempt for our department. Under the pretense of "taking inventory," he had offered everybody a high memory computer, but infrequent users were left with antiquated ones. (I was among those.) In time he became known as "Sir Walter." His regime had prevailed for nearly five years. Then, in the fall, he apparently had gathered in two or three offers from start up dot-coms but had been cautious. When a well established communications outfit offered him the CEO position, he accepted. Julianna had been right; the rumors had been reliable.

My mission was simple: secure final approval for hiring young Relling. As I walked through the opened door the dean waved his hand, "Com'on in, Jack," as he was bent over his chair staring into an oversized monitor surrounded by several computers and what looked like speakers. A very large man, with a shock of black hair encircling a shiny, large bald spot, Walter Scott Livingston created a presence in his office. He more than occupied its space, literally and figuratively. Indeed, whatever vacuum there might be anywhere around him he amply filled. No matter what the season he wore short-sleeved shirts, and his suit jacket lay crumpled in a corner chair.

"Listen, Jack, let's cut to the chase, I can't give you this one-year-plus appointment." Now he looked up and his clear, hard blue eyes stared into mine. While I respected the dean's no-nonsense efficiency, I distrusted his motives, his voluptuous lust for power that lay behind almost every decision, good or bad. In time I saw Walter Scott Livingston as a caricature of the evil dean in an academic satiric novel, someone neither to fear nor hate but to be wary of when you crossed his path. So I had come to expect the worst from him, but the ambush about Relling staggered even me.

"What are you talking about? That's ridiculous. Why? For three semesters?"

"Ah, yes, why? Why, why, why? The faculty question ad infinitum, eh? Like two year olds! Because, Jack, we cannot see our way to bringing in a fellow for a year and a half at an inflated salary when the courses Adler had can be taught by you or Habers or anyone else, and those courses that are given up can easily be shelved—yours because of low enrollment, and others because the curriculum in your department is getting a little too fulsome—'disgustingly excessive,' I once looked it up. Your department offerings read like a Chinese menu, for God's sake! Besides you're doing fine right now, no?" He had spoken without taking a breath. And now he grinned.

"That's unfair—"

"No, Jack. Here," and he held a stack of papers in his hand. "Go on, look at 'em."

I took them and turned pages. Course enrollment numbers for five years; courses offered for five years; number of majors for five years. And more. The blessings of a dean who worshiped at the altar of the computer printout. And clearly the numbers were declining in each category except in courses offered.

"Whatever these papers say, they're numbers, that's all. These days some classes will get smaller, it's the culture, a trend. That doesn't mean you stop teaching them. Student tastes come and go as quickly as—as a spring shower."

"God, Jack, what poetry! You guys have such a way with words! A 'spring shower'?"

"Don't mock me, okay?" My voice was hoarse with anger.

"How large are the upper level Physics classes? Besides, why make us go through the charade? It cost you and us time and money to get this guy to come and give a talk and—"

"Ah, fratricide among departments. Tsk, tsk. Should I take from Physics and give to English? As for 'charade'—that was an unavoidable delay. Janette, poor thing, was out with the flu, and I got these figures this morning. Sorry."

"But I—"

Walter Scott Livingston interrupted. "But? But whatever it cost is chicken feed compared to a year and a half of salary and benefits. Had I had these printouts last week, I'd have saved us all time and money. Sorry." But the "sorry" rose in an ironic trajectory. "I've called Edith. She could have told you. For Chrissake, she almost cried. What's up with her anyway?"

"Edith is trying hard. I'm not accepting this." My hand was shaking. Though in a rage, energy seemed to be flowing from me.

Walter Scott Livingston swung his swivel chair, got up, turned the chair around and embraced its back with his huge arms, leaning his massive body into his chair so far, my muscles twitched to hold him at bay, expecting him to lunge forward, tip the chair and fall straight into me. I even stretched out both hands in anticipation. But the chair did not tip, the dean did not fall.

"Look here," the dean said calmly, "I know you're an old hand, and I respect you, Morris," reverting to last name, which always signaled hostility, "but you can go to the Pres if you want, or to the Board, or to the student newspaper, because frankly, I don't give a damn. This is what it is, okay? No replacement. Now if you guys can clean up your act down there, maybe in a couple of years we can look for a tenured replacement, eh? I mean your place is a goddamned mess. Look at your wife's department? Tightly run ship. No nonsense. And, yes, they also get replacements, now and again. It's leadership, you know. Julianna's fantastic. What a dean she'd make!" And he opened his blue eyes wide and stared me down. His bushy eyebrows were raised to make him look almost comical, and his shirt collar was unbuttoned, his tie loosened, and beads of sweat stood in little pools on his bald spot.

Swallowing, I passed by the remarks about my wife's department and dismissed mention of Julianna and the deanship as only one of this man's flip comments meant to sting. I knew that any appeal to higher quarters would be politely turned down. One thing this dean had achieved was final say, especially on small matters like a temporary replacement. In fact, no one could point to a single decision that, when appealed, had ever been overturned.

"I'll take it to the department." I spoke quietly, knowing that this would be of no use either. My anger subsided, and slowly I calmed down. There were no alternatives. So I added, "But first, for the record, and I'll do so in writing, I register my protest—my personal protest. You're treating us shabbily. And also, why the need for all the personal abuse? I think I've always been proper with you?"

For an instant the dean looked genuinely contrite, but I recognized the disingenuous facial expression, something like a mock grimace. Rising from his oversized chair, on which he had resumed sitting, with two large steps Walter Scott Livingston had reached me and now placed his huge right hand on my shoulder. "God, Jack, I meant nothing by that. You know me? I'm a New Yorker at heart!

No, honest, you know I wish *you* were Chair again. I like Edith, but she sort of can't hack it. If *you* were there—"

The hand was hurting my shoulder so I disengaged by turning my body ninety degrees, like a running back eluding the tackle of a burly linebacker. It was rank flattery, I knew that and said so. "Edith is just fine. And don't flatter me because it won't get me a replacement. By the way, we fought a lot. You didn't always think me a good Chair. So let's drop that."

Again the dean looked hurt. "But, no, I meant it. Anyway, I know you're the bearer of bad news, but such is life," and he was opening the door. "Take it easy, and hey! You'll all survive. Besides, I have a feeling something good will come of this, don't you? Department's too big anyway. Need to make wise choices in future. Any retirements in the offing? Don't think so. Never know, of course. One day someone'll get tired of it all and decide to go golfing, eh?"

I made no reply. "Wait," the dean said, "you left the stat sheets. Take 'em. Good for the department. Get Edith to convene you all, and then you can digest these stats. Okay?"

And I took the envelope of "stats" and walked with melancholy steps down toward my building, feeling a heaviness in my arms. The paths, I noted, were gathering more litter every day. Cigarette butts, half eaten pizzas, parts of newspapers, Styrofoam cups still full of black coffee—they overflowed the trash cans and made an unsightly border on the grass.

God, Leon, this place is looking like a pig sty! They won't even let us get a temp! A lousy temp! Can you believe that? Calm down, Leon said, save yourself. You know him. But those stat sheets worry me. Got to get the department to become more lively! Yeah, sure. With you gone there's little chance of that! I'm miserable, Leon. I know. Can't you help? But there was no reply.

Just past the library, I caught sight of David Kominsky, a former dean who, virtually collapsing with an ulcer and nerves, was ordered by his doctors to avoid tension. So he resigned in mid-year, some seven or eight years ago and returned to his chemistry lab. The ulcer was gone and the nerves were calmer, but the man had been damaged for life. You could see it in his sunken eyes, and for someone not yet sixty he walked with a pronounced stoop of his shoulders and dragged his feet pushed into sandals, barely lifting them off the ground.

Initially I had no intention of saying anything, but outrage kept inflating like a balloon. For an instant, I was convinced I would be victimized by an aneurysm (still at times a threatening word) if I did not let go. And so I told Kominsky the whole story, in great detail, from beginning to end.

"The dean's a shit," Kominsky said, "what can you do? Maybe the next dean—"

"Well, and who will that be? Julianna has heard rumors. She's worried. And some of her colleagues in History, too."

"Jack, you want to end up like I did?" He placed his hand on his stomach. "Stop worrying! And Julianna, too. It'll only be a change of deans!"

"Have you ever thought of retiring, David?" I had not meant to say it, but the words simply leapt out of my mouth as if I had no control of them.

"Retiring? No, not once. That bum isn't putting thoughts into your head? You're still young, what—sixty one—two?"

"Sixty-five in December." The sky clouded over and it was getting chilly.

"You look younger. Probably because I feel ancient."

"Nonsense. No, no. No such thoughts. But the time will come. And I'll know?"

"Maybe. But they'll carry me out! I'm staying out of spite," and he laughed. "Besides have they *suggested* retirement? You know it's illegal to do that."

I shook my head. "No, no suggestion." But I recalled the dean's remarks about whether there were any retirements in the offing in the department and the snippy remark about someone maybe getting tired enough to opt for golf. But I decided to say nothing of that. Instead, I laughed at myself. "I'm making it sound like premature death! Anyway it's an idle thought I had about the future. I'm nowhere near it. But you know sometimes the whole profession—I don't know. Am I showing signs of senile nostalgia, David? Sometimes—sometimes I feel my shelf life is up—'use by such and such a date.' I mean there are days—"

"You, bitter?"

"Yeah, well. Maybe not bitter but at the least, used up. Ever feel that way these days?"

"No. But you know me. I stay in the lab most of the time and deal with Asian grad students. It's different for you. I've tuned out. Still—" and he placed a hand on my shoulder and I could not help comparing Walter Scott Livingston's heavy paw that pressed me down with the soft small hand that belonged to the gentlest of human beings.

"Don't worry. I guess I'm reacting to Sir Walter. Got to run and tell the department the good news."

"Good luck. And hey, remember," and he put his palm over his stomach again. I managed a wan, reassuring smile and continued to head for my building. If not exactly trudging the Via Dolorosa, it was a difficult walk, and I wished I could have avoided it. Raindrops began to fall. Then my body stiffened as I heard a familiar voice, "Hi, Professor Morris!" With a slight turn of the eyes I saw its source, Milicent L. Jacobs, clad only in a white long-sleeved blouse and jeans. It was to trouble me later for months, and I never found a clear answer, but I did not turn my head, did not reply, pretended not to hear or see her. I even quickened my step, as it was beginning to rain steadily, and walked right past her, so close that if I had moved a few inches I could have touched her. But rain was not the only reason I kept silent. Soon enough I was to rue this slight, but then I had no way of knowing what events it would set in motion.

Straight to Edith's office. The door was shut. I knocked.

"Come in." The voice was agitated.

Edith Sellers was bent over her desk, writing. She looked up.

"Jack." There was a trace of belligerence in the way she said my name. Her eyes were bleary and the tip of her nose a little red. The dean had been right. She looked as if she had been crying.

"Edith, now don't let this get to you, we'll manage—"

"Let *what* get to me, pray tell?"

"This Relling thing. The dean's a bastard."

"Yes, he is! But it's not the dean." She got up and closed the door, turning the knob twice to be sure it was locked.

"You don't think I'm upset about that idiot up the hill? Oh, no. The guy's a bastard, all right, but it's not him I'm thinking about."

"Then—"

"Your friend, Stanley Habers!"

"What happened?"

And Edith proceeded to tell me how Habers had treated her like a one night stand, how he had stormed in and told her their tryst had been "comfort treatment," and it seemed to him it had worked, hadn't it? Anyway, no more, okay? Better all around. And he leaves as fast as he came. I agreed this was not exactly elegant behavior, but did she not want out? Yes, but not thrown away like refuse! Last night, when she left her office, she saw him with Carol—well, heard them—oh, nothing, she wailed, it's beginning to sound like a French farce. And it was. But she did hear them giggling in Stan's office, she said, and Gunderson whispered.

"Let's drop it," she said. She'd have to call a meeting about this Relling business? She had recovered some of herself, not all. Her mouth was peculiarly twisted as if she were holding back words she wanted to say. Yes, she will have to call a meeting. But I would make the call to Relling. Stanley, I said, was not worth her grief. No, she said, he definitely was not. Her mistake to have started up. "You know, he can be a bastard, a real prick. And my God, Carol is half his age!"

I was pleased at this unexpected candor of language; I had never heard her say more than "damn" or "hell." Her mouth was back to normal. Yes, he can be a bastard. And a real prick. Carol was hardly "half" Stanley's age, but it was best to let that go. Then I walked up to Edith (she had resumed her sitting position behind her desk) and gave her a gentle pat on the shoulder. She acknowledged it by placing her cold, smallish hand on mine, and I feared she would cry again, but she didn't. She looked up and said rather wistfully that they're ruining us up there, the dean. It's going to cost us. I nodded. But what can one do? Last time we all marched down we came away with less than nothing, remember? She remembered. Yes. They, too, are bastards. And pricks. She grinned like a child having dared to say something naughty. Twice.

The department met briefly and vented a good deal of low intensity outrage. Even Stanley Habers did not muster up much of a passionate response. "Jerks!" was as good as it got. Marvin Golden said, "Well, maybe the dean would have approved if our candidate was a better prospect," and then dropped his eyelids. Carol Gunderson was the most upset person in the room, and her face turned angry-red to match her hair. Actually she looked very attractive when ticked off. "Boy, am I ever pissed," she said, but having her own tenure to think of that was as far as she was going to go. Morale was descending into the shadowy realm of indifference among us, that much was clear. Only Robinson and Bentwick sat quietly, their faces expressing perhaps just a little *Schadenfreude*, but no one seemed to notice or, if they did, to care. Hal Muzzey had taken to combing his mustache with his little comb, and everyone expected him to speak. But he didn't. Ann Rosenthal had brought her knitting and remained silent. Edith revived the Search Committee (with a glance at Carol she added her) in order to "strategize" about the curriculum, how we would have to shift courses, drop some, and somehow survive without any replacement. In the end we comforted ourselves into believing that Relling was, after all, no bargain. Bless cognitive dissonance! I left the meeting feeling only tired.

That night I told Julianna the whole messy story, and we got into a little tiff when she said rather off-handedly, "Well, Jack, I must say you guys don't seem to get *any* respect up there. Too much disarray in the department?"

"Oh? I suppose you run a tighter ship, the dean thinks so."

"What did he say? Anyway, that's not what I meant—"

"Said you were a great Chair."

"Sorry, Jack. Let's forget it?"

"Okay, let's." And we did, but I nursed my grievance and pretended to be asleep when she touched my shoulder and turned out the light.

In a very confusing dream I saw Stanley Habers stroking Carol Gunderson's bared breasts, but then suddenly it was I doing the stroking, and I tried to wake up but couldn't. In the morning, when I gave Julianna a make-up kiss on the cheek, what coursed through my head was, I had lusted in my dream, but by the time I was in the car I had persuaded myself that the stroking was Stanley Habers' all the time and I was only a witness. Edith's tale of whispering and giggling, what nonsense anyway! And I had to admit, the dean had a point, Julianna had a point—the department *was* beginning to fray at the edges.

With daylight-saving time gone and winter preparing its way into our lives (although the last week had been mild and sunny), a gloom fell with the darkness. Colleagues continued to snap at one another, to sigh impatiently when someone else was using the Xerox machine, to pass each other in the hallways with barely a hello.

When I saw Stanley Habers I wanted to speak to him. Against my better instincts, I would interfere. It hardly occurred to me that Carol Gunderson and my dream had anything to do with this. In his office, which was only two doors down from mine, I noticed some changes in dress. The boots were gone. Wearing loafers, khakis, a blue turtleneck and a black sweater, he looked spiffy. I complimented him, adding that it made him look younger, spring-like. It's late Indian Summer again, or hadn't I noticed? I stood like a fool, caught in the act. What was on my mind? Class starts in seven minutes. Speaking in a low voice, I said I didn't want to interfere, but it was hard to see Edith hurt. Habers genuinely looked perplexed. Edith?

Something told me that I needed to change direction. Well, yes, the whole affair of Relling and all that stress, she needs support, I guess. "What she needs," said Habers, grinning a little, "is to get laid." I hesitated—he had given me an opening, but I stopped myself. Habers looked at his watch. Hey, he had to go and teach the little buggers. Anyway, tell her to get over it. She's old enough. Just shut the door, okay? And he walked out of the office leaving me stranded.

Lingering briefly, I remained motionless, then followed Habers out and closed the door. Actually, I had to admit Stanley Habers was right about Edith. And I was glad I had not interfered, glad I had resisted that bad habit of meddling when it was simply not my battle to fight. I was not Edith's *pater familias*. (And yes, it *was* I who was stroking Carol Gunderson's breasts in the dream!)

On the ninth of November I went for the follow-up visit to Dr. Julius Hoffman. I concentrated and made an effort to review the past month, but it was difficult to make a good chart. Was I feeling better? Worse? The same? Twinges here; twinges there. Often I was fatigued. But still, I had traveled to New Haven, to New York and back without too much difficulty. At the very least, I was functioning just fine. Well, there had been that one incident driving back from Seth when I felt cold, then hot. So some momentary discomfort, if that, but that was about it. No big deal, little change. "Watch, observe, report back," had been the doctor's orders, but I would not have much to "report." So trying to prepare for Hoffman I could honestly say there had been no dramatic turn for the better or for the worse. I was living my routine, day to day, and in fact had been so busy lately that sleep was better, my thoughts less morbid. But still I felt uneasy, something buzzing me like an evasive fly, and the inconclusive diagnosis was the proverbial sword of Damocles.

Turning my car onto Commonwealth, I noticed that some trees were still punctuated with a little color, while others had not withstood the wind and rain of the past few days and were fully naked. It would have been unusual to be otherwise on November 9th; in fact that any leaves were left at all, tired and dry as they looked, was the blessing of unusually warm days and cool nights, and some light frost in late October and early November. I parked the car a block from the doctor's office and again rehearsed what I would say. More tests? More speculations? I was wearied and almost wished I didn't have to face Dr. Julius Hoffman.

Hazel said the doctor was running a little behind, so I sat down and picked up a late summer *Newsweek* and began to turn pages without really reading. I gathered up some of the medical pamphlets. Grow your hair back, erectile dysfunction cured, fix your heartburn, and for each I strained to read some of the small print side effects: vomiting, high blood pressure, low blood pressure, strokes, fainting spells, nausea, diarrhea, lightheadedness, rashes, vertigo, death. Do not take if pregnant or allergic to aspirin or if nursing. Consult your physician.

And here he was. "Jack." I hear Dr. Hoffman's gentle voice, "Come on in," and he waves his hand, this time toward his office, where I try to tell him how things are going—inconclusive. Probably all in my head? No, no, he protests. I mustn't blame myself. I had *real* symptoms and was absolutely right to come to him, and we did all the appropriate things. Calm words intended to be reassuring. No doubt reassuring for himself as well. What now, I wonder, and the doctor says, well, you've said things are no better but no worse. That's good news, though obviously "better" would be even more encouraging.

Hoffman suggests a consultation with an orthopedic colleague. Specializes in necks. Necks? Yes, and he explains how sometimes those fellows are whizzes at reading nerve problems, and though the original MRI report of my back had been pretty clean, some arthritic degeneration, that's normal at my age, he's been thinking and now wanted to have me take an MRI of the neck. Then he offers some technical explanations, but frankly I'm tuned out. All I say is I don't like those machines. He'll tell Hazel to find one of those newer open, less noisy ones. Resigned, I shrug. Intent on getting it over with, I ask that it be as soon as possible. He calls Hazel. Done. I'm pleased.

Finally I have something specific to tell Julianna. When I stepped into the street a cold rain was starting up, and I just hoped it would not turn to sleet. God knows, it was cold enough. I pulled up the collar of my fall jacket, right now too thin with the wind—and by the feel of it invading from the northeast, the ocean—slicing into my bones. Driving to campus I had the wipers on high speed, and when the car fogged up I pushed the air conditioning knob and put the fan on, full blast. The dark would be coming faster, winter time. Even if the meeting ended by five it would be very dark. I shuddered.

Dreary November was always a sad month, and at once it registered—November 9th, Kristallnacht, and though I was too young to have clear memories, the smell of fear was always there, always retrievable, and its very indistinctness was perhaps worse than having real images I could seize and conquer. Not exactly the now popular post-traumatic stress, but a shudder without name or shape. The drawn faces, the tears on my mother's cheeks, sudden changes. Memories. And the silence and the dark were memories too. In some ways, my not remembering was more frightening than had I specific images and a time-line I could summon and identify.

I sat quietly and held Julianna's hand, telling her everything. She took it in calmly and reassured me that Hoffman was no doubt right—nothing serious. A pinched nerve in the neck was no big deal, right? And we would take a nice spring vacation, somewhere warm, and that would help. Perhaps go south, Savannah, or Charleston, maybe both. We had agreed the mid-year trip to the Southwest was out, and this would make up for it. We needed it, and having unburdened myself I breathed more comfortably.

On a Friday I was to be squeezed into the MRI machine, the open and less noisy one. Image West Center had an antiseptic look to it. I sat down and did not even bother to take a magazine. After a few minutes I heard, "Jack?" and decided to ignore it, because sometimes I resented the familiarity, which I knew these people were told would put patients at ease, was used for the sake of that ubiquitous "privacy." For me—well, it gave me hypertension. "Jack?" came the voice again. Now I worried: what if she canceled me? "Jack Morris?" I rose slowly, "Hello, you called? I'm Mr. Morris."

The attendant was an ample woman, and as she smiled her face looked like a carved pumpkin, with the mouth slit like a half-moon. She said cheerfully, in a sing-song Jamaican voice, "Hi, Jack, how we feeling today? Follow me." I gave up.

The technician, having read her paperwork, did not call me "Jack" but "Professor." After asking whether I had "voided my bladder" (I had), she handed me earphones. "Professor, we have music to mute that awful banging noise. They say these are quieter, but between you and I—they're not. You seem like the type for classical?" Did she have any Sinatra? Sinatra? She was about twenty-five. Had heard of him? Never mind, classical is fine.

As I lay like a mummy in this white magnetized coffin, I thought of anything to distract me from the infernal banging, for the technician had been right, not much muted after all. Music made some attempt to come through the tiny, flimsy ear phones—"The Blue Danube" and Strauss waltzes, Image West's idea of "classical." In any case it was barely audible as it fought unsuccessfully with the jackhammer *rat-rat-rat-rat* of the machine. "You're doing fine, got a twelve minute one coming up," and that loudspeaker voice from the technician was the clearest sound I heard above the incessant banging. I wanted to remove the earphones and to stick a forefinger into each ear, but of course I couldn't, my arms locked into place against the steel curves of the machine.

Among the images that flooded my mind was that of cheery Milicent L. Jacobs' face, and I felt sorry for having ignored her friendly greeting. She will probably think I'm angry that she dropped my course. God, was I? I had complained enough about it. Well, her demeanor, right? Where, I wondered, was she burning Norton these days? I would find out, soon enough.

When Dr. Hoffman's call came into the office, he sounded cheerful. As he had suspected there were some damaged vertebrae up in the neck. Nothing severe but enough to make trouble. And this was the cause of all the symptoms? Quite likely. He couldn't be sure until I did some therapy. But, yes, his orthopedic friend, Aaron Schulman, thinks that the MRI shows deterioration consistent with my complaints. I was stunned. Rather than relieved I was annoyed. Why couldn't we have done this initially? And why did we go through all those other tests? Because, the doctor answered patiently, your symptoms were also consistent with a lot of other possible problems. Tone of the good doctor now a little cold. Deterioration? I asked, with a sneer in my voice. We all have it after age forty he said, he could have said "degenerative," but he thought I would like that even less. Well, I would have. What now? Physical therapy. Hazel will make an appointment. And I ought to work on my posture. No medication unless Schulman says so. I thought he was scolding me, as if in the final analysis this thing, whatever it might be, was *my* fault? Never mentioned my posture before. Fine. I would go after Thanksgiving. Yet another doctor! Is this what the future holds?

Our Thanksgivings had always been family affairs. They did not fit the pattern of the conventional holiday gatherings of fiction, movies or television. Truly they were neither the silly feel good affairs of comedy or Hallmark, nor did they reach those tragic meltdowns where everyone quarreled, great truths were revealed, and doors were slammed to family relationships. True, the children sometimes reverted to sibling behavior. Miranda would bully Helen ("There's a real world out there, dear sister. Better get ready for it! It's not the Peace Corps!"), and in turn Helen would lecture Seth ("No college? Now that's really stupid, you know!"). Some unpleasant moments at the last few gatherings, nothing irreparable. At the end of the weekend everyone had made up, everyone embraced.

Seth had called and asked whether he could bring a friend for Thanksgiving? Was Helen coming with anyone? No, she was solo this year. Of course, bring. His name was Manny. They had met through work. Fine, there was plenty of room, bring. We were happy to see him socializing, feeling Seth did too little of it.

Seth had come for an overnight for the Rosh Hashanah holidays. He sat impatiently during services. Dinner was eaten mostly within those disturbing sound waves of silence, when stillness itself cries out to communicate its pain. We spent most of the time apart from Seth who retreated to his room pleading exhaustion. In the morning he was off after breakfast, quiet, almost too cordial. He insisted on taking the "T" to Logan, did not want to impose all that traffic on us, all he needed was a lift to the Green Line. I drove him.

When we were alone Julianna and I had taken a long walk. Out of the blue she said, "I hope it won't snow on Thanksgiving." It seemed to be a non sequitur, but then I realized it was not. She was hoping nothing would keep any of her children from coming. She needed their protective presence. But Seth obviously—one more time—had settled in our hearts and made them sore and heavy.

The next Monday the University's office of Human Support alerted "Dear Professor Morris" to review his status on Social Security and Medicare, which sent a card. The university literature urged me to get medigap insurance to fill in the balance not covered by Medicare. Even in medical care Julianna and I would no longer be together.

All of this perplexed and irked me, but I did as I was told. Out of curiosity I attended a Retirement Seminar. Sitting in the large room I was astonished at how crowded it was and how many familiar faces I saw. It was a little like going to a porn flick. "*You* here?" was the implicit question. "Yeah, *you* too?"

Reality—of which Eliot said we could not bear too much—was pressing in. The larger world took notice of my age, without asking. Out there they were telling me: Morris you're as old as you are. Live with it. It sobered me some, but I did not visit the "T" to get my senior I.D. card. I hardly ever took the "T" anyway. When we're young we can't wait to get older; but it did not work that way in reverse.

For a while I assessed my "deteriorating," or degenerative vertebrae and glanced at the text I was preparing for the poetry class. We had reached Auden and my eyes fell on

> O season of repetition and return,
>
> Of light ...

This was a spring poem. I could hardly wait, but winter had not even begun. For some time now, I had been developing this growing resentment of the cold and all its relatives—snow, wet, icy winds, gray skies. But even as I was silently reading Auden's words, like musical counterpoint, into my head stormed these lines from Yeats, written in his early sixties,

> What shall I do with this absurdity—
>
> O, heart, O troubled heart—this caricature,
>
> Decrepit age that has been tied to me
>
> As to a dog's tail?

7

When life wants to get you it will, in ways you can count on. Or sometimes in ways you can't. When I removed the mail from my bin I recognized a letter from a journal to which I had sent a long essay I had labored on over the past summer. It had taken months to get a response, which nowadays was considered fast. In the old days you could predict a rejection because they would return the manuscript, but with computers it had become a disposable world. Manuscripts were never returned, and in my heart I knew this envelope carried a rejection. I wanted to explore why Yeats asked so many questions in his poetry. Clearly, when I wrote the essay, I was myself a man with questions—more questions now than ever. Sooner than I ever expected, my whole life was shaping itself into a colossal "Why?" I went to the office, sat in my swivel, and taking my letter opener slit the envelope with two swipes and read:

Dear Professor Morris:

We regret to inform you ...

The letter was long, but I read no more of it. So was this the beginning of my orphanage? Professionally, who was dying, I or they? It will be among my posthumous unpublished works, and I laughed out loud.

Another letter came from a university press for which I had read a 500-plus-page manuscript on modern English poetry, which I had recommended for publication provided certain revisions were made. They offered me two options: $100 honorarium or two hardcover or four paperbacks chosen from enclosed catalog. If choosing cash payment, please don't forget to include Social Security number. I glanced at the hardcover list: *Gender and Culture in the Mexican Novel*; *In the Closet: Gays and Dolls in Victorian fiction*; *Performance Arts and Scandalous Impulses in the 1890s.* (Just for Ann Rosenthal?) Closing the catalog I checked the box for $100 and wrote in my Social Security number. What the hell, dinner with change to spare, as Stan Habers might say.

Then I reached for the rest of my mail. Minutes of the faculty meeting, minutes of the department meeting, fliers announcing lectures, two University Press catalogues (one cover promised "Up to 75% Off on Selected Titles"), and there was an envelope marked "Confidential." I looked at the sender: Walter Livingston Scott, Office of Dean of Faculty. No doubt official notice of the refusal to appoint the replacement. Even though addressed to me, it should have gone to Edith, so I went back to the mail room and slipped the letter into her box. Then I headed for my seminar, which was going well just now. Everyone had settled down, and reports were being presented, discussion was lively, though I was, to my chagrin, sometimes absent-mindedly absent.

Checking my box again before leaving for the day, I found two more fliers and the letter marked "Confidential" returned, unopened. No note or anything. Edith was careful. She saw my name, assumed an error and re-routed it. After all, my box was in fact close to hers, and mistakes happen, even with Angel. I held the letter in my hand, decided to bring it to the office, and sitting in my unzipped fall jacket, I opened the envelope with my fingers and felt the sharp zing of a paper cut on the knuckle of my right thumb.

> Dear Jack:
>
> This is an unofficial letter, a courtesy, to inform you that you have been accused of improper sexual conduct by one of your former students. Her parents have retained attorney, and you may do so, but it is our hope that the matter can be resolved without legal presence. I cannot name the accuser at this point, but Associate Dean of Affirmative Action, Phyllis Bentley, will be sending you a copy of the "Complaint" today. We are making every attempt to keep this matter confidential, in fairness to all parties, but I fear the student newspaper has already got wind of the story, though I assure you not from here. I have been told that the alleged victim went to the paper before filing her "Complaint." I regret this turn of events and make no judgment of any kind. You are familiar with the process, and in any case details will be forwarded by Dean Bentley. This is, as I have already stated, an unofficial notification. You will continue your teaching and other duties.
>
> Yours,
>
> Walter Livingston Scott
>
> Dean of Faculty

The initials WLS were writ large above the typed name. This time my heart reacted. During the first moments of reading the letter I was convinced I would pass out. Everything turned blurry and for a split second I lurched forward.

When my eyes reached the end of the letter, I was gasping for air. Still in my hand, the sheet of paper fluttered and I realized I was trembling. "Milicent L. Jacobs!" I cried out, "What have you done!"

Who else? I knew it with absolute certainty. Immediately it passed by my closed eyes, that fated moment when I brushed past her greeting and refused to acknowledge her. Oh, I saw her now in her jeans and white long-sleeved blouse, smiling as she had so often done in class. In my office, that day she dropped the course, she had said something about burning Norton, and now she was burning me. And the next breath I drew was more like a sob.

The phone rang and startled me so that my whole body twitched. I hesitated. Julianna? I placed the receiver to my ear.

"Hello?"

"Hi. Professor Morris?"

"Yes. Who is this?"

"My name is Julie Hannover." The voice rose. "I'm with *The Crier*. I wonder whether you have any comment on—on—about a sexual assault matter—I guess, like a student has accused you—" The voice rose with each word and became nervously fainter.

I was lost. *The Crier* was the student newspaper. "No, of course not. I have no idea what this is all about."

"So 'no comment' on the sexual misconduct matter would be a fair way to describe your—your response? We want to get it right, professor."

"I have no comment on anything. Look, young lady" (wrong phrase, idiot!), "look, Ms.—I'm sorry I forgot your name—"

"Hannover."

"Ms. Hannover, I have no comment on *anything*. I never said I had no comment on the 'sexual misconduct' matter, is that clear? I don't want to be rude, but I'm late for dinner, so I'm going to hang up. And please—no more calls." And before there was any chance for Ms. Hannover to say anything I dropped the phone in its cradle.

Things like this happen to other people, not to me, but they *are* happening to me and what do I do now? Julianna has probably been called. Oh my God! I grabbed for the phone but withdrew my hand. This I must tell my soul mate face to face. And I shut the light and closed the door and fled like a thief to the parking lot. It was cold; I shivered as a nasty wind swept by. The car heater, which had been giving me trouble, would kick in just about when I drove up the driveway.

To say that I was thinking would be a poor description. I was driving and being very careful as usual, for the dark streets that led to my house were full of dangers during these November dusks—bicycles, often with students on them who wore no visible markers, huge, high SUVs with their halogen headlights pointed menacingly straight into my windshield, wet dead leaves. So concentration momentarily focused my mind on dangers lurking rather than dangers already announced.

Then it happened, so fast I could never react, even were I a younger man with quicker instincts. A thud as I started to turn left into my street, I hardly felt it, and then for a second the flow of time ceased. When I looked to my left I saw another car. Clearly I had been side-swiped, though not hard by an oncoming car turning right at the corner. My glasses were knocked off my face, but no airbag deployed. Otherwise I was unhurt. There had not even been any sensation of whiplash. As I sat motionless, I heard a woman's voice and a banging on the window, more a tapping perhaps. Though physically not injured, the bump had jolted and unnerved me. Feeling my throat tightening, I imagined some hand had gripped it fully intent on choking me to death. I knew I had to make some kind of decision: survive or surrender. Innocent as I was, the shame of the accusation colored my cheeks; I could barely swallow. All the events since Leon Adler's death had coiled themselves menacingly, ready to crush me. So tempting to give in, what the hell! But I heard myself yelling, through sealed lips, No, Milicent L. Jacobs, no, Dean Walter Livingston Scott, no, Father (Father?)! Trapped in darkness, I could hear the rain and the tapping on my car window. I, the accused, sideswiped, sitting in this sealed car in the rain, in the dark. Without glasses everything looked even fuzzier. What was going on? I bent down and quickly found my glasses, put them on, and in a burst my mind cleared, my throat loosened. Rolling down the window, obscured by rivulets of rain (was this the great decision?), I made out the face of a frightened young woman on whose cheeks tears (or were they raindrops?) were falling down.

"I'm so sorry! So absolutely sorry! I didn't see you. I was—I was just—" She sobbed.

"We better exchange licenses and write down the info. That all right with you?"

"Sure, sure. My God, my parents are going to kill me for this." We took each other's licenses, standing in the drizzle, and as I read her name she no doubt read mine for she let out a screamish, "Oh, Jesus! Professor Morris!"

"Julie—. You called from *The Crier?*" and I barely formed a smile. "Have you been to see my wife? Never mind. Of course you've been to see her."

I was about to put a paternal arm around her shoulder to comfort her but realized just how bad an idea that would be, so I tried verbally. I dried my glasses with my handkerchief.

"You have a job to do, but let's get this car business over with and then we'll be in touch. You must have been going a little fast. I never saw you. Deadline?"

"Sort of," she almost whispered. "Your wife was very nice. She didn't have any comment either. I shouldn't have come. I'm so sorry, really I am! It was sneaky. Are you mad at me?" she asked in a pathetic voice. "Please don't be mad at me." Now I *was* her father.

"No, no. But let's have a look at your car to see whether you can drive it." Walking over I tried to get a sense of the damage by carefully sliding my hand over the side of the impact until I felt a minor dip in the metal. Slowly I rubbed the damaged surface. What I felt was a small dent, nothing major. "Try to drive a few feet, I think you're fine." She went into the car and very slowly moved forward. "Okay," she said. "Try yours?" "Okay, I will." On the left fender of my car I made out a bump about equal to the one I had stroked with my hand on Julie Hannover's car. I got in and moved forward a few feet. Getting out I walked over and leaned into her open window. "Just fine. Are you all right to drive? You still seem pretty upset?"

"No, no. I'm cool. I'm good. I'm *so very sorry!*" She was almost wailing. "I mean it. And Professor Morris, I've made no judgments. Maybe I can get them to hold the story?"

"No, how would that look? I'd be accused of blackmail, no?" Now I was teasing her. "Do your job. It will all get to be public anyway. Academe more than most places is like a sieve. Talk of leaks!" She laughed. "Just do your job in an honest way. Right now there are allegations, so be sure you use the word 'allege' everywhere. Fair enough?"

"Absolutely, absolutely. And no names, never! By the way, I'm not just saying this because I killed your car, but I've heard you're a really nice man. I mean it. And we'd never use names—"

She was repeating herself. "Well, that's good. You seem like a nice girl." (I ought to have said "woman"). "Go on, or you'll miss deadline. And drive slowly!"

"Cool. I will." And she was off, and I was sure I heard tires screeching, but perhaps the sound was still the remnants of the screech of the collision embedded in my ears. Or so I hoped.

Julianna met me at the front door. Her eyes were swollen and the tip of her nose was red, not from crying but from a cold. In fact she offered up five successive sneezes, carefully caught in a wad of Kleenex, before she could say a word.

Then she embraced me and said, "I heard a bang down the street? Are you all right?"

"Just a fender-bender. The student reporter who was hurriedly leaving to make her deadline. To say that the Professors Morris had 'No comment.' Is that the way you found out?"

"No, no. Stan Habers called."

"Stan? Oh, well, no surprise there. He knows everything that goes on. Before it happens."

"Jack, he was very sweet. He said that he would walk the plank for you. This, he said, is a trumped-up charge. In a million years Jack would never—and in that vein."

I opened my eyes wide. "Well, a bit melodramatic about walking the plank, but I appreciate his support. He's right about the frame-up. And I know who it is. Almost one hundred per cent certain." We had entered the house and I had taken off my wet jacket. We sat on the sofa and I put my arm around Julianna. She kissed my cheek and sneezed in the process.

"Why, Jack? God, I'm giving you my cold. Hell! What do you mean you know? Why would anybody want to do this to you?"

"Why? Well, because I didn't say hello to this student a couple of weeks ago. I snubbed her. The one I told you had dropped my class. And then got a bit sassy when I tried to dissuade her." Realizing how silly that sounded, I recounted the whole tale of Milicent L. Jacobs, from the beginning, when she sat outside my office door before classes began. I had never bothered to tell Julianna all the details.

"But the girl is neurotic. This is absurd."

"Whatever ails her," I said, "these days, as you know, an accusation is all that's needed, and the wheels start turning. Oh, got a courtesy note from Sir Walter," and I fished it out of the briefcase and handed it to her. She read it quickly.

"He might have called you on the phone. Some courtesy."

"Well, better than a subpoena, or whatever will come."

The phone rang. "That's going to happen a lot. After this let's put the machine on and screen the calls." Julianna nodded in agreement. She picked up the phone.

"Hello? Oh, Edith, didn't recognize your voice, sorry. Yes, I've got a lousy cold. I know it's ridiculous, but it's also awful," and for the first time her voice faltered. She cleared her throat. "I'll get him." Cupping the speaker part of the phone she said, "It's Edith Sellers." I nodded.

"Hi, Edith. Well, that's all you needed, huh? Well, thanks … Well, thanks. I know I can count on your support. The whole department will? Even Gunderson? Just kidding. Actually I like her, and I think she's fair-minded. Well, I'm glad of that as well. Yes, shock. By the way, *The Crier* will have it whenever they come out. Tomorrow? Oh, yes, Wednesday, right. Apparently she went to the paper. No, I don't know. No names. Don't get agitated, it's out there anyway. So you know that? Oh, and I got a private note from Sir Walter. The one marked Confidential, I thought it was about the Relling business so that's why I had put it in your box. Well, glad you put it back unopened. You got a copy? All right, don't fret, Edith. This will come out all right in the end. She's fine. Well, yes, of course she's upset. Not to worry. See you tomorrow. By the way, how is this already common knowledge? Rumor mill. I see. Okay. Stay calm. I will." And I hung up.

"Well, it's nice to have friends. Edith says she's sure they'll all back me. Do you think, deep down they'll believe me? Always some doubts in people's minds with things like this. Nothing I can do about that, is there?"

"Jack, darling," she took my hand between her two and held it tight. "There's nothing we need do because I honestly don't think that anyone who knows you would *ever*—"

"No, not those who know me. But then, don't forget, not everyone really knows me."

The phone rang and we let it go to message. It was Natasha. We were tempted to pick up but decided to listen instead. "Hi, I guess you're not home. Obviously not. Just checking in. Got some news. I hate leaving long messages. But not to worry. My parents have asked us all to stay with them for a while, and I've taken them up on the offer. More when I catch you. Bye."

We looked at each other, and as if in unison: "What will she do with Benjamin and Rachel?" Rachel was in her senior year at the high school, Benjamin a sophomore. "I'll call back tomorrow," Julianna said and the phone rang again. "Hi, it's Stan. You're not out looking for a high bridge, are you? Jack, whoever did this is gonna pay! I'll personally see to it! Sonofabitch! This is over the top! *You*? They might as well start accusing Robinson or Bentwick. Come to think of it, they're more likely candidates. *You*! Okay, talk to you tomorrow. And I'm doing some networking here. Want to know who's doing this. Keep your chin up. Ever try yoga?" Click.

Again we searched each other's eyes and nodded knowingly. Stan, yoga? "But you know," I said, "I'm not sure I like the depth of doubt that *I* could ever do anything like this. Do they think me totally incapable of screwing around?" My voice truly sounded sardonic, but a part of me meant what I said. The judgment of the impossibility of my transgressing felt too dismissive for comfort. Julianna made a face.

"Well now, Professor Morris. So you want to be considered potentially 'naughty'?"

"I just wish they would phrase it differently. Their certainty makes me sound like a eunuch!"

She threw me a mischievous glance. "Poor Jack. They don't know, do they," and her red eyes twinkled.

"No, in fact, they don't!" Then I suggested we go out to dinner. "I just have a dent, but we'll take your car. I know you feel lousy with that cold of yours—"

She nodded. "Right. It's just a cold. I'll take tissues! Just let me get into something comfy. Spanelli's?" After we left, the phone did keep ringing. When we put the machine on after dinner we ran the messages. Two people hung up. One call was from Seth. "Hi. Guess you're out. Nothing important. Got a call from Uncle Paul. God, he hasn't called in more than a year. Asked me what I was doing for Thanksgiving. Did I want to come out to Santa Fe? Of course, I said, no thanks. Do you think he's angling to come *here*? I mean to our house? Just thinking. A little weird, no? S'long." The last call was from Julie Hannover. "Hi, Professor Morris, Julie Hannover. I just wanted to see whether you're all right—about the accident, I mean. And I'm very sorry. I'm sure my parents will take care of all damages. And—and I just wanted you to know we're using the word 'allege' a zillion times, I made sure of that! Bye."

We were glad we had not been home and had made sure to linger over dinner as long as possible. No one minded. On week nights the place was nearly empty. We shared a bottle of inexpensive Chianti, leaving some, Julianna saying she could not really taste it. Anyway, as I had told Seth, the days of whole bottles were pretty much over. When I finally got to sleep, I dreamt I was in a very large room, one that seemed to grow as I sat in a corner on a wooden chair, surrounded by a mob of people, but they were all quiet, there was not a sound in the room. In the morning, I thought about this dream. The trial? Of both my own predicament and of Kafka's novel?

As I shaved next morning, I remembered Seth's call. My relationship with my brother was fractured. We had not spoken directly in years. The last time we were together was when we brought Father to Birch Manor, and even then few words were spoken. Lately I had begun to feel as if Paul did not exist.

I think it had all fallen apart—and nothing like this can ever be dated—at our mother's funeral, a gray day in August, hot and humid. Both of us were grown men, and communication had already been sparse, if not hostile. Our quarrel was about our parents, more specifically about Father. At mother's grave I watched my brother's grim face. Standing by himself, a few feet from me, tears rolling down his cheeks, I heard him mumble under his breath, "Tyrant, tyrant!" I chose at first to identify "tyrant" with God, but he had directed that word elsewhere. Paul and mother had been very close; she always appeared to be protecting him from unknown assailants.

Paul was only two years younger, and this had helped us to stay close for a long time. We were almost like twins. In our teens this changed gradually, not suddenly. We grew apart because at seventeen I was ready to drive a car, and Paul, in my eyes, was now immature. Then girls—as always—were the decisive line of separation. We now had little in common.

Perhaps he felt betrayed, bereft, lonely. Sensitive herself, in poor physical health, my mother suffered the developing fissure between us with helpless sadness and compensated by focusing her attention on her youngest. At the same time, though they had never shared much, my father and Paul became antagonists. Paul resented his coldness, his imperious treatment of mother. He felt she was his showcase wife at university teas and functions, his dutiful Rolodex, his proofreader, his home secretary, his concubine—or worse still, his slave. Quarrels in the house became more frequent and verbally violent. Once when Father reprimanded my mother rather harshly for forgetting to tell him about a phone message (this was before answering machines), Paul dared to say, "Why don't you hire yourself a student, and then she can be your secretary!" Father was enraged, walked across the room and slapped Paul's cheek. Hard. Paul simply quivered and stared at his father, finger marks reddening on his pale face. He looked at Father not with fear but hatred in his eyes. Then he straightened himself and said very slowly, "Father, don't *ever* do that again." There never was another slap. But the damage had been done. Father and son would never reconcile.

After high school Paul went to college in California, as far away as he could. He studied engineering out of spite, because in his heart he cherished history. My mother was devastated, and Paul's absence grieved her. Apparently they wrote to each other often. One day, after sorting her things after her death, I found bulky envelopes tied in a packet with a ribbon, like love letters. I never read them.

That was a long time ago, that day when I thought I lost not only a mother but a brother. Eventually Paul kept in touch only with Seth, who remained a favorite. Wherever Seth was during the past several years, Paul had thrown him a lifeline—postcards, phone calls, once even a visit. The invitation to Santa Fe did not strike me as very unusual, nor did I think my brother was angling for an invitation. When Paul wanted something he came out and said so. I washed my face with cupped hands and then slapped some after shave lotion on my soft cheeks. Then I dressed myself and joined Julianna who was already finishing breakfast.

"Jack," she said, looking a bit pale and frowning, "I know this is hell for you, and it's silly for me to say it, but you mustn't let this get to you. This sort of phantom accusation has unfortunately become all too common. It happened to someone I know at Wellesley. A woman accused by another woman, a student. It was in the papers, and I know someone who knew all about the case. It was all the talk at the conference."

"I know these things happen. But, to quote Job, why to me?" I actually smiled. "What happened to the woman?"

Julianna frowned. "Well, Job's story ended well. She resigned."

"Oh? So did Christ's! His story ended well? He rose, right? But I don't think he enjoyed being nailed any more than Job enjoyed his boils and losses. Resigned, eh? Maybe there are better options." My smile had faded as I began taking all these analogies a little too seriously.

"What do you mean 'options'?" She sounded hesitant.

"Oh, we talked about retirement long before this happened."

"'Talked'? Well, in any case, surely, you're not going to let this drive you into *retirement*? What an absurdity!"

I resented her tone. But true, if I had five years left she had at least ten!

"I don't see retirement as something I will be driven into. I've been thinking about it a little as a way of preparing for the future. You know there are all kinds of things that have to be planned. But don't get me wrong. No one is going to force my hand. I have time."

Julianna looked a little miserable as she sneezed. "Of course. Years," she said smiling. "And do we need all those years to prepare?"

"Well, I wish you wouldn't sound so peremptory." I must have looked sullen.

"Sorry. I meant to be reassuring. It came across the wrong way. But first things first, all right?" She placed her hand on my cheek and I savored its warmth and put my hand over hers. "Let's be cool, as the kids say?"

"Yes, you're right."

"Sorry. I was sounding a little too—I've got to run. Meeting before class with Curriculum Committee. I want to see you for lunch. Off-campus? Can you make it? And we need to have Natasha for dinner. I'll call?"

"Yes, to Natasha. As for lunch, depends on how many boils this Job gets between now and then. I'll call." She bent over and kissed me on the cheek. Twice. "Bye. I hope you don't get my cold," she said in her nasal voice. "Call." And she was off. I heard her sneezing all the way to the car.

Alone, I stared at my cereal bowl and decided to skip it. Pouring some coffee I chose to pass up the bread and jam as well. Truly I was not hungry. After all, this was not my last breakfast, was it? A half hour later I was off, too, looking again at my car. In the light of day it was barely a minor dent, probably smaller than that on Julie Hannover's car. Strangely the paint was not broken. Of course, the deductible would make sure so that there was no coverage. Out of pocket. I might just leave it. A reminder? It was still drizzling.

As I walked through the main entrance to my building, I tried to look as normal as possible, smiling a little as I visualized the large "A" on Hester Prynne's dress. Or was it her cape? I must look that up. As a teenager there was the old saw about how everybody would know by looking at you when you lost your virginity. Now I understood why. But people I knew just passed me and nodded, said "Hi," so perhaps nothing extraordinary showed? I knew I would walk past the table where *The Crier* was stacked, and when I got to it I took the folded paper quietly, surreptitiously, and tucked it under my arm. Once in the office, I closed the door, sat at my desk in my jacket and opened the paper, still feeling I was being watched. There it was, front page:

ENGLISH PROFESSOR ALLEGED TO HAVE SEXUALLY ASSAULTED A FORMER STUDENT
By Julie Hannover

The Crier has heard directly from a student who alleges to be a victim of a Professor in the English Department, who—she alleges—sexually assaulted her. Neither the name of the student or the name of the professor will be revealed at this point, since it is only an allegation. However, *The Crier* believes it is its duty to report the news, and this is certainly news. The student alleges that the professor, a long-time member of the department, invited her after class to help her get through some difficult texts. He allegedly took her to his office, and closed the door. After a few minutes of discussing the text he remarked on her tight blouse, she alleges, and then suddenly lurched at her, groping her breasts and even, she alleges, tried to put his hand under her skirt. She was so upset that she could not move, she alleges, but she finally regained her composure and pushed him away. The professor, she alleges, warned her not to say anything, for she would certainly not pass the course if she did, and anyway she was already close to failing, even though, she alleges, this happened very early in the semester. When she returned to her room she e-mailed him and warned him never to do this again. After the initial groping, she walked out of his office shaken and, she alleges further, afraid to tell anyone until now. She received an e-mail in which he apologized but warned her to keep this to herself. The only person she told was her boyfriend who immediately advised her to drop the course. She did so the next day, and her boyfriend did as well, the same day. After telling *The Crier* her story, the student then went to the Dean's Office and filed an official complaint.

The Crier called Dean Walter Scott Livingston, Dean of Faculty, who would neither confirm or deny that a complaint had been made. He did say, "All such complaints, should they come here, would immediately be passed on to the Office of Affirmative Action and the University Counsel." Calls to these offices received a "No comment" response. *The Crier* is committed to keep its readership informed as this story unfolds. At this time, however, it should be remembered that we have reported an allegation, and caution that, in the interests of fairness, everyone keep an open mind.

That was it. That was enough! Hard as I tried, I could not recall what Milicent L. Jacobs wore that day when she wept in my office. The first sentence of the story was garbled, but I appreciated all the "alleges" and was glad that Ms. Hannover had taken that seriously. On the whole the story was not bad English ("neither" takes a "nor" but that was being pedantic) and free of misprints. To be in print as a groper, in public, even nameless! Everybody knew or soon would, even though few among the faculty took the paper seriously. But now it was out there. It would spread quickly, like the flu, and then I would be a marked man.

I hung up my moist jacket. I am not impulsive, but I pulled out a piece of university stationery from the top drawer and inserted it carefully into my printer. Then I rolled my chair close to the computer and sat for a minute or two staring at the blank screen and began to type, addressed to Dean Walter Livingston Scott, undated, for I would show it to Julianna first:

Dear Dean Scott:

In view of recent accusations, it has become clear to me that the wisest course I should take is to tender my resignation effective the end of this semester. I believe this to be in the best interest of my department and, to be honest, in my interest as well. In addition it is

A knock on the door. I hesitated and then shrugged. Go on as usual, I told myself, for anything else would only make matters worse. So I opened the door and there, standing side by side, Robinson and Bentwick, both in three-piece suits, Robinson in black pin-stripes, Bentwick in a subdued plaid (did they still sell these, or were they just well preserved from who knows when?), starched white shirts, muted ties.

"May we come in?" Robinson asked.

"Of course, of course," and I ushered them in, grabbed an extra chair from the corner of the office, and asked them both to sit down, please. They did.

"Morris," Robinson said (only last names: it was not disrespect, quite the contrary), "we think you probably know why we've come?"

"Well, to be honest, not really." I leaned forward, and then added quickly, "*The Crier*?"

"Yes," Robinson said solemnly.

"Well, they don't mention my name—"

"As people are saying, Morris, It's 'out there'?"

"People are saying that?"

Bentwick said his first word. "Yes."

I knew what was coming and was on the point of telling them that the matter was already in motion. These venerable gentlemen would not wish to be associated with a department in which, however allegedly, one of its members is a public spectacle, exposed as a possible groper, an assailant! So what are they here for then? What the punishment? Resign? Of course. Spare us the shame and the humiliation. I was beginning to sweat. Didn't Edith say everyone was aboard with me on this? But what followed was something very different.

"Morris," Robinson began again, "we have come to tell you that you have our full and unqualified support in this unfortunate matter. We neither of us believe a word of it. We have known you a long time, and one thing we know is that you are honorable."

"Yes," Bentwick said, "we have disagreed on policy matters, that's not news, but as a person you have treated us honorably, correctly, respectfully—"

"More than can be said of some others," Robinson added. Especially Stanley Habers, whom I knew they detested.

"Furthermore," Robinson said, removing his glasses and polishing them vigorously with his starched, folded handkerchief, "we cannot imagine that you would ever do any of those things to *anyone*, let alone an undergraduate!"

"You're very nice to Ms. Gunderson," Bentwick said, "and heaven knows she baits us all, but on occasion you've had the worst of it." Though I didn't see the relevance of how I treated Carol Gunderson to the sexual assault story, I was grateful. But indeed, I again admitted that in my dream I groped her breasts. Really!

"Anyway," said Robinson, "we are in full support of your character, and if it gets that far we will bear witness to that character as impeccable. We are very sorry you have been put in this situation."

"Yes, very sorry," Bentwick echoed. They rose and extended their hands, which I shook, first Robinson's, then Bentwick's. I was moved. It occurred to me that for the first time I had seen these men as human beings, and the blush of guilt spread in my cheeks, how often I had, without saying so, dismissed them, as did so many others, as ridiculous vestiges, two clowns. Habers was more honest perhaps, but I could never be rude to them in public, that much was true, and I had often defended their right to speak—or to remain silent, to abstain, literally and figuratively. Perhaps they were appreciative of that, and this was the payback? Suddenly it did not seem so ridiculous at all to have the support of two conservative, upstanding members of the department, and I was moved by the way they had come to me.

I was looking at them and really seeing two physical beings. Bentwick looked younger. His full not-yet-gray hair was ample and combed into a pompadour in the style of the Fifties. (Did he make it that way? Did he make it grayless?) His eyes shone clear blue, and he wore no glasses; his ears were small and neatly tucked to the side of the head. The nose was straight and below it sat just a tiny line of mustache. Robinson, on the other hand, was heavy-set. The stiff shirt collar appeared to push up his neck skin. Gold-rimmed glasses protected rather bleary looking eyes, and his face was spotted with small red splotches; the mouth seemed too small for the oval shape of his head, which was quite bald.

"I am truly grateful for your support," I said, "and to have it this early. Of course, I do also assure you it is not misplaced. I never did any such thing, as alleged, but the department will suffer; and let's be honest, so will I. Already feel it. It's ugly."

They were about to leave. "Well," said Bentwick, "it's some world isn't it, when anyone can make an accusation and it's immediately a *case*? It could happen to any of us!"

"Yes, it could." And I was astonished to realize just how true this was, and how these two admittedly often fuddy-duddy men were on the right side. Indeed the same side as Stanley Habers! They nodded, bowed actually, and I opened the door and they left. I sat there and squeezed some tears back before they could even enter my eyes. Damn it, why me? Then I deleted the letter on my screen and wondered how I had been foolish enough even to think of such a thing!

Another knock and an open door, simultaneous. Stan Habers.

"Hi. Had the machine on? Don't blame you."

"Actually we were out to dinner."

"Oh, where?"

"Just a place, I forget the name." I knew Stan Habers didn't approve of Spanelli's, and I didn't want to argue.

"So, Stan." I didn't know what to say. The last thing I wanted was to communicate self-pity.

"'When sorrows come, they come not single spies,/But in battalions.' Damn, but my guy had it right for any occasion."

Delighted to be bailed out by Shakespeare. "*Lear?*"

"You flunk, my good friend. *Hamlet.*"

"Figures. Ever think of going back to your 'guy'?"

"As a matter of fact, now that you mention it, yes. Seriously. There's also, 'One woe doth tread upon another's heel'—"

"Stop showing off. But go back to him. Another backyard book sale?"

"Could be, you selfish bastard. Now let's cut to the chase. The first thing is the e-mail accusation. I checked with the computer guys. They can retrieve her alleged e-mail, no matter you deleted it or not. And they can go to her—"

"Stan, I don't have e-mail."

"What the hell are you talking about?"

"I don't have e-mail. Remember when Sir Walter first came into office and sent around that so-called 'inventory' questionnaire about computer use? Well, I was one of those who had to say that I didn't use it much. That's what the questions were meant to flush out. Then last year I was told by Computing Central that the new e-mail system the university had installed needed stronger—modems, newer windows, I don't recall. I said, no thanks. So that was that."

"Holy shit, Jack. How can you do without e-mail?"

"It's a relief! Everything comes in hard copy eventually. When I need it, which is rarely, I use our home computer. Obviously Julianna is up to speed. So when they offered to update me I said no. I still write notes. Or I type them out and print them." But the real reason why I had refused e-mail was that colleagues had been complaining for a few years now that students flooded them with e-mails: questions about the class, excuses for lateness, requests for extensions, everything they used to come into the office to ask for. I wanted none of that. Already students were few enough. Without e-mail, I figured, they would at least make occasional visits, and I could salvage some sense of proximity with them. That lost, and it would make the distance between me and them even more unbridgeable. As it turned out, I was not overwhelmed with students, but a few did drop by when e-mails might have saved them the trip.

"No e-mail? That lying bitch! Well, we can prove that easy. Even better! Less work—"

"Stan, I truly appreciate your interest. But can I ask you something? Please, just for a while? Back off? Until I know what lies ahead. Because I don't know. It all just hit the fan. I have to wait and see what happens. Promise?"

Habers looked a little hurt, and whenever he did his face turned solemn, as if it had been slapped. "What lies ahead? Yeah, what *lies* are ahead! Okay, okay, I'll back off. I mean—this is scary stuff, you know?"

I could see that it was indeed scary stuff, especially for Habers, and that though he genuinely anguished over my troubles, his motive to help was also to ward off the fear that such a thing might happen to *him*, for Habers flirted with undergrads, harmlessly yes, but these days? Perhaps Robinson and Bentwick, in their way, were also motivated by fear. Who could blame any of them? I imagined myself as some infectious disease that had entered the house and scared everybody in it.

Julianna and I lunched at the small Thai restaurant across town, where we could be pretty sure about privacy. I told Julianna about the visitors of the morning and mentioned my lack of e-mail that would, according to Stan, clear me at once. Julianna was skeptical. "They'll claim you used mine."

"So can't they trace yours?"

"Yes," she said, biting into a chicken satai dipped in peanut sauce, "I think Stan is right about tracing, but you could be e-mailing her from your wife's office?" She was still red and sniffling, but the sneezing had abated.

"Logically speaking? No. Is it all set for Natasha tonight?"

"Oh, yes, forgot to tell you. All set. But let's take her to Spanelli's? Twice in a row, I know, but I feel like hell, not in the mood for cooking."

"Sure, I don't care. Did you tell her?"

"Said I would check with you and call her back."

"I meant about all this—"

"No. Of course not. But you can."

"Fine. What did you think of *The Crier* piece?"

"A few too many 'alleges'? Sounded a bit alliterative? But that's only for consonants, right? Anyway, takes the flow of narrative away." She snorted a laugh. "Oh, it's fine. They tried very hard to be journalistically moral, that's nice."

"It's worth a dent in the car. If this reporter hadn't bumped into me, it might have read differently. I told her to be sure to make clear this was an allegation."

"Right. Well, then, definitely worth a dent!"

Natasha had not heard anything, so over dinner we filled her in on the details. She was genuinely shocked, offended. "If only Leon were here to help. He was so good at things like that." Yes, I agreed, he would have helped me see this thing through. But we reassured her. Natasha was moving in with her parents in Grosse Point, she said, because they felt she needed a change and she agreed. And she had worked things out with the high school so that Rachel and Benjamin could finish the year there. Benjamin would come home for graduation and march with his class. It would be good for all of them. Michigan weather was not much better than Boston's, but she couldn't face the cold winter alone in the house. David had gone back to Oberlin, skipping the second semester abroad to be closer for visits. Thanksgiving, Hanukkah, New Year's Eve—too much. She decided too late to join her parents for Thanksgiving, but that was fine. Of course, we immediately implored her to join us (we had often exchanged Thanksgivings with the Adlers, especially when the children were younger), but she begged off. "You have enough of a crowd. No really, it's better to be at home with the kids. Besides I'm not feeling festive right now. But Julianna, let's get together Friday morning. The weekend is packing." They agreed. She sat there, small, petite, dressed elegantly as always, with her black hair in perfect place. But again I was sure she had shrunk a little. We talked about the "problem," about Leon, about the children. She was effusively thankful for our company. Yes, she would keep in touch from Grosse Point, of course. She would leave after Thanksgiving.

When we got home, Julianna put her arms around me. "God, Jack, don't you ever leave me in the lurch!" The mention of Thanksgiving had stirred something within her. "Thanksgiving in this house without you—" and without meaning to she began to cry. I patted her on the back and then kissed her on the lips, lightly. "This business in school is nothing, right? I mean when you think of other things that can happen?"

"Yes, yes, of course, nothing."

I promised never to leave her in the lurch, knowing how silly it was to make any such promises. And knowing that she knew it too.

8

I had been to see Dr. Aaron Schulman, who was somewhat older than Julius Hoffman, very quiet, business-like. He asked me to walk back and forth, stand on my heels and then my toes. With a long thin wooden fork he scratched the soles of my feet and then my legs. Measuring sensation. He told me to roll my neck this way, then that. Then he repeated essentially what Hoffman had said, degeneration of neck vertebrae, pinching nerves, nothing very serious. Writing a script for physical therapy, he advised me to wear one of those cervical collars, whenever it felt comfortable to do so, especially in the evenings. They were available in the lobby pharmacy. I bought the collar and made an appointment for physical therapy.

My first of several sessions set the pattern. On a Monday I arrived in the brick Medical Center not far from the university. PT was on the second floor. After filling out some forms, having the impression of my insurance cards taken, I sat—one more time—aimlessly thumbing through magazines, until someone called out, "Jack?"

"Mr. Morris?" I asked.

The woman standing in front of me, in slacks and blouse, seemed taken aback. She was about forty, her dirty blond hair tucked in the back, a freckled face, the picture of physical well-being.

"*Mr.* Morris," she said with some "excuse *me*" sarcasm, and led me into a room. "I'm Wendy, and I'll be your therapist," and she smiled nicely. "Why don't you sit down here," pointing to a fairly narrow bed, more like a gurney without wheels, covered with a white paper sheet and two thin white paper pillows at the head.

"Now let's get a read on this problem of yours," and she sat down beside me with a clipboard on her lap. Then she took my history, made notations, asked if I was allergic to any medications. Finally, "Lie down please, on your side, and pull your slacks down just a bit so I can feel around your back," and she began a long series of pushing here and there with her rather bony hands, always asking, "Does that hurt? A lot? On a scale of 1-10, what number?" This time I responded docilely, and by the end of the session, she had began to chat a bit personally. "So you teach. What do you teach? English? My favorite subject in college." We had made up, and in succeeding sessions we became chitchat friendly. Twice a week, I dutifully set out for my three week regimen: she gave me instructions on exercises: "Turn your head like a spiral, so as to loosen those neck muscles. Then the back. It's all connected." Often I was horizontal on the stationary gurney with the "electric stim" machine next to me, listening to the timer clicking away ("Tell me when you feel the tingling"), and feeling the ice pack lying like a loadstone on my back and buttocks. Sometimes Wendy would massage my neck and back, "Very tight through here, let's loosen that up a little," and that felt the best of all. When we parted I held a portfolio of exercise sheets and we shook hands. A final admonition, "You've got to do these religiously, Mr. Morris," and nodding, to make her feel better, I said that things had improved a lot. Actually they hadn't.

Julianna had a busy schedule; I did not. So I gave up my preparation—which lately I was beginning to think came to nothing anyway—and decided to take a drive.

I headed out west on Route 2. Fall was just about dead. A few yellowish leaves hung on, but black branches were everywhere. Harvard, Groton, the usual leaf-peekers' paradise, were empty of color; even the sky was light gray, not even a haze of sunlight. In fact a light drizzle hovered, almost a low, frozen fog, and every once in a while I had to swipe the windshield clean.

My mind was disorganized. Leon Adler. Milicent. L. Jacobs. They had nothing to do with each other, and yet here they were competing in my head. Competing! How could that be? Leon, a friend ripped out of this life, Leon, who meant so much to me, dueling with Milicent L., a disturbed young student who had dropped my course and accused me of sexual assault? Leon won. For a time. Someone's death close to you is supposed to make you ponder your own mortality, but Leon's death did not have that effect on me any more. Instead, I just couldn't understand its irrationality. And that was a surprise since literature embodies the irrational, repeatedly forces you into a "willing suspension of disbelief," because if you didn't have that, the whole edifice would collapse. I knew that intellectually, but my feeling self refused to cooperate. I simply couldn't process the absurdity of this death, so the only course was to let it go. I knew that somehow, someday, I would be able to grasp it, but now I just couldn't.

So as I drove past Groton, Milicent L. was easier. I wondered, what was she really like? Was she dropping because of her boyfriend—her ex-boyfriend? Actually that made no sense. So it was the course? Too hard? Or was it me? Did she find me a bore? Well, what of it. And a small slight pushed her into such revenge? I was getting closer to Leominster; malls and industrial parks were beginning to ruin even the leafless scenery of Harvard and Groton, with its quietly lonesome expanse. It was time to turn around, not so simple a task on this highway, with its concrete dividers. But soon I found a way where they allowed a left and as I was heading back, Milicent L. stubbornly refused to retreat. She kept popping back, like a Jack-in-the-box, and now she was becoming an irritant. I turned on the radio in the hope of losing myself in music. It didn't work.

What was this, what Auden called this "neural itch"? I had thought it was sadness; or anxiety; or regret; or frustration. It was probably all of these, but no one of them seemed quite to fit. With something of a shock, I recognized anger, passive rage. Leon's death and this disaster with Milicent L. merely opened spaces that had been shut—or only slightly ajar. But what was I in a rage about in the first place? It would take more time to understand that, but the first, tentative reply was: I was not who I used to be. Missing pieces. I had lost—what had I lost? Energy, sense of achievement, contentment. In their place had come impatience, some self-pity, much frustration. And anger. At myself?

I pulled into a rest area and watched a light wind picking up brown, dead leaves. It was abandoned. A peeling picnic table and benches stood in lonely seclusion amidst high, browning weeds. In this desolate place, with bare branches everywhere, I was as alone as the landscape. Scarcely a car passed by in either direction. Like my surroundings, I, too, was desolate. Leon, this girl, look what she's doing to me? I mean it was raining, and I was in a hurry. I *might* not have seen her, she couldn't really tell, could she? Well, she obviously could. Assault? That's a serious charge. God, I could go to prison! Leon was quiet. But he might have told me that my pride was getting in the way, feeling sorry for myself. Lighten up!

I drove back into the road and happily let a few cars pass me. As I headed back to the university, the drizzle turned into a light rain. By the time I arrived at my office door, I shut it carefully and slowly for fear of slamming it to smithereens.

Thanksgiving was closing in. Even without looking at the calendar I could feel it. Of course, one had only to look: the trees, the late November gray, the cold that bit its way through your outerwear. But it was the students who showed all the signs, already displaying that pre-holiday restlessness, a certain irrelevance, an indifference glazing their faces, a shifting in their seats, a look in the eyes that said clearly: Sorry, professor, I'm not with you any more, I'm half outta here. (And it was only Monday.) Their silent messages embodied a sensuality, and in their excited chatter with one another, a feeling of joyous expectation barely subdued underneath the obvious anxieties. And why not? I was always guilty for keeping them that last day before they all would disappear. "Yes, I'll be here, no matter if just one of you comes," went the usual day-before-speech Thanksgiving speech. Most students had begun leaving on the Sunday before, and with each day the ranks thinned appreciably until on Wednesday only a few who lived locally might come, and I would be in class, but it ended as an informal, nice chat for a half an hour or less and I would send them off with, "Have a nice turkey day, come back in one piece!"

Before leaving, I retrieved a letter from my mailbox from the Associate Dean of Affirmative Action. She was a fairly recent appointee, Phyllis Bentley, and I didn't know her. A few years ago Marge Keefer, whom I really liked, left for greener pastures. I had worked with her on appointments when I was Chair. My luck! The letter enclosed some printed guidelines, a three sheet packet headed "Complaint" and marked "Copy" accompanied by a brief note:

> Dear Professor Morris:
>
> I am enclosing the Guidelines, "Grievance Process," updated last September, and a Complaint sheet by a student, Ms. Milicent L. Jacobs. As you will see, the complaint concerns allegations of sexual assault, and I direct your attention to the relevant sections in the Guidelines. Our policy is, at least initially, to resolve such matters informally by inviting all parties to sit with me (and on occasion some other persons, whose identity will be checked out with me) to review the issues at hand. However, there are to be *no* attorneys present, though we do not prevent either party from seeking legal advice outside the university venue.
>
> In the interests of all concerned, this meeting should take place as soon as possible, but I have been informed that Ms. Jacobs has already left campus for home, so I suggest the Monday after Thanksgiving. Meanwhile, will you please send me a formal response to Ms. Jacobs' allegations within ten days of receiving this letter (which in this case would mean immediately if we are to have a meeting on the date suggested). If you have any questions, please feel free to call me at Extension 370.
>
> Sincerely,
>
> Phyllis Bentley
>
> Associate Dean, Affirmative Action

After reading the lengthy "Complaint," which elaborated on what *The Crier* had reported, I swung myself in circles on the swivel. First smoking gun confirmation of what I had known already—Milicent L. Jacobs. No surprise. I looked out the window. Through the spindly branches of the bare trees I could see the highway beneath the building, cars speeding by, making a rumbling noise that I heard only in winter. Perhaps the leaves acted as a buffer during other seasons? It was neither sunny nor cloudy, just gray. Oh, yes, Milicent L. Jacobs, spelled with one "l," I knew it all along. On a piece of university stationery from my drawer, I wrote in pen the following to the Associate Dean of Affirmative Action:

> Dear Dean Bentley:
>
> I categorically deny all the charges outlined in Ms. Jacobs' "Complaint." The Monday after Thanksgiving is fine, so long as we can make it after my seminar which begins at 2:00 PM? I will require no other person on my behalf, but please feel free to permit Ms. Jacobs to bring anyone you and she agree on being there. By the way my computer has no capacity to generate or receive e-mail.
>
> Sincerely.
>
> Jack Morris
>
> Professor of English

I signed and folded the letter, slipped it into an envelope, sealed it, stamped it "Confidential" and dropped it into the departmental "Out" box.

When I got home a feverish head pain pounded me. Julianna insisted I take my temperature, and I stuck the thermometer into my mouth until it beeped. When I held it to the light it registered 102! Damn it!

"I've given you my cold," Julianna said, head hanging in sympathy and guilt. "And stress has compromised your immune system."

"No, this is just a flu thing. I haven't sneezed all day. Just chilly and achy."

Julianna suggested I go up to one of the children's rooms, and I chose Miranda's. "It's roomier, I'll just open the trundle bed."

She agreed and I walked up slowly, aching all over, undressed, and urged two Advils to cascade down my throat with a huge glass of water, courtesy Julianna. She brought me liquid every half hour—juices, water, chicken soup. I drank constantly and complained that this just made me run to the john, but Julianna was a strict caretaker.

"That's fine, just drink, you must!" After a few hours the fever had subsided, down to 100.4.

"Just a twenty-four hour bug," I insisted.

"Let's keep it that," Julianna said sternly. Since I was not teaching the next day, I had Julianna call Angel, just to say I wouldn't be there, in case students came. "Tell her to put a note on my door."

"Do you have office hours?" Julianna asked. "No, but sometimes they come anyway." Not much any more.

I spent a restless night. Guessing that the temperature had probably risen again, I progressed from shivering to sweating, as if I were being yanked from a cold bath and pushed into a steam bath and back. Dreams, but I could not recall them. In the middle of the night, dripping with sweat, especially around my pajama collar, I lifted my upper body with a start. I had dreamt about Leon. For a long time I could not fall back, and during those hours, in probably a febrile state with aches in my body, for the first time I was really able to grieve for my dead friend. What a calamity! What a loss! How unfair! I sat up, wide awake, propped myself upright against two pillows. Through closed eyes I saw Leon Adler clearly, saw his agile, dark-complexioned face, his black hair, his dark and soulful eyes, his benignly ironic but genial smile. Then I heard him talking, laughing, earnest and witty. Why? The simple three letter word would not go away. Why? Why? Why? But I knew there was no answer.

I remembered my moments with Leon Adler in a state almost hallucinatory. What was this pressure? My bladder. Urgent. And I trudged to the bathroom, but too weak to stand, I sat down and heard the attendant at the MRI telling me (or had she ordered?) to "void" my bladder. Now the voiding came in fits and starts, but when I was done I did not immediately get up. Fact was, I couldn't. Again the word "void" rang in my head, and sitting there, in a heavy sweat with who knows what fever, I felt a void in my gut, and knew I was being dragged into a void, disappearing. Taking my hands to my cheeks to keep myself steady, now I was heaving, tears running over my trembling hands. Wiping my face I ran my fingers across my lips and tasted salt. Pain stabbed, and I realized my heaving was making my body move, ever so slightly, back and forth, as if I were a praying Hasid. As I wept, I understood only dimly what later I would see with much greater clarity, that at last I was weeping for Leon Adler, yes, but weeping also for myself, for what I was aware so deeply I was losing, for a past that was slipping from me like a fading horizon and a future that held so much unknown, so much fear, so much terror for being unjustly accused of a terrible act. A void. No tissues, so I grabbed at the end of the roll of toilet paper and tore off a handful, wiped my face and blew my nose. After a while, it all stopped. Shivering again, so

I downed two more Advils, shuffled into bed, covered myself halfway up my face with blankets and fell into a dreamless sleep.

When I awoke, I knew the fever was gone. So I had been right: in twenty-four hours it was all over, though I felt a bit shaky. Getting out of bed cautiously, I remembered little of my heaving in the bathroom, but doubted I had shed real tears. Must have been sweat. Of course, I would be well enough to go in and teach the next day, but this day I remained in bed and mostly slept.

Poor Julianna, however, was still sneezing and blowing her nose. Her cold would last for a week. That day we agreed not to call any lawyers yet, though by our wordless looks we also agreed "assault" was indeed a very serious business.

At the last moment, Helen called: she was indeed coming, grabbed a dirt cheap fare off the Internet. She sounded ecstatic. We threw each other wistful glances. Well, who is she bringing this time? No one, it seemed, coming all by herself. First time in ages that ever happened. But she sounded happy? Yes, very. Seth was coming with his friend, and Miranda and Robert, of course. So all the children would be together again. Julianna was awash in pleasure. We made an unspoken vow to forget, at least for a few days, my state as an accused groper of undergraduates.

Preparations for Thanksgiving were Julianna's province, and her cold had all but disappeared. She organized her time so that each day—when she could—she would buy whatever was not perishable. The "free-running" turkey, already perished, was ordered early, and that was my job, to pick it up on Wednesday, when the store would be unimaginably crowded, since I waited until after class, such as it was, but I enjoyed the chore—it was just about my only one. Except I also put together the dining room table which needed all its extension boards, and I was assigned to choose the wine. Seth had lately expressed a preference for red, so I added a couple of bottles of Côtes du Rhône. The rest were whites, mostly Chardonnay and a Gewürztraminer for Julianna. Cooling the whites was always a problem. There's no room, I would wail, where do I put these? Oh, stop fussing, Julianna said with a touch of impatience, just squeeze them in. In the end, I always managed, though the turkey got the worst of it.

Our house was an unexceptional colonial, almost indistinguishable from thousands of others in the middle class professional suburbs of Boston. When the children left they wanted to keep their rooms intact for home visits, so we took out a home equity loan and built a two room extension over the garage. It was almost paid for now and served as adjoining studies. Robert and Miranda would be a bit tight in Miranda's old room, but after they bought the trundle bed there were never any complaints. Helen and Seth were grateful to have their old "comfort station," as Helen called the bedroom in which she slept away her childhood and adolescence. Whenever Helen brought a boyfriend, he would sleep on the living room couch, which had occasionally generated comparisons to Miranda's privilege of sleeping with Robert, but the grousing didn't last long. After all, Miranda and Robert were engaged, older, and in a steady relationship, right? The dining room was a bit small even when the table was pulled to full length, but the wood-paneled family room with its couch and easy chairs and a few bookcases was cozy, even when crowded, or especially when crowded. People brought it to life; it had that feel about it that said, please use me. Only the kitchen was problematic. Small to begin with, never modernized, it simply couldn't stand the strain of too many people, and there would be the usual exasperated pleas from Julianna, "Everybody out!" But we managed.

They all tried, as best they could, to arrive on Wednesday, but only Helen managed. The crowds would be so bad we told her to take a cab, and to make sure, we dispatched one to the airport and paid extra fare, well worth the frayed nerves of having to go to Logan on the day before Thanksgiving.

Even the cab arrived nearly two hours after touchdown. We would wait until the morning for Seth and his friend Manny, they would take the train up; and for Miranda and Robert, whose flight Thursday morning from Washington would be a breeze. I picked them up at a nearly deserted airport.

By noon the whole family was together. Seth arrived last with Manuel, or Manny, a shy young man with swarthy complexion, too thin for looking healthy, who greeted the family with the same "Hi, I'm Manny. Glad to meet you," as he shook one hand after another. They had grabbed a cab from the 128 Station.

The day began cold and a little windy but sunny, and by early afternoon the gift of a southern breeze brought such mildness we all assembled on the patio in sweaters and commented on the gorgeous weather. Everyone was dressed casually except for Manny, who wore a sort of purplish shirt with short collar and a very thin dark green tie fastened with a tiny knot. Over the shirt was a dark linen jacket. Robert wasn't wearing a tie, but he *looked* as if he were. In fact he was wearing a white turtleneck. His handsome light-toned face was notable for its topping of very blond hair, carefully parted on the right. He sat upright, shoulders straight, perfect posture.

I leaned back on a patio chair and surveyed my progeny. Miranda looked most like her mother; she had her dark hair, skin color, and the bright eyes. And she laughed in the same full-throated way and could scowl like Julianna, too. Lately she had lost weight, too thin perhaps, but still healthy looking, bright, feisty, always our brave new world. In her gray wool pantsuit, she looked very fetching.

Then Helen, physically more like her father, never any extra weight, just built square, Helen whose face also betrayed more of my seriousness, which belied her wit and wickedly funny mouth, her mischievousness, her fast repartees, communicated as much with her arched eyebrows as with words. But despite the appearances of sarcasm, Helen would always be an idealist. It was what had brought her to the Peace Corps; it was surely to dictate the rest of her life as well.

And finally Seth, a beautiful, smooth face, a perfectly formed nose, a shock of dark hair. Yet his face could survive, inexplicably, a day without shaving. Despite his slim body, he was built like an athlete, resembling most his uncle Paul, but he lacked all that anger Paul projected. Seth merely exhaled anxiety or glumness, and lately that had diminished. Yet when I looked at him now I sensed this worried look had, for this day at least, returned. Some heavy thoughts were weighing on that boy, what were they? Altogether, I considered myself fortunate, and for a brief, languishing time, I took in these children, enjoyed a soothing and reassuring sensation of weightlessness that made me figuratively stretch my body as if I were on some secluded beach basking in blue sky, gold sand, enveloped by an emerald-green sea. Then for an instant I was aware of the fourth child, Nathan, lying in the earth, not far away. My body twitched and the magic of the moment was almost broken.

Closing my eyes I saw the word "assault." That sealed the end of my soft reverie. My "trial" was days away, but already I felt what accused innocents must—panic, despair, certainty that I would be convicted.

That time of day, in the deep fall or early winter, the sun swarms over the patio. Sipping wine, we talked, and our conversation was animated, everyone catching up on details. We had not been together since last July. Helen talked about her classes: she had finally decided to major in Spanish, it was the language of the future, and besides she was already fluent from her Peace Corps years. She would do something with it, perhaps teach English as a second language. Miranda offered endless anecdotes about the difficulties of living in the District, all the graft and waste, while the kids struggled with books that were falling apart, and sometimes none at all. But she would stay and fight, she had no intention of quitting. Anyway Robert's job would keep him in Washington. Later I found out that Julianna had asked her in the kitchen whether she was any closer to getting married, and to her astonishment she replied, nonchalantly, yes, they were thinking of a date for the summer. Julianna told me and we both were surprised but happy. Miranda was never casual about such matters. But any further questions would be seen as grilling, and we were determined to keep the house happy.

Seth was quiet, but despite his shyness, his friend Manny talked a lot, probably to ease his anxiety, which was obvious. What did he do? Well, he was a geek, like Seth, and in fact they had met at some computer conference. No, they didn't work together but close enough to keep up. Liked each other and began to hang together soon after they met. What did he think about the Internet, Miranda asked, "Was it a threat to literacy, privacy, an addiction?" It was a little too much for Manny but he stammered, while Seth sent a glare in his sister's direction. No, he didn't think computers, or the Internet, would take the place of books, but, yes, privacy was a big issue. Actually, he, Manny, was more of a computer hardware guy, well it was all very complicated. "I'm not a Luddite," Miranda insisted, sipping her wine, but there *are* issues. Poor Manny obviously didn't know what a "Luddite" was, and Seth tried to rescue his friend, let's not get so deep on Thanksgiving, okay? But Helen weighed in. "It's not computers replacing books, that's not the problem," she said, facing Miranda, wine glass in hand, "it's artificial communication, which was to be honest a new loneliness. All those people chatting and e-mailing and instant messaging and not even seeing each other! Well, except on those small screens on the new cell phones! What a new lonely crowd that was!" Did Manny agree *that* was a danger? "Well, maybe," Manny said, "maybe." Seth had the look on his face that said: right now, I wish I had two brothers.

By three the warmth that had so teased us was gone, and we appeared simultaneously to look at one another and by agreement reassembled inside. The brief cheat of full sun had put us in good humor, and though we were now rubbing our hands, that hour or so of warmth had been worth it. Anyway, Julianna, who had left earlier, was signaling that dinner was almost ready. I threw some logs into the fireplace, and the flames leapt lustily, making for a full-blown conflagration.

No one knew about my university problems. Julianna had agreed there would be time enough to talk about that. Once in a while, through the slight high of the wine, thoughts and images from all directions kept returning, like a final invasion by hostile armies. Throat dried up, heart skipped a beat. Days, yes, but Monday was not far off, and I had received a phone message from Dean Bentley's secretary that the conference, as she called it, could take place at 4:15 Monday, after the seminar, was that all right? Yes, I replied, I wanted to get it over with. I would release my students a little earlier.

Dinner was a pleasurable time, not only because the food was tasty, but because the repetition of the meal somehow reawakened each year a silent compact within the family. Year after year, the turkey was soft and succulent, its taste heightened by mushroom gravy; and the home-made cranberry sauce was tart, the candied sweet potatoes with raisins and a touch of Grand Marnier and lots of brown sugar were a delight, the apple pie a wonderful finish, the wine soothing. But it was not the individual parts of the meal that pleasured, it was the ritual, the reassurance the eating of it bestowed, like a gift. Manny was very polite, saying at every opportunity that this or that was the most delicious he had ever eaten. And the wine, he said, was "awesome." Who knows? Perhaps Manny never enjoyed a proper Thanksgiving. (My family had never understood this holiday. Our parents would take us out to some inexpensive big barn of a place, and I recalled how unpleasant the meals were, with lots of loud families crowding the restaurant, children crying and fussing, and bald, nasty waiters hurrying you to eat so they could clear the table for someone else.)

All hands helped to clean the table, and by tradition the males did the dishes, but the pots were filled with hot water and detergent and allowed to soak. Julianna had noticed that Manny had not brought an overnight, and she let it pass until Seth all at once announced, well past dinner, "I have to bring Manny to the station. He's catching a train home. Take your car, Mom?"

"Of course, but oh, but why?"

Julianna said, "We have plenty of room here, Manny. Why not stay the night? What's the hurry?"

"Yes," I quickly joined in, "please do stay!"

Manny looked at Seth, a little pained, then at me. "Well, thanks Professor Morris—and Mrs. Morris" (he had forgotten she, too, was a "professor"), "but I have some family stuff back in the city."

"Oh? So you're from New York?"

"Yep. Born and raised there. But thanks for the offer. And thanks for the meal. It was really *great*! Best Thanksgiving I've ever had. I mean it." And he sounded as if he did. Then he said his goodbyes the way he had said his hellos, shaking everybody's hand with a "Goodbye, nice to have met you."

"Back soon," Seth said and they were out the door.

There was a brief silence, and Helen said, "Nice geek, isn't he?"

Everyone laughed but we agreed that Manny was a nice young man, well-mannered, a little overcome by this high-powered family, Robert offered, but a good "lad." Why he said "lad" was probably the same reason he didn't want to be called "Bob." In any case we watched football for a while, Helen joined us, and Miranda and Julianna went for a walk, even though the light had vanished long ago. Seth returned in about an hour, and we repeated our approval of Manny, which seemed to please him. Into the evening, until nearly midnight, we sat and talked, agreeing with Helen that phone and e-mails are still no match for face-to-face conversation. Seth went upstairs first, and finally one by one we all peeled off to our respective rooms.

Miranda and Robert seldom stayed more than an overnight. So Friday after lunch I drove them to Logan where they caught the shuttle. The airport was eerily deserted, and I made the round trip in little less than an hour. Robert had been especially affable at breakfast, as had Miranda, and there was some expectation that more would be said about the wedding date. Both looked fresh and flushed, like a couple that had just made love. She is happy, we were thinking, each separately, though we exchanged a look. But nothing more was said about wedding dates. They talked about their friends, and Robert told some stories about his thriving law practice. He was full partner now in a small firm of about two dozen, and his specialty was patent law.

Helen was off to see classmates in Cambridge, a Friday-after-Thanksgiving custom. She was two years older than her fellow students in her class at Berkeley; her high school friends had all graduated and were settled. Some had married and one had already borne a child. Last year Helen complained to her mother that she had increasingly less in common with them, felt like an outsider. Still, there were enough singles, and she was off early borrowing Julianna's car. That left Seth. In truth he would often stay the weekend, sleep late as he did this morning, "chill out," as he put it, to "get my head together."

Julianna and I were abandoned, as we sat and read the morning paper. Still with her eyes on the print, Julianna said softly, "Jack, will we ever have grandchildren?"

"I hope so! But what brought that on?"

"What? I mean it seems clear that Helen is not even thinking of marriage. Seth? Not for a long time—if ever. And Miranda and Robert? Well, to tell the truth, that summer wedding could be years away. In the light of day, frankly, I now think she was just shutting me up." She sounded weary, sad.

"You're tired, darling. Don't be such a pessimist. It will happen. You'll see. We'll have a whole bunch of them."

"Well," she said, putting the paper on her lap, "I don't want to be an old granny in a rocking chair when we do. Do the math." And she rose to clean up the breakfast dishes.

Honestly, I had given little thought to grandchildren. After all, no one was married yet, but when I did do the math, yes, Julianna was not so wrong in worrying. Almost sixty-five—by the time grandchildren arrived how old would *I* be?

And once in a while I had thought about a grandson. If they were all girls that would also be all too lovely. Of a sudden I, too, greeted a pang of melancholy. Once I read that heavy dinners can make for depression. But I chuckled. More than food was on my plate to make my breathing occasionally labored, as I blew out some deep sighs, fending off unwelcome reminders headed toward me.

Julianna, her car gone, was waiting for Natasha to pick her up. "Why don't you and Seth do something?" she said.

"Don't worry, he'll sleep till noon! We'll rake. Having dinner with Natasha?"

"I'll see. Maybe I'll take her out somewhere. No doubt the children are saying their good-byes." A honk in the driveway. "Call you. Bye."

But Seth did not sleep late. Shortly after Julianna left, I was surprised to see him standing on the bottom step.

"Morning, lazy bones. Breakfast?"

"Not hungry. I'll get some coffee."

"You're losing weight. Eat!"

Seth didn't bother to answer. He made himself a cup of freeze-dried instant and cut half of a banana hanging from a plastic tree. Still chewing he came into the living room.

Thanksgiving had its chores. In the old days, before we could afford Gustav Anderson, and when the children were still at home, we would all go out and I had to replace heavy wooden storm windows into hinges and the children raked. In those days I would still climb and everybody held the ladder and watched. Julianna, afraid of heights, was always anxious and kept saying, "Be careful! Be careful!" When we built the two new studies, we installed combination storms and screens, so now only some raking was left. Before Gustav Anderson, only Julianna was spared from the raking: she was allergic to dead moldy leaves. I would watch the children and shake my head. Each personality translated to raking. Miranda was slow, methodical, a prim raker; Helen sort of raked wildly, putting one pile from one corner to another. When Miranda criticized her, she would throw down the rake and run away, either in tears or in anger, or both. When they got older, she sometimes stuck out her tongue. Seth was resentful, but he was the best and most efficient raker of them all. He hated it and said so, but he did a great job and quickly: the sooner over the better.

Gustav Anderson (don't dare call him "Gus") was a peculiar man. He fancied himself a horticulturist and dictated the terms of his engagement: "I will come once, when *all* the leaves are down. Don't forget, the oak trees keep their marcescent leaves till spring, when new buds push them out." (Even Julianna had never heard of "marcescent" until she looked it up: "withering but not falling off," but it was intended she be impressed—and she was.) "But come twice and we'll pay extra." "No, no. Once is just right. If you need me a second time, I'll come, but you won't." But of course, since he came before Thanksgiving, there were always leaves after that, and by then Mr. Anderson was off on his month long vacation to Florida. Always, Mr. Anderson performed in a denim jacket, a blue denim shirt and a slim, clip-on plastic black bow tie, the sort soda jerks and gas station attendants wore in the 1940s or 50s. Julianna had spirited disagreements with him about the garden, but he would prevail most of the time. In truth he *was* good, if too stubborn, yet no one in the neighborhood dared wake his ire for fear losing him.

So each Thanksgiving we raked. Even today, though there wasn't too much, some clean-up remained. In recent years, with Helen and Miranda off sooner than later, Seth and I raked together. Seth still didn't like it, but he remained the efficient raker of old. "Com'on, it's a father-son thing," I teased. "Yeah, right," Seth replied, rolling his eyes.

Because of some nasty, windy early November days, the additional deposit of leaves was light. "Let's rake a little, Seth? There isn't much."

"Fine. But let's do it now."

"No problem."

We put on old shoes and sweaters and I gave Seth the new rake and took the old one, and then remembered that with my fragile back I couldn't do much. The raking motion always stirred up trouble. "I'll take it easy, my back." Seth nodded and began what would be no more than an hour's job at most. After a while he walked towards to me, as I was gently scraping the driveway.

"Dad, how long did Nathan live? I know you told us once, but we were young, at least I was, and I don't remember."

Ambushed, though the question was perfectly reasonable. It was just that Nathan had not been spoken about for a long, long time. I leaned on the old, almost toothless rake.

"Why do you ask? So suddenly?"

Seth seemed irritated. "Why not? He was my brother! And I just want to know."

I took off my work gloves and flattened my hair with my bare right hand two or three times, but I was almost unaware of it. "Nathan? Barely two months. Just about seven weeks."

"What did he die of?"

"He was premature. His immune system couldn't make it. In those days they didn't have all the fancy words they have today. They just told us his heart gave out."

"He would have been my older brother," Seth said, as if he were working out the dates.

"Yes. He would have."

"Dad—Dad, I want to see his grave. I know we all went there once, but I must have been six or seven. I want to see it again."

"Well, we'll do that someday."

"No, not someday, Dad. Today. Please?" The voice was tight.

I wanted to say something to derail Seth, something like, this is not the time for me, it's always very painful, and it's a holiday, I'm not feeling great, and I've some body aches that are very current. I've been falsely accused of messing with some undergraduate. *Assault!* I've a hearing on Monday. But as I silently heard all this, I recoiled with revulsion at my selfishness, and swallowed the words. Instead, "Seth, why today? What's so urgent?"

"Because it just is. I'm home. You're home. It's nearby, I remember that. What's the big deal. I'm done," and he pointed to a leafless lawn.

"Then go alone. Take my car."

Seth was offended. "I don't know the way. Besides, maybe it's time we do something together for a change? Other than raking? Father-son thing?" Sarcasm in the voice. Reproach.

"This isn't exactly going to the movies, or the ball game." I was beginning to fret.

"Dad, do I ask you for that many favors?" More reproach.

Truth was Seth almost never asked for anything, which at times had hurt me, for I took it as a form of withholding, as if asking was a way of showing love, making connections. And now that he asked, even if it was a request to see a long buried brother, could I turn him down?

"All right. Let's go then. Let me leave a note for Mom, in case we're late." We changed clothes. I left a note: "J—Seth and I out. Back after lunch. J-"

The drive to the cemetery was longer than usual because the roads were crowded with Friday shoppers speeding to the malls for the after-Thanksgiving sales. We were silent in the car. To me Seth's face appeared drawn, but perhaps I was projecting my own. Eventually we arrived at the cemetery, and when we got there it didn't take me long to find the grave, though I did go to the little administration house and had them draw a map: "Morris, Nathan," I said to the woman behind the counter. Cars were lined up for a funeral, a small cavalcade, but once beyond them, the narrow roads were deserted. A few people were standing at graves, one could see them through the headstones, here and there, figures that looked hidden because one saw only parts of them. The scene reminded me of a surrealistic painting, even comical in its way. We had to walk a few yards from the road, and when we arrived at the grave site, my body went limp. Although the sun was out for a second day, it had turned much colder, but there was scarcely a breeze. In this cemetery there was a full vista, and it was not particularly pleasant. No Sleepy Hollow, no Mt. Auburn, not many trees.

The small headstone and grave were supposed to be cared for—"Perpetual Care"—but I immediately noticed weeds and dandelions. I would complain before leaving. After Seth and I placed small pebbles on the headstone, I bent down to pull at the more obvious growths, pulled them out with a force out of proportion to their size. The engraving on the stone was simple: "Nathan Isaac Morris, Beloved Son," and the dates were partly obscured by high grass. The more I pulled at the offending weeds, the calmer I became, though to look at my rapid arm movements and powerful pulling one would have thought I was unearthing the grave itself. Seth began to help, and in five minutes we managed to have most of the obvious overgrowth cleared. I looked at the partially cloudy sky and followed some birds circling, eerily silent. There was no pattern to their flight—they just flew this way and that.

"They're supposed to keep this clear, the bastards!"

"When were you here last?" Seth asked.

"It's been a while." Guilt.

"Why is there this custom of putting small stones on the gravestone?" Seth asked.

"I'm not sure. I used to think about that myself. Once I asked a fellow in the Religion Department. He was a bit stumped. 'Perhaps to unload the stones on your heart,' he suggested, the heavy weight, and I liked that so much I never pursued it again."

"Sounds possible. Dad, do you know why I wanted to come?"

"Frankly, no." My voice was resentful.

Seth looked me in the eye, not sternly but with hesitation and fear. "This brother of mine, this innocent little Nathan, he's been between us all my life!"

I was so shaken I stood upright with a jolt. "What do you mean? What do you mean!"

"I mean what I said. He was the great joy of your life, wasn't he? Even if he lived only seven weeks. *He* was your son, the one to carry on the name, and I was sort of a defiant gesture, something you and Mom had to do to prove you could have another healthy child!" I froze. I was looking at Seth as if I had been struck and became aware that both our eyes were brimming with tears.

"How *dare* you—" I took a step forward.

"Don't." Seth stuck out a hand as if he were fending someone off. "Don't! You know what I mean, and don't pretend otherwise. So please, no speeches. I got to be the oldest son because this little guy died, but you never really got what you wanted. I've been a disappointment, for you and Mom, except you the most. I never even went to college. I was not that happy child you had hoped for after Nathan died. I was always your problem, your underachiever. I know that bible story, Dad. But this time you gave your blessing to the older brother, but he was dead, so by not giving it to me—by not giving it to me," and Seth's body was unsteady, his voice choking. My son a Karamazov? At this moment he wanted to kill me and wanted my blessing, both equal in his desperation. I made another move toward him, but this time he thrust both his arms out. "No, not until you hear me out! I've waited so long to tell you what I feel. I've been choking. So by not giving me my blessing, because I was the oldest son now, you did just like the bible story, only poor Nathan had nothing to do with it, and Mom didn't help you, like in the bible, but you did it. You pretended to bless me, but you didn't, you blessed *him*," and he pointed toward the tiny grave. By now Seth was nearly wailing his words, and his bible story was all muddled.

Again I moved, this time with imploring eyes, toward Seth. Again I was repelled. Seth was drained of blood, his face white in contrast to his black hair. "I will not give you any sons, Dad, no children at all, and you know why?"

"Yes, I think so," I said calmly, in a whisper.

"Oh, all-knowing father, you do? You do? You do *not*!" He was shouting.

"You're gay, Seth. I've known it for a long time, in my heart of hearts. So has Mom. Perhaps not *known* it, but guessed. We've never talked about it, Mom and I, that's true. Maybe we were waiting for you to tell us. We should have made the first move. Parents make many mistakes."

Now Seth looked as if he had been hit. His arms hung limply at his side. A copious stream of tears flowed down his cheeks, his nose was dripping.

"Well," he said at last, as if he were a condemned man speaking his last words, "so now *I've* told you."

"Yes. So now you have. And it's been a burden you've been carrying for too long. We love you, Seth, more than you can ever know. I know that sounds like a cliché, but sometimes there are no better words than simple ones. All that about you disappointing us, and giving our blessing to this poor dead infant, that's simply not true."

"Yes, it is!" And Seth stamped his foot into the grass like a child.

"No, it's not. I'm no psychologist, but you seem to need it to be true. Why? Because if it's guilt, forget it! Do you think I give a damn about my name being 'carried on'? We love you whatever you are, another cliché, sorry, but it's true. That's what parents do, most of the time—"

"Something I'll never be able to understand, right?"

"Perhaps not, no. But you need to believe. Our hearts will be broken by knowing what a hard life you will have, because Seth, this culture, it's a lot of pretending—it's hypocritical, much of it. Once doors are shut and lights are out, people whisper the truth to each other. What they really think and feel. You will suffer. But we will love you, whatever—"

"Dad," and now there was a sudden imploring tone in Seth's voice, "Dad, I want so much to believe you!"

"Well you must!"

"What about when you and Mom shut the doors and close the windows and put out the lights? What will *you* whisper? What's *your* truth going to be like?"

"A fair question. We'll probably cry a little to think of the pain you might have at times, but embrace you even more fiercely. We'll want to protect you, and I think you'll need to watch out that we don't overdo it!" And I believed the words I spoke.

This time my arms succeeded in surrounding my son, as if protecting him from the perceived attack he had twice fended off with outstretched arms and once with his eyes. Seth was limp, and we embraced and Seth cried, and my eyes moistened, and we stood there wailing and slightly rocking back and forth to a wind that was not there. Because we were in a cemetery, the scene was not strange at all. Mourners do that. And we were, in our way, mourning, mourning over a wasted past and a frightening future. How long we did this no one can say. Probably no more than a few seconds. Then we walked to the car and drove back to the little cemetery office, where I quietly but firmly registered my outrage at the "mess of weeds on my child's grave," and received an apology and a promise of immediate attention.

On the way home Seth sat quietly. At one point he said simply, "Manny? Is that when you—?"

I shook my head. "Manny? No, long before that. Parents sense things, what can I say?"

Seth laughed. "Because, you know, Dad, Manny is a friend, not a lover! Manny's straight as they come."

Now I, too, laughed. "Oh, really? Well, he's a nice fellow."

"Straight. Just a fellow geek. And uncle Paul. He's straight, you know that. Sometimes I thought you thought—"

"Paul? He's a womanizer! No, no. I never thought. Before we married he once made a pass at your mother!"

"At Mom? I don't believe it."

"Why not? To be honest, I think he was just out to rile me, and as I remember, he succeeded in charming her. But no, no. Your uncle is certainly straight—in that way anyhow." I hesitated and then said, "Did you tell him?"

Pause. "Yes, I did."

"When?" Unavoidable sternness in my voice.

"When he came out to Seattle. You're angry, aren't you?"

"No, not angry. But you trusted him before you trusted us. That hurts a little."

"It shouldn't. I was scared, Dad, okay?"

"I understand. But not of uncle Paul?"

"No. He's not my father. Anyway he didn't seem too surprised either. He told me to cool it and wait for the right moment. But if you want to know, he also told me it would all be okay with both of you. So don't think so badly of him!"

"I don't," I said softly, "and I'm glad he told you that. That it would be okay to tell us. I mean it."

"Good. Now can we drop it?"

"Sure."

For the rest of the drive we sat in silence, but between us something had changed that we each felt in our own way. Perhaps Seth would never totally believe that he was the blessed one, and perhaps I would never altogether forgive life for taking my first born son, but a wall between a father and his son had been broken, and while there may forever remain rubble on either side of that wall we had together breached, we both knew that we would be closer than ever before. And so I was grateful to have one son beside me, just as I would be forever wounded to have another in the ground.

When we arrived home, the note was still there and the answering machine light was flickering red. I crumpled the note and pushed the button. "Hi, it's me. Natasha and I are off to the mall, so don't worry about me. I'll be back before dark to avoid the main traffic. Bye." But I was worried, not about the traffic but about how to tell Julianna who, I suspected, was not so close to knowing about Seth as I had said. We had not talked about it, except by indirection, by making comments that Seth was so shy with girls, that kind of thing. That part was true. But did she really suspect?

"Do you want me to tell Mom? I think *you* should." There was a studied commonplace in my tone, as if I were asking him to tell his mother about some good restaurant.

"Yes. I should. Or maybe—"

"I'll do it, of course, if you want, but I think you should do it."

"Dad, can the rest of the family wait? I mean Miranda and Helen—and Robert. God, Robert, he'll break off with Miranda!"

"Don't be foolish," I said, though I figured there was a distinct possibility that Seth was right. I never liked Robert, ever since he asked not to be called "Bob."

"But sure, you tell your sisters whenever you want, but tell Mom next time we're together. When are you leaving?"

"Saturday night. I have to be back. Have a date."

And that stung. A lot. I refused to let my imagination go where it was pulling me, so I shut it off like slamming a door on forbidden sights.

"All right, then. Don't rush it." I was going to say, It's been such a nice holiday—and what? Don't spoil it? Words would need to be watched now. Seth had a way of picking up on every word, often misunderstanding, but still, care needed to be taken. Everything was raw.

"You know what, tell her in a little while. There's stuff in school right now, nothing that much, but our minds are—well, we're preoccupied. Maybe we'll come down to New York in the near future. Anyway you'll be here again soon?"

"Maybe. What's in school?"

Had Seth heard anything about sexual assault? About his alleged groping father? "For Mom? Nothing that much. Department stuff. She's got a lot on her plate. You know what it's like being Chair. Remember when I was? I was awful!"

"Yes, you were!"

"Well, agreed then? Just wait a few weeks."

"Sure, sure. The dark secret can wait a few weeks," Seth said with trace of coldness. "Dad, did you know Nathan was going to be a boy?" he asked out of the blue.

"Well, they didn't have fancy tests then, but the doctor thought so and turned out to be right."

"And me?"

The doctor had predicted a girl, but I held off and quickly said, "You? Actually, he said fifty-fifty. Played it safe."

When Julianna came home, just as dusk was about to turn into night, she was in high spirits. "We had a good laugh and a good cry and then I thought we'd go to the mall and I bought her a necklace as a goodbye present. Well, a 'so long,' I hope. Was that a good thing, dear?"

"Yes, a very good thing," and I kissed her on the cheek and then held her.

"Anything wrong? What have you two been up to?"

"Nothing's wrong. We've been driving, it's so nice out. Just driving around a bit. And we raked. Didn't you notice?"

She looked a little quizzical. "Getting too dark. All right, then. Helen not back, I take it?"

"No, but I think I see the headlights," and I was indeed right.

Seth kept his promise and did not say anything to his mother. Saturday night he took the train back before sundown. At the station platform I embraced him hard and looked at him, man to man, as if to seal our secret. Helen left very early on Sunday from Logan.

Sunday night I could not fall asleep. To me it seemed I was awake all night, because twice I raised myself to peek at the digital alarm—once at two and again at four-thirty. But toward morning I must have dozed off because I dreamt about a large chamber again, only this time there was no silence but many noises, and in the midst of the ever growing crowd I thought I saw Seth, not me, standing in a corner. As in the previous dream, this time it was Seth, not I, who looked a little forlorn and frightened, and as happens in dreams I realized it was Seth as a child. When I awoke, I recalled the dream and acknowledged with a painful jab in the pit of my being, Oh, yes. He will suffer. I hope not too much. And for a second time in the last few days, I asked with a touch of self-pity, Why me?

And now the trial.

9

Monday morning dawned with a cold drizzle, and the forecast warned of possible sleet at midday, turning much colder by nightfall. I got myself together quietly, as an artificial calm enveloped me like a protective skin. For the proceedings, I had no script, no notes. There was nothing to say other than deny it all, as I already had in my letter. What preparations would that need? By silent consent, Julianna and I performed our routines without much talk. She came down to breakfast, as always, soaked in sweat from her stint on the treadmill, and I decided to eat the usual, though I was hardly eager. Conversation, sparse as it was, concerned the weekend.

"Did you think Seth was all right? He looked drawn to me. I mean I know he always chills out here and works like hell at his job, but—"

"Seth is fine. He's twenty-three, as you always remind me. Let it go. I thought Helen was in fine mettle."

"Yep. And no boyfriend," she said. "Too much trouble right now. How long will that last?"

I laughed. "Not long. Miranda seemed fine, too. Robert was okay." We were forcing it now and knew it.

"Yes, yes. Both fine." She had finished eating and was coming over to put her arm around my shoulder.

"Jack, promise me—," but she didn't finish the sentence. I detected fear.

"I promise, whatever it was you meant."

"Call me right away. I'll be home by then. Thin day today."

"I will. And don't worry. Truth shall prevail, or make you free, or whatever," I said mockingly.

"It will, Jack. This is an absurd business. I really can't believe it's happening."

"It is, love. Go on now. You'll be late." And she went up to shower and dress, returning as always so quickly I continued to be astonished by her efficiency. She blew me a kiss and was off with her rapid steps, in her smart suit, black leather jacket, briefcase swinging jauntily at her side. I washed the breakfast dishes and cleaned the table.

Today I had office hours, and though probably no one would come, I needed to be there, force of habit. When I arrived, a note was taped to my door. It was from Edith Sellers. "Jack, I'm in. Please come to chat. Edith."

I phoned her. "Hi, Edith? Jack. I've got office hours. Well, no, not too many. Probably none. No, no appointments."

She asked me to leave a note on the door and come anyway. Well, the Chair had spoken. I taped a piece of paper to my door: "Won't be long. Write your name below if I'm not back."

I knocked, she opened the door. She looked put together, a light blue blouse, heavy navy sweater and slacks. "How was Thanksgiving?"

"Fine." I sat down. "Everybody made it in. Yours?"

"Oh, fine, too. I decided to stay at home. My folks are in Florida, and I just didn't feel like the trip. Too crowded at the airport, and no direct flight to where they are. But it was good. Rested and caught up. But have you ever tried to find a place that doesn't serve turkey on Thanksgiving? You know what? I loathe turkey! Tried the Chinese place. Closed. Tried Thai. Closed. I finally raided the fridge for ice cream and jello!"

I laughed. "You look rested." I meant it, but it sounded perfunctory.

"Well, guess what? Our friend Stan made it all better." And she told me how he had taken her to "L'Espalier," had again suggested that they stop these private meetings for the sake of propriety, and so it was on *her* terms, and she felt a whole lot better. Of course, they both knew it was a bit of a charade, but life is a game, right? Consensual makes everything right. Even if it's play-acting, or something like that! But it was enough for her. "You know, Jack, pretense, even when both parties are aware of it, is an elegant face-saver. History now, all right?" She looked at me as if she had said something very wise. It sounded as if she had rehearsed it.

"Sure. You called me in to tell me this?"

"No. I called you in to tell you that we have sort of spoken informally among ourselves, and some may have spoken to you privately. And we are solidly behind you. We wanted to let you know that before the hearing today. Not a single exception."

"Well, Edith, that's reassuring. You told me that the first day, but I don't mind hearing it again. Seriously. It's nice of you to tell me, nice of everybody to back me. Robinson and Bentwick came to see me. I was touched." I began to get up.

"One more thing, Jack. After my term is up, would you consider chairing again? There's a real consensus."

It came as an untimely surprise, and it was so obviously meant to lift my spirits. Too obviously. "You know, Edith, that sort of reassurance I don't need. Thanks, but no thanks. 'I've done the state some service, and they know it.'" I was sure I had been too artificial quoting Othello, but Edith let it go. "Besides, you know what? But don't tell anyone, and this has nothing to do with the current mess. My slope heads downwards. One of these days, in a few years, I'll leave this place."

Now it was her turn to be astonished. "Leave? God, no Jack! You can't mean it?"

"Why is this such a touchy topic? I don't mean anything imminent, but you know, at sixty-five you begin to think about the future? Just prudent to do that. Why are people so surprised when I even mention it, as if 'retirement' is some sort of dirty word?" I was genuinely out of sorts.

"Because I suspect that no one sees you anywhere close to that?"

"Well, I'm not. But someday. I'm going to have to be the judge of when. I'll work it through. You know they say that when the time comes, it will be clear and unmistakable. And all I'm saying is that I've had—I've had some thoughts about the future," and I pointed to my forehead. "Now I'm waiting for messages from here," and I rather dramatically hit the left side of my chest. "Right now, it's probably far off. My wife always teases me about planning ahead. Did you know I buy four or five tubes of toothpaste?" And I broke into a grin and we both laughed and I left.

The Scotch-taped note I had left was blank. I sat for a while staring at the floor.

I skipped going out to lunch, having brought a bagel, some slices of low fat cheddar, and a cookie. I dropped a tea bag into a cup of hot water I had boiled in my little electric kettle. The seminar was heading toward conclusion, as was the semester, with only two meetings including today's remaining. The lanky young man with the shoulder length hair, he who had been so unpleasant at the start, remained in class, an intelligent and active talker. In fact it was his turn to offer his report today. Mont Blanc had dropped out long ago.

I told the students I would have to cut the session short but promised to keep my remarks to a minimum. As I eyed the faces I wondered: what did they know? Graduate students tend to shun the student newspaper and, living off-campus, as almost all of them did, separated them so that mostly they were ignorant of current news. Certainly no one said anything or made any show of embarrassment. I held to my promise: I scarcely said a word. Elias—that was the young man's

name—gave a fine report, but the words sank like rocks into a deep hole. I had
listened but not heard. What awaited me did not permit attention to anything
else. I looked at my watch and it was time to stop. Grabbing my papers I hurried
to the office. At my door, Stan Habers.

"Look, I hear you can have someone with you? How about it?"

"No, no. Thanks. Really, I can handle this."

"You need a big mouth like mine!"

"I'm innocent, Stan. That's all I need."

"Okay. Suit yourself. Break a leg."

"Thanks." And I opened the door, slipped into my winter jacket, placed a
manila envelope containing the copy of the "Complaint" and all other pertinent
matter into my case and almost ran down the stairs. Can't be late for my own
execution! At the last moment I rushed to the bathroom and, washing my hands,
seeing myself in the mirror, I winced and muttered under my breath. Some
groper, gads! This accused looked more like a better-dressed homeless man.

Outside it was cold, but no sign of sleet, just gray and threatening. I stepped
lively up the hill to the administration building to answer the summons. Room
202. Arrived, I was a little out of breath. But once I got to Room 202 there was a
note in large computer generated letters on the door: FOUR PM MEETING
TO BE HELD IN BOARD ROOM. That was on the ground floor. It was a
huge place, and I had been there only once or twice. I hurried back down the one
flight of stairs, but when I opened the door of the Board Room no one had
arrived. My watch told me I was about seven minutes early. Not knowing where
to sit, I remained standing, having thrown my jacket on a chair near the wall.

On the austerely dark wood-paneled walls hung the portraits of the university's eleven presidents, all male. With identical poses, they looked as if they had
all been painted by the same artist, which I knew to be impossible. I gazed at the
portraits more closely, one by one, and when I got to the seventh president, one
Frank O. Eldridge, I heard the door open, turned and saw Phyllis Bentley and
Walter Scott Livingston striding in, engaged in lighthearted banter. I saw them
before they saw me, but when they did the dean, wrapped in a dark suit, winked
a hello, and Dean Bentley of Affirmative Action said, in a friendly voice, "Professor Morris?" And she reached out her hand. "Phyllis Bentley. You're nice and
early. Thanks for accommodating us. Why don't you sit over there," and with
her hand on my arm she led me gently to the middle of the huge table to a chair
facing the window. I thanked her and sat down, but as I did a pain shot up my
back—or was it down my neck? That little raking and trouble already? Or was it

bending down to pull those weeds off Nathan's grave? Probably nerves, and I shoved the pain away.

Within moments a young woman accompanied by a man walked in. Milicent L. Jacobs and that boyfriend of hers—what was his name? It would come to me, but for now it was a blank. They were told to sit more or less opposite me, and instead of going to the head of the table, as I expected, Dean Bentley moved about three chairs in, and next to her, Sir Walter. Phyllis Bentley was professional in demeanor. Tight-fitting gray suit jacket, white blouse, and moderate make-up—she could have passed for a CEO. Looking up, she cleared her throat a little, and said, "Sorry that we have to meet here in this huge room, but 202 has a heating problem, so this was the only available alternative. We sure won't feel claustrophobic here!" Only Walter Scott Livingston chuckled.

Milicent L. Jacobs had not raised her head, she was staring at the table. Her friend, however, was gazing at the portraits, or so it seemed.

"First, let me explain the dean's presence. He is here to answer a technical question, that's all. Any objections?" Silence.

"Well, good. Then before we start I want to make sure: do we all understand why we are here at this informal hearing? And that what takes place here is to be kept confidential?"

I nodded. Milicent L. Jacobs appeared to nod. Her friend said, "Yeah."

"Well," Phyllis Bentley began, "let me repeat that I am entirely neutral. My purpose is to set out the facts and try to resolve this issue before it goes any further. Shall we see whether we can achieve that?" It was not a question.

"So," she continued, "for the record let me ask each party whether they have read the copies of materials sent. Professor Morris, you have read Ms. Jacobs' 'Complaint'?"

"Yes."

"Ms. Jacobs, you have read Professor Morris' reply?"

For the first time she looked up and faced Phyllis Bentley. "Yes," she said audibly.

I looked at her and saw an entirely different person. She was dressed to the nines. She wore a pinkish suit, a blouse with ruffles at the neck and sleeves, graced by some sort of beaded necklace. Her hair seemed put in place professionally, and she wore designer eyeglasses, those horizontal oval-shaped ones, which I could not recall ever noticing. (How do they see anything with those?) She looked two or three years older.

"Now, Mr. Schell, you are here to lend support to Ms. Jacobs?"

"Yeah."

Mike Schell sat slouching in his chair in battered jeans and a thin crumpled turtleneck, deep maroon. Looking a bit unshaven, his hair short and uncombed. "All right. Let's begin." Dean Bentley's voice was calm and firm. "Ms. Jacobs, in your 'Complaint,' if you will get it out please, on page two, top paragraph, you assert that you sent an e-mail to Professor Morris and received a reply from him?"

Ms. Jacobs turned to the page and read earnestly. "That's right."

"Well, Dean Livingston is here to set something on the record. Now Dean Livingston, Professor Morris wrote in his response, there is only one page, last sentence, 'My computer has no capacity to generate or receive e-mail.'"

I thought Mike Shell guffawed. In any case he raised his hand and let it drop on the table. Ms. Jacobs removed her glasses.

"Dean Livingston, you have a list of everyone's computer? The type, the strength, the capacity etc.?"

"That's right," said Sir Walter. "Have it right here." He slapped his hand on a folder.

"And what does your list indicate about Professor Morris?"

"That he is correct in saying he has no capacity for e-mail in his computer. He requested not to be updated. Owns an ancient aunt Tilly, but when we offered to upgrade him with Windows, he declined. His computer cannot send or receive e-mail. Or get to the Internet. Deprived, I'd say, but then there's no law that says he must have it."

Ms. Jacobs looked at Mike Schell, who shrugged.

"Thanks, Dean Livingston," and he got up and on his way out I was pretty sure I caught a wink.

"Ms. Jacobs, in light of this information, do you want to alter your recollection?"

"No." She said it with self-assurance. "I thought you were on *my* side."

Dean Bentley's cold voice came slowly. "Let me repeat, I am neutral. I am on no one's side. I am trying to get at the facts and resolve this matter. Clear, Ms. Jacobs?"

"Yes." Self-assurance missing. "I sent that e-mail, I *did*!"

"To what address?"

"I don't know. As usual. His name, dot.edu, whatever."

"But Professor Morris does not have such an address. Your e-mail would have been returned to you as undeliverable. As you heard he can't receive or send."

"Well, you're confusing me. I was pretty upset."

"Understood, but this e-mail business is a little messy. If this gets any further, Professor Morris would have the right to have your computer examined. And of course his."

"What for? It's mine!"

"In order to see whether your message is there as undelivered."

"I delete that stuff all the time."

"The technology can find even deleted e-mails. It would be nice if we could straighten that part of it out?" Dean Bentley's voice remained even, professional, now with just a hint of sympathy for the young woman, who was in a bad spot. So Stan had been right.

Ms. Jacobs sat and stared into space. She had put on and removed her glasses several times. Now they were in her hand, which rested on the table.

"All right, then," Dean Bentley said, "let me move to a different point. Your 'Complaint' details the events so that you dropped the course *after* Professor Morris' unwanted advances?"

"Right."

"And indeed you state, page 2, paragraph 4, that you did find the course hard, and that Professor Morris invited you to the office to help you. And that's when the alleged assault took place?"

"Yes. You have it all there. Why do we have to go through this again and again? I should have brought my Dad," she said sullenly, as if the boy slumped in his chair next to her would be of no use at all, as she looked furtively at him for help he obviously did not know how to give.

"Ms. Jacobs, we are doing all this to be fair. A man's career may be at stake. Assault is a potentially criminal charge. Now tell me this: what were you studying the day you dropped the course?"

"God, I can't remember."

"'Burnt Norton,'" I said. It fell out of my mouth.

"Yes. Right." Ms. Jacobs nodded, as if she were in fact remembering, which she probably was.

"'Burnt Norton,' then," Dean Bentley said. "Now we have the date you dropped the course as the same day you were studying that work. I have a piece of paper from a spiral notebook here. It was sent to me this morning. It comes from a fellow student in Professor Morris' class. It's dated the day you dropped the course. The paper is titled BURNT NORTON in capital letters. With it is a note. I will hand it out to the principals," and she gave me and Milicent L. Jacobs a copy. I silently read with her, "It says, 'Dear Dean Bentley: I am sending you this because I think it may help the Professor *The Crier* says was accused. I know there were no names mentioned, but I pretty much *know* it's my Professor. This is a notepaper I took in Professor Morris' class. I took some notes on the poem which we were doing that day. Milicent Jacobs sat next to me and leaned over and wrote this on my notebook.' And I will now read this: 'I don't get this stuff. My boyfriend's dropping. Me too, after class. Loyalty, even though we're break-ing up. I *really* like the nice old man.' The name of the student, and I called her to say I would not, could not, conceal it, is Elly Smitherson. Do you have such a student, Professor Morris?"

I had listened and read intently, and when I heard "nice old man," there was the pain in my back again. "Nice old man!" I would rather be a groper than a nice old man! Ah, yes, "That is no country for old men…." I had not heard the dean's question so she repeated it. "Yes," I said simply, "she's a student in the class." So she and that loser were breaking up at the time, some truth there. Dropping the course, was this to reunite them? I sighed. Then I first noted the student had a problem spelling professor.

"In light of this note, Ms. Jacobs, might you wish to reconsider your allega-tions?"

"Why?" Ms. Jacobs looked utterly confused. I mean so what? I did write that, maybe. I did think he was a nice old man—" A stab of pain again. "But what's that got to do with anything?"

"Well, if you wrote that on the day you dropped his course, and you originally said you dropped it *after* he allegedly groped you, then would you be writing that you were dropping the course because it was hard, because you wanted to follow your boyfriend since you were trying to get together again, and would you call a groper a 'nice old man'? It seems just not to add up. Ms. Jacobs?"

"After I wrote that note, then I came to drop, that's when he did it!"

"Sorry," Dean Bentley said, "but the time-line of your narrative in the Com-plaint says otherwise. It states clearly that you dropped the course a day after the alleged event."

Now my back felt locked. I knew that if I moved a thousandth of an inch I would never move again, never. Bent over a little, I raised my hand, like a student in class.

"Professor Morris?"

"Dean Bentley, may I speak?" She looked a bit doubtful, but then she nodded and cupped her face into both hands, leaning her elbows on the table.

However this played out, I had been thinking of saying something confes-sional, something like: "Milicent, I am truly sorry I snubbed you. You see I had some lousy news to carry back to my colleagues, and I was very upset, and it was raining, well, beginning to rain, and I did sort of see you, that's true, and I don't really know why I snubbed you, why I turned my face, but it was not meant to offend you, certainly not, I'm not that sort of fellow, so I can understand why you were hurt, why you lashed out with this totally absurd accusation—really I can see that, I understand ..."

But what came out was very different. Turning my face toward her, locking my wide open eyes onto hers, I still had the sensation of not seeing her. Cheeks flushed, neck throbbed:

"You may just about have ruined my life at this place with your foolish fantasy! Do you have any idea what you've done? Play with someone's life as if I were one of your Barbies! I could face prison!" I was shouting, but I could not hear it, and I slapped the table with open palm. Hard. "How can you do anything so *vile* and stupid! What makes you think that I would ever want to fondle *you*?" Dean Bentley was speaking, but I did not take it in. A voice I heard, stern, and she had gotten up and was walking toward me. "You're nothing but a narcissistic *child*! Grow up. What do they say, get a life! Do you actually think I owed you a hello? What the hell—," and as I slapped the table a second time, the weight of a strong hand rested on my left shoulder. "Professor Morris, I think Ms. Jacobs gets the point."

There was profound silence in the room. I heard some freezing hail-like pellets hit the window; it was now totally dark outside.

"Can I leave?" Mike Schell said.

"Whenever you wish," Dean Bentley said. She had returned to her seat.

He got up and shuffled his way out, head down. Milicent L. Jacobs had taken out a pretty pink lace handkerchief and was sobbing into it, quietly, her body heaving up and down. To me it sounded more like keening. For an instant I really felt empathetic pain, as I watched her dissolving composure bring back to me the image of the smiling, needy, imploring-for-approval face I had seen so often, beginning with that day in late August outside my office door.

For the first time Dean Bentley looked a little unsure of herself. "Ms. Jacobs? Does that crying mean Professor Morris is right? Do you take back your accusations?"

She never said a word, simply nodded and blew her nose vigorously into that laced lavender handkerchief.

"Ms. Jacobs, if that is a 'yes,' then may I ask that you apologize to Professor Morris?"

Ms. Jacobs stopped her sobbing, her glasses were off and still on the table, she was rubbing her eyes with her hands. Then she turned to me, placed her two hands on the table, and as if she were a leopard ready to attack, cheeks red with tears and fury, she flung out her words like primal howls.

"You couldn't even say hello, could you! I mean I dropped your damned course! It was b-o-o-o-ring! Half the class wanted to drop. They just stayed for the requirement! Take a poll! Ask them! I had no bad feelings against you! But you couldn't say 'Hi' to me! Walked right past me! You hurt me! You hurt my feelings. A lot! You—" Milicent L. Jacobs was not accenting her sentences with question marks but with bitter exclamations, and they came from deep, deep down, from the deepest part of her misery-filled interior.

Dean Bentley had heard enough. This was turning into the soap opera she was there to prevent. "Please, Ms. Jacobs, compose yourself. And apologize."

Milicent L. Jacobs drew a deep breath, then said something in a low voice I could not hear. But she said it so feelingly, I believed her—whatever she had said—and was touched. For all that she had done to me, I was angry at myself. My careless dismissal of her—was it on some level anger that she had dropped my course?—had brought me to this, had brought her to this. I actually flailed at my vanity with silent curses. And for the first time that afternoon our eyes met. She looked collapsed, her shoulders tucked in like a bird's wings in a storm. Mascara was streaking down her cheeks. She was really blessed with a very beautiful face, and I wondered why beautiful faces, when they were falling apart, looked so terrible and so appealing all at once. Gazing at her, I barely nodded in assent, and then she got up and exited so quickly it was hard to tell she was ever there, except that I sniffed a trace of perfume in the air that I had not been aware of before. She had also left her glasses and all her papers.

Dean Bentley had returned to her chair. She looked at me from across the table and simply shrugged. "I guess we have a very troubled young woman here. I'll see what we can do to steer her into counseling." Then she got up and walked over to me slowly "I am truly sorry. These things happen. But you know, unfortunately, very *in*frequently, compared to the *fre*quency, when the story turns out to be true." She had put her emphases in such a way that she was, however subtly, blaming me for the *fre*quency, rather than commiserating for the *in*frequency, of which I happened to be a victim. Payback for my outburst? Her weak smile, her accusatory eyes, communicated something, perhaps a warning to all lechers, young and old, who really had groped? I resented it. Marge Keefer wouldn't have done that.

But then my pain was killing me, and I ceased to see Phyllis Bentley clearly. As a matter of fact, I was half sitting half standing at an angle, from which I saw the portrait gallery of presidents, their eyes piercing me reproachfully. When I tried to straighten myself to stand, I immediately fell back with a scream.

After that I can't recall what happened. I might have lost consciousness for just a moment, for it felt as if a blade had sliced me in half. Next I was aware of a scene resembling recent dreams: a crowd gathered in a corner of the room by the door and someone yelled, "I called 911. Anyone here who knows CPR?"

"It's not my heart," I managed, as I lay on the floor in a heap. "It's my damned back!"

But it was too late. I heard the insistent siren of the university emergency ambulance, and two student EMCs rushed in with a collapsible stretcher on wheels. When I repeated that I was fine except for my back, I was treated summarily: "Please, sir, let us do our job. Any pain at your age can be heart or worse. Even back pain. So relax, we'll take it from here."

I gave up. After taking my pulse and blood pressure, they lifted me onto the stretcher on a three count, wrapped me up like a mummy, then snapped my head into place so I couldn't move. Slowly the room had emptied. Dean Bentley, who had turned rather pale, was looking at me with concern.

"Dean Bentley, will you call my wife, please, and tell her my back went. She'll know. It's happened before. And please begin by conveying the outcome of the hearing?"

"Yes, of course. Is she home?"

"Yes, by now," I looked at the imitation grandfather clock standing in the corner of the Board Room, "definitely at home." The medics were still fussing over me.

"Where are you taking me?" They mentioned the hospital twenty minutes away. I turned to Phyllis Bentley, "Tell her I'm in the usual hospital, and not to worry. It's my *back*. And sorry for the outburst." She nodded.

They carried me out and placed me into the van-like truck, and I said, "Please, fellows, no sirens."

"Fine," one of them said, "just flashing lights."

"Good."

When we got to the hospital, Julianna was waiting. She had obviously not believed the message about my back because she looked tight and grim. She walked into a cubicle where they had put me in the Emergency Room. A nurse came in and took my pulse. "On a scale of 0 to 10, how would you judge your pain?" She was very earnest. Without meaning to sound like a wise-ass, I said, "Eleven." The nurse was not amused. Gray-haired and wiry she looked me in the eyes, as if saying, "We have a lot of people here in worse shape than you," and left abruptly. Julianna looked pained. "Honest, honey," I said, "I wasn't trying to be funny. Anyway it's my back. When I sit all tensed up you know what sometimes happens."

"Well, they want to test you for everything anyway," she said, in full support of the doctors. I fidgeted on the narrow and hard table that served as my bed. Just desserts?

"Nonsense, but I have no intention of fighting them, it's a lost cause. They have to cover their proverbial behind!"

"Well, better that—"

They did now begin to test me, EKG; automatic blood pressure machine, again and again; blood samples. The young resident was giving orders. Turning to Julianna, he ignored the patient. "I think this is not his heart, maybe just extreme muscle or nerve pain. Any trouble like this before?"

Frustrated at being ignored and talked about in the third person, I said *I* would be glad to answer that, and then recited my medical history concerning my back and neck, right up to the latest MRIs.

"Tell you what, if these tests prove negative, and everything so far has, we'll give you a shot for the pain. Ever had one?"

"Sure," I said, thinking of some of the shots which had struck my body.

In less than an hour the resident returned, cheerful. "No sign of heart trouble. We'll give you an anesthetic shot at the trigger point. If that doesn't work we'll go to the facets next. Let's give it a week or so. I did a turn at the Pain Management Center, I know about backs."

After establishing precisely where the pain was in my upper buttock (I almost screamed), the doctor said, "Good," and he drew a circle on the spot with a black felt-top. Then he injected saying, "It won't hurt and the effect is pretty quick. Feel all right?" I nodded. "That was the anesthetic. Now the shot. I'll check back in a few minutes."

"I could have had him last year in class. He looks twenty-three or four," I said when Julianna returned to the cubicle. "Oh, they just look younger each year. Don't be such a curmudgeon." She held my hand. "No," I said a little ruefully. "We're getting older."

The resident came back, still cheerful. "So you've had this before, Professor—" he looked at the chart, "Morris? Keep in shape?" My face gave the answer.

"Well, you ought to. Get those stomach muscles tight and all this will go away. Strengthen that back! And range of motion. Move, move, move." I sighed. Then I told him about my neck again.

"Oh, yes that explains a lot. Yep, more PT, and do it religiously. Make time in the day. I promise, it will help." I had heard it all before.

"Well, I'll discharge you and good luck! Put some ice on the spot if you want. No more than fifteen minutes, maybe twice an hour at first, then less. Here, take these. It's a muscle relaxant. I've given you four. It'll make you sleepy. No driving, okay? At least it's not the heart."

Oh, I objected, but it *was* the heart. With considerable sorrow I knew that, as my new friend Yeats said, now all my ladders, too, were gone, and I was lying in "the foul rag-and-bone shop of the heart." *My* heart. Julianna had brought my old cane, and I was wheeled to the exit and then walked gingerly to the car, which an attendant had brought to the front.

"How is it?" Julianna asked. "Maybe that cervical collar would help if you wore it more often?"

"It's damned uncomfortable. Besides, I didn't want sympathy today. If I had worn it, someone would have thought, 'Look at the guy. Milking it all for what it's worth.' To hell with that."

"Yes, darling, but today is over. Oh, and I'm so relieved it went well. First thing Bentley told me. Imagine the stupidity of it all!"

"I know. But you know the girl—she *is* troubled, fine. But I didn't help things. I was very stupid, too." And I described my angry diatribe. "Anyway, it's over. When does *The Crier* come out?"

"Wednesday. I'm sure that woman who hit your car will have the story."

"Hmn. Hope so. But I also hope it's short."

"And no 'alleges' this time?"

I forced a smile. "I don't think so."

When we got home I stretched out on the bed and iced my buttock, and with the muscle relaxant kicking in I fell asleep almost at once. Nothing but numbness came as I recall Julianna quietly slipping the ice pack from under my back. A long day and, in all ways, a painful one.

That night I spiraled into a deep sleep of uneasy dreams, but when I woke I recalled nothing. Julianna sat on the bed, dressed.

"My God! What time is it?"

"Ten. How's the pain?"

"I don't know. I haven't moved yet." I turned my body, as I was taught and then swung my legs over the side of the bed, rubbed my eyes and began to stand up. "Ouch, not gone. But better." I took a few tentative steps. "Better. What's today, Wednesday?"

"Tuesday."

"I have to teach tomorrow! We're getting to the end, the slackers are beginning to drift back."

She didn't think that was a good idea, but when it came to holding class I was stubborn. "Tomorrow," I said, and Julianna knew I meant it.

Next day I was much better. The pain had eased and the grogginess from the muscle relaxants was gone. If not overdone, walking was good for the muscles, the doctor had said, but Julianna insisted on at least driving me to and from class. I grudgingly agreed. She helped me dress, tied my shoelaces, but insisted I wear the cervical collar, which made me look pathetic. Then, after a brief breakfast, she asked me to take my cane, ever mindful (as I had been with my father) of calling it my "stick." Except just now that was the wrong word, too.

"No!" ("a paltry thing,/A tattered coat upon a stick …") "—No way, please!" I was beginning to wonder whether Yeats was the right poet for me to have fallen for at this stage of my life. Julianna shrugged. Looking for all the world like a "paltry thing," I walked stiffly and slowly into the car, and she drove. We made arrangements for her to drive me back during a window in her own scheduled day.

Outside my door Stanley Habers was pacing up and down, waiting. When he sighted me his face almost contorted itself into a self-satisfied grin.

"Ah, the collar of the hanging to hide the marks! But they didn't hang you after all, so I hear?"

"No Stan, they didn't."

"What happened?"

"We were all asked to keep everything confidential," I said. Besides I really didn't want to talk about it.

"Yeah? I heard she recanted, no?"

"Well if you know, why ask?"

"Details, man, details."

"There are no details. I ended up in the emergency room. My back caved in."

"I heard. Hit those exercise machines. I hate them too—"

"Strengthen my stomach muscles, I know. Stan, thanks for your support. I want to prepare. I've had little time. Don't mean to be rude."

"Just one thing—was I right about the e-mail?"

"Yes, well there was more than that, but yes, you were right." Satisfaction, ear to ear, broke out on Habers' face. "Okay, my man, prepare, prepare," he said waving his arm in an exaggerated farewell, and he was gone.

Before facing my students I removed my collar and actually hid it in a drawer. Someone might come. Fifty minutes aren't going to make a difference. During class I did feel a little wobbly, so I sat at, rather than on, the desk, something I had done more and more frequently of late. The class went slowly, the students were restless, already anxious about their take-home essay final. More work for me, but at least I would be able to read their work, which is more than I could do with their scribble in blue books. In the back row, I spied Milicent L. Jacobs' face smiling at me, or rather grinning. But, of course, it turned out to be just another smiling student. Perhaps those muscle relaxants were making me prone to hallucinate? In any case it had startled me.

When I got back, I opened the envelopes gathered from my mail cubicle and one was on official department stationery, handwritten, brief but gracious, which said, "We're glad the ordeal is over, and we never believed the outcome could be otherwise." It was signed, "Sincerely, Robinson and Bentwick." I opened another envelope, a folded white piece of paper, torn from a spiral notebook, from Hal Muzzey: "If you want to sue, I know a good lawyer. The idiots!" A third letter was a card I removed from a thick ivory envelope, the inside of which was a pattern of blue on blue. The card greeted me with a beautiful arrangements of summer flowers. Letting my eyes move to the writing, I had guessed correctly, recognizing Ann Rosenthal's clear and elegant hand: "My dear Jack, Words cannot express my relief and my outrage. I shall always be your friend and colleague, and I cannot believe that anyone would make you go through all this. I heard your back is hurting. Here's to a quick forgetting—and a speedy recovery from your aching back! Affectionately, Ann." Good old Ann, she would have lived a better life in Victorian England. Then I opened the last envelope, message typed. "Dear Jack: I hope you don't think that my personal views ever blind me. I am a professional, and I would never compromise my activism for a personal relationship. I was particularly glad that the process worked, for I feel that this is, for me at least, the most important thing. Carol Gunderson." I was struck by something and reread. The words "I" and "me" occurred seven times in this little note. Its odd, cold officialese was probably a reluctance to appear to be brown-nosing so close to tenure decision, for Carol Gunderson's future would be decided by the department during intersession. Still. Edith had called Monday night whilst I was asleep and sent a potted plant. Also she had called me Tuesday and we had a brief chat during which she wished me well, expressing her sincere sympathy "for your poor back." She would not be in Wednesday, going to Boston for a conference of department heads. Habers had given his view in person. Everyone had been heard from except Marvin Golden. All in all, a decent bunch. I thought myself lucky. When the phone rang it was Julianna coming over to take me home in an hour.

I remembered that today *The Crier* would be out, so I walked over to the table in the office and grabbed one of the last remaining papers. If I could have I would have run back, feeling foolish as I passed the departmental office. Angel was out, and the student helper made a happy face, but then she always did. She was Vietnamese, her English weak, but smiling was, I knew, a cultural habit of respect. The first page had nothing, nor the second. Turning page after page I still found nothing. Impossible, and I repeated the routine, slowly and calmly. This time, on page four, bottom, I found a brief two column piece.

PROFESSOR CLEARED
BY JULIE HANNOVER

The Professor of English who, we reported in a pre-Thanksgiving piece, was accused by a former student of sexual assault has been cleared of these charges, according to reliable sources. Associate Dean of Affirmative Action, Phyllis Bentley, when asked to confirm, said she could neither confirm nor deny. Asked to elaborate, Dean Bentley said, "I am unable to say whether any charges were made. That's policy. Sorry. There will be no further comment from this office." *The Crier*, to whom the student first came with her story, attempted, without success, to contact her. Her roommate said she thought she had left campus for home, though she could not confirm this. Dean of Students, Mark Prokoff, asked about the student's whereabouts, said, "We do not release any such information."

End of story. And not a single "alleges." I folded the paper, ran my fingers across the crease, and slipped it into my briefcase when the phone rang again. Speak of the devil. It was Julie Hannover.

"Hi, Professor Morris? Julie Hannover. Did you see the story?"

I hesitated, wondering whether I should say no; that was true the first time I looked. But then I wanted to make myself feel virtuous and said, "Yes, I did. Just read it."

"Was it all right? We are real sorry you had to—"

"Thanks. The original story was page one and this one was a little hard to find." In spite of myself I could not let it go.

Silence. "Uh, well, yes. You know follow-ups are always shorter."

"That right? Well, I'm no journalist. I just thought the finding of innocence might match the accusation of guilt. 'Alleged' accusation, I should have said."

"Uh, well, not always. Anyway—"

Take her off the hook. "How's the car?"

"Good, good. I mean I haven't fixed it yet. Waiting until intersession. How's yours?"

"Okay. Haven't fixed it yet either. But I did tell my wife."

"Hope she didn't yell at you?"

"Oh, just a little—"

She laughed. "Oops, gotta run. Sorry. Hope we meet again. Bye." Click.

Well, I nodded, you're a nice kid, but I hope we don't run into each other again. By foot or car.

My office door was half open when I looked up and saw a woman and a young man behind her standing somewhat uncomfortably, hesitant. She was clad neatly in a maroon wool suit, and over her right arm she carried a matching wool coat tucked against her body. Her hair was black with some streaks of gray smartly arranged to blend in and give her a chic look. The young man was dressed like all such young men, except I noted how tall he was and that his jeans were a bit too short.

"Hi. What can I do for you?"

"Professor Morris, I'm Amy Levinson—used to be, that is—and this is my son Josh. We're looking the place over."

I was puzzled. The name rang no bell. "Yes?"

"Well, I can't expect you to remember me, it's been a while—quite a while! I was your student nearly thirty years ago?"

Speechless at first, for I had no memory of either face or name, but I didn't want to say so. So I scrutinized thoughtfully and pretended. "Oh! Amy—"

"Levinson. It's Grossinger now. You can't possibly remember? I was an indifferent student. And I sure don't look the same!" Her face smiled generously.

"Yes, yes. I must say, it's been a while, but you majored in English? Please, do sit down."

"Thanks. No, actually I majored in Sociology. But I loved to read. I took your poetry course. We did a lot of Eliot. Over my head, some of it, but I stuck it out."

"Oh, gosh, yes. Long time ago. And here you are, married. And children."

Amy Grossinger, née Levinson, looked at me with abstract eyes. "Yep. Time goes. Josh's the oldest. I have a daughter in middle school. Anyway Josh is enrolling somewhere next fall. We're pretty sure it's here. If so, I told him he has to

take you. I have never forgotten your class. It was just about the best class I had
here. I wish I had been a better student."

Blood was rushing to my cheeks. "Well, that's awfully nice of you. I'm sure
Josh will have a great time. And what are you interested in, Josh?" Josh was silent
and wanted to be somewhere else. He was looking down at the floor and chewing
gum. His lips closed, but he *was* chewing, the mouth moving in slow motion.
And his mother gave him a quick stare. The chewing didn't stop, but it became
almost invisible unless you focused on the mouth. But I wasn't doing that,
instead fixing my eyes with more interest than I had on my former student, trying
hard but unsuccessfully to squeeze a memory of the face into my brain. Josh said,
in a low voice, "Aw, not sure yet."

"Of course, you're not. And a good thing." And I knew my question had been
silly, my language banal. To be fair, I had been startled and didn't know what to
say.

"So what are you up to, Amy? May I still call you that?"

Of course. She said she had been a mother first, then dabbled here and there,
and was now working on a modest graphic art business, out of the house, with a
partner. She was happy.

"Well, that's great!"

"And you? Everything fine with you?"

Oh, yes. Children have grown up. My wife teaches here, chairs the History
department. Things change, of course. New people all over the place. You know.
I was running out of things to say. Amy Levinson must have sensed this, for she
held out her hand.

"Great to see you, Professor Morris. Josh will come around to see you
if—when—he arrives, right Josh?" Josh nodded dutifully, his mouth reactivated,
the chewing vigorous.

"Well, nice of you to drop in. And I look forward to seeing Josh, if he decides
to come. He'll have a lot of choices. But if I can help once he's here—I do know
the joint, you know," and I was aware I had said "joint" for Josh.

She thanked me, held out her hand, which I accepted with relief. "Bye."

When they had left, I stared out the window through the bare branches onto
the nearly empty highway. And I was in some denial. I can't believe that my students are bringing their sons to me! And she had gray in her hair! When she was
my student all those years ago I never dreamt—to paraphrase Yeats—that I
would see her combing gray hair! My God, I'm ancient. But then I recalled my

early days, all full of energy and the rush of pleasure. How I had loved teaching, every class, every student. What a time!

Time present and time past

Are both perhaps present in time future ...

I don't think so, I think time past is time past. At least right now, that's what *I* think, Mr. Eliot.

Julianna was at the door. I didn't immediately tell her of Amy Levinson's visit. How could I bring myself to confess I had just spoken to a former student who was perhaps only ten or twelve years younger than my wife? And she handed me my cane.

But that evening I told Julianna about Seth. Despite what we had said, I knew that Seth was hoping I would pave the way. We were lounging on the couch after the news, and I had been searching for the right moment, but there would never be a right moment anyway. To my astonishment, she appeared to be taken even more by surprise than expected. She paled a little, looked grim, bit her lips, fought off her tears for a while, but then let them flow, heaving her chest as I held her tightly. Few words passed between us as we comforted each other.

When the tears stopped, she looked at me and wondered whether, just between us, we could be honest, honest to say that it was not merely the hard life Seth would face, the prejudices and dangers, that made us sad? Wasn't there a sense of loss here, too? No matter that we would love him as ever, if not more, were we not mourning the loss of someone about whom we had dreamt the dreams of parents that would never come to be now? Yes, I nodded, yes, and no one would feel differently, there was no shame to feel that. And that was what Seth had feared, that is why he had kept silent, as I imagined so many children did. Somewhere deep down they all knew that such news would at first cause a reversal of expectations for parents, a shock, a shattering of what they had day-dreamed for them, their child, or more honestly, for themselves. This, too, then was a coming out for the parents, this too was an honest confession of pain, and it was a balm for them both. But then I also had to say it, and Julianna agreed, was it not haughtily self-righteous of us to *expect* our children to conform to comfortable images we invent for them? What right had we to do that? To feel sorry for ourselves because our son was living a life that made him happy? No right. And yet also, having admitted that, we might allow ourselves our corner of regrets, which we knew would never go away, but now we also felt cleaner, as Julianna put it, less the hypocrites. Love for Seth had nothing to do with it, but loss was loss. We would need to love a different Seth now, a new Seth who was not new except in our image of him, and such images are powerful, icons of identity that could not be changed overnight. Readjustment.

A new line was there for us, and we would need to take care to negotiate it, to be honest with our son, to love but not to overindulge, not to overcompensate, for if anyone in the world would spot this it would be Seth—Seth who had, after all, become a true wanderer. She now had a good reason to go to New York and be with Seth; there had been an invitation to her to serve as an outside examiner at N.Y.U. and she had held them at bay. Now she would say yes. And she would let Seth tell her, and she would pretend that we had not talked. Yes, I agreed. I told her because I had to, it was too much to carry alone, and besides Seth half expected it. She not only understood but said she was grateful, and now it would go a lot easier with Seth.

As we shut the lights that night, Julianna turned to me and stroked my face and wondered out loud whether too many strange things were happening to us lately? It was beginning to feel like a pile-up on a foggy road. I said oh, yes, a pile-up all right. Lying there as she fell asleep, I recalled Stanley Habers' quotation from *Hamlet*, and I repeated it to the walls,

> When sorrows come, they come not single spies,
>
> But in battalions.

10

After the second story in *The Crier*, they all said it was over. Julianna hugged me, rubbed my back with open hands and said, "I'm so glad it's over. What a relief!" My colleagues said it was over. Stan Habers sat in his office feet apart, very pleased. "Well, man, it's over, and you know what? It's kind of an interesting story, and I heard how it ended, and what a nut case she is. God, I hope they get her outta here!" And he got up and slapped me on the back, pretty hard, as I was standing near one of his bookcases. Edith Sellers striding down the hallway one day actually shook my hand and squeezed: "Good that it's over, Jack." And she walked away smiling. For a little while I myself was thinking it was over.

But it wasn't over. In some ways it had just begun. No matter how sweetly people smiled at me, I sensed that small corner in all their minds that harbored some doubts. Paranoia? Maybe, but they looked at me too quickly and then turned their heads to escape my eyes. Or so I heard them through their smiles: "Wonder what *really* happened there? Never will know the whole truth." In classes I was sometimes convinced female students looked at me differently—some appeared to leer, some frowned, some turned their heads away. Was I imagining all this? As for the male students, some of them, I was sure, offered a wink, a fatuous and almost envious glint in their eyes. In my dreams I kept hearing laughter but could make out little else. Milicent L. Jacobs had done a number on my life, that's for sure. There were times when I thought, rather sardonically, that for all my troubles I might as well have fondled her. But whenever I summoned up her image, any thought of that collapsed. Other moments I had the feeling that I saw her everywhere—in the hallways, on campus walkways, by the water cooler. Though I had heard she had left campus, it didn't matter: I could feel her presence, saw her rapid steps, saw always the back of her, of course, never the face. Because she was not there. But she was.

At first I nursed only profound sadness; then I pitied myself; finally I felt pure rage. When I met Habers again, he slapped me on the back a second time, "You look worried? What's the problem? Thing's got no legs!" Well, with time I saw the "thing" becoming a centipede. But I tried hard to forget, to make it all be "over," and I might have succeeded if it had not been for the letters and the phone calls.

The first call rang in the office.

"Hello?"

"Professor Morris?" The voice was muffled. It sounded a little like Marlon Brando in *The Godfather*.

"Speaking. Who's this?"

"We don't believe this shit that you didn't do anything to the girl. We think you did, prof diddler, and we're gonna see that you get yours!" The phone was slammed so hard that I jerked the receiver from my ear. First I laughed out loud; then as I sat still, seething with anger, I felt blood rising, ears ringing. In my Directory I thumbed the pages and found Police, which sent me to Campus Security, and there I found everything from Emergency to Front Gate to Parking. Was this an "emergency"? Well, it wasn't a parking issue, and the Front Gate? Fingers resting on the phone; then I picked it up and dialed 111 for Emergency. A gruff voice, "Officer Molloy, what is your emergency?"

"It's not really an emergency, officer, but—"

"This is an emergency number, sir. If you do not have an emergency, please call the proper number."

Again the phone, bang! I banged down my own receiver, as if officer Molloy could hear it! Searching for the Director of Security number I found it and dialed again.

"What is your call about, sir?"

"An abusive phone call."

"Well, professor, there are loads of those. We can't trace it. Nothing we can do, sorry. But if it happens again, call back."

I thanked her and placed the phone into its cradle, more gently this time. Of course the woman was right, and now I was embarrassed.

But I did not believe this was "Bonnie" Jacobs' doing nor her "Clyde" boyfriend's. But who? And then I targeted a prime suspect. Last spring I had failed a plagiarist, a senior who could not graduate, forcing him to come back this fall for a course to meet the credit minimum. Dressed like the Great Gatsby, he had been arrogant, even threatening. On several occasions I had seen him in the hallway or on campus this semester, and though our eyes never met, I perceived a definite chill as we passed each other. No love lost there. Yes, I was certain. All this was John Strozzi's work. But could I prove anything? Clearly hopeless. This wannabe rich boy, with his white V-neck knit sweaters, who was on the tennis team but rarely came to play (so the coach had told me), who thought he was another McEnroe, he had a grudge all right. Must have been. I recalled the day he played with a toy revolver facing me across my desk, the day I had called him in to show him the evidence. "My brother's," he had said, "he's eight." I threatened to call the police. He guffawed and retreated. Oh, yes. Strozzi.

For a few days there were no calls, but then about ten one evening, Julianna shouted up the stairs, "Jack. It's for you. Sounds strange." I took the call in my study and waited until Julianna had hung up downstairs. "Hello?" This time it was not a muffled sound, but a gruff New York area accented voice. Tony Soprano had replaced Marlon Brando. "Hi there prof diddler, we're not forgettin' you. Watch your back, man." Click. I knew better than to tell the police, but the next morning I called the telephone company. Exaggerating a little, I told them I was the victim of countless obscene phone calls and wanted something done. They said they would gladly give me an unlisted number and facilitate a way of letting me inform friends and family of the change. We were both annoyed.

"I thought it was over," Julianna said. "Could it be about something else?"

"What? 'Diddler'—?"

"Okay, of course. Then let's do it." And so we did, and that was the end of phone calls at home. Marlon Brando called once more at the office, but then there was quiet.

But now they took to the mails, and somehow I thought of the source in the plural, because the phone calls had said "*we*." The first letter arrived in my office box, typed single-spaced on plain white paper. "Prof diddler—you'll be exposed! We got the goods on your previous diddling!" Nothing else. I decided to take the letter to the Director of Security, a no-nonsense fellow from East Boston, Al Cappalucci, and I had known him for years, though there had been little reason to see him.

"Professor Morris, there isn't much we can do. I'm awfully sorry. It'll stop, though it may take a while. They get tired out, know what I mean? It's a fuckin' game for 'em, pardon my French." I sat and nodded slowly. "I hope so. Thanks."

Cappalucci had been right. For the time being there were no further letters, and the unlisted number had stopped the phone calls. I was tempted to say it was over but dared not. Had I not thought this once before? Anyway, in some ways, it would never be over.

And I had been wise not to celebrate too early. One last letter arrived at home addressed to Julianna, so she had opened it. She showed it to me more with a distressed "When will this stop?" look than with any comments about its contents:

Dear Mrs. Morris,

Your husband has been having loads of affairs with students for years. Millacent Jacobs was not the first. She backed down because she was scared of him. He threatened her with all kinds of things. We think you should know this.

There was no sign-off. After all, "anonymous" was old-fashioned, and they might have been unsure of how to spell it. They couldn't spell Milicent, and it wasn't the one "l." I was helpless, yet I had been right.

"*We*," I said to Julianna, "I always knew there was more than one person."

"Does it make any difference?"

"I don't know. Maybe."

"Perhaps that girl Milicent what's her name is behind it?" "Don't think so. I still think that plagiarist is somehow involved. And maybe that boyfriend of hers—Milicent's. Not she." Julianna lowered her head.

"It's become more than a nuisance, Jack." She stared at the floor.

"What do you want me to do about it? A public disavowal in *The Crier?* A day in the stocks? Walk around campus with a sandwich placard?" I sounded raspy.

"Jack! Look, I know you've tried. But it's beginning to get to me. In my department—"

I looked at her sorrowfully. "Oh, my dear! And what about you? Do you think I've had loads of affairs with students?"

"Jack!"

"Impossible, right?"

She looked at me not knowing what to say. "Yes, impossible. Do you regret that?" Now her voice was raised.

"That I didn't have any affairs? Sometimes I resent the 'eunuch' implication. I've told you that before. No. What I regret is what I've done to you."

Julianna managed a sympathetic face, though it came hard just now. "We'll survive this. It *will* all go away."

"Maybe," I said simply. "Maybe."

She wrapped her arms around me now and placed her cheek next to mine. So we stood silently and she wiped some wetness rolling on her cheek, while I was inert, breathing slowly and evenly as if I were asleep.

When we were graduate students, we were ruled by certain tyrants against whom, in those days, there was no recourse if you wanted to survive. Some of us were summoned to their office, a confrontation—some trivial transgression. Usually they had heard about "it" from so-and-so. So we students committed to memory the opening sentence of Kafka's *Trial*: "Someone must have traduced Joseph K., for without having done anything wrong he was arrested one fine morning."

That sentence now involuntarily jumped out at me. I was returning from class, and since I had been carrying an old record player to play a recording of Eliot for my students (it hadn't been converted to a CD), I knew I would have too much in my hands to fumble for keys. So I had left the door almost shut. When I pushed it open with my foot I saw a man and a woman standing in front of my desk: he in double-breasted raincoat with belt, style circa 1940 Bogart; she in shiny leather jacket.

"Who are you?" The man spoke first. "Professor Morris? Sorry to trespass. We assumed it would be unseemly to loiter outside? Forgive us? My name is Roger Jensen," and he took out an ID and held it up. "And this is Ms. Higgins," and he turned toward the woman. "Susan Higgins," she smiled and raised a laminated card.

"You'll excuse us, but this is just a formality. The parents of Ms.—" His cadence was sing-song. The man looked at a slip of paper.

"Jacobs?" I helped.

"Yes, Ms. Jacobs. Her parents retained us. Private investigators. Gosh, this sounds like a bad movie. We're almost embarrassed. May we sit down?"

I did not respond and left them standing.

"Anyway, look, we're uncomfortable—"

"But," Ms. Susan Higgins chimed in, "we're obliged to ask some questions. With your permission, of course." She never stopped smiling. I was struck by her bleached blond hair and deep red lips hiding large teeth, her rather large handbag. Out of a gumshoe movie. She might have been from the 1940s too. The two of them, a couple from central casting.

I spoke slowly.

"Just out of curiosity, have you been in touch with our administration?"

"Oh, no," Jensen said, "not necessary at all. Keep it amongst ourselves, you know."

"I didn't ask because I was fearful. To the contrary. I think you *are* trespassing, and the administration should be told of your visit. Perhaps I need an attorney?"

The man Jensen made a surprised grimace and folded his hands like a supplicant. Susan Higgins just stared, her face turning color a little. "Oh, Professor, if you do not want us here—I mean we'll go at once. Our trip is just a friendly way of saving you the trouble of—well, of inconveniencing you in any way."

"What exactly do you want? The case is closed, you know."

Jensen: "Well, yes. But you see Ms. Jacobs, you know, she is very upset. She now recants her confession of guilt. Says she was terrified. So what we want to know is—"

But I stopped him in mid-sentence.

"Never mind. I don't want to hear any more. We'll do this right, okay. If you want to talk to me you'll have to ask permission from Dean Bentley and Dean Livingston Scott first. And I may want that attorney. What the hell do you think you're doing, coming into my office like this and confronting me?"

Both of them seemed genuinely startled. They looked at each other, then at me.

"Well, we *are* sorry, indeed sir. We will leave you. No intent of criminal trespass. We know the law. The door was open. Anyway, you'll hear from us through the mail."

Jensen actually bowed so low it was clear he was wearing a toupee, which had moved sideways. I said nothing, stood up and opened the door wide and held it while they walked out together in two-step like dance partners.

Two weeks later I received an apology from Heep Investigation Agency in New York. It was all a mistake. Their people had acted unwisely. And besides, they had received word from the Jacobs family that their services were no longer needed. I cursed the day I had turned my head from Milicent L. Jacobs.

Stan Habers' long strides suggested he had every intention of tackling me. Instead he gave me a bear hug, smiled and winked.

"So how does vindication feel? Haven't talked for a while. Let's go to my office," and he grabbed me by the arm and just about pushed me through his door which he shut or, more accurately, slammed.

He stood supporting himself on his desk. "Ok. It's done with."

"It's not done with. I've been getting phone calls and letters."

"Oh?" He shrugged. "But listen, Morris, I'm an old pal. I've been meaning to ask you. Tell the truth, what *really* happened here? I gave you my full support and would have walked the plank for you, but now that it's over with—hey, you know me?" He had obviously ignored what I had said.

"I love details. I've been dying to ask you. I hear she was a looker. So what *really* happened here? A little encouragement? An innocent hand somewhere? Was this a woman scorned thing? Honest now, you know you can trust me—"

I listened to his words and they were far away, a hollow sound. Of course, he was yanking my chain. He loved to do that.

Then I heard him, closer, clearer. "You know Morris, I never went for the undergrads. Too dangerous. Oh, they trip themselves up, like yours, misunderstand the slightest touch, I flirt with words only, but there was *something* going on here, right?"

No. Habers was not kidding around any more. He meant it. What happened next was not very good for either of us. I lunged at him and swiped my hand across his face, hard. I must have hit his nose, because streams of blood were exiting both nostrils and running down his beige, open-collared shirt. He looked at me in disbelief, stunned. So was I. Quickly I pulled out my handkerchief to stem the flow of blood, but after taking the white flag, he gently yet firmly pushed me away.

"Hey! I could interpret that as the man doth protest too much. What the hell—!"

Something menacing in my eyes must have stopped him.

"Okay, Okay. I guess you meant it. No harm intended." He held his right arm out, palm upward, like a school guard signaling a stop sign.

I was totally unable to understand what I had done. This was not like me, and I remembered almost hitting that basketball player who took my parking spot back in the fall. Only this time there was no friendly Shaunessy to stop me.

"God, Stan, I'm *really* sorry. I don't know what possessed me!" The bleeding had almost stopped. Stan bent his head backwards.

"You sure are sensitive. I mean—oh, forget it. Shit, this hurts." He blinked his eyes and then shut them.

"Did I break it? Your nose?"

Stan gently took his right forefinger and touched his bloodied nose, while my blood-soaked handkerchief dangled from his left hand.

"Yeah. I think so." And he started to laugh.

"Listen, let me drive you to the hospital, please. I don't know what happened to me. All the stress. I just can't explain it. But, there was nothing going on, Stan. *Nothing!*" A woman scorned? Well, he might have been right there, but I didn't volunteer my snub of Milicent L. as an explanation.

"Well you sure made your point with emphasis. I believe you, man, I believe you." And he laughed again.

"Stan, the hospital? You need that looked at."

By now he was sitting on his oversized lounge chair, with his head bent back. "I think I'm supposed to have ice? Anyway, they can't do much with a broken nose, can they? Can't put a cast on it!" By now he was sounding worried. A hypochondriac who hated doctors. A dilemma.

"Stan," I pleaded. "Let's clean you up and let's go to the ER. Please?"

"Oh, all right," and he handed me my blood-red handkerchief. I took it at a relatively unstained spot between my fingers, not knowing what to do with it.

"Dump it in here," and Stan pushed his waste paper basket toward me. He was wearing boots again. I let it drop in.

As we drove to the ER, the same I had been hurried to with my collapsed back, I tried small talk, though actually I was feeling lousy about what I had done. Still, why did he provoke me?

At first the nurse thought I was the patient (she recognized me), but then she saw Stan's bloody face. He was bleeding again, just a trickle.

"What happened to *you*? If it's broken, we can't do much."

"I blew my nose too hard."

She didn't laugh and led us into a cubicle where she cleaned Stan's face and nose with some moist cotton, it looked like, and brought some ice.

"Told you," Stan mumbled, looking at me rather forlornly. She told him to put his head back. Pretty soon a young, white-coat came in and introduced himself politely.

"Let me see if it's broken." He touched it gingerly, bent it this way and that, looked at Stan's eyes, smiled and said, "Doesn't feel broken. Face would be swollen. Just a little bleeding. That's abating. You look fine under the eyes. Any trouble breathing through your nose?" Habers took a deep, fairly silent breath and shook his head.

"Well, then, that bleeding will stop. Let's keep the ice on for a half hour and I'll check back."

After less than that the white-coat came back and looked things over and seemed satisfied.

"You'll be fine. No break, I'm certain. Of course if it starts to bleed heavily, come back, and we'll stuff some gauze up the nostrils."

It didn't start bleeding. I brought Stan home. He had no classes, and the office hours he canceled by cell phone while we drove.

We sat on his plaid couch, and I still must have had a guilty look because, having changed his shirt, Habers came in smiling. "Hey, Morris, I'm kind of glad to see you can actually slap me around. I bet you've wanted to do that forever—" I raised my hand in protest, but he went right on, "Come on, Jack," and I was glad that for the first time in the course of this episode he called me by my first name, "we all have that wish. If it makes you feel any better there were times when I wanted to sock you!"

"Really? Often?"

"Well, let me count the ways." Then he smiled. "Yeah, really. Now that you socked me, I feel free. Watch your back, Morris!" And he laughed heartily. "Want some red wine?"

"Actually, yes," I said, and he came back with a bottle and two glasses and poured. "Expensive stuff. This 'coming out' deserves decent vintage, right?" He squinted to read the label but it must have hurt, so he just said, "Take my word. It's a French Burgundy, I think." I took the bottle and turned it by the neck to the label. I nodded. "Burgundy. Rest of it too small to read. Stan, I'm so—"

"Hey, stop apologizing. That would take it all back. No, no, no. Just drink." He poured, like an experienced sommelier. I was going to say how decent he was and understanding and all that, but I knew he would just shut me up. I was certain he knew I appreciated his forbearance, and I guess he took some genuine pleasure in seeing a side of me neither he (nor I) was used to.

We said no more about the incident but instead exchanged tidbits—the department, just fluffy gossip, until he said, nonchalantly, "Listen, I hear it whispered that you're thinking of packing it in. Anything to that?"

We were on the second glass of wine in early afternoon and my tongue was dry. I stared at him.

"Now don't hit me again," he said and then laughed. So did I.

"Well, I'd be lying if I denied I hadn't thought about it."

"Jack, you'd be nuts. I mean for what? That stuff with the girl will all go away. Department needs you. I'm not crapping around here. I don't give free compliments. Hey, you want me to work harder? For God's sake, man, who else is there? With Adler gone?"

Leon's face flashed by me through a slight haze, just for a second. I admitted the department was a real consideration, but downing the second glass I confided, "It's more Julianna."

"Julianna?"

I nodded. "Julianna is five years younger." He knew that. "And she's going on all engines." My speech was becoming a bit slurred. "And I think she looks at retirement like a divorce. I mean that's ridiculous! Isn't it?"

"No," he said to my surprise. "It's perfectly normal. The two of you—and then suddenly you flake off and sit in your retirement chair. *Rocking chair*," he added mockingly.

Habers poured himself a third glass, but I began to place my hand over mine, knowing I had to drive, but he waved me off. "There's always cabs," he said, reading my mind.

The notion of retirement had disturbed something in Habers; he was getting angrier by the minute, slouched in a leather armchair, his eyes narrowing. Not angry only at me, but at the whole idea. "God's sake, Jack, we're not *old*, you know! We can stay forever. You know that. I couldn't survive without seeing those young faces, yeah, the gals!" Sorrowfully I thought of how even that was no longer true for me. The young faces made me think of my graying and thinning hair.

Habers: "This damned throwaway society—they'll throw you away, you wait and see! Old age is garbage in our country 'tis of thee. Read the other day about an 'elderly' man, hit and run—turns out he was sixty-three! Those boomers! Some twenty-year-old reporter thinks sixty-three is 'elderly'! Want to make everyone else old and stay young forever themselves, the bastards!"

"Yes," I said, "of course." And I realized he was talking out of fear, for himself now, not me. His voice was steadier than mine. For a while he drank and we said nothing.

"Well, you just can't run out on me, that's it! Shit, man!" He rose and slowly walked toward me, and in his teary eyes I could see it wasn't to pay me back with a punch. Then he spread his arms. Instinctively I got up and spread my arms. We met in the middle of the room and fell into each other, embraced. He was sobbing now. I think I shed a tear. "Yaknowaluvya!" he mumbled. "Me too," I whispered. My head on his shoulders, I saw the living room wall was papered peppermint stripes. (It had been long since I had been at his house.) I tried counting the stripes—red, black, white—but I couldn't. "Stan, Stan—it's not a done deal. Anyway, we're getting drunk." He pulled back and grinned. "Yep, we are Morris, we *are* drunk." We disengaged like two boxers and moved unsteadily, each back into his corner where we slumped down into our respective chairs.

I let the wine settle, and for quite a while we were silent again. Then I started to get up. "Time to go. And, well, you know," and I pointed to his nose and shrugged. But he motioned with his hand. "Down!" he commanded. I obeyed.

Stan had opened another bottle.

He was looking miserable now. Some red puffing appeared on his right cheek, but that may have been the wine, though the nose trauma probably contributed.

"We need to settle this right now. No quitting, okay? I won't let you!" He stood up again; he was shouting. Now his words were coming out thick. We were both really pretty tipsy.

"Okay, okay. You know I said—I said I was only *thinking* about it anyway. But some days I hate coming in. Why did you take Julianna's side? What's it got to do with her, anyway? Peppermint wallpaper? She's the one who likes rocking chairs! I *hate* 'em." By now I was belligerent, confused. He insisted on making black coffee, and we drank several cups. We alternately used the bathroom. When I saw myself in the mirror, I shuddered.

"You're an asshole, Morris," Stan hollered. "Or, as one should say correctly, an *arse*hole!" He was swaying a bit. "This is a throwaway society. I said that already, didn't I? Morris. You retire, you're done. Forgotten. Kaput!"

"That's ridiculous! I mean when you get to a point, you change"—I was groping for a word—"change direction."

"Yeah, sure. Direct into the hole, the black hole, man."

"Stan, I think I need to go home."

"Okay. I'll call a cab. Can't let you get away with killing yourself, that's a coward's way out!"

"Well, I had no intention of driving," I said imperiously.

"Good. *Arse*hole!" Then he smiled.

After a while, the cab honked.

We were at his door. The coffee had helped. "One last thing," I said. "Did you *really* believe something had gone on between me and that girl?"

Habers covered his face with both hands and stepped back. And I knew that, despite his mocking gesture, he had really thought so. But in the midst of sobering up, I was actually delighted that he had thought me capable of—well, at the least of flirting with Milicent L. Jacobs. As I bent over to get into the cab, I heard Stan's shouting. I turned my head.

"Hey, Morris. Edith? She made out I did it with her? I never laid a hand on her! She should be so lucky! I kissed her on the cheek! Hahhahhah." And I believed him, and ducked into the cab.

When Julianna saw me at the front door, she looked simultaneously concerned and bemused, since I greeted her by blurting out, "I'm drunk! I almost broke Habers' nose and we drank lots of Burgundy after I brought him home from the ER, he was bleeding." She just nodded, ministered to me, I can't recall it all, and I fell asleep on the couch. Next morning on the way to school we drove by Habers' house (he was discreetly absent) and I picked up my car. I had told Julianna everything; she just laughed.

My sixty-fifth birthday fell on December 7, a Monday, two days before the final classes of the fall semester. In the past there were always comments about Pearl Harbor Day, but after a while people forgot the connection. That day was not so infamous as mysterious in my memory—my fifth birthday unceremoniously interrupted by a world war. Strained faces and whispers and the phone ringing. I knew that something bad had happened. When Father and Mother whispered in German, it was always a bad omen.

Julianna had suggested a small party, but almost at once we agreed that Leon's death was too near, and that we could never keep these parties small. I was staring at our one good carpet, my eyes getting lost in the pattern. Maybe the detail in the pattern *was* in the carpet?

Julianna had given me a boxed Yeats *Variorum*, and on the Internet she found some antique dealer selling a first edition of an early volume of *Poems*. It came with a blue cover with gold leaf design, and in the middle rested a Rosicrucian rose on a gold cross. Its beauty took my breath away. Looking at my face, Julianna beamed. The children called. Only Seth had done the math. "Special day, Dad!" To tell the truth, I said, I'd rather forget its specialness. They each sent cards and books, and I wondered—for the first time—should I be accumulating or thinking of downsizing?

Students dropped off their final papers, but I knew there were always one or two problems. And the first one appeared like a wan apparition at my threshold. Jane Smollet. She pleaded. Hers was a different case, honestly. *Real* trouble. She'd been dumped on. A thirty page history paper and an art project and this in-class math final and—I interrupted, reminding her that the paper had been assigned a month ago. What's the saying these days, "prioritize"? Well, she had tried, so absolutely tried! It's been *so-so-so* crazy. She was up all night. Just couldn't seem to get it done. Could she have a few days' extension? No, she couldn't. A day?

I looked at Jane Smollet. She was the antithesis of Milicent L. Jacobs, for her face exuded misery. Every time she spoke, she had pulled her chair closer. I pondered her red, sleepless eyes, a pleading, fear. Jane Smollet looked like a poster child for anorexia. Dressed indifferently, her ripped jeans full of paint, there could be no doubt about her art project. Everything about her supported the story of an all-nighter. Paint smell mixed with body odor. I rolled my chair backwards as unobtrusively as possible and shook my head. All right, we'll compromise. Tuesday by nine, but that's it. Otherwise she'd fail? Yes, unless I gave her an incomplete, and she was a senior. She did not even smile. "Nooo," she wailed. I wilted at her ragged honesty, ragged like her jeans. You have no choice. Get on with it, Jane. She wanted to know what her grade was up to now. I knew she was probably a C+ or so, opened the grade book, moved my eyes left to right. More like a C and I said so. A C! She sounded incredulous. But what about class discussion? She had talked a *lot*! Yes, I acknowledged, but she interrupted, I meant she said dumb things, right? Now had I said that? It's implied, she said, her head hanging. She took a tissue from what was left of her jean pocket and sniffed with her nose, which she patted. I sighed. Get the paper to me by nine Tuesday. I offered help. She shook her head. No. To be honest, she hadn't started it. I had figured that out before she admitted it. But again I did like her openness. She was composed now. Thanks, she managed, and said she was sorry. She clearly was, knowing she had screwed up. Okay, I nodded. We each managed a smile. She began to leave. Your books, I shouted. She rushed back to grab her scruffy green book bag.

Taking a deep breath, I felt sorry for this scrawny, unhappy girl. Sitting for a while, I was on alert for another supplicant. None came. On the due date I would sit and wait well after five, and someone would be running up out of breath, saying their printer was broken, the computer crashed, there was no paper left. Eventually, Jane Smollet did get her paper in, smelling of turpentine. Later than we had agreed. I graded it a C.

Winter

11

Intersession was a between time. The campus emptied, or nearly so, library hours were curtailed, the Faculty Lounge was closed, and sometimes the heat would not work. Silence fell celebrating the end of something; a special kind of hibernation began. Still, it was a time to catch up: order for the Reserve Room, bring back library books no longer in use, straighten out debris from last semester, write that book review, and work on the remaining graduate school recommendations, those not due before the Christmas break, always too many. You walked around in a baggy sweater and corduroys, and for me, who still wore sport coat and tie when teaching, this was a delightfully rebellious act. Informal dress filled me with pleasure, a peculiar sense of privacy and freedom, which could also be shared. Those colleagues who came in during intersession were equally casual in dress and mood, and we formed a loose confederacy, like children out of school. The prevailing sigh was, "Thank God, much as we love 'em, they've gone for a while."

This was also a time for a trip to Jordan Hall to hear a Quartet or a Trio, or a visit to Symphony, or a dash to the A. R. T. in Cambridge to catch a play. If the Museum of Fine Arts featured an exhibition we went. In the old days this was a time for dinner parties, but now few went to the trouble any more—everybody agreed they were too much fuss and bother. So that left take-out or meeting at a restaurant and splitting the bill down the middle. Now that Leon was dead and Natasha gone, most of our socializing was with Julianna's friends from her department and friends made, over the years, from other corners of the university, or neighbors. I did not socialize much with my colleagues any more. They had, it seemed, better fish to fry. Years ago I would invite Stanley Habers with some woman he was going with, and we even hosted Ann Rosenthal to join with Leon and Natasha. Occasionally we invited graduate students and one or another assistant professor, who would eventually leave or never make tenure. All that was over with.

On the first day back at the office, I labored over the recommendations piled on my desk. After a while I became aware of the bitter taste of envelope glue. Relief. That was done. Next, some office housekeeping.

But that was interrupted by a knock. "Yes," I said still bent down over my desk, and when I lifted my head, before me stood Mike Schell, Bonnie's Clyde, and he appeared exactly as I recalled—washed out jeans, a crumpled T-shirt, uncombed hair. Hanging from his hand a very worn-out, brown leather jacket, with white-line cracks, which he nervously waved back and forth.

"Well, hi! Come on in. Take a seat. What's on your mind? No drop slip this time?"

Mike Schell slouched in the chair he had once before declined, looked a little sad and said, "Professor, I didn't come for trouble. I came to get out of it. It's about Milicent Jacobs?"

Why the rising question? Had she infected him with that? "Oh, how is she doing?"

"She's not here. Not for a while. She went home right after that meeting in the big room."

"So I heard."

"Well, look, I came to say that I went along with her because I felt sorry for her. You know she's a sicko. I mean, man, she's *weird*."

"How so?"

"She just kept on me about this molesting. You know there were times I think she believed it all happened? Anyway I didn't know what to think. So I went along with it. But at that meeting—"

"In the big room?"

"Yeah. Well, I could see it was all a lie, and I made a run for it, remember?"

I remembered. Looking at this fellow and listening to him, I thought, my God, I'm talking to Huck Finn!

"Well. Okay, then. So I just want to say I dropped your course because I was hopeless. Just *too hard*. Everything else *she* did—well as I said she was nuts. She had this thing for me, so she followed me around and—"

I wanted to put an end to Huck Finn's suffering.

"It's fine Mike, it's fine. I'm very glad you came to tell me this. And forget it. It's all over. Doing okay? Good." And Mike Schell even said thanks and then walked out as he came in, bent over and scraping the floor with his squeaky sneakers, his heels on his torn jeans, shoelaces from one sneaker lapping up the floor. I sat quietly. I was running out of suspects. Not Milicent L. Jacobs, not Mike Schell. But there was still John Strozzi.

This intersession, the department had agreed to debate Carol Gunderson's future. The dean wanted a decision before the Spring semester began and said rather pointedly that this was already a concession, since most departments had sent up their recommendations by early December. Stanley Habers told me it was a slam dunk, but I had learned that there is no such thing. Difficult cases in the past had gone through smoothly; "slam dunks" had led to blood-letting quarrels. No one could predict the outcome of tenure meetings.

We were scheduled to meet on the second Monday in January, and Sunday the evening forecast was ominous: snow beginning midnight into early morning, up to 8-10 inches in the suburbs, more further west. Edith called around nine, desperate. What should we do? Nothing yet, I advised. They can be wrong. Have been, often. See what the morning brings.

Monday morning, I got up early and drew the curtains. It was snowing lightly, but the accumulation appeared to be just a few inches, enough to be a nuisance but not sufficiently serious to cancel the meeting. Edith called at 9:30. Hoped she had not woken me? So we meet? Yes, why not. Storm's gone out to sea, haven't you heard. Yes she had. Fine. See you.

The sun glistened on the dusting of the evergreens. On my way to the garage, I was greeted by Betsy's yellow-stained gifts in the snow. I thought I had heard "Betsy! Betsy!" early in the morning and had been right.

We assembled in the usual room, and because it was intersession, there was no need to be secretive. Carol Gunderson had gone home to the deep snows of her native Minnesota. Now that's winter. By ones and twos they arrived. Marvin Golden came last, just a little late. Luckily, the heat was on, hissing in fact, but Ann Rosenthal kept her heavy down coat hung over her shoulder and wrapped an ample green and purple shawl around her neck. Robinson and Bentwick wore high black rubber boots, though by now the walkways were cleared, and it was warm enough in this January thaw for the snow to melt in the bright sunshine. Stan Habers sat in his cable-knit green sweater, laced snow boots covering his corduroy pants, hitting the table with his pencil in nervous taps and looking at his watch every few seconds. Edith Sellers had her coffee and cookies at the ready. She flung her arm nervously in the direction of refreshments, which some in the room had already taken to their chairs.

Edith reminded us of absolute confidentiality. Even her dress was relaxed, comfortable slacks, sweater, and heavy snow boots. The meeting went without any real surprises. Habers reeled off three points in the candidate's favor, tapping his eraser-end of the pencil for each. Ann Rosenthal immediately seized on each point to dispute it, politely. Marvin Golden, who was doodling, remarked that the book's cost was absurd, $79.50 and no illustrations! Hal Muzzey, having vigorously combed his mustache, exploded, saying that we were discussing Gunderson's tenure, not book prices!

And so we haggled on. Robinson quite agreed with Professor Rosenthal. Bentwick followed. But here was a shock: for the first time in memory he did not second his colleague's view. Rather, he said somewhat wanly in his mellifluous voice, he was of an older generation and would not be around long for Gunderson's tenured life, should that happen, and he was therefore inclined to leave the future to "people my junior." With that last phrase he held his right hand out with spread fingers, like some oracular shaman who had said his piece and needed to say no more.

After an awkward silence, Golden, who leaned back in his wooden chair, stretched out his legs and looked up at the ceiling. Gunderson, he offered, would be all right, but she certainly could have profited from more theory, but no matter, she'll do. He'd seen a lot worse. Irritated with this arrogance, I spoke even more enthusiastically of Gunderson than planned. I let it be known that in my opinion this was one of the most creative and freshest voices to appear in the department in more than a decade, and that, of course, meant she was in my higher esteem than Golden, who would not miss the point. Finally the Chair said that while she had her differences with Gunderson on a personal level, she agreed with the majority. Gunderson, drawing both students and critical praise, was needed. Robinson and Rosenthal voted "nay"; Bentwick abstained; the rest voted in favor.

As we dissolved our meeting, Habers caught up with me. He ventured that the little speech by Bentwick had touched him, he meant it. But that Robinson remained a jerk. I agreed. We parted and filed out into the afternoon sun. A chill had invaded the air. After all it was January.

Driving home I became glum. If Bentwick says *he* is the past, am *I* far behind? Then I wondered what Leon would have said. Voted for her, for sure. But I missed hearing that even voice, that measured tone, those words quietly coming out with certainty, but earned certainty. Leon, you would have said, Yes?

It was not that Leon Adler's death had been forgotten, but the second semester began on a happier note than the first. They say time heals, but it was perhaps less healing and more the necessities of having to continue because there was no other choice. I always loved the first days of a new semester. Even now. Students laughed, their cheeks flushed red with eagerness, their eyes spoke innocence and curiosity. Politeness and bubbling enthusiasm were palpable everywhere, even among colleagues who had not seen one another since the tenure meeting. And some good news, at least for the majority: the dean had appointed an *ad hoc* committee. By informal polling, the unanimous decision was to send Edith Sellers as the department's advocate.

January weather had behaved like a roller coaster, from thaw to cold to thaw, but most of the time it had been sunny with little snow. Now came February, always cold and snowy, luckily a short month. Julianna was busier than ever. She had accepted several commitments to conferences, was writing a paper for a late summer mini-symposium in Toronto, and attended to her duties as Chair. Rumors were beginning to circulate that she was on a short list of potential successors to Sir Walter, but we danced around it, I because I feared hexing it, she out of genuine modesty. Seth seemed happy for the first time in ages, his phone calls were frequent, with a bounce in his voice. Julianna had been to see him when she went down to New York to fulfill her commitment at N.Y.U., and her time with Seth was obviously a success for both. "He's so happy and relieved," she said when she came home, "I can hardly believe it." Helen was still dating the English Department T. A., and only Miranda sounded a little low-keyed, hesitant, as if she wanted to say things but always, at the last moment, changed her mind. My visits to my father were more spaced. "He's disappearing," I said to Julianna after one of them. "There seems so little left that holds him together. He's also losing weight."

My back was much improved. I finally took seriously the doctor's advice and was moving more. Walking was sometimes difficult on icy winter sidewalks, so I ascended, very suspiciously, Julianna's treadmill. At first I walked so slowly and held on so tightly to the front bar, that there was no rhythm, it was a real effort. I looked like a clumsy clown. In time, Julianna tactfully helped, and laughing with me, not at me, she taught me how to get into the swing. One could not say I was working up a sweat, but my heart went aflutter, and after a while I began to get the hang of it. Though I never enjoyed it, I conceded that my more rapid heartbeat was a new experience, coming as it did from moving my body rather than vexing my mind.

Julianna often spoke with Natasha, especially on Sundays when I added a few words of my own. She was happy to be with her parents, and the children had adjusted in school. Definitely, she had done the right thing. Would she be back by summer? She guessed. The house? She didn't know what to do. She'd see. Many times during the course of a day at school, I would think of Leon and sense loss in the presence of absence. Mostly I wanted to talk to him: Leon, when should I retire? I think about it more and more. What about Julianna? She's nowhere near it. Not for another five years or more. Not even thinking of it.

What do you think, Leon? Since the dead have no other answer than their gone-ness, I continued imagining him in our conversations. Leon had been about a decade younger than I when the merciless aneurysm decided it was its time, so he would never have the chance of considering retirement. Perhaps this was by itself an answer?

One afternoon I opened an envelope and removed a folded letter, watermark stiff. I read, "Dr. Murray Jacobs. Practice of Psychiatry." The address was Fifth Avenue.

> Dear Professor Morris:
>
> On behalf of my wife and myself, we wish to apologize for our daugh-ter's misstep, for which she is truly sorry. We thought it best to remove her from campus for the rest of the year, but she has committed herself to return for Summer Session. We hope you bear her no ill will, and that all difficulties are now behind you.

It was signed, Murray and Thelma Jacobs.

Removing my glasses I rubbed my eyes. "Misstep"? Dictated between patients? What arrogance! And "difficulties behind you"? I stared at the letter with amused disbelief. "Committed herself"? I wish that were true. But I understood Milicent L. Jacobs much better now. As I was about to crumple the letter and throw it into the waste basket, I changed my mind, folding the paper back in its creases and slipping it into my briefcase. Julianna would want to see it. A Fifth Avenue psy-chiatrist! What else?

Second semester began well, though I continued to experience the distance between myself and my students. Sometimes I fancied that the undergraduates were diminishing in size and appeared younger and smaller when in fact I knew they were getting taller and always remained the same age. Once a pleasant, smil-ing young woman held the door for me as I was rushing toward it into the library, and afterwards I nodded, Yes it's obviously showing.

Yet strangely enough, just when classes were going well, when my physical ail-ments seemed under control, thoughts of someday leaving all this stubbornly pushed themselves into my head. It was as if my self had waited until the turmoil had subsided some, so that in relative peace I could now contemplate the once unthinkable. As if mind and body said: Now is your chance to take a good look at your life without prejudice, so that later you won't blame whatever you do on a bad back, or on quarrelsome students, or on any of your children. Any decision you make now is cleansed of what you might regret as having been excuses. The less baggage the better. And yes, better make up your mind because you know this won't last. The body will rebel again, despite the treadmill; the students will become restless in a few weeks, especially just before spring break; one or another child will cause your heart to ache. So carpe diem—for decisions with no revisions, to play on Mr. Eliot's words. But just as strenuously I repelled these thoughts, counter-attacked, pushed them away as intruders. What an absurdity, that's what Julianna had called it. Retirement? Not yet.

But on a Sunday evening, sitting in my study, I turned my chair in semi-circles and my eyes fell on the A-O volume of the *Oxford English Dictionary*, in which I had some time ago looked up "aneurysm." I had left it on the wooden stand, open in the middle to balance the weight. Through the magnifying glass (supplied with the set), I turned to the letter "E" until I found "emeritus." Latin: " … that has served his time (said of a soldier) … to earn discharge by service." To my surprise, its first application to a professor was listed as 1823, not that long ago. What word did they use before then? Well, I had been a soldier for nearly forty years, counting T. A. teaching. Had I not earned my discharge? I had done the state some service, as Othello had said (and as I had told Edith Sellers), and whether or not *they* knew it, *I* did. On that note I experienced a delicious rush of the past.

Coming home early one day, I find Julianna in her study.

"Disturbing?"

She is startled and turns her head with jolt-like quickness.

"Oh, no. Just reading proofs."

"You didn't tell me proofs had come?"

"Well, what's the big deal? I thought I had. They came yesterday. To the office. I work better here. Fewer interruptions. Or so I thought!" But she is smiling.

"Nothing important."

"No, stay. Only teasing. I'm tired anyway, and I want to talk."

"Oh? Funny, I came to talk too."

"Me first?" She removes her glasses and stretches out in her chair. "I'm beginning to get stiff. I heard about this aerobics class Phys Ed is offering, late afternoons, twice a week. I think I'll go. So. Me first?"

"Sure. What's up?" I leaned against one of the walnut bookcases.

"Well, I heard—it's just a rumor—that I'm on a short list for the deanship. You've heard it too, but I know you—you don't want to put a hex on it, so you've been mum. I won't get it, honestly I don't think so, no false modesty, but I'm flattered."

Her modesty has been overruled by expectation. Good, I say to myself, good. "You're right. I've heard it around, it's 'out there.' Why so pessimistic?"

"They need a woman. But they also want youth. I'm still academically young, but there's an insider who's a lot younger. And, being an insider, I hear she has the inside track, even though officially she's not on the list."

She asks me to guess.

"Phyllis Bentley," I say without an extra breath.

"You're so good at that! You've had dealings with her. What's she like?"

After some hesitation, I reply.

"Well, my trial, yes. She's tough and business-like, not a charmer, and too cozy with Sir Walter. Somehow I don't trust her. She'd be a mistake. You'd make a much better dean. I mean that. Do you want it?"

"I'm not sure, that's what I wanted to talk about. I'm just getting done with this monster book," and she slaps her hand on her massive pile of proofs. "Honestly I'm a bit weary of writing now. And teaching. And chairing. Maybe deaning would be a change?"

"Absolutely," I encourage.

"Anyway, let's think about it, yes? I need your advice. It's just all rumor now, and as I said, there's little chance. But it's sort of fun to consider it, I have to admit. We would get richer! Your turn?"

"Oh, nothing important."

"No, something's on your mind. Fess up!"

"Well, should I send that paper on Yeats out again? I'm worried about another rejection."

"Of course you should. It's a fine piece. Rejection? Come, you mustn't lose faith. Have you shown it to anybody?"

"Yes, Leon. He liked it. But then he's gone."

Her face responds with a shared sense of sorrow. "Yes, true enough. But Leon would want you to send it out."

"Okay, I'll think about it."

The paper on Yeats was a last-minute inspiration. It was not what I wanted to talk about, but the timing was bad. Just as Julianna was dreaming about being dean—how could I talk of forsaking her, academically speaking?

The first faculty meeting of the second semester was called to consider a proposal: students, if invited by the instructors, would visit classes as "peer reviewers." So far the suggestion for their official title was "consultants"; they would be paid, just as if this were a work study job. This would take the pressure off being visited by one's faculty peers, much more stressful. After all, students were in a better position to judge a class from a *student's* point of view, their suggestions would be based on a genuine desire to tell the instructors what *they* expected in a class, where the instructor fell short in hitting the mark. There appeared to be sharp division among the faculty.

I decided to skip the meeting, which surprised Julianna, since I was a loyal presence. "You go and tell me all about it. Sounds like a dumb proposal to me! We'll meet at the usual place?" She shrugged. "Okay." We never sat together but always met afterwards at a bench not far from the meeting. I'd stroll over; meetings always ended by a time certain—more or less.

I waited longer than usual. A long meeting. At last she appeared, walking swiftly toward the bench. Well, how did it go? How had she voted? She had debated. But she figured it could be made to work, provided they dropped that silly name for the students and did it right. Right? And what did that mean? Oh, she complained, she had a headache from all the haranguing in there, and she placed her hands to either side of her head. Let it go. She'd fill me in. It was lively. I should have gone. No, I thought, glad I didn't.

At this moment, walking side by side with my wife to the parking lot, I had the uncomfortable sensation that, in this venue, we were already beginning to occupy opposite sides of the street.

12

Julianna's corrected proofs arrived in mid-March, and despite my nagging, she refused to hire help. Three summers ago, with the help of a grant, she had immersed herself for two glorious months in Paris. Of course, I tagged along.

Three summers ago? Only *three*? It frightened me because it seemed so much longer—more like ten! I had felt so young and sprightly, so happy, so full of expectations. Julianna devoted herself to archival research in the Bibliothéque Nationale, while I walked and read, sipped great cappuccino and savored croissants with strawberry jam, luxuriating in solitude—voluptuously, as Montaigne had advised. By any comparison it turned out to be one of the most stressless summers in memory for both of us. A small but perfectly adequate flat on the Left Bank parked us within a short walk to wonderful bistros and cafes, and on occasion we splurged and upscaled to a fine restaurant for lunch. Often we feasted for hours and drank too much. "Not Spanelli's," I would say, and Julianna shook her head and laughed. We walked around like lovers. And we were. Julianna was exultant about her work and its progress; I was proud of her exultation.

Alone, I walked the streets of Paris recreating scenes from novels I had read and taught. That summer, my senses were so sharp. Sights and smells and taste: everything was more in focus, punctuated, new. I discovered the facades of buildings, both awed and lured by the detail of masonry, its designs of flowers, birds and other animals carved into the outer walls, especially the high and wide window frames. Food tasted calibrated, I singled out ginger from garlic; and to Julianna's delight, I often identified smells coming from bistro kitchens that I had seldom paid attention to. Even the birds sang with distinctive clarity.

We traveled to Chartres on a mid-morning train for the hour ride. The cathedral's overpowering cobalt hues, sun bursting through the stained glass windows; we would remember it forever.

Another time we headed for Ginervy to take in Monet's water lilies, though we agreed the paintings were more passionate. In August, when the natives fled and the tourists poured in by the busload, Paris was less attractive, but we succeeded in not letting anything bother us.

The second week in August, I flew to London to visit with Richard Leary, whom I had befriended at the university when I brought the family to London for a year on my Fulbright. A bachelor, my friend had settled into a small but neat flat near Hampstead Heath. The weather was as sunny as Paris, if a little cooler. Leary an Anglo-Irish expatriate, had dropped the "O" and the apostrophe. He had a wry but gentle sense of humor, told richly textured anecdotes delivered at great length and with expansive arm motions. He was older now, shorter, an added pot belly, but his hair was still bushy and mostly black. Well, I wondered, how do *I* look to *him*? We prowled the pubs, talked literature. (Leary was mainly a Shakespearean, and yes, of course, he knew Stanley Habers' book and was respectful and amused by its outrageousness.) Afternoons, after tea, we took long walks, mostly across the Heath; on occasion we lunched at The Spaniards. I called Julianna almost every day. She was fine. Enjoy! I did, but by the end of the week, homesick and a little guilty, I was ready to go back. Great visit, we said to each other when we parted. As I walked into our Paris flat, I had come home. Little time remained.

I continued bumming leisurely in museums. One day, in the Louvre I became aware of a beautiful Eurasian woman standing next to me in front of a Corot painting I did not know. She was tall, wore a tightly fitting mauve dress graced at the modest waist by a thin back shiny belt. Around her neck hung a double-stringed golden necklace with a pear-shaped opal descending toward a barely visible cleavage. White heels, a matching white handbag, a mauve parasol to complement her wide-brimmed mauve straw hat—she might have stepped out of a portrait. I recall it now still somewhat befuddled because when she turned to me with a smile to ask a question, in French, I literally fled, nearly in a panic; I behaved like a schoolboy. But her beauty and youth had pained me and cast a small shadow over my happy state.

When finally we had to leave Paris, Julianna shed some tears, and I put on a proper melancholy face in empathy, though in truth I was now anxious to go home. For me at least, this trip was over. We landed at Logan in the midst of a late August heat wave, and by the time we entered our stuffy house and turned on the air conditioners, attended to the business of mail and cleaning and the garden—it was all gone, a dream-like memory. Still, a good memory; one recalled it in color.

13

A knock on the door. Neither faint nor Stanley's. But I have become uncommonly guarded about knocks on the door. A moment of hesitation, and the knock is repeated. I rise, walk toward the door, which is closed, and open it.

"Seth?"

"Hi, Dad." Seth looks straight into my eyes.

I pale. "What's wrong? You all right?"

"Fine. Honest. I'm good. Came to see you. Let me in?" Seth breaks into a forced smile. Relieved, I regain some color and usher my son into my office, shutting the door. Seth looks disheveled, though he is nicely dressed: maroon turtleneck, cable-knit white sweater, corduroys. But he needs a haircut, the black mane curling over his ears. And his face is a bit flushed.

"Seth, what's going on?"

"Nothing. I came to talk to you."

Visions cross my mind at a gallop, none of them reassuring. "About what? What's the matter?"

"Nothing, really." Seth looks at the floor. "I came to talk about this business you've been accused of." Arm into the air, palm pushing toward me, "Mom didn't tell me, Miranda did. So don't jump to conclusions. Mom doesn't even know I'm here. Had to sneak around to make sure she didn't see me. I don't want her to know, not especially."

"Then how—?"

"I already knew when Miranda called. A friend. Al Halpern. He was actually your student a couple of semesters ago. And he showed me *The Crier*. It's obvious it's you, Dad. I read both stories. He happened to be in New York to see his folks. Anyway, look, it doesn't take a rocket scientist to get it. Seems a lot of people guessed."

"Did they? Well, that's comforting!"

"Dad, you must have known—"

"Yes, yes. Of course I did. But what—I mean just why—what do you want to know beyond what you know? I'm happy to see you, Seth, but—" I shrug in resignation. "Consolation visit?"

"Not really. But what has this woman done to you!" He is shouting, and I place my finger to his lips. "Walls are thin here. Turn it down."

Seth nods. "Sorry. Just think this is too much, that's all. How can she do that!"

"Seth, the girl's very—how to put it? Disturbed?"

"Oh, yeah? My heart bleeds for her." His voice is rising again, and this time I put my finger on my own lips and Seth lowers his head.

"She's emotionally unbalanced. Have compassion! My guess is that she just needed attention. She had broken up with her boyfriend." And I tell Seth some of the story. It agitates me, but I need to settle him down.

"Don't get any ideas," Seth says defensively. "I mean I see and like lots of women socially, I have lots of women friends." "Good!"

"But could you sue or something? It's your whole life in this place, it's a rotten thing she did to you!"

I am touched to see one of my children—especially the reluctant Seth—so loyal and concerned, though I have not the slightest intention of legal action. Never thought of it, not even in passing.

"And another thing." Seth hesitates and begins squeezing his hands, like a shy schoolboy. "Will this make you think of quitting here? Because that's what I'm *really* upset about!"

I'm startled. "Quit? What, you mean resign? Whatever makes you think that?"

"Well, because. I think I know how you feel, and your rep—that means everything to you. You can't quit because—"

My "rep." I hear from *Othello*, "Reputation, reputation, reputation! I have lost my reputation." (Later that night I will look up the rest: "I have lost the immortal part of myself, and the rest is bestial.") I hold up my hand. "Seth, hold it! I have no intention of quitting, where did you get that from? As for my 'rep,' I have the support of my colleagues. All of them. And I'm innocent. Why in the world? I just don't understand. Methinks this trip has more to do with your fear of me 'quitting' than with this business about legal action?" I show some impatient anger. "I appreciate your concern, Seth, but why is everybody telling me what to do with my life? It's mine you know. If I want to 'quit'—whenever that may be—I'll do it, and 'quit' is a lousy word, you know. It's perfectly respectable to *retire* at some point. Huh? I'm sixty-five. That's when Father retired."

Seth loses some color, looking confused. "Hey, Dad, I didn't come here to fight, okay? I came because I care. You do what you want—" Tears lurk in the voice, and he is about to get up.

I say I am sorry, I don't mean to be ungrateful. But Seth must understand, it's been stressful. And this visit is a bit of a surprise. "So, okay, let's be honest, was it your fear of my 'quitting' that brought you, yes?"

Seth still squeezes his hands. "Okay, to tell the truth, yeah. Maybe. That's the number one thing, you're right. Don't quit!"

I listen, not convinced I have yet heard the real reason for my son's sudden appearance. "Still don't think I know your agenda. How did you feel when you read that stuff in *The Crier*?"

"How? Awful!" Seth's hands are quiet now.

"Ashamed?"

Seth raises his head and stares at me. "'Ashamed'? Of what?"

"Of having your father, however innocent, mixed up in all this?" My voice is even, almost too much so.

"*No*, Dad! Never ashamed."

"Okay, embarrassed? Your friend, what's his name, must have been a bit excited with such gossip?"

A long silence. Seth bites his lower lip and strokes his overgrown hair. "No, Dad, not ashamed, not embarrassed."

"Then—?" I let the word hang.

"*Scared*, Dad. I heard you were arrested and spent a night in jail, but then that just turned out to be some stupid rumor. But, yeah, I'm still scared."

I listen. What have I got into? Poor Seth. I shake my head slowly. "Seth, there's no reason to be scared. Do you hear? No, I was not arrested, not in jail. Though some private investigators came, her parents hired them. Seems the girl recanted her confession of guilt, but that lasted the life of a mayfly. And all that happened months ago. Last December, I think." (How had that rumor of arrest and jail started?) "But, yes, these two people came to chat. They were perfect gentlemen—well one was a woman." (I papered over their unctuous unpleasantness.) "Now it's over and done with. All of it. I could have done without it, but life has its speed bumps, or whatever."

Seth blows out a deep breath, as if he has been under water for a long time. "Okay, Dad. Okay. His hands are on my desk, and I notice some signs of a nail biter.

"I know. And I'm sorry you had to find out the way you did. Maybe I should have told all of you. I intended to at the end of the year. I did." I have come from my chair and am standing over my son with my hand on his head. "You need a haircut, young man!" But perhaps I have finally given him the blessing he so yearns for?

Seth laughs. So do I. But in my head I hear myself saying, "I'm sorry. So sorry." It is, I'm aware, something I've been saying too often lately.

Seth has touched some nerves in me and now regrets the whole thing. You can tell as his body collapses into the chair.

"All right, then. Let's reveal you to Mom? Lies have short legs, and you know she wants to see you, always. How about it? It's silly not to. We'll have lunch. Have time for that? You haven't lost your job, have you?"

"No," Seth protests, "just taking a few days off. Okay, call Mom, but don't get into all this stuff we talked about."

And I promise I won't and then phone Julianna who is surprised but happy. We eat a lovely lunch at Seth's favorite Chinese haunt on Route 9, but I have little appetite. As promised, the reason for Seth's visit never comes up. Seth says he had a few days and felt like surprising us. He stays overnight to the great delight of his mother. But that night I lie awake a long time and hear the words "quit" and "sorry" more insistently than I would have liked.

One night (it was actually closer to dawn), as we were in heavy deep sleep, we were startled by a sound that parents dread. The phone rang. The first ring sounded distant like a very loud and shrill scream, as if in a dream, but by the second ring, I was fully awake. Since it was on my side of the bed, I groped for the phone, and as I lifted the receiver my mouth dried up instantly. "Hello?"

"Yes, hello? Is this Professor Morris?" Julianna was leaning on my back, and I could feel her deep breaths and the slight tremor of her body. "Yes. Who is this?" Not Tony Soprano again?

"I'm Dr. Aaron Shapiro, Professor Morris. I'm calling from Birch Manor. It's about your father."

I covered the mouthpiece and said, "It's Father." I could feel Julianna's body relax. It was not one of the children.

"Yes? How bad?"

"Well, pretty bad. He's had a major stroke. I don't honestly know for sure, but it's unlikely he'll make it through the night." Then, as if for emphasis, "*Very* unlikely."

I looked at the radio alarm-clock: four o'clock. "All right, I understand. I'm on my way. It'll be about three hours plus. Obviously I'm not even dressed."

"Of course. No rush. Anyone else we should call?"

I hesitated. "Yes. My brother. I'd appreciate it if you would call him. It's in your records. Paul Morris in Santa Fe. It will save time."

"I'll do that. And Professor Morris—again, please don't rush. I make you a promise. We have lots of ways to keep him going until you arrive. Only one question. Our records show no DNR from your father. Was there one?"

"No what?"

"No 'Do Not Resuscitate'—we ask all our residents whether they want one."

"Oh, sorry. Still sleepy. No, no. We asked him about it some time ago. He said he wanted to think it over. When we raised the issue again, he became very agitated, so we just thought we'd leave it. Is that all right?"

"Yes, that's fine. Absent any instructions from your father, the family makes the decision. Your decision?"

"Given what you said, no. Do not resuscitate."

"Fine. I'll call your brother."

"And you'll just keep whatever you're doing going until my brother arrives, okay?"

"Will do. And, of course, I'm very sorry. About your father."

"Yes, thanks. Bye."

"Bye."

I told Julianna the details. After I hung up I instantly understood that, although he was technically dead, they were keeping my father alive with machines. Julianna, already up, was laying some clothes on the bed. She offered to come but I said, no, I'd be fine. "Call the children in the morning."

The sky broke out with the first shimmers of dark light.

Anyone who has ever driven highways at breaking dawn knows it is a feeling like no other. I wondered whether truck drivers felt the same, the dark was theirs, they owned the road and the night, and I heard their roar. From our house to Route 128 was not far, and some cars were already heading for early work shifts. Fewer of them were on the road once I swung onto the Pike west, though the closer I got to the Connecticut border, the more traffic. With early light, the artificial illumination of gas stations, towns, and other spots where the night was alive was beginning to shut off, here—there—as if someone were blowing out candles. For a brief few minutes natural and electric light engaged in a strange competition, until finally the changing of the guardians was complete. Gold, yellow, and the orange of dawn. A Turner landscape. I had left shortly after five, and it was now six as I plucked my ticket from the toll machine and turned toward Interstate 84 to Hartford at an even seventy. Oak trees were finally crowned with some red, and I noticed some promise of blooming forsythia bushes by the roadside. For a change I shifted into cruise control, but even without traffic, after a few minutes, I disengaged. I needed to feel mastery over the car. The straightaway toward Hartford and the bridge that evaded the city's center would be coming to life. I had already passed Vernon and the Rines New York Style Deli, where we often stopped on the way home from New Haven or New York and guiltily downed tip-of-the-tongue and corned beef. Time hung. I briefly listened to a repeat discussion of the AIDS crisis in Africa from BBC World News. Statistics overwhelmed me. I stopped at the pre-set music station. Sounded like Sousa marches. Impatient, I shut the radio. Quiet was best. Would Paul come? Surely, yes. Paul would be there soon. Yes, *I* should have called him.

For the remaining time I had this febrile vision of my father being kept artificially alive by machines for sons he would not know, for one son who might not even come. Some tears were urging to drop, but the urge was as far as they made it. Pulling into the familiar pine-lined driveway, an immense feeling of peace overpowered me. This would be my last drive on this pebbled road. Samuel Morris, a.k.a. Morisohn, had left strict instructions, unusual for a Jew: no funeral, but cremation, and no memorial services except any Yale might wish to hold at some time after his death.

Dr. Shapiro, who had been paged, met me. A young man, perhaps late thirties, he was pleasant and solicitous.

"Good to see you, sir," he said respectfully, "your father's condition is the same."

"No chance of any reversal?" I was intent on asking, even as a formality.

"None." Dr. Shapiro said it with firmness and certainty. "You understand, I had to call you as soon as I was sure—"

"Of course, I understand that."

We took the elevator to a separated wing I had never seen, the "Special Care" unit, top floor, Hell. My father was in a private room. He lay on a hospital bed, an IV stuck in his thin arm covered with spindly veins, and I was besieged by the sound of machines with their steady noises making strange, but timed, dissonant music. Father's breathing was labored but set to a regulated rhythm by the machines. Looking ashen and his face slightly contorted, with the lower lip sagging, eyes closed, Samuel Morris was clearly never to awaken again. I sat down next to him and clasped his frail hand which had turned bluish and was cold to the touch.

Yes, I was told, they had reached my brother. He had said he would try to be here around noon. Heading for either Hartford or New York, depending. They hadn't heard since. And, I ask again, they could keep these machines intact? No problem, as long as necessary. Had I eaten breakfast? Did I know where to go? No and yes, I hadn't eaten, I knew where to go.

After breakfast I wander over to the fish tank and sit down and give a salutary nod to those fish and their back and forth swims that had so bedeviled my father. Then I fall into a half-sleep; I wake with a start as a woman in white nursing uniform lightly touches my arm. The nurse asks whether I want to return to my father's room. I nod, still a little groggy.

Nothing has changed. The chair has been moved to the side wall, so I again pull it astride the bed and take my father's lifeless hand.

For a long time I sit, listen to the insistent pings and clangs of the machines, and think about this man whose life is being sustained only by the mechanics of modern medicine. What has he really felt? What has he thought? He has been lonely, but also, until recently, so self-sustaining, so much still Father. Perhaps I ought to have visited him more often, but lately our time had turned into a futile confrontation with nothingness. Often I doubted whether my father even recognized me, since sometimes he would not speak for a whole hour, and simply to keep my own sanity, I talked endlessly about myself, Julianna, the children, but I could tell that nothing registered. Eyes straight ahead, my father had sat motionless except on occasion to rub his ample forehead as if some pain had alighted there and he was trying to swipe it away.

Dr. Shapiro enters so quietly I don't hear him. He carries a little tray with a needle. I look puzzled.

"Morphine. For the pain. Just in case."

Rubbing my father's arm between elbow and shoulder with an alcohol swab, he injects. When I continue looking at him in astonishment, he shrugs and says, "I know it looks silly. Medical protocol. You understand—?"

Knowing he means well, I keep silent except to say, "And the rubbing of the alcohol? To protect against infection?"

"Yes, of course. We never inject without it." His face is deadly earnest, and I nod with the same gravity on my face. When he leaves, I don't know whether to laugh or cry.

After some time, I withdraw my hand from my father's and close my eyes. Once a figure of such power and presence, this shrunken corpse—for that is what it is—becomes an image unrecognizable, unfathomable. Shuddering, I hope I will not go this way. It is, of course, not so hard for the dead, who have even ceased dying, but for survivors it's like bearing witness to memories dissolving before one's eyes, the past and the present locked in mortal combat, each attempting to gain the upper hand, each fighting to overcome the other. And the present always wins: perhaps the machines and their noises are simply too much. If Paul does not come soon, I will ask Dr. Shapiro to disconnect. I look at my watch. Past noon.

Involuntarily I close my eyes again and ask my memory, no, command it: Think of a slice in time with Father that is precious, an experience between the two of us that lingers as happy and carefree, think of love between us. At first nothing comes. Then a memory.

I am ten or eleven, Father takes me to lunch for a special treat; mother has taken Paul to New York to see a specialist for what they think is asthma. It is summer, a bright and sunny day. White tablecloths, waiters with black bow ties, a huge menu card in French, which I can't read. I eat whatever he suggests—turbot, not steak; strawberry shortcake, not chocolate eclair. But I do so with awe and love. What a gift to be alone in this cavernous, fancy dining room with my father, who is translating for me what he deems the best food. How can I not agree? He is in an expansive mood, smiling, urging me on, asking me, do I like this? Do I like that? Was he not right? And I am bathed in warmth, saying what he wants to hear—"Yes, great, Father! Wonderful!"

"Jack."

I open my eyes and turn sharply to face my brother and put my arm around Paul.

"Paul. I'm glad you made it."

"Any doubts?"

"No, none."

"How long has he been like this?"

"Well, they called me at four. A good while, I guess."

"And—?"

"You haven't met Dr. Shapiro yet?" Paul shakes his head. He stands there with a small overnight bag in his hands, dressed smartly in a blazer, open light blue shirt and khakis.

"Well, they kept him going for us. To say goodbye."

"He's dead, Jack."

"I know, but the heart beats and the breaths are pumped in and out. It's grotesque, but they truly believe it's humane."

"I know." Paul takes a chair and pulls it to the other side of Father's bed.

"You look dazed. Sleeping?" Paul asks.

"No, no. I was thinking back—I willed myself to think back to a special moment with Father. Remember the time Mother took you to a specialist in New York about your asthma?"

Paul shrugs, but then, "Oh, yes. We took the train."

"Right. And Father took me to lunch in a fancy restaurant. I have no idea what the name of it was. But it *was* a special day for me. I can see and smell and taste it as if it were yesterday."

"Did it bring comfort, the memory?" A trace of irony in the voice.

"Yes, Paul. It really did."

"Well, good. I mean that."

"Paul," and I pull my chair around the bed to sit next to my brother. "Paul," and I put my hand on his shoulder. There is no resistance. "I know that it was bad, but you know, he did love you. He did."

Paul shakes his head slowly, and three or four tears roll down his cheek. "No, Jack. He really didn't. He was indifferent. But you know, guess what? *I* loved *him*! I loved him all my life, even when I hated him. Does that make sense? I so much wanted his approval, and never got it. *Never*," and the voice is sad, not bitter. Helpless, I take hold of my brother's hand. (Oh, Seth!) Nothing I can say that would be anything but banal. So instinct guides me not to press my brother closer, to say nothing, to allow it all to stand. And it is the right thing, for Paul turns to me, and for the first time in decades, we embrace as brothers and weep silently in each other's arms. I place my hand on my father's black and blue forearm; Paul in turn places his hand over mine. Somehow the three of us are, however briefly, united.

Then we summon Dr. Shapiro and ask him to silence the machines and thank him for his sensitivity. Later we would concede that the doctor had been right, that the time we had to say farewell was worth preserving: for ourselves. Arrangements for cremation were already signed, everything had been prepared long ago. I call Julianna in her office. We exchange a few words, all that is necessary. Julianna has always admired, if not loved, Samuel Morris, and she expresses her sorrow quietly. Yes, she has called the children. Miranda said she might come in for a weekend. Perhaps to talk about her future? Julianna is so happy Paul has come, and especially when I later tell her that at least for this occasion we are reconciled. Well, I wouldn't exactly say "reconciled," I had added, as if revising myself, "We embraced briefly over the corpse of our father. And we did shed tears together." Sad, rather than bitter.

From Pine Manor I call Yale. There is just not enough time to make the necessary preparations. Unfortunately, just now, they're homing in on Commencement, and surely all sorts of people from around the world will want to come to this "memorial celebration" (the tone is that of quotation marks). Next fall? It's fine, of course, I understood. "If we do it we'll have to do it the right way," the dean says. That's the way your father would have wanted it. He did not know him personally, but from all he'd heard—. It is agreed to schedule a day at the start of the next academic year.

"Why not come home with me, Paul? I will sit a modified Shiva. A symbolic one. It would mean a lot."

"I can't, Jack, but it's not what you think. I need to go to L. A., absolutely need to. I'm starting a little business out there. I'll tell you about it when it's done. Retirement is getting to be a bore. I'm only sixty-three. I'm not being unfeeling, but I must go."

"Is retirement a bore, then?" I had caught that bit.

"For me. Everyone is different." After a pause, "You're not thinking—?"

"No, no, nothing immediate. But it begins to enter your mind, you know?"

"All I can say Jack, don't rush it. But then you can keep working, writing, yes?"

"Well, yes, that's true. Only the teaching goes, really." Did I say "*only*"? That's the heart of it! "I'll think about your advice when the time seems nearer."

"Do that. Anyway, I must go. My best to all at home."

"I will. I understand, no hard feelings." And once more, but more quickly, we embrace and go to the Administration Office to sign papers. An hour later, the details sealed, we each leave on separate journeys.

I did offer up some gestures for observing my father's death, gestures Samuel Morris would probably have scorned. I did not cover mirrors, nor did I sit on a cardboard box, but each morning, early, for a week, I drove to a local synagogue to say kaddish. That much I owed not to my father, but to myself. Only a few older men were there, putting on their teffilin, prayer shawls over their heads; they were barely enough to make the necessary ten. But the shul was small, damp and dark, for morning service was early. I guess it was "almost Orthodox," as people were now wont to say, but the men were friendly and gave me their deepest condolences. I was welcomed. When they prayed they were all business. But afterwards, they were chatty, wanted to know all about me and the family. One of them, a man surely in his nineties, made a special effort. Sitting next to me, he gave off the odor of after shave lotion and something else, elusive, but it was not unpleasant. "I'm so sorry for your loss," the man said in unaccented English, "a *tate*, a father, that's a serious loss, very hard, very, very hard," and he put his weightless arm over my shoulder." And I would nod and think how right he was, yes, a *tate was a serious loss.*

Sitting every morning in this small chilly little house of worship was a visit to a strange land for me, but it provided comfort. It was hard for me to imagine how some observed this kaddish ritual for a whole year, twice a day. One morning I found myself silently praying, not from the book, not anything prescribed, just a private prayer. But even while I was in the midst of what for me was an unusual event, I realized that my prayer was hypocritical at best, something along the lines, I supposed, of what some very secular people do as they face disaster, when they might be sitting in a plane making an emergency landing and hearing, "Brace! Brace!" What did I pray? I prayed that I should not change because I felt so often that I was becoming someone else. In the midst of mourning my father, however ritualistically, I was praying for myself.

When the week was done, I shook the hands of the morning worshipers, and they all nodded with understanding, and a few said, "Don't be a stranger," "You're always welcome here," "It was good to honor your father, even just for a week." Slight reproach? I thanked them.

Meanwhile, Julianna was quietly supportive. She let me be reflective, and I spent many hours, more than usual, in my study, reading or just thinking. Some lines from Eliot, handy from the previous semester in my marked up copy of the *Four Quartets*, I read over and over:

> There are three conditions which often look alike ...
>
> Attachment to self and to things and to persons, detachment
>
> From self and from things and from persons; and, growing between them, indifference.
>
> Which resembles the others as death resembles life ...

At first, the lines frightened me. Was I in a state of indifference? Of death? My father's death had affected me, but not the way I had expected. I felt neither sorrow nor relief but a kind of indifference, a numb, painful indifference, suffused with regrets, with guilt, even some anger. Not indifference, then? What in the world was I doing, reading Eliot? Was this grieving? Was I a pedant, even in the midst of my father's death? Someday, I knew, I would be ready to weep. But the time simply had not come, and to force the issue now would make me feel even worse. So I continued to read and to reflect. Actually, most of the time my mind was empty; or fixated on the trivial, the irrelevant. When someday I retired, I would need to move my books from my office. Where would they go? No room here.

Preparation, office hours, grading papers were, for the week, set aside, and though I taught my classes, my heart was not in them. News of Father's death soon became known. Colleagues sent condolence cards to my home, and some slipped envelopes into the mailbox. I opened a particularly ornate card from Robinson and Bentwick, black-bordered with an ecumenical verse about loss and grief rhyming with dross and belief. Very decent of them. Another card came from Marvin Golden that had printed on it, in capital black letters surrounded by quotation marks, the following: "I can't go on, I'll go on." A few lines down, Samuel Beckett was identified. The card was signed M. Golden. I arched my eyebrows. On the back of the light blue card, I looked for a trademark, and found: Famous Quotations Ltd., Inc. Below the bar code I made out the price—$5.00! Angel hugged me and said how sorry she was, and how she remembered her own father's death. I was grateful.

The children called. Seth asked whether he should come up, but I said no, it really wasn't necessary, though I would love to see him soon. Just now I liked being alone for a bit, "need my space," I kidded, but Seth merely said he understood.

In a few weeks I was back in the rhythm of my life.

Spring

14

When I saw the dusk falling on Hill 4, I had harvested some insight about the ever growing emptiness between myself and the world I had known. At times, I felt a stranger to myself. And earlier, that late autumn afternoon when I had driven down the leafless Route 2, I had seen the shape of my anger because I was no longer what I had been. Pieces of the puzzle were beginning to fall into place. But if I was no longer who I was, then who was I? That I began to understand better the day of the early April blizzard. But let me start at the beginning.

As a child, I had loved snow, sledding and ice skating with Paul and, although Father raised his eyebrows at the huge snowmen which he thought unseemly, these white creatures gracing his front acreage. Once we had stuck one of his wide-brimmed black hats from his walking tours in pre-America days on an ample head of a very large snowman, but he had scolded us, and from then on we made sure never again to take any of his "garments," as he called them. Sledding was my favorite—the speed, especially when the snow was a little slick with ice, the cold air hitting the lungs with painful pleasure, exhaling smoky breath through my nostrils. We were recruited for lots of shoveling but didn't mind. Shoveling was an occasion for snowball fights, with each other or with some older boys on the block. Marvelous winter, soft snowballs exploding on my face, a sensation of ice cold against warm, red cheeks. A time for laughter. On occasion, of course, Paul or I would get nasty, pack the ball hard and aim for below the head, and when the snowballs hit it hurt, even through winter jackets. But neither of us ever cried or complained to our parents. These were the days of solidarity between us, and now I regretted how short-lived they had been.

As I grew older, I didn't exactly begin to suffer from chinophobia, but snow and I were (gradually) no longer on such good terms. Over time I developed an aversion to snow, except, of course, when gazing at it through my windows, lovely soft snow fluttering down, gathering steadily to build cones on the evergreens. What a beautiful sight, so quiet an interval, sitting and staring into the nothingness of white, the relentless steady fall of flaky rain—that's what Helen had called it as a child.

But then some powerful nor'easters killed the power lines, and we had to sit in the cold for hours on end, covered with blankets, watching smoky candles, feeding the fireplace. Having an electric stove, we had to make do without even a cup of hot water. That's when the glamour of winter began to wear thin. When we lost power so usually did the Adlers, and our two families would commiserate over the phone. The snowplow man came at all hours, often in the middle of the night, waking us from uneasy sleep with his harsh scraping noise, back and forth, further and nearer, a repetitious motion that, through the narcosis of half slumber, sounded threatening. On occasions the plowman had his radio on, loud enough so you could hear the distant grating sounds of nighttime AM rock. I had tried, without much success, to get him to do his business before midnight or after six in the morning. But snowplow men, like gardeners, had their own rules, and offending them was risky.

Driving in a snowstorm was what I most dreaded, worrying about myself and, once home, if I happened to be first, pacing around an empty house anxious about Julianna. Always, when the flakes began to fall and I was at the university, I would look warily at the sky and make every effort to escape before it turned serious. Just getting off campus could take an hour. In the old days I had tolerated all this better, but now my patience was threadbare, if that. Every time I swore never to be caught in one of these storms again. But it did happen, the day after April Fool's day.

Actually the initial morning forecasts were still on the fence. The local TV stations were pretty much in collusion: three to five inches, but mostly in late afternoon. Flurries in the morning, a little windy later. Then they went into all that useless detail that I listened to as if these meteorologists had ordered me to sit and wait out their oracular prophecies.

My last class ended at three, so I should be fine. Julianna was leaning over the kitchen table in her lightweight jacket, sipping coffee and going through some papers.

"Late day?"

"Well, I have a tenured member meeting scheduled for three. Why?"

"The snow."

"Oh. Bad forecast?" Julianna never watched or listened. She relied (if that is the word) on me; she knew me as a compulsive weather watcher.

"Oh, not bad until late afternoon, but I'll be home by three thirty. If you have a meeting—"

"Look, dear, if it looks bad I'll cancel and cut out early."

"Okay. Drive carefully."

"I will. You too." She said it remotely, as if she was listening with half attention, which she was. Soon she left, throwing a kiss. I pondered the graying sky warily. No one said this one would go out to sea altogether. Julianna always thought storms would go out to sea; she couldn't be bothered with them. I should stop fretting. Of course, she was right. The sight of Julianna, cheerful and efficient, resolutely walking from the house with an energy that left its trace behind, like perfume, struck me. Only five years' difference between us! Was I so much older? Or was she so much younger? Was there a gulf between us that was beginning to show? So many distances now. The students, Julianna, Leon, even the children. I slowly put my books into my case and shut off the kitchen lights, and with labored steps walked toward the garage.

In the office, I brushed the snow off my mind and held a busy office hour. I still liked talking to students. My swivel chair turned with my back to the window, I never saw the large wet flakes swirling until shortly before noon, when I began to prepare for a luncheon appointment with a graduate student. Then I was surprised to see the flakes beginning to cover the tops of some trees in the distance. Walking to the Faculty Lounge, I saw the grass turning white, but the pavement remained bare, the snow flakes dissolving as they hit concrete.

The student, whom I did not know well, sat down gracefully at the table. Meticulously she spread a linen napkin over her lap. I could not help glancing furtively at the huge picture windows of the Faculty Lounge, and what I saw made the thought of lunch less appealing. Her name was Jane Wheaton, dressed in plaid skirt, white blouse, and maroon sweater. More light brunette than dirty blond, her hair cropped but neatly styled. Though it was difficult to see through her rimless glasses, the eyes looked blue, the lashes long. I guessed she was in her late twenties, but she had a round, girlish face. We ordered the pasta special; she added a Diet Coke; I asked for coffee. "Really coming down," I said to her, and she looked up smiling. "The snow," I gestured toward the window. She gave a glance and simply nodded. While waiting for our food we passed the time with small talk. She was Habers' teaching assistant, and she spoke with adulation. "He's different. Not fussy or formal. He makes you feel at ease. And he can be funny. Of course, he doesn't suffer fools and all that." I wondered briefly whether she was drawing a distinction between Habers and myself? When the food arrived, she ate with calibrated appetite. As she lifted her fork in a steady rhythm, I found myself observing her hands, small but strong, her fingernails well cared for, and I noticed a touch of colorless polish on them. She shifted her fork occasionally from left hand to right, and on the ring finger of the left hand she sported a good-sized diamond, but no wedding band. Engaged, obviously.

As I ate with diminished pleasure, I kept stealing glances at the window and saw it snowing harder and harder, though no one seemed to know or care except me. Finally we got around to her dissertation. We both declined dessert. For about fifteen minutes, Jane Wheaton, unassuming, seemingly shy, outlined her plan. She scarcely stopped talking to catch her breath. All of this was so engrossing, for a time I forgot all about the snow. And for that alone I was grateful. But as I listened attentively and with genuine enthusiasm, I also knew that I might never work with Jane Wheaton, not to the end—that might be three or four years. But I was not yet prepared to admit even that, shook it off.

I ordered a second cup of coffee and complimented her originality and could tell she was pleased. Then a tactful glance at my watch conveyed the obvious: it was time to go. We parted at the door of the Faculty Lounge bound in opposite directions.

My walk back to the office was very different from an hour ago. Now the snow was beginning to stick, and I could feel my feet sliding. I took measured steps. Students were cheerfully delighted in the snow, some of them running, then letting the momentum carry them forward on the slippery walkway. Once I was almost on collision course.

Within sight of my building, I saw her. No doubt about it. She was walking slowly, her hair covered with a wet white sheen. But my God! She looked naked neck down. I strained my eyes through my wet glasses and wiped them with bare fingers. Oh, she was wearing a fuzzy white turtleneck jacket, yet it all seemed so seamless. What was she doing back? Beginning to stride now, reckless on this slippery surface, I was right behind her. "Milicent!" I said, and actually placed my hand lightly on her shoulder. Then I lost my balance and both hands landed not so lightly on both her shoulders—they were holding me up. She turned abruptly and stared at me. It was not Milicent L. Jacobs. Nothing like her. But I could have sworn? Then it came, quickly, as if someone had pressed a button, a slap in the face. It wasn't hard, more like an involuntary pat. Stunned, I placed my hand on my cold cheek. "Sorry. I took you for someone else," but she was long gone, disappearing into the whiteness.

When I reached Grover Hall, I was shivering. I took the few steps to the front door slowly and with great care. It wasn't Milicent L. Jacobs, not at all, yet had that girl a voodoo doll? I had been slapped for placing my hands on her surrogate's shoulders? It made no sense, none whatever, unless I was recognized as the accused? Not likely. Passing by Angel's office, I tried to compose myself. "Well, are you seeing what I see? They said a few inches!"

"Yup. Sure am. Sticking to the ground. Slippery yet?"

"Yes. Leave early!" She waved. She had work to do.

But I couldn't get that slap out of my mind. In the bathroom, I looked in the mirror. It had not hurt, no mark was left, no scarlet letter "D," but I felt branded.

When class began, I was surprised at the turnout. Students marched in with a jovial air, the shoulders of their jackets decked with snow, their hair crowned in white. The wet jackets soon made puddles. But the class seemed more cheerful than usual. To them snow was fun, and at this age they were fearless. In fact today they were lively. I was mostly quiet, allowing the excited voices to make their points with a passion I had rarely seen lately. Good, good. All that for snow?

One side of the classroom was lined with two large windows, and almost mesmerized I watched the snow falling with increasing tempo. It must be windy out as well, because at times the snow was driven horizontally, and the flakes were no longer big and wet but the kind you get in mid-winter. There was a bit of road that could be seen, and it appeared to be snow-covered, while the pace of cars was increasing. At least some people were getting home early. Finally, about ten minutes before the class was to have ended, I said, "Folks, it's snowing out, and I have to drive home. See you next time." They looked happy and packed their things. I rushed to avoid the inevitable student who would want to go on talking, feeling a little foolish as I bolted from the room. I called Julianna. The secretary said she had left just a little while ago and, yes, to tell me she had canceled the meeting. So I called home. No answer yet. Gathering myself together, I left the office in such a hurry I wondered whether I had properly closed the door.

Outside I immediately noticed how much colder it had turned. Feeling the wind hitting my face was painful, like pin pricks, as snow was again blowing horizontally straight at me. Underfoot at least three inches had fallen, but when I got to the car it looked more like five or six, especially on its roof where the pile was neatly conforming to the metal shape. I opened the car door, which allowed some snow to accumulate on the driver's seat, and turned on the motor and the defrosters. There was far too much snow on the windshield to start the wipers. I brushed the roof. With the scraper, I made some headway on the windshield, but I couldn't keep up. As I cleaned one spot and moved to another, the one I had just cleaned picked up more snow. Some of my colleagues in the lot were performing the same ritual in orchestrated pantomime. It struck me as a funny sight. Finally, having done my best, slowly I backed out, and in a rush of panic thought of returning to the office. And then what?

I made for the gate. The backup was already considerable, faculty not staff, unless they had called things off in the interval. Everyone was converging at the steel-lined double gates that were always open. It was easy to tell the university had not yet officially closed, because there were no campus police waving their flashlights to control traffic. It was first car first, though most people were polite and waited their turn.

Finally I made it to the road leading into the highway. There was no other way than slow driving, because it was already crowded, but when I gingerly negotiated the ramp into the highway, I was aghast. Bumper to bumper, cars, SUVs, and the ubiquitous trucks, which would predictably jackknife and cause all sorts of chaos. Without realizing it, I was banging the steering wheel with my right fist.

I hit the AM radio button until I found local news.

"Well, folks, this is Mike, if you're not at home, you should be. This was not supposed to happen like this, so blame the weather guys, including our own Larry Bowers. Hey, Larry, what in blazes is going on? Go tell our listeners. And straight talk. Leave the warm air meeting the cold air and all that jazz to the TV guys. Eh?" Larry was apologetic: it looked as if we were having a blizzard. The National Weather Service put us on a winter storm warning a little while ago, blizzard conditions were developing, heavy snow and winds gusting to fifty. He was asked how much snow we'd get and as usual he hedged. Outside of the city—well, maybe a foot, more, further west and north. The traffic report was no better. Cindy Coletta said, "Folks, if you don't need to be out don't go out. And call your mate on the cell phone, 'cause you're going to be *very* late for dinner." Despite Julianna's nagging, I had resisted getting that cell phone. It was a mess: reports of dozens of spinouts, one rollover on 495, cars on the side of roads with drivers cleaning snow off windshields, and a clogged 128 north and south. 128—that was my road and I needed no news of that: I was witness to it all: a mess—in front, in back, and on either side. The voice belonging to Mike wailed, "Oh, my," and he promised an update in twenty minutes or so. Meanwhile, to relax us, back to some soft rock, and I shut the radio.

Now I needed to concentrate. Despite the frantic swipe of the wipers and the whirr of the defrosters, the windshield was picking up a film of dirt and wet snow, mostly from the cars in front, and I found myself bending over and squinting. The seat belt pressed against my chest. Too risky to use wiper fluid. It could make things worse. Still I gambled, and it actually helped, though some of it glazed a little on the glass. Side windows yielded no visibility. Again and again I rolled them up and down, in a swirl of driven snow, and it helped for a half minute or so, but no more. Thank God the tank was still half full.

We were crawling, stop and start, stop and start. And each stop required delicate footwork with the brakes. People generally left more room than usual between themselves and the car in front, but once in a while there was the idiot trying to weave in and out who inevitably skidded. Some cars fishtailed. If I got off one exit early, I would avoid the large curvy part of the highway. But there was always the chance that the narrower secondary road would be worse. I debated it and decided at the last moment in favor of fleeing the highway. Now I had to maneuver quickly over to the outer lane, just one lane over, and this would take more faith than skill. I put on the directional, and after a few minutes managed to get there, but the off-ramp was clogged. By the time I realized the extent of the chaos, it was too late. Again I punched the steering wheel. Standing on the ramp and trying to get traction was nearly impossible, especially as cars in front came sliding down perilously close to collision point.

Somehow at last I found myself off the ramp, and though all the signs were covered with snow, I still had my markers and knew where to turn. Now it was narrow, single file where the treads of tires had made their indent. There must have been eight inches on the ground. Maybe more. God, what a way to end an early April day! Here, on this road, it was trail the red lights in front of you. Pied Piper. Somewhere there was a first car, and if that car veered off into the abyss, we would all follow. A few cars in front I saw the blinking lights of a plow or a sander, but it would make little difference.

With the snow continuing to swirl in all directions now, I became aware of shadows of darkness. To the right I looked at what took on the appearance of a Whistler painting—indistinct hues of black and white, a fuzzy outline that made it difficult to demarcate any boundaries between meadow and sky or meadow and road. This was the meadow side. To the left, set back a little, were private homes, far apart, smoke pluming from the chimneys, that was all I could see. I stole a glance at the digital car clock on the dash—4:30. And I had left my building shortly after 3:00.

At the same time I was beginning to feel pressure from my bladder, my feet were cold, despite the heat which, to keep alert, I had now turned down. But I was not far from home, conservatively a few minutes from the traffic light at the Four Corner crossing that was just ahead. Once I passed by that—perhaps ten minutes more to safety. Right now the light went from red to green to red without more than two or three cars ahead moving a few feet before the light turned red again. The hanging traffic light was shaking in the gusts, as if some unseen hand were signaling desperately with a lantern. Four Corners was a bad spot in good times. In bad weather it was a disaster, with cars turning every which way.

As I sat there staring at the red light, full stop, I dreamt back to my sledding joys, recalled the day my sled grazed a tree and I sideswiped my nose on the bark and, transfixed, watched the red blood spreading out on the white snow in sinuous waves, like red ink on a white blotter, while Paul ran, frightened, and shouted for mother.

The wipers almost put me to sleep, and then I heard a horn behind me and felt a slight bump. Had I been asleep? The light turned green and there were two cars ahead. Without warning, a sense of direction abandoned me. Which way to turn? All the landmarks were gone, and though I knew I should go straight ahead—knew it somewhere—now, for no apparent reason, except the car menacingly close behind me, I hesitated. No, in the past I would have acted. I was no longer what I had been. Everything had slowed. Suffused with doubt, not certain of anything any more, I sat paralyzed in the middle of a blizzard. I had lost not only my bearing but my mooring as well. Like the swirl of snow enveloping me, I was adrift. The horn blew again. Twice. The light turned red and the horn blew in anger, the driver was leaning on it. I felt as if I were being pursued. When the light turned green, without any rational reason, I turned left and made my way to the Mercedes-Benz dealership close to the corner. Where am I? Where am I going? How can I have lost all sense of direction? My heart pounded. Was Julianna stuck in this, too? I prayed she would be home when I got there. (If I ever get there, I mumbled in passing.)

Managing to enter the driveway of the dealership, I stepped out and sloshed through deep snow, my feet soaked by now. Hardly believable: I saw lights. They were open! Or was it just for security? They always had some lights on, even when closed. I pushed and the door gave way. Two young men in the back of the showroom sat laughing, feet up on their desks. They saw me and came to attention, smartly.

Acutely self-conscious, I walked through the small showroom past a shiny new white Mercedes convertible. Even in my bedraggled state, my bladder bursting, I eyed it with admiration. Years ago Stan Habers had marched into my office, "Hey, Morris! Got myself a mid-life Chrysler," and he practically dragged me into the parking lot to show off his trophy—a white convertible with red leather seats, girdled by chrome, spoked aluminum wheels, shiny all over, a well-preserved car of older vintage. Of course, Habers volunteered the price. A bargain! And I had made a patronizing remark, had he really need of such things? And he replied with a line from *King Lear*, "Oh, reason not the need ..." But now it was I looking at the sleek Mercedes with regrets. Ah, retribution! (The beauty of Habers' mid-life Chrysler was all outer. The innards kept breaking down, and within a year he had sold it to an antique car dealer, for a profit.)

I told the young men I was relieved they were open but, smiling, they said they were just stranded. They had taken off their suit jackets which hung on the backs of their chairs, and their ties were loosened, but they looked well groomed. Could they help?

"Yes. First I have to use your john, please. Then I need to make a call?" One of the young men politely pointed to the rear. "Men's room is right through there, sir. Phone on my desk will do. Just dial 9 for out."

I thanked him and went straight for the bathroom. Standing at the urinal longer than I could ever recall, I remembered that I forgot before I left campus, but why should I have remembered for what ordinarily was a twenty minute drive? But smart to have turned left! Never could have held out until home. Instinct? Subconscious? What matter? I washed my hands and dried them on a blower. Looking into the mirror, I was shocked to see my image, white face, wet jacket, tie loose, hanging forlornly. More lines spread across the brow than this morning.

No, I was not who I had been. What didn't help was the fluorescent light, which was flickering ominously and caused my image in the mirror to light up and darken in surrealistic spurts, like an action painting. (Surely we would lose power at home, if we hadn't already.) Then I walked out and headed for the desk and to the phone one of the young men pushed in my direction. Julianna picked up. Relieved to hear her voice, I told her where I was and yes, I would drive very carefully.

Grateful, I thanked the stranded men and even shook their hands, a gesture that brought smiles to their faces. There was yet another question, and I hesitated. To get home I had to backtrack? Or could I get home any other way? I gave them my address, and one of the men tore a page off a Mercedes-Benz pad and drew a simple map.

"Just keep going down the end of the block, turn right, one block, then left and you're on the way. Second right, that's your street."

Were they so obliging because of my disheveled looks and graying hair? Had that anything to do with their good manners? Of course it did. I followed the directions, and although it was slow going, there were few cars, and at last I saw my house and opened the garage door with the remote. I had made it home.

I shut the motor off, my hand on the remote for the garage door, but I hesitated, wanting just for now to sit in silence. The snow had slowed to a steady fall of very large snowflakes that were clinging to all the car windows. Soon I was enveloped, had no vision in any direction. It was comforting. I plundered my memories of the afternoon, and yes, the puzzle was again taking shape. I knew better than before who I was now. By no means was it just age (sixty-five was hardly old these days), but time had placed me on the other side of a certain space. All those exultant feelings about my life as a teacher had moved away from me, or I from them. If only I could begin adjusting my vision to this new space, perhaps I would stop missing things and start taking notice of what this new territory had to offer?

But right now I could see nothing, not even the garage door in front of me, for stopping the car had stopped the wipers. Leaving behind, parting with what was, embracing what is and will be—that was the answer, yes, I was sure. But such acceptance was not something we're taught, we must learn it, will it, seize it: here you are; there you were. That would be a lonely place to be, at least for a time, until, like the streets of a strange city, I would master navigating them. I started the motor and the wipers whirred and cleared the windshield, and a sheet of snow cascaded off the slowly lifting bay door like an avalanche. Even through closed windows I could hear the door's groan. The car barely made it in. Drops of melting snow crawled down both my cheeks and down my collar, as I shivered feeling the wet on my neck. I trudged my way to the house door.

That night the last words I said to Julianna were, "I saw Milicent L. Jacobs today in the snow. Except it wasn't her. But the girl I mistook her for slapped my face and disappeared into the snow." She groaned, but we embraced, not yet the embrace of full understanding, that was still to come, but enough to bless us both with peaceful sleep.

15

The next evening, after dinner, I sat in my study, Julianna in hers. Staring at the ceiling, I decided to get up and walk across the hall. I lingered in front of her open door, and she turned to me with a questioning look. "Jack?"

"I need to talk."

"Just preparing. You look bushed. That storm did you in. What's up?"

"I'm not even sure. Sorry. Bad timing. But lately it's always been a bad time. It can't wait any more. It's oppressing me." "You've been looking down. Sad. What's the matter?"

"I don't know. A weight. I feel a weight on me."

Julianna drew her palm across my cheek. "I think you're still shell-shocked from what that girl did to you. You're obsessed about her. Maybe?"

"Maybe. But that's not exactly it. There's lots more." My words came slowly. "Yesterday, sitting in the car in front of the garage, all the windows were covered with snow, and I thought I was really much closer to understanding everything, but today, that's all gone. Well, not *all*, but—"

"Have you thought of—well, I mean if it's—maybe some help?"

"A shrink?"

"Maybe? Just to see what may be up, no? You've been through hell."

"Perhaps I could call Patico?"

"Good idea. He's retired but still around. You're no stranger to him. Maybe he can recommend someone?" Dr. Albert Patico had helped us both when Nathan died. To my surprise (and by the look on her face apparently to Julianna's as well), I said, without hesitation, "Okay. Sure. Why not?" I wasn't certain why I had agreed so quickly, for I honestly thought it a complete waste of time.

She seemed pleased and kissed me on the lips. "Let's go to dinner. *Not* Spanelli's again! How about *Kasaki*?" It was a Japanese place (with Korean accents), a town away, where Julianna devoured her beloved Tekka Maki tuna sushi, which I wouldn't touch ("raw fish! God, no!"). "You can have those lovely white Tempura Udon noodles you like, with chicken, and then we both love the beef bulgogi?" Although it was not my first choice of food, I agreed and we went. It turned out to be a bad decision. The bulgogi—grilled on a gas range at the table and spread out on green fresh lettuce leaves—looked appealing. But I had no appetite even as my stomach murmured as if begging to be nurtured. Absent-mindedly I seized the bulgogi with my chopsticks, planted some on the lettuce leaf, curled it with my fingers and guided it reluctantly into my mouth. And then again. The Japanese beer tasted bitter and too cold as it flowed down my dry throat. Perhaps I drank it too fast, because I soon found myself in the small bathroom where I entered a stall, kicked up the seat, bent over, and with closed eyes heard it all come up in three loud wretches. After flushing, I washed my hands and face with soap and water. When I returned, Julianna, with concerned voice, said I looked ghastly white, was I all right? No, I said, could we leave? Of course, and she abandoned her sushi half eaten. I signed the credit card slip and we left. In the car I told her I had chucked it all up, and she held my hand and felt its moist, almost lifeless cold. Poor Jack. It will be all right, she promised, it will. Sure, I said. Who knows, probably it was the beer. Maybe drank it too fast. Perhaps, she agreed, in an unconvincing tone of validation. I may have forgotten the tip, I confessed, as if afraid of being overheard. Not to worry. We'd make it up next time. Okay, but for an instant it was touch and go, for I had the urge to give up more. But there was no more. I was empty.

In the morning I called Dr. Patico. Well, came the deep voice, he'd see me himself but he's out of practice now. And there was a coughing laugh. He had been a heavy smoker. That's what you fellows call a "double entendre," eh? He recommended a "young fellow"—everybody seemed young to him these days—Saul Golomb, fine credentials, and he'd sent a few satisfied customers there. Cambridge, last he looked. Spacing his words with slight pauses, he gave me his phone number and wished me luck.

Immediately I made an appointment with Dr. Golomb, who indeed still had his practice in Cambridge. Parking might be a problem but Julianna, who knew that part of Cambridge corner to corner, sent me to a parking structure a few blocks away. The garage, close to the Square, was half empty. As usual, the Cambridge streets around Harvard were unevenly shoveled after a snowfall, and even though the calendar was almost spring, it had been cold, and the recent snow, now coal black, was stubborn in melting in shaded spots, lurking near buildings where the sun had not yet done its job. There was nothing charming about bulging red cobblestones. For some reason I had not zippered my jacket, and the wind, though refreshing, bore into me. I had left myself plenty of time and arrived twenty minutes early.

Dr. Golomb's office was on the second floor of an unassuming three-story brick town house. The wooden steps still had islands of sand. I opened the front door, wood frame and glass windows, and climbed the staircase one flight. Its steps creaked a little. Below the small gold nameplate ("Dr. Golomb") was a sign: "Please Ring Bell," so I pushed the button and a buzzer sounded that released the door. The waiting room was high-ceilinged and pleasant, wine-colored walls, a few easy chairs, a small couch, a coffee table laden with *New Yorkers*, *The Best of Boston*, and the usual news magazines, and one rather old *New York Review of Books*. A large green plant stood watch at one corner of the room; if Julianna were here she would immediately have touched the leaves to test their authenticity. I reached for a *New Yorker* and began flipping the pages looking at the cartoons, some of which were inside jokes I didn't get. Without warning I was struck by a tingling, as if an alert had sounded in my system. Why was I here? I didn't like the whole business. Stay or flee? *The New Yorker* danced in my shaking hands. My mouth dried up. What was I afraid of? Had I not seen enough doctors lately and endured MRIs? Had I not weathered them all boldly and calmly? Well, this was an MRI of my heart and soul. A bolt coursed through me, and my back, ailing as ever, stiffened against the chair. Yes, I would flee and was about to rise just as a door opened and a man (about fifty) wearing a modest dark gray suit, blue shirt and tie came toward me to shake my hand.

Did the professor park all right? I accepted the outstretched hand and nodded. Yes, just fine, thanks.

The doctor waved me in, and I was perfectly calm now. Dr. Golomb closed the door and invited me to sit in an easy chair directly facing one where he sat down. I took in a clean, sparsely furnished office, professional, indifferent, walnut bookcases lining most of the wall space. What looked like an original oil painting of a young, beautiful woman hung on the wall on the left side of the desk, topped by neatly stacked piles of papers and pamphlets. The only anomaly, at least in my vision, was a black computer tower with a matching black monitor standing on an angle at one corner of the desk.

Well, how could he be of help?

And I began, systematically, telling my tale. First, of course, I spoke of Leon's death and how that had so deeply affected me. Yes, I had felt worn down, well no, burnout would be too strong, considerably singed perhaps, certainly tired, and well, yes, there were still some unresolved physical problems, but none of these was the main issue. What was? Well, I just knew that after nearly four decades of teaching, one way or another, counting from my years as a Teaching Assistant, it may be time to let go. Four decades? Yes, four. And now I perceived an ever widening gulf, a chasm, a deep space between myself and my students, between my expression and their comprehension. It made for a mismatch between what I gave and what I got in return. Of course, it was still sometimes fun to teach but fast becoming no fun at all and often downright depressing. I glossed over Milicent L. Jacobs, said there had been some unpleasantness with a charge of sexual misconduct. In fact, I had been charged with sexual assault, but it's all over now, fabricated accusation, of course. Well, then, seems understandable that you're thinking of retiring. *Four* decades? Where's the problem? I had thought it out beforehand. For one thing, I had not told my wife how close I was to thinking of retiring. Oh, we had danced around the subject, but she would be surprised to know how far I've come. And while I was leaning toward letting it all go, I hadn't finally decided, was having second thoughts all the time. Many issues. There was, of course, my wife, who seemed very distressed to become, so to speak, partially widowed so early. Had she said "widowed"? No, no. But she was five years younger and in full stride. Enormous energy. No, "widowed" was my own word. Then there was the untimely death of my friend, which inflicted a personal wound, and also left the department thinned out, and I was concerned about that. Yes, of course I was sad, but also there was a responsibility, nothing to do with sadness. No one is indispensable, but—well, I was a very senior member. Also there were graduate students. Although I could finish up the ones who were writing dissertations, there were others I felt close to, and I would need to cut them off, rather abruptly. And then there was my father. Died recently. He'd been pretty out of it this last year. Oh, well, not really relevant. Laughing: yes, my father had more or less ordered me to retire at sixty-five, just as he had! Famous sociologist at Yale. And how can one be sure of such a momentous decision? And especially since the law permitted me to stay forever, and this was all voluntary. It was Dr. Patico who had suggested the name. Who had suggested I come to see somebody in the first place? Actually it was my wife. I had told her I was feeling low. She thought I needed help.

I had stopped. Dr. Golomb had listened carefully. A clipboard with yellow lined paper rested on his lap, and occasionally he had unobtrusively made a notation. Once in a while he appeared to be nodding. But with a patient so willing to talk, he had not interrupted often. Now he spoke.

He didn't know me, of course. And any therapist who pretends he could "know" anybody after a half hour or so is a liar or a charlatan. But my story certainly indicated some trauma, starting with my friend's death. As I spoke he had been struck by a couple of things. Yes. Well first off, voluntary retirement would give anyone pause. After such a long and active professional life, and obviously a successful one, who wouldn't have hesitations, whatever the decision? If one leaves there is loss, certainly. Routine, familiarity—these are not minor. If one stays perhaps there might be nagging regrets. The doctor would find it abnormal if there were no second thoughts—either way. But second thoughts appear trumped by a firm decision, whichever way it goes. And one more thing. The professor had glossed over the matter of being accused of sexual assault. Unpleasantness? More than that, he should think?

My shoulders slumped. Was I being admonished? Had I not given a well-prepared, articulate presentation of the problem? I thought I had. In fact I was astonished at the clarity and calm with which I had delivered myself of a complex issue. No hemming or hawing, full sentences. Like a very good lecture, the kind I used to deliver with regularity. And was it so necessary to detail the Milicent L. Jacobs matter? Was the doctor suggesting I had not been clear? Or that I really knew which way it was going? No, to both questions, he said. All he had meant was that one noted some things. For instance, all the reasons the professor cited for having doubts are not internal but external. One hears a lot of guilt, too. And a bit of anger and resentment. I was puzzled. How's that? Guilt? Anger? Resentment? A touch of irascibility in my voice. Well, if one scrolls down the list of reasons offered for maybe having what were called "second thoughts"—and with each point he lightly placed his right forefinger into his left palm—some things emerge. First your wife. Then the department. And then students who would be deprived. Also a conversation with a father who is dead now and hovered between reality and unreality—and he did in fact approve of retirement? Sounded from what was said he almost—well, "ordered" it, I believe was the word used? So the hesitation to retire could possibly be an act of rebellion? But that's a different door. Let's not go there for now. Also heard a note of apology, as if how could you make a decision on your own, especially when all those other outside issues weighed on you? What he had *not* heard was anything about my own firm decision to serve *myself, my* needs, and Dr. Golomb now lightly tapped his pencil eraser on the clipboard. But silence on that issue was communicated in the implicit anger and resentment when the reasons against retirement were offered. They sounded plausible, and I had certainly faulted myself for not being sensitive to others—should the decision be to retire. But the tone sounded otherwise. By the way it occurred to him, maybe far-fetched, that retiring was an unconscious desire to meet up with my friend? But never mind that now.

I became defensive. As for internal reasons, I meant—in fact I *did* say, right at the start—that I felt kind of burned out—well, tired, dissociated from the students—Dr. Golomb interrupted and said I had actually said "burnout" was too strong. Wasn't the phrase "considerably singed"? Yes, okay, but those were all reasons for someone rationally *wanting* to get out. But there was no affirmation saying, "You know what, *I* want out." Not, "I think these are good reasons for *wanting out*." See the difference? One might have said, "Yes, there are people and reasons for not retiring, but they come from outside me." As *he* saw it, those other things—in the end—they're irrelevant to the immediate issue at hand.

This time I produced a grimace, an expression of consternation. But then that's a contradiction. If the doctor heard all those reasons he called external, and never heard—what had he called it—an "affirmation" that *I* wanted out, then how could he conclude that this is precisely what I did want? Dr. Golomb's face curled into a very weak smile and he looked deeply into my eyes. He hadn't said he knew what the decision was. Only that perhaps I was closer to knowing than I knew. And I understood that what he was really saying was: I know things because, my dear fellow, that's why I have a shingle out there. That's what I'm trained to see. It's almost always what the patient does *not* say that counts, not what he does say.

But I have second thoughts. Often, I protested. Of course I had. There's hardly a decision we make when we don't. And this—this is a big one. It is! I seemed to be reproaching the doctor. Well, then, what made him so certain I was decided in the direction of retiring? This time Dr. Golomb looked hard at me, I thought, even a little mischievously, but I could have been imagining that. He repeated he did *not* say he was certain which way it would go, but it interested him that I should keep thinking he did. Did I want official reassurance?

Resigned, I looked toward the floor. No pattern in any carpet, Just black linoleum. All right. I take the point. Dr. Golomb: A man of your intelligence and verbal skills? Oh, yes, he was certain I had taken the point. Dr. Golomb leaned back, and this time he did smile.

But surely some kind of guilt about, say, my wife or the department—absolutely. Perfectly normal, he said, raising his hand. And considerate. But in the end we're alone. We know that all these people—the department, the graduate students, even the wife—should I decide to go through with it, well, all of them will survive. By no means did he intend to minimize my importance to all these people. On the contrary. But we both knew that life goes on, even after death. Yes? And this is hardly death? No. But some people think of it as that! For a time, maybe. Not for long. We tend to get used to the reality as we see it. More quickly than we can imagine. The doctor seemed to have come close to resting his case. Yes, I said, thinking of Leon Adler, we do go on. There was one more thing. Had I already mentioned it? A teacher of any kind, but at least one facing year after year these eighteen- to twenty-year-olds, that was a special trial, no? After all the doctor, I was sure, sees patients of all ages; so does a dentist (unless specializing in kids), so does a lawyer, so does——. But college age, that was when the hormones no longer flamed as in adolescence: they just stayed at the peak for four years, solidified, strong and exultant. It was the very thing that gave one so much strength and pleasure, seeing those young people that way, but eventually it was also capable, by comparison, of giving so much pain, so much sadness. I was sweating.

Dr. Golomb nodded in agreement, and stealing a glance at a little digital clock on a bookshelf, said he needed to stop now. But he suggested that if I wished we could talk about this again, however many times I wanted. He had a feeling I would finalize this decision, with more visits or not, and that when I did, I would be at peace with it.

We rose together and shook hands. Dr. Golomb walked me to the door. Once in the fresh air, I thought to myself that this was a very clever man, but like all of these fellows just a trifle too sure of himself. No, I wagered, I would probably not see him again. But right now I was far from feeling any peace. Right now, I needed time for myself, time to sort this out. When I reached the garage, the doctor's words were all jumbled. What was this "guilt," "resentment," "anger" all about? I was beginning to feel less irritated and more confused. Perhaps I should have skipped this trip. Did it really help? I sat in the cold car for a while and then started the motor, having no idea what I should do, where to go, knowing only I was not ready to go home. Without much debate, I decided to drive to the office.

The office. How strange that in American academia we call it an "office," as if it were a business. (During my stay at Oxford, I visited colleagues in their "rooms"). Yet this office is a kind of second home. After three decades and more, it has become a place where part of me acts out a second self, a second, parallel life? It is not a very comfortable or cozy place. Its gray steel desk and cabinets, the peeling corners where the computer wires are tangled like a nest of snakes—these hardly brighten one's heart. And yet. True, home, too, has an "office," but that is called a "study" and what a difference! There I prepare, read, think, write. But here, in this office, I am the "professor," this is the official sanctuary where I perform the last rites and rituals before professing in front of a class, where I scribble final notes on cards, where I meet students (Milicent L. Jacobs!), where hundreds of class-worn books line the walls, where colleagues drop in and chat. Sanctuary. Yes! That's a good word. I sit at my desk, not having removed my jacket. This is a quiet Friday for me, no classes, no office hours, and only Ann Rosenthal has greeted me with a look of "Why are you here?" Should I call Julianna? She might worry. I decide not to. For a while I don't notice that I have not even turned on the lights or the heat, so I reach behind my chair and push the heat button and welcome the blower's noise. The office is ice cold. Enough light still comes through the blinds.

So: give this up? What sanctuary then? Does not everyone need two sanctuaries, one balancing the other? Have I ever totally thought it through? Oh, they might let me keep the office for a while, and I might come in, but eventually—? Then what would I *do*? I hear the chatter and laughter of students as they pass by my slightly ajar door. No more of that? No more of being the giver of knowledge? No more professor professing? And I think what an empowerment it is to stand in front of a class and act as expert witness to precious texts with scores of pens and pencils poised to bear witness. Earnest faces, anxious eyes. That, too, would be gone. But Golomb is right. Although people will say they miss me, eventually they would politely salute with a smiling hello and disappear into their busy lives. Cut off from that as well.

So I begin inventorying all the losses, and they appear staggering. For what feels like a long expanded moment, I truly believe I have been won over by "second thoughts." Why are these doctors always so arrogantly certain that they knew what you are thinking? Surely Golomb sounded as if he knew I had decided to get out, period, he was just pretending to be neutral, winking at me. The light begins to fade, and I sit in near darkness.

I call Julianna, and practice allows me to see the phone pad just enough to hit the right numbers. Yes, in the office. I have some papers to pick up. (A small white lie.) Yes, I would be home soon. The doctor? It went fine. I'd tell her when I got home. Then a change of words. Truth is, darling, I need some time to think. Of course, she agrees, quietly. I'll not be long. Fine, drive carefully. "Drive carefully"—we had been saying that to each other lately, more often than ever before. Perhaps since the fender-bender with the young reporter from *The Crier*? No, before that. Since Leon Adler's death.

I sit quietly staring in the dark out of my window, and I see headlights of traffic beginning to pick up the pace. Never have I felt so numb, so alone. It appears as if I sit there a long time, my mind unable to settle on any one place for more than a second or two. My eyes come to rest on a pile of grade books. Getting up from my chair is like an awakening, and I flip the light switch. Why have I saved these grade books? Like tax returns there is a statute of limitations, but I have preserved these grade books going back over twenty-five years, or more. and they are gathering dust. They are part of my sanctuary, too. My (sadly) inedible madeleines. Proof of my professorial existence. Of my past. Over the decades their colors have changed, from green, to black, and most recently to light blue. Amy Levinson. The name comes to me in an instant, Amy Levinson, who stood in my office with her son, after nearly thirty years. Carefully I bend down to the green pile until I think I have reached the possible years she had been my student. After looking through three books I find her. Straight B. Closing my eyes I try, but there is no young Amy Levinson materializing. Too long ago. I take some black grade books from fifteen years ago, and open them. Neatly printed names: Jason Weil, Emily Frazier, Helen Mobolinsky, Eve Tully—even then, mostly women. Stephanie Auslander.

I stop, place the grade book on my desk, and this time I remember. Oh, yes, Stephanie Auslander. Tall, dark, flashing eyes, black hair past her shoulders, looking older than she was. Very, very precocious. Undisciplined. How often Stephanie sits on that chair—and my eyes fall on the empty chair where students sit (where Milicent L. Jacobs had once sat!)—defiant, but her dark eyes asking for yet another rescue. Never tears, but inside she is suffering, reading current fiction or poetry, but missing her due date for some assignment. Writing poems, which she gives me to read; they're derivative, but brilliant. Love affairs, all of them going badly, a dying mother, perhaps an abusive father? She talks mostly in riddles, but she talks. I know students who make up or embellish their personal agonies, but Stephanie Auslander never tells a lie, I am absolutely sure of that. Stop smoking pot, I beg her, it's a temporary fix. Get help. She has mocked the university's counseling staff, they're idiots! She probably runs circles around them. Get *real* help, I say, trying to entice her by my tacit agreement with her judgment of the university's Counseling Center, but she has no money for that. I offer to help financially. No, she says without any embarrassment, she doesn't want any.

She's a senior when she takes the third course with me, and I begin to feel worn down. Her mother dies. Her lovers leave her. Her father is becoming an alcoholic. This time she seems broken, but she becomes less defiant and more of a listener. Finally, in her last semester, she somehow pulls herself together, comes to my office one day, sits there smiling, announces she is going to graduate school, to Iowa, where she has been accepted to their writer's workshop. I am so pleased. She hands me a slender volume of poetry (from an author and press I've never heard of), wrapped in a deep yellow dust jacket.

I move to the bookcase where I house my poetry and scan left and right, up and down for the yellow spine. After almost giving up, I actually find it. Had I read it? Yes, surely I had done that. Opening up to the title page I read her inscription: "For Jack Morris. Thanks! Stephanie Auslander." That was Stephanie, she would never write "Professor" or gush with words. And the hand-

writing is stylish, large and steady, nicely formed letters slanted to the right, bely-
ing her otherwise discordant state. She has promised to write. Well, you're in a
writing program! No, write to *you*. All right, I hope so. But she only writes once.
A brief note on a card with some abstract painting on its reverse side. The card is
in the book. Something about doing fine and hope to see you. But that is all. No
return address, and I lose her after that. Where is she now, Stephanie Auslander?
What is she doing? Has she found her own poetic voice in flat Iowa, or does she
live with a husband and three children on a farm? Or both? Or neither?

I run my eyes down the last class list on which she is listed, and at least three
other names ring bells. Not as loudly as hers, but bells. Then I place these grade
books back and look at more samples from recent years. Light blue ones. With
each grade book, similar results. Nothing. Names and faces are impossible to put
together with any certainty. No one stands out. Even last year's names are distant.
Now and again a name and a face join fleetingly, but there is nothing special to
remember. Is it the students? My age? Both? I replace all grade books with care.
Yes, they are part of my sanctuary, part of my personal library, part of my quilted
life—even those booklets in which scores and scores of names mean little or
nothing. The official biography of Jack Morris. Well, a good part of it. They have
meant something once. I treasure them still, even if lately the names are just
names. I shut off the heat, then the light.

But something draws me back to the chair. I turn it sideways and again am sitting quietly in the dark. Through the window the headlights now swipe at my
vision in staccato rhythm. I hear the faint rumble of the cars, tires on pavement, a
rhythmic swish, swish, swish. Sight and sound mesmerize. How often I have sat
here surveying the same ritual homecoming, never hearing and seeing as clearly. I
become aware I am running two forefingers down my cheek. The face burns, still
very smooth, because I have taken a very close shave for Dr. Golomb. Almost half
a lifetime in this very small office, and what would a fly on the wall have to say?
Oh, it would take generations of flies! I make an effort to shape a balance sheet:
pluses and minuses. This time staying on is virtually a blank slate, while leaving is
full—time to do what I want, rest from all the tensions, release for the tingling
nervous system, no more meetings, no more deadlines, no more disappointments
in the classroom. Most of all freedom and joyous irresponsibility, pleasurable solitude. No more students, no more books ...

But is this, too, a way of "voiding"? A surge of nausea overcomes me, like the
night I had the flu and sat on the toilet too weak to stand and pee. But the nausea
is not in the stomach: it possesses me, as it does that character in Sartre's novel, I
can't recall his name. All right, what is left? And again I try to fill in the pluses of

staying. What is left? The affection and respect of some colleagues, even of some students, still; the responsibilities given me because I'm trusted to carry them out, because I'm still efficient at getting some things done. Being engaged, doing, staying connected with the world I have known for so long. Now I have stopped noticing the headlights and hearing the cars. These intrusions are back to normal, a very far away din. But then to stay sharp one needed energy, and of that I seem drained. God, how weary I feel! Yeats is an optimist. *My* soul cannot clap any more! Tired of fighting with deans, tired of meetings and committees, tired of colleagues, tired of students, tired of emptiness. Yet this emptiness is also freedom, free of feeling the pounding heart of pleasure: an ashen freedom. O God, all that work, all those years. But has not Eliot said experience is overrated? That old me should explore, go on? Where is the joy? It has fled. I begin to feel a chill; the heat has been off for some time now, and the cold quickly fills the small space of the office. I find myself cupping my ears with both hands staving off the sound of something awful, when I realize what I fear hearing is the soft wail of my weeping. But I am not shedding tears, no febrile salt from my eyes this time. In fact, all is dry and hard—hard as the feel of my blottered desk on which I have placed my forehead. All those grade books. All those students. All those children. Now, for the first time, I know I am, in so many ways, an orphan.

It is time to go. As I am about to walk out, I am startled by the figure of a man in the doorway. It is only Jaime, the custodian, who has been around so long he was once called the janitor.

"Mr. Jack" (Jaime calls everybody Mr. or Miss followed by first name—except for Robinson and Bentwick). "Reading without light? Bad for the eyes. What you doing here on a Friday?"

"Oh, just cleaning up a few things."

"Cleaning? That's my job. Trying to get rid of me?" We have a good relationship, and I like Jaime's Latin humor, relaxed and delightfully silly, always accompanied by a broad smile on his olive-skinned cherubic face as he grins at his own jokes.

"No, not that kind of cleaning up. Your job's safe. How's things with you, Jaime?"

"Can't complain. You, Mr. Jack?"

"Oh, not bad. Fine. Fine. Tell me, Jaime, do you ever think of packing it in?"

Jaime grins. "Every day! No, just kidding. Not yet. Maybe soon. But I don't mind the job. Why you ask, Mr. Jack?" He is holding himself up with a dry mop.

"Well, I'm thinking of it. I'm just not sure. I don't know how to be sure." I wonder why I am beseeching Jaime for wisdom, but there I am, earnestly asking: really, Jaime, what should I do?

"Well, Mr. Jack," says Jaime, "I think you know when you know. Get what I mean?"

"No. Tell me."

"Well, I figure this way. If money's no problem, then you gotta ask, where do I like it better, here or home?" And he points his mop first in one direction, then in another.

"That simple?"

"Yep. That simple. 'Cause if the answer is you like it better home, then that's it. There's the point. You know, Mr. Jack, we all like it home, but if you like it *better*—you know what that means?"

"No. What does it mean, Jaime?"

"Well, I'm no expert, Mr. Jack, but to me it means you really don't like it *here* any more. Not so you're looking forward to it. It's heavy on the other side," and, leaning the mop against the wall, he pushes both of his outstretched arms into space, to his right.

"Jaime, you should go to Cambridge and hang out a shingle."

"Mr. Jack?"

"Never mind. Tell me, Jaime, do you look forward?"

"You know what? Yeah, I do. For all the bullshit I get, I like to come in and do a good job. Yeah, I still like it. And you?" "Well, maybe not that much. Anyway, you helped, Jaime, a lot." And I think, Jaime you've made more sense than Dr. Golomb. Simple and clear. And I gently slap Jaime on the back. "Let me get out of your way. You have work. Take care, okay?"

"Sure, Mr. Jack. You know, I'd hate to see you go!"

"Thanks. No decision yet. This is between us, all right."

"Sure, Mr. Jack," and Jaime places two fingers against his puffy lips.

We part, and as I walk down the stairs to the front door of the building I know that I'm not looking forward to coming back to this sanctuary as I once did, not the way Jaime does, still doing a good job and finding satisfaction in the regular tasks of emptying trash baskets, mopping the floors, wiping dust. Honorable work. He does a better job than I, I hiss to myself. So a chance conversation with the custodian has sealed the issue? At least that's what I want to think right now. But in my depths, though I would not now admit it, Dr. Golomb's words have also come home, even though meeting Jaime is a wonderful confluence of events, and—who knows?—Jaime's questions may in some way have determined my fate, one way or another.

I push against the heavy wooden door. The building is so old it is exempted from handicap regulations, so nothing is automatic. Anyway I do not like automatic doors. Not even the ones where you push the metal square with the handicap logo on it and wait. Like cruise control it deprives you of making a choice. What if you change your mind? The doors would automatically shut again, by themselves. I feel the muscles strain in my shoulders and arm, and as I push down, my hand wrapped over the steel handle, and I feel in charge, I am making a decision. Perhaps to exit here is better than to enter? The April wind hits my cheeks. So be it.

Had anyone run into me just now, they would have seen a man taking rather jaunty strides with a slight smile on his face. To be honest, I compare myself to Sisyphus until I remember that the rock he pushes keeps falling down before he can reach the top.

16

That evening I walked into Julianna's study. She was reading. The doctor had helped. A little, maybe. I repeated a few of the details, so she wouldn't be hurt, feeling excluded again. Julianna nodded and said, "Good. I'm glad you went. I won't press right now. Maybe later. Whatever more you want to tell me." She hugged me tight. But words and hug are both tentative, a little forced. Julianna was not sure of what was happening, easy enough to tell. But if I did not win her blessing, I would founder again, suffer an inner war wholly destructive to my sense of who I was and would be. I told Julianna about Stephanie Auslander, and how I had revisited my past, my "other" life. Did she remember, I had spoken of this talented but unhappy girl? Yes, she thought she recalled it. The name was unusual. Auslander. Yes, she remembered. Lamenting, I mentioned how recent grade books were mostly names whose personae I had forgotten—or never known. She listened, holding my hands. And I was convinced that her hands grasping mine firmly was confirmation of her assent. What else was there for me? Or for her? But assent to what?

"Julianna, I went to see this doctor to unburden myself about—about getting out." Her face formulated a question. "Yes, retirement. I think I'm coming to some sort of decision."

Now she paled. A long silence. "Can we talk about this downstairs? More room to breathe. It's not a matter of timing so much, but—yes, you've taken me by surprise."

"Julianna, we've talked about this before. Several times. I had no intention of an ambush!"

"Let's not get dramatic. Oh, sure. Yes, we've talked about some distant future, but not the way you're about to. I can tell. You've made up your mind, haven't you? You're not thinking of 'future' anymore, are you, Jack? I so hate being side-blinded."

"And you said not to get dramatic. No, I'm not certain. Well sometimes I think I'm sure. Some days. Then I waver."

"Downstairs?" It was more of a directive as she walked ahead of me down the stairs to the couch. Julianna had stiffened. She was always empathetic in her relationships, never one to play the prima donna. But anyone who tested her—and I was certainly doing that—she made it very clear that she would not be a *secunda donna*.

"I need a glass of wine. You?"

"Please."

When she returned, she sat on the other end of the couch, and the space between us now was real. For a painful instant, it felt as if my heart was out of body. She placed two glasses and an open bottle on the coffee table and poured for herself.

"So. When, how—what's this about?" Julianna sipped her Chardonnay.

"Now do be honest, Julianna, we *have* talked." I knew that she could not have missed that much, she had after all seen me go through the year, one crisis after another. No, she knew, and knowing was reality now, why shock? "It's just that I feel tired, and it's never one thing. It's not Leon or Seth or my father. It's not driving in a blizzard. It's not Milicent L. Jacobs. It's everything. You still enjoy it all, true?" I didn't wait for an answer. "Well, I don't. I'm tired of writing, too, and have no stomach for chairing. Edith said the department wants me again after she steps down. I don't really enjoy teaching any more, either. Not the way I should. I like the kids, I just don't want to teach them any more. Does that make any sense? It's too hard. We're getting out of sync! And that's not fair to them. And, yes, my body has taken a beating, and my pride—a little. The other day a former student came in with her high school son, who may be coming to us next fall. She had streaks of gray hair! You know how the OED defines 'emeritus'? As something you get after service, a discharge. Well, I'm ready for a discharge. And, yes, okay, I'm probably obsessing about Milicent L. Jacobs and all that stuff a little. Isn't that normal?"

I had said it all in a single breath, there was no punctuation in my speech. Julianna had been silent, looking at me between sips, without expression. My glass remained empty.

"It's true we have talked, just—well, anecdotally." Words came quietly and slowly. "But the way you've come at me with this, it's a decision. It's not a discussion any more, is it?"

I tried hard to escape this net of wounded words.

"Well, if we put it to a vote, I think it might be a tie."

But Julianna was not amused. She poured herself a second glass of wine. "I think you might have gone about it so that I'd be in on what we call 'the process.' Don't you?" Now her tone carried sarcasm.

"But you were. You are. I'm not coming in with a signed contract. But I've come to tell the truth, to bare my soul, if you wish. Or heart. What did Poe say, 'My heart laid bare'?"

She sat for a long time in silence. Finally she said simply, "What poetic language! Frankly, I don't give a damn what Poe said. I can't retire yet. Not ready!"

I was hurting. The dean, too, had mocked me about 'poetic language.' "But I know that! Your energy, your lust for your work, your relentlessness—that's what I love about you! I'd never expect you to drop that. And why ever should you need to?"

"I won't." Her eyes were brimming with tears now. "And cut the rhetoric!"

"Look, it'll be a sort of professional divorce. We won't be doing the same thing any more, not during the day, that's all."

"So I'll have visitation rights, evenings and weekends?"

At this I burst out laughing and perhaps I saw a trace of a smile, the way her lips were parted?

"Yes. And I can meet you for lunch?"

She got up and paced around the room. "You know, Jack, it's like a blow to the gut," and she fisted her stomach. "All right, I do understand, I try to. But—" She had taken her glasses off and held them in her hand. Without them I was clearly able to detect her reddening eyes. In her hurt she looked so vulnerable, tears came to my own eyes.

"You suddenly feel you're married to an aging man, that's it isn't it?" I was almost shouting. "I wonder whether that's what my students think. Probably. You were right when I had that tiff with Seth. I have lost touch with the young!" I threw the words at her, laced with unusual bitterness and the self-pity I so loathed.

And Julianna recognized it immediately. "Now you're just feeling sorry for yourself. I better get back to preparing," she said, in a voice I knew after all these years. It was pain, it was anger. She picked up her glass and left, and I was left abandoned on the end of the couch, staring at an empty wine glass.

Even the best relationships are sometimes interrupted by painful quarrels. I knew this would last a couple of days, during which we would speak to each other in neutral tones, and only about essentials: pass the water, please? When are you coming home? I have to bring the car in. So I'll call you if it gets late.

Usually I had three reactions:

First there was self-righteousness, self-justification, self-pity, feeling very sorry for myself, as Julianna had already said. After all, she could be more sensitive to *my* needs? And what about the time I gave up my grant so she could start *her* career earlier? There was no need for her severity! In any case I *had* talked about retirement. Several times. She conveniently forgets. What? Thought I was talking about ten years from now? Thinks she's going to have to wheelchair me and lose her great opportunities? Well, what if it came to that? What if I were struck down with a real illness, needed her help? I mean, I've always tried to be a good mate. What's so terrible about being married to a retired person? She's been a member of AARP herself for years!

Second there was guilt and remorse. I'm a stupid bastard! Why am I acting so silly? Retirement for her is a faraway mirage. And all of a sudden to be stuck with someone hanging around and not be able to talk shop? To see a kind of aging while she still has all that youth and energy! It was a terrible predicament, and I had handled it clumsily. Obviously I should have saved my speech till the end of the semester. Doused cold water all over her. God, what a lousy thing to do!

Third, the adults awake. Usually, in Julianna first. A signal. Better take the cue. We would get through this, as we had so many other trials.

But first there was another storm, quite accidental, literally. A domestic affair bloated with meaning. It was Saturday, Julianna was washing up the lunch dishes as I was trying to get at the garbage bin under the sink when I bumped her. She dropped a plate, and falling to the hard tile floor it broke into many pieces. Before I had a chance to say anything, Julianna turned on me: "God, Jack, look where you're going! Lately, I don't know, you seem to be in some kind of sleep walk!" I was already on my knees picking up shards of broken plate with my fingers and dropping them into a paper bag. "Ouch!!" I had cut myself on the forefinger, blood was dripping at a good rate on the fragments of white cheap china pieces. Julianna immediately came to help. "Jack, stop, I need to sweep this up. What made you try to pick up by hand!" She led me to the downstairs bathroom, washed my wound by letting water gush over it as the sink turned red. Then she pressed hard with a piece of gauze and placed a bandage on the finger, tight.

"Does it hurt? I hope I got any small pieces out."

I merely said, "No, you're right, lately I don't know where I'm going." She said she was sorry.

In the afternoon I brought back three bunches of daffodils, and when I handed them to Julianna, she again said she was sorry, and I knew this time she really meant it. "Hard to find anything else this time of year," I said, as she was placing them into a vase. "It's been so cold."

"I know," she replied, in a soft voice. "How's the finger?" "It lives." Sitting beside her, I curled my arm around her and squeezed her body next to mine.

"Forgive me," I pleaded, really I hadn't meant to surprise her, but the pressure was too much. It sort of slipped out, and I pulled her cheek close to mine. It had been tough lately. Sorry, but I was feeling older than I should—older than I am! A stranger to myself. No, right now I didn't know where I was going. I might still reconsider, but as I felt now—we must both accept that. She understood. Did she truly? I hardly understood myself. It was not sudden, this feeling of almost total collapse—total, I insisted, and I involuntarily exhaled a deep sigh. I was so weary. She brushed my lips with a kiss.

"Oh, Jack," she said, "I knew it was bad, but not *that* bad." "That bad," I said. "But if it's to be retirement, it's not death. I'd keep busy. And refreshment will come, I will come back to life." To myself I thought, perhaps my soul *would* clap again? "Of course, of course," she said reassuringly. Then she asked almost in a whisper, "When, Jack? Been to the dean yet?" Her voice was resigned.

"You *know* I wouldn't do that before talking to you. Never! I'm thinking after next year. And next year I have that sabbatical coming up. Maybe I'll take that in the spring. Teach the fall semester." It sounded good to her. Can't leave the department in a lurch, can I? No, no. Of course not. Though she is clearly empathetic something about the words is still crisp. They stab like little icicles.

"I'll make an appointment to see Sir Walter, okay?"

"It's your decision now," she said. Did I think a sabbatical would—might change things? She was looking for a life raft. I'd thought about that. But I didn't think so. At least at the moment. Couldn't ever know for sure, but I'd played it out in my head over and over. And, no. I doubted it would change anything. Honestly, though, I may change my mind. Let me see the dean first.

She merely pursed her lips. "Sounds good." No conviction.

I lay with eyes open in the dark for a long, long time. When at last I fell off, still on my back, I dreamt wildly. It would have been impossible to say how often I had dreamt about Milicent L. Jacobs after that first dream when she appeared with Stanley Habers and her boyfriend, and they assaulted me with drop slips and threatened me with that giant silver revolver. Some mornings I was certain I had dreamt about her, but try as I might, I couldn't recall a shred, nothing, just a feeling I had seen her. But then often I had gone to sleep and, with eyes closed, seen her clearly in one venue or another: the classroom, the office, the pathway where I walked past her, the Board Room. But now I recalled, in great detail, my dream, nearly a nightmare. Like all dreams, with its rapid kaleidoscopic pace, it was confused and illogical.

At first Milicent L. Jacobs sits in the grass plucking petals off a daisy—he loves me, he loves me not. A child. She does not speak. When she looks up at me she has grown older, much older. Gray streaks pattern her hair, and wrinkles visibly fold over her brow. Then she cries and I bend down to comfort her, but she evades me with a scream. I think it is Julianna grown very old. Another transformation. Milicent is a child again, about eight or nine. She is dressed in a pink flowery dress, though it might have been another color. Her hair is curly, she looks like Shirley Temple. Head lifted toward the sky she sings the nursery rhyme,

> High diddle diddle,
>
> The cat and the fiddle,
>
> The cow jumped over the moon.

Then she laughs uncontrollably, gets up and runs off singing over and over, "High diddle diddle ..."

I bend over my wife in the dark. Hearing her quiet breathing, I am desperate to embrace her, but I can't. Too soon. Though it is not altogether a myth that lovemaking resolves quarrels, that night Julianna and I are not in passionate embrace, yet I yearn to be close; we have made up like that many times. But Julianna has remained too distant. Not angry. Not resentful. No more reproaches. Worse—non-judgmental silence. And as if some shadowy image in the distance has moved close and its shape now emerges, brilliantly clear, as I still emerge uneasily from my dream, I understand. Julianna is terrified. (As was Seth.) There can be no intimate sharing until the fright leaves. In time we will have our genuine forgiving embrace, but now, astride the fright, my senses absorb a withholding that troubles my already damaged spirit.

17

Next morning, I call the dean's office for an appointment, and (as Dr. Golomb had predicted) I am at peace. The secretary asks, "Can I tell him what this is about?" I hesitate and then reply, "Computers." The word leaps out. To which the voice on the other end says,

"Did you say *computers?*"

"Well, I did. Hard to explain on the phone."

"Okey-dokey, tomorrow at 9:00?"

"Sure, fine." Computers! I laugh. After I hang up.

A cold and gray morning, and the snow storm has left its mark on campus, though the roads, of course, are clean. Sunshine has accomplished most of the melting a day earlier, and the snow plows had neatly flung piles to the sides of the walkway as I make my way to the administration complex. Actually what little snow is left still looks remarkably white, and I eye it approvingly. As I get closer, I register a twitch of anxiety, but I attribute that to my last visit in this direction, Milicent L. Jacobs. One of the younger secretaries asks me to take a seat. At 9:15, the dean emerges and waves a friendly "Hi, Jack. Com'on in."

When we are both seated, Walter Scott Livingston says, "I hear you want to talk computers? I could show you a few things, I've got all the latest technology, voice recognition, really! Practiced with the kids last night. Brought them here."

"Have you ever read Arthur Miller's *Death of a Salesman?*" I ask.

"Death of what?"

"Salesman."

"Nope. Should I?"

"Oh, never mind."

"Well, Morris, Jack, professor of English, you didn't come to talk about computers, did you? Or dead salesmen? What's up, Jack?"

"Walter, I came to talk possible retirement."

"Retirement?" His voice conveys pretend surprise.

"Yes. Maybe at the end of next year."

"Goodness you're a young fellow for these days, Jack. I mean what, off-hand—sixty-two? sixty-three?"

"Oh, you know damned well I'm sixty-five."

Mock amazement. "No! Still, young for today, no?"

"Retirement isn't always motivated by how old one is."

The dean makes a face of gravitas, nodding. "Well, no. You're right. So. Where do we start?"

"We've had a death of a senior member with not even a part-time replacement. If I retire, that's two senior people gone. Department can't survive that. It needs new blood."

"You mean to say you're falling on your sword for your department? Put them on empty, but then get something out of *me*?"

"No, nothing to do with swords. Anyway, I don't consider retirement as a death. No, I don't want to leave them on 'empty,' as you put it. There are obligations."

"And so you want to dump those obligations on *me*? I mean what the hell, it's *you* who wants to retire!"

"Well you never know who might be dean next year. And I thought some sort of assurance—I mean at least we know each other—"

The dean actually stands up, his large frame emerging like some colossal being in a sci-fi movie, because in rising he seems to be growing.

"Oh, well. The next dean. Well, there's lots of talk. Lots of lists. Lots of names. Your wife's a good prospect. Maybe she's on a list? Make a damned good dean, as I've told you before, but—"

He was toying with me. "Just in case, then—"

"If she became dean, then she would think it a conflict of interest to give your fellows an appointment?" The dean clears his throat.

"Well, I hadn't come in even thinking of that, but perhaps. It just seems prudent before I make the decision final, well, I'd feel better if there were a letter of commitment allowing us to search for a tenured appointment when I go. Maybe just an associate?"

Walter Scott Livingston laughs hard and loud. His whole face expands, especially his eyes, which he opens in an exaggerated show of surprise. I think he will explode, like some huge balloon, so vigorous is the shaking of his massive frame. His face is totally red.

"'*Prudent*'? You'd '*feel better*'? Why you've come to blackmail the dean! Morris! Really, what the hell are you thinking? What will you do when I say no way, José? Eh? What will you do? So you stay, so what? Stay. Go. Either way, it's no skin off my nose! So what?"

"Well, nothing 'so what.' Anyway—'blackmail' is an ugly way of putting it. *You* mentioned Julianna, I didn't. I just thought I'd be better off dealing with someone I know."

"Now, now. You sure were thinking of Julianna, no? No *quid pro quo*? Don't look so shocked. After my parents left New York for these parts, I went to Boston Latin for a couple of years!"

"Did you? Good school. But no, no *quid pro quo*. But you and I know how much money matters around here. A young replacement, even with tenure, is cheaper than Jack Morris for another five or ten years. Right? Let's be honest, you wouldn't exactly weep if I retired. You've been telling me about my declining enrollments for years."

The dean is sitting again. He stares at me. Clearly the mere mention of salary makes him think. I have hit on something.

"You know, Morris, you're a sonofabitch! Of course, you're damned right about new blood—the department needs some. But it's illegal for me to say anything about anyone's retirement—"

"You haven't said a word. *I* raised the issue."

"So you did. So you did. A letter of commitment from me? You've been around here long enough to know that's a joke. Things change. New dean comes in—whether your wife or someone else—and you know, when the numbers don't add up, they'll blame me, of course, and they'll rescind or put on hold all or some commitments. And if they're going to be triaging, believe me, your department will be the first to be last. So what's the use?"

"I'm aware of that. But a commitment is better than nothing. Look, there'll still be a year's grace for the search, if I do retire. So the position—assuming we'd find someone—won't be filled until the year *after* I've retired. Almost two and half years from now. That's not unreasonable?"

"You know why you really want this piece of paper? To bail you out with your department, that's the *real* reason, isn't it? It's not that silly thing about 'we know each other,' is it? Own up! No, not even bail you out with your department; it's bail you out with yourself! You want to feel moral and ethical and all that crap, so your colleagues won't accuse you of blowing a hole in the ship? Right? I know you, Morris. Full of guilt and hand wringing. Yes? Am I right? We'll let you keep the office for a year. With your junky computer?"

"No. Actually I want one with e-mail potential."

The dean stares and I laugh, but the dean isn't laughing, just a hint of a smirk. "Bang!" and he slams his short stubby hand against the wall, "Like it or lump it, Morris, you're getting one! *Everyone's* going to be up to speed, even you—or the fellow sitting there when you're gone. Coming right at the end of semester. So, so, so. Death of a professor, eh?"

I wince. I am silent. Whatever else, Walter Scott Livingston is very clever, crude but cunning. And he's right, of course. My conscience is a reason (if not the only one) for urging him to make the commitment, and I have been stupid to fall even for a second about Julianna's candidacy for dean, I have half believed in it. Yes, my adversary is right. My selfish righteousness (a variation of self-righteousness) is driving me to this suggestion of a "bargain," and the only reality is they would welcome my retirement to get someone cheaper and younger, that I know. Still, maybe I'm being too harsh on myself. Honestly, as I nudge my better self, I genuinely want to help the department and shrink from the thought of making it weaker, if I retire. But still I sigh.

So I try the confessional. "You're right, that's the real reason. No, I'm not anxious to be seen as destructive. It intrudes on my vanity. Yes, I want to bring them my retirement in one hand and something in return in the other. Is that so strange?"

"Not a bit, not a bit! But why all that crap about getting it from someone you know and then the possibility of your wife being in conflict if she were dean? Yeah, I brought it up, you finished it. You've wasted my time. Okay. You retire and I'll write a *'letter of commitment'*—sounds like sending someone to the loony bin! Well, Morris, it's no skin off my nose. But I'll be gone! I'll give you your damned letter *when* you make up your mind. I'll let you have until July 1 to decide, end of the year for *us* here. If I know your department, it might be years before you people can agree on someone anyway. But don't think this is a game. It's an insult to think you can blackmail me with that dumb approach you came in with. An insult!"

And now he actually seems angry, but I know even this, too, is part show. Sir Walter could care less. He just relishes demonstrating his smarts and his power.

"Fair enough. It's doesn't matter how we do it. The result is the same," I say, a little shaken. "You should also know me well enough," I add almost as an afterthought, "that, yes, I do care about the department, despite your psychoanalysis of my motives and my contrite admission."

With curled lips and arched eyebrows, the dean manages another sneer. "Oh, sure Morris. Altruistic to the bitter end." Into the phone he barks to his administrative assistant, "Get me retirement forms for Jack Morris, English. *All* of them." Then he leans against the back of his chair and looks at the ceiling. The forms arrive in an instant.

"All right, Morris. Here they are. Read them. If you have any questions get in touch with the university counsel. When you've signed, just return. But remember: no later than July 1." He glances at his watch. "Bye. It's been fun chatting computers with you! But I have decanal matters to attend to. Got to use big words with you, Morris. Need your blessing. Ha, ha! Oh, and by the way, don't let your wife get her hopes up." And he grins, baring his large teeth. He offers me the forms and raises his other hand in departing salute.

Once outside, I felt relief and self-consciously foolish. But it has the same results, no matter how badly the rest had gone. So I rationalize. It was certainly dumb not to have leveled more with Sir Walter, but then we both knew the real motives were more complex than guilt. Were they such bad motives? What's wrong with a conscience? Walter Livingston Scott wouldn't know a conscience if he tripped over one. Oh, he could recognize it in others, precisely because he lacked one. And death of a professor? That one hit home. Did I damage Julianna's chances? No, no, I reasoned, Julianna was no doubt right. Youth would win out there as well and, after all, nothing I had said could identify any complicity by Julianna. Unless the man suspected she had put me up to it? But then *he* had raised it all. Feeling uncomfortable, wanting to drive away these thoughts, I was saved by Edith Sellers trudging up the hill in boots.

"Hi, Jack. Just on my way to the Big Man. He wants to look at our projected courses for next year," and she held a folder up. "Can he really tell us what to teach and what not?"

"Well, yes he can. Really. Of course, whether he *should* is another question. Edith—I want to see you, soon."

"Anything wrong?"

"No, no. Nothing wrong, but we need to talk some business. There's time."

"Fine," she said cheerfully, "whenever you're ready. Toodle-do!" And she walked off in her rather strange gait, her feet, in oversized boots (no longer necessary) stepping outwards, as if she were learning how to ski. She looked droll, a little comical.

I needed to get off campus, so I walked straight to the parking lot, went into my car, put on a Sinatra disc and drove away to *"Put your dreams away for another day/And I will take away their place in your heart./Wishing on a star/Never got you far,/So it's time to make a new start."* The retirement documents are in a manila envelope next to me on my car seat. When I got home I tucked them into my desk drawer in my study. Eventually I will Xerox them, so that I would have a set in the office.

A few days later I sat down with Edith Sellers to tell her of my decision. Though our conversation was brief, she did not respond well to my possible retirement. When I first saw her sitting behind her desk, she appeared to have been crying. Her cheeks seemed puffy, her eyes red and swollen, her nose red. She looked awful. Then she began sneezing and wiping her nose with endless tissues yanked from the box next to her, and I realized she must have a cold.

"Sorry about the cold," I said empathetically. "Those spring colds can be nasty."

"I wish it were a cold! Those have a predictable lifeline. Allergies, Jack." Her voice was nasal. "Get them every spring. This grass, that flower. But it starts before even a blade is out. I mean there's still snow around. They told me when I was a kid that I'd outgrow them, but each year seems worse. Ahh," and she blew her nose again.

Then I told her. First she scowled at me. "What? I mean, Jack, you're needed here. You *can't* do this! No one has ever retired in the department, have they? My God, you'd be the first one! Of this group, anyway. *You?*"

I had never thought about being first. Truly, I would be the first, at least that I knew about. But I was taken aback by her belligerence. She was telling me what I could or couldn't do with my life? And hanging me with a reminder of my conscience? What the hell!

"Edith, it's my life, no? I have thought of the department, by the bye."

"Well, I didn't mean to imply, Jack—I mean—"

"You did imply, Edith," and I heard my voice rising. "I've a right to a personal decision. For God's sake! And I feel it right to give you a heads up. I am seriously thinking—but have not decided. Dean gave me until July 1."

"Of course, Jack. It's just—Leon's death—"

"Now don't you rake that tragedy up. You act as if I were fifty! I'm sixty-five!"

Edith must have realized that she had overstepped.

"I'm sorry, Jack. It's my allergy," and she sneezed and ripped some more tissues from the box. "Of course we would miss you. We've never quarreled. Not now, please. As I said, I'm sorry. No, it's just a bit of a shock. We'd miss you," she repeated and sneezed some more.

Edith had meant what she said, she was a good heart, but within a year or so, if I retired, she and the others, in some essential present tense of their being, will have forgotten me. Again I heard Golomb's words. Even when they saw my presence, they would smile, say hello, ask after Julianna and the children, say, "How does retirement feel?" and then they would rush to their offices, shut their doors, and attend to business.

"You would all do fine. Counting my graduate days, I've been in front of students for almost forty years. Right now I believe it's time I spared them."

"Oh, Jack, don't be so self-effacing!"

"I'm not," I protested, "just telling it as it is. Today a voice says, 'It's time.'"

"Oh, you make it sound so portentous, Jack." She exploded in a multiple sneeze attack, and she must have used up half a box of tissues, grabbing at them so rapidly it looked like a speeded up video.

"You're right. Here's the truth: I feel right now that I've had it, that's all. How's that for simplicity."

"Now you're mocking me." She sounded rebuked.

"No," I protested. "Again, just telling it like it is. Or should I be more 'portentous'?"

"You're an old scoundrel, Jack." Edith was almost blushing.

"Right about 'old,' Madame Chair."

Edith Sellers looked embarrassed. "Oh, Jack, I'm putting my foot in my mouth."

"Edith. Let's leave it there? It'll be fine, I promise." And we dropped that part of the conversation, but not before Edith, trying to make up, hugged me with the sincerest press of her body, in the midst of another multiple sneeze seizure.

I decided to say nothing about the letter of "commitment": it was premature.

"It's best not to make any announcement just yet about my possible intentions. Time enough once I've signed on the dotted line?" She assured me she would keep it all under wraps. Then she threw me a bombshell. It was Edith's turn to surprise me. "I've sort of been harboring a secret, too. I have a Fulbright for next year—England!—and I asked Walter whether I could leave after two years as Chair, and he agreed. I tried to postpone it, but the Fulbright people weren't crazy about that. So we need a new Chair. After you said absolutely no—and now I know why—I confided in Stanley, and you know what? He *wants* it! What shall we do?"

A little twinge of hurt that she didn't tell me earlier. Already?

"Great! He'll be fine. And congratulations. On your Fulbright. That's wonderful! Where to in England?"

"Thanks. Exeter. Nice countryside, I hear. As for Stan—Jack, we all like him, but he *can* be a loose cannon! He's capable of alienating them all—the department, the administration—!"

"You'll love England, provided the weather holds. As for Stan, no, Stan is a big boy now. And you underestimate his ability to sober up his tongue, even if that may be a mixed metaphor. I've been on university committees with him. When necessary, he can charm the pants off anybody. He's a very shrewd fellow. He'll do fine. Besides, it's time he did something for the department besides be its shining light of authorship. It'll do him a world of good."

Swollen red face and all, Edith looked thoughtful. "Really? Maybe you're right. I'll think on it, as they say. But only the three of us and the dean know. Of course we have to vote, and so far I see no other viable candidates. Do you?"

"No." We spoke some more about the future, and I made a few suggestions. We were at peace again, and when we parted she hugged me affectionately again, this time with no allergic interruptions.

As I bumped into her walking to my car—rather as she bumped into me, striding briskly and talking fast to a male companion I did not recognize—my glasses fell off on impact. But she got the worst of it. Through a haze I saw her sprawled on her back, high heels swinging up for a moment, searching hopelessly for safe harbor. She looked like a huge insect on its back.

"Professor Morris! Last time our positions were reversed. As I recall *you* were on the floor, and *I* hovered over you?" Her lips parted into a smile.

I had retrieved my glasses, undamaged, and put them where they belonged. "Dean Bentley? I *am* sorry. Yes, I recall that!"

"Don't you be sorry." She had risen with the help of her male companion and was brushing her dark gray pin-striped suit. "My fault. I wasn't looking." She introduced her companion. An interview, she said. He looked shamelessly young and embarrassed.

"By the way, that student? I hear she went home for treatment. We were in touch with her parents. I don't know details, of course. Not my bailiwick."

"Of course. Well, good. Glad to hear it. So you're all right? Sure?"

"Sure. Bye." And she was off, limping a little as her heels clanged unevenly on the asphalt. I was uncomfortably reminded of Milicent L. Jacobs. For some time now I had made a real effort to forget her. Would I ever? *Could* I ever?

Seth alone said he would come for the Passover holidays, if we wanted him to come.

"If *you* want," I had said. "It's your call. Of course, *we* want."

So Seth did in fact come, not enthusiastically. "This is the second holiday that I'm the only one," he said on arriving, and Julianna and I, on cue, shrugged and acknowledged, "That's entirely true. You're also the closest. Anyway, let's make a go of it!"

We celebrated a Seder for three, and I must admit it did seem lonely. We had not yet completed the journey to what articles referred to as the "comfort zone" with Seth. Yes, we had been on the lookout for articles on "If Your Child Is Gay" and the like, and there was no shortage of them, in magazines and on the Net. On the one hand, we feared that almost any questions outside his work might be construed as interference, just as silence could easily be taken as indifference or worse, disapproval. So we skirted the edges. How is life treating you these days? What interesting plays have you seen? Met any people worth your while? And Seth was laconic. Life's fine. He didn't like the theater that much. He had met a few people worth hanging out with. Yes, Manny was fine. In turn, he did not ask us many questions, so we volunteered.

Did you know that Natasha has taken Rachel and Benjamin to her parents' house in Grosse Point? David's back in Oberlin. Well, she was lonely. Mom's finished her proofs on her big new book. Wonderful stuff.

The time passed slowly, and gradually the strain was obvious to all three of us. By Saturday Seth had lightened up, and he told a few funny New York stories. That evening he took the train back. "Sorry, but I need to get going. Friends on Sunday." Of course, we said, but spent a lonely Sunday, saying little, reading the papers and taking a long walk. Passover celebrated exodus from enslavement. It blew through us more like winds of exile in the suburban desert.

18

Now it was May, only a week remained before finals, and the academic year would soon end. It was always the same: the end of another year. And, like a curtain, everything will close, and the stage will be bare. Commencement, which I was thinking of skipping this year, was a fortnight away. Always it was a frantic time: urging seniors to complete their theses, prizes and awards to recommend, and, of course, reading papers of graduating seniors in time for the Registrar's deadline.

One morning I was about to set forth for my ten o'clock when I noticed a tremor in my hands as I gathered my books and folders. My first thought: Damn! I'm coming down with something. Apprehensively, I placed my palm to my forehead. Not hot but moist with sweat. Leaning against the office door, I took a deep breath. Then another. A third. But again I must have taken them too deeply, because I noticed I was getting light-headed and had to catch the swivel chair armrests to keep from falling. Bending my head down, allowing the blood to flow back, the dizziness subsided. Stomach muscles tightened and a swell of nausea came and went. My tongue felt sewn to the top of my mouth in a way I had never experienced. I was hurled into spatial isolation—desk, bookcases, chairs—all seemed in some distant place from which I felt separated. Actually I couldn't feel my hands on the chair either: they seemed disconnected from the rest of me. It was time to go to class, and I was already a little late. Slowly I opened the office door and stepped into the hallway. The classroom was only a few yards away. My legs were unsteady, and now I was feeling an unpleasant wetness under my arms. Unbuttoning my shirt collar, I loosened my tie a little, and made it into the classroom, to the desk, but the students seemed not to notice and kept up their chatter. For an instant I had the urge to scream out at them: Notice me! But I realized that their notice was the last thing I wanted. Surely I would not make it through the hour, I was certain of that. So I prepared the class: "I think I'm coming down with something, so if we stop early you'll understand." Now they quieted down.

On some faces I convinced myself I saw a little sneer: "Come down with something, Prof, we don't mind." But a few faces showed concern. Or was it puzzled uncertainty? Most were indifferent. I tried hard not to pay attention to my body. As I began to speak the words sounded distant, out of body, and my heart now began to thump so loudly and rapidly I was certain the students could hear it. As if to stifle the sound I placed my hand over the left chest cavity, but that only made it worse since now I could feel this thumping in my hand. Get them to talk—but I knew that would only invite a response, and I felt unable. My mouth tasted acrid. If *I* talked I would be in some control. Waves of vertigo swept over me, and they were sudden, as if I were losing my balance, my head jerking forward. My hands were leaning on the desk, but I began to talk. Later I had little memory of what I'd said, but it was flat and whispery, and what I did remember was faces looking at each other and at me with puzzled stares. Longingly my eyes reached for the door. After almost fifteen hellish minutes, I could not continue. Slowly, still propped up with both hands on the desk, elbows stiff, I managed, "Sorry, folks, no more today. Should have stayed in bed, as they say. See you day after tomorrow." I left the classroom, shaken. Fled would have been a more apt description. Walking rapidly back to the office, my legs were still unsteady and my feet when they hit the floor did not feel that they did. Angel passed me taking a stack of papers somewhere.

"Jack? You look terrible! Are you all right?"

"Yeah. No. Coming down with something."

"Do you want me to call Julianna?"

"No, no, no. I'll be okay, really. Thanks." The familiar voice and the sight of a sympathetic face worked wonders. Feeling much better, I stopped by the water fountain and allowed the parabola of water to cool my throat. By the time I sat in my office, I was breathing almost normally. I felt tired, as if I had been through some terrifying event, but no longer shaky. For some time I stared at the closed door. This had never happened before; I knew damned well it was not the flu. Certainly I had gone through something awful, for which I could find no earthly reason. The sweat on my forehead and under my arms had dried, and now I felt a little cold. Walking out to the hall I drank some more from the water fountain. Pretty soon I was in the men's room, but I was so tight, nothing came out. I washed my hands anyway and was astonished to see how sunken my cheeks looked. Removing my glasses I cupped my hands and filled them with cold water that I swept over my face, not once but twice. It felt good.

I taped a note canceling office hours on my office door and made for the parking lot. Gripping the steering wheel, I was calm but drove slowly. Once home I found myself alone. Good. Julianna need not see me like this, she would only worry. And I recalled she had an invited speaker and dinner afterwards. So I would fend for myself. In time I would tell her. Now the only concern was: would this happen again?

In late afternoon I set out for a little hill not far from our house, protected conservation land, from which one could see some of the skyline of Boston. You could hardly compare it to the famous three hills of Boston (honored by the naming of Tremont street), but those in the neighborhood, who were in the know, lovingly called it "Hill 4." In the past, Julianna and I, sometimes the children, too, had driven up on summer nights to catch a sunset, or to marvel at eclipses—sun and moon—but I hadn't been here for years. Narrow and badly paved, the road curved modestly for about half a mile. In places it was not wide enough for two cars, but none came my way. There were no official parking spaces, and mine was the only car, so I just nudged it close to a woodsy side of the hill and walked over to a large, flat stony place, perfect for sitting. A number of bushes had broken out with green and red buds, and some trees sported light green shiny leaves. It was a mild afternoon as the sun was beginning to lower over the skyline.

The increasing space between myself and my students that I had been noticing for some time was now real, an emptiness between me and a whole world in which I had roamed so comfortably for decades. At times now even Julianna appeared to be on the "other side." Space. A matter of physics and philosophy. I had often held forth about "spatial" problems in my teaching of novels and poems, thinking I understood, but my experience of spatial distance now—well, it was a sensation impossible to translate into words. It was what I had felt this afternoon, something very frightening. Perhaps once I internalized it, it would become better. Space between me and my students, that was clear. Or was it? As I had told Dr. Golomb, they stayed the same age and I grew older, so the space between us widened with each year. Though I had been in the habit of saying the students were leaving me, it was I who was leaving them. But that was logic. The space was not just age, it was internal space. Literally the students seemed to be so far away sometimes, so much in the distance, that my mind could not reach them. On occasion, I was beginning not to see them. Their world was diminished, as if I were backtracking and they were disappearing. Like a bad dream.

Recently I had read something about how Chinese science, especially geology, was stopped dead in its tracks because artists painted without spatial perspective, creating those elongated mountainsides, one-dimensional, trees hanging down over rocks, the scroll flat, if beautiful, but no space, no perspective. A theory, but interesting. Perhaps that was a way for them to avoid those scary spaces that European philosophers began to lament after they knew the world wasn't flat and not the center of the universe? When we discovered perspectives everywhere, and painters made it a mission to paint distance, was that the beginning of western panic? Looking out beyond the barrier of trees at the tops of the few high rise buildings, I felt no sense of dread. Yes, distance also defined the space between past and present, for that distance now seemed far greater than it had when I had looked at it so cheerfully in years past. Was it all a sign of moving away? From? From life itself, a measure of the journey to its end? And with clear recognition I realized that this was it, this was what it was all about. No wonder I had panicked. Breathing a sigh of relief, I took one last look as a few lights glimmered on top of the scrapers. It was later than I had thought.

Then I had the best conversation with Leon since his death. Actually, it was a monologue, and I no longer pretended to hear his answers, I knew what they would be.

Leon, you have been at my side, even though, true enough, there were times when I did not think of you as often as I should have. No, don't protest! Dead friends deserve as much attention as living ones. You remember the times we all spent up here? Good times. Gone. But this hill has made things a lot clearer. I know for sure now what this space business is all about. You probably would have dissuaded me from getting out, maybe even persuaded me, who knows? And I am not sure yet what to do. Honestly. But I am in new territory now, where I no longer possess that nearness to the students. They don't hear me. It's words rising into the air and silently falling, like snow, unnoticed by the ear. I thought it was a kind of death, something you're more familiar with, of course, but you know I realize now it's just a different part of life, that's all. As I said I've moved on to new territory, uncharted so a little scary, but all shall be well. Where I was there was no longer room for me. Where I will be—? And the shrink was right, in a way. I need to do this for myself. Yes, I worry about Julianna more than anything, but if I step away she will need to adjust, and you know she will. Not widowed like your poor Natasha, just looking at me from across a barrier, perhaps, which we will both need to get closer to in time. At least we live to embrace. Yes, if I go through with it—in time all shall be well. If I stay I will adjust, embrace a new vision, like new glasses.

With that I walked to the car and snaked my way downhill.

Once home, I decided to call Dr. Hoffman. Office closed. I tried the voice mail and left a message. It was returned within the hour; he was just leaving. Hesitant, I described the episode before class. Had I been taking those mild tranquilizers prescribed last fall? No, I admitted, I had not even filled the prescription. Totally forgot. All right, he would call in a new script to the local pharmacy. And he wanted me to "drop in" soon to check out the "vitals." An hour later, I actually drove to Walgreens to get my small bottle: "Take Twice Daily as Needed." Sitting quietly in the car I read the printed side effects stapled to a little bag that housed the bottle: "Do not take if pregnant. May cause dizziness, dry mouth, irritability, sleeplessness, nausea, constipation, diarrhea, vomiting ..." Great, pills to cause what they're supposed to cure—and then some. Well, it said "as needed," and I'd see whether I would need them.

A day passed and the first class since the "event" was unavoidable. I dreaded it. The bottle of pills was in my briefcase; the class went badly. A few students came up and asked how I felt.

"Fine. Twenty-four hour thing. Thanks for asking."

When I dropped in to see Dr. Hoffman, he gave me some news. After taking my blood pressure twice, the doctor said matter-of-factly: "I'm afraid you have pretty high blood pressure. We need to control that at your age. Too high, even accounting for the white coat effect—you know, a little anxiety?" My first reaction, strangely enough, was amusement: now *I* would have a number I could spring on Stan Habers. "More pills?"

"Afraid so. But these you have to take." Not "as needed," I thought.

"Ignore the list of side effects. I'm giving you a mild one—shouldn't have any appreciable fallout. And you don't have to read the labels in the supermarket, but stay away from the salt shaker." Well, better salt than sugar.

"Back in two weeks. Under stress?" I shrugged. I could have recited it all: I've lost a dear friend to an early death. Then you put me through so many tests I lost count, stuck me, had me probed, photographed and scanned in all sorts of positions, had me lie in a magnetic coffin listening to jackhammer noises. I've been falsely accused of sexual assault, and my colleagues were so eager to defend my innocence, they made me feel like a eunuch. Marlon Brando and Tony Soprano honored me with obscene calls, and I was also given gifts of poison pen letters. I threw my back out, then had a high fever flu, despite the flu shot you gave me. My son cried out at my dead infant's grave that he was gay. My father died without being conscious enough for me to say good-bye, his poor bony body hanging on tubes and lines from pinging machines. My brother cried and embraced me, but he's off again. While I'm professionally waning, my wife is at full moon. I became disoriented in a blizzard. My classes are not going all that well. And I had that anxiety attack, but that one you know about. And it looks as if I might pack it all in. Instead, I said simply, "Yeah, some stress. Nothing that unusual."

Dr. Hoffman smiled. At what it was hard to say.

Edith had called a meeting to preside over the election of a new Chair. Stanley Habers was the only candidate. What sometimes had been a difficult occasion became a shoo-in. Some had lobbied that I take the chairmanship for the last year, but I had adamantly declined. Edith had kept her word and not said anything about our conversation. That left Habers, and he had been lobbying himself, talking to everybody, even to Robinson and Bentwick. When the vote came, it was unanimous. I was a little surprised. How had Habers managed to win over his two adversaries, I asked after the meeting. Habers said it had been a piece of cake, he had chatted with them, hinted that he was sorry he had sometimes seemed to be rude, but he would be a fair and even-handed Chair. "And I will, you know."

I nodded and knew it to be true, and I was glad Habers had talked to them, that was the right thing to do. Habers said he also promised to be more respectful, though he hadn't used that word. And he was serious. That little speech by Bentwick during the Gunderson tenure meeting—that had certainly impressed him. He still couldn't stand Robinson, but, hey, he'd deal with it. Anyway, they said they welcomed his coming to them, and that was that. "I gave them a mental enema. Always works." I was both startled and amused by the image of a "mental enema," but I wished Habers good luck and extended a high five. In my own mind, I knew the honeymoon probably would not last, that after a while, Habers would lose his patience, unleash his tongue. But that was no longer my business.

Then one day an announcement came to the mailboxes:

> You are cordially invited to attend the Farewell Party for Dean Walter Scott Livingston next Tuesday, 4-6 in Bradford Lounge. Refreshments.

I didn't want to go, but Julianna said she had to, first as Chair, second—I understood. Fine, of course, but I'll skip it, thank you.

Final days of the semester, and I was still trying, not very successfully, to teach. It had turned unseasonably warm. The air conditioning was still not on, awaiting, whatever the weather, its scheduled day of May 30th. Students had no such calendar. They now came to class in meager dress. The women wore tank-tops, the men T-shirts with cut-off sleeves, and almost everyone was in shorts. Already their minds were on summer, or on each other's exposed body parts, and few paid attention. Once again, they were restless.

End of May, and the campus was swarming with cleanup personnel. After all, Anderson's "marcescent" leaves were finally ready to be harvested by leaf vacuums, as new buds at last evicted these winter survivors. Lawns needed to be reseeded, branches sawn off, hangers downed from towering trees, new flowers planted. Machines whirred and made the campus noisy; the smell of gasoline was everywhere. Wherever you looked there were rakers, sawers, pruners, planters. At this time of year they almost equaled the faculty in number, and they mostly spoke Spanish and laughed while at work, engaged in good-natured sing-song banter. Well, it was spring cleaning time. Everyone understood that this coordinated and massive restoration was mainly to ready the campus for Commencement for the parents, the Board of Trustees, honorary degree recipients, Alumni.

Meanwhile there had been cleaning to take care of at home as well. The April snowstorm had caused tree limbs—some of them more the size of small tree trunks—to snap and cover the garden and back yard. Julianna phoned Gustav Anderson. It looked like a war zone, blasted trees around trenches, as they appeared in some of the old black and white World War I movies. As the last dirty snow in the shadows melted with the late April rain, more and more debris surfaced. The garden was littered, and Julianna shook her head. "What a mess!" she sighed, "I'll probably lose half my plants." Gustav Anderson arrived with his tinker's truck—for "an initial look-see"—rakes, shovels, scissors, mowers loaded neatly in all the available spaces, and in late April, the tree men finally came with their power saws (it took them two days of endless sawing). Then Anderson came and worked, and after a week or so the garden and yard were clean. Soon flowers sprouted everywhere, olive green and red leaf-buds urged their way from the branches, and Julianna again was at peace with her handiwork. At last, stretching its barely green tendrils, Spring asserted itself.

Preparing to leave on the last day of classes, standing in the driveway in late May, I smelled the soft still air and looked up at a clear blue sky. Quiet. I listened to a bird trilling. Of course, I couldn't see it, and if I had, other than a sparrow or a robin?—but I knew its song was sweet. By now the garden was almost in full bloom with spring plants. Julianna was such a happy gardener, and I sent myself a mental note to be sure to tell her this again.

My eyes caught Betsy, hind leg raised, yellow stream cascading onto Julianna's flowers. Then Betsy squatted, she was fertilizing. But where was Mrs. Dentist? Gazing at the dog's black, teary eyes, I understood—for all this time I had not hated poor Betsy but her dog walker. After all, I did not begrudge Betsy's good digestion. It was her mistress who was my *bete noir*. My heart softened, as Betsy's somewhat puzzled eyes beheld me. She raised her black, wet, quivering nose and emitted something between a growl and a bark and, I was sure, a lamentable fart. She was not certain whether I meant her harm. I was about to bend down to reassure Betsy, who had finished her business, when Mrs. Munken appeared.

"Nice day," she said.

"Yes, but you know, I'd appreciate less fertilizing on my lawn, driveway, and garden. My wife's a great gardener. No extra help needed."

Mrs. Munken simply stared at me and then, more shrill than ever, she screamed: "Betsy! Betsy!" and disappeared with such haste that, alas, she stepped into Betsy's lawn gift and nearly lost her footing. I smiled in indescribable triumph. Walking briskly to the car I slipped in a Sinatra disc and listened joyously all the way to campus.

After all this time, last days were still difficult. Separation anxiety? Hardly. What then? For one thing I always looked back and wondered—had the class been a bust? Had I succeeded, at least a little? On the last day of class almost everyone showed up, even those intermittent attenders who thought their final appearance would do them some good. I had learned not to make a "real" day of it; they were in no mood. And one piece of business saved for the last day was handing out the questionnaire for *How to Choose Your Professor.* Doomsday, Judgment Day, Day of Awe. My colleagues had jokingly invented different names. Some of my Jewish friends called it the semi-annual Yom Kippur. Who would be written and sealed into the book of life at the university for another year? Who would be condemned to oblivion? But I knew that all of us were apprehensive: what would the students say? That student who always seemed so friendly, so nice, so approving—that could be the one to kill you with a snide comment. Would all the hard work of the semester pay off, or would this be another middling judgment, appearing in September with the worst comments, usually what student editors thought were the wittiest barbs, published for all the world to read? Those who said they no longer took these booklets seriously were kidding themselves. Words and stones *did* break, if not bones, hearts. Stan Habers told me recently that someone had created a new web site, "Pick-a-Prof," so help him. Students could subscribe and get the whole story, including how many drops there had been in the course (did Milicent L. Jacobs subscribe?), grade distribution, and individual reviews. Lucky me! I was not a browser.

In the past some students would drop by and say good bye: "nice semester, great course, see you again?" Today no students came, but Carol Gunderson did. Her *ad hoc* committee had voted her tenure, and the dean had accepted its recommendation. All this was no surprise and had been unofficially communicated to her and to the department by Edith Sellers. The remaining business was for the Board to sign off, but that was a formality.

She looked radiant, her red hair flowing to her shoulders, her blue-green eyes, looking more aquamarine, aglow with delight, like a child who has just been given the toy of its dreams. She came in to thank me for my support, which she knew she wasn't supposed to know about, but let's face it, these things get around, the buzz you know, and she particularly wanted to thank *me*. I gazed at her sitting with legs crossed, in a flowery summer dress with a respectable V-line neck, looking younger than I knew she was.

She assured me that she was not making the rounds. It would be improper. Honestly, she beamed, mine was the support she had wanted and valued most. Oh? And why was that? Because she truly respected my work and me as a person. I was a role model! I held up my hand in protest. No, she said earnestly, she meant that. After all she wasn't one to bullshit, and she quickly put her hand over her mouth. What's the matter, I said, did she think I would be shocked? She laughed. Well she hadn't heard it much from me. She saw me in a certain way—. Like an old fart, who would be offended by "bullshit"? Now she was laughing with her whole body, and her breasts heaved, and I recalled my dream. "You're funny," she said. Well, she couldn't help it. Yes? Yes, she didn't see me as a fuddy-duddy for sure, but well, it's more like talking to her Dad. He had a great sense of humor, he was cool, but you just don't say certain things to him. And so—well—oh, she sputtered, better let it go. Well, I dropped it and myself as well, sinking into a stooped position, as if I had been pressed down from above, by force. So Carol Gunderson saw me as she did her father. How nice! Managing a smile, I thanked her for stopping by, again congratulated her. She embraced me—like a daughter—and planted a kiss on my cheek and left with a wave.

Just as I was about to leave myself, the phone rang. It was David Kominsky. Did I have a few moments to spare? Of course, come on over. He knocked on the door and shuffled in on his standard sandals. To me he looked even more slumped than the last time we had met, when I had come from Sir Walter's office with news of the Relling fiasco. His eyes, always sunken deep into their sockets, looked lifeless.

"How're you doing? Sit."

"Want an organ recital? Naw, I'm okay. You?"

"Fine, fine."

Then he told me how Julianna was passed over as dean. Bentley, of course. Hadn't been on the list, but when Julianna gained more and more support, the big guns drifted away. Experience, they argued. Chairing was rotation, not a long term post. So the white smoke came, but not for Julianna. Anyway, it's a disappointment, he was sure. But she had lots of support. And tell your dear wife how many were behind her. (Yes, I thought, just enough to push her down into the pit.) I promised to tell her and assured him that she's prepared for it. Really. She never expected. Anyway, she's a busy bee as he knew. She'll get herself involved. But, hey, thanks for doing this. It's very decent.

David Kominsky nodded, waved his hand, and said, "God it's good to be over with the year. I thought it would never end."

"I know the feeling," I sighed.

"Is it true you're thinking of retiring?" Kominsky frowned.

"Yes. It's true. How did you know?"

"As they say, Jack, 'It's been out there.' But why?"

"I have until June to decide. But there are times when I feel too much, too soon, I guess."

Kominsky looked puzzled. "I thought it was 'Too little, too late'?"

"Well, not in my case. I got too much too soon, too much from all of it here," and I swept my hands in circles like a helicopter blade, "and sooner than I'd have liked."

"Well, their loss, if you go, I must say. You sound a little bitter?"

"Not really. I didn't mean to, just tired."

"Take care, Jack."

"You too. And David, get yourself some sun. You look positively white!"

"Sun?" he spoke the word as if it were foreign, and he didn't know it. "You know what," he said cheerfully, "I'll do that."

We parted and I drove home in sadness, for I knew that, after all, Julianna would be disappointed. She was. A little. But not for long. She was on her knees in the garden doing what she loved most. Her sweaty and dirty face, her gloved hands, her mussed-up hair, sweat running down her forehead—she looked beautiful. I stopped in front of her and she raised her head.

"Trying to get some of these annuals in."

"What's the difference between annuals and perennials?"

"Oh, Jack, I've told you a hundred times. Never mind. They both grow. Besides you damn well know." And she grinned.

I could not keep it in. "You're right, I was just teasing." I asked her to give me her hand. She took off a glove and stretched it out while looking puzzled.

"What's up?"

"They've passed you over for dean, honey, the jerks. David Kominsky just told me. You had a lot of support."

She withdrew her other glove and wiped her brow.

"Oh, well, Jack, we guessed. Bentley?" I nodded.

"Stop looking so glum. It's no tragedy. I mean it. I shall just continue to cultivate my garden!"

I bent down (despite the twinge in my back), took Julianna's head between my hands, and kissed her on the lips. Smelling the mixture of soil and sweat stirred me. Julianna was a good trouper. She would never whine or stew about this. Never say anything regretful or envious. Did I realize how lucky I was? Sitting in my study I retrieved the retirement papers and just stared at them. Then I decided, for the first time, to really read them: on retirement you lose your tenure; all benefits are canceled; no more contributions by the university toward retirement. There was more, but for now I replaced the papers into the manila and returned it to the drawer.

That night Julianna and I were at last embracing with conviction, forgiveness and new love. Yes, I was still on that other side, but it was becoming more familiar now. Julianna was not quite there yet, but she would meet me halfway in time, I was sure, and we would meld again to be even closer. After all, I was just beginning to explore this new space, it will take time.

One evening, a few days after classes had ended, Miranda called. Could she come down this weekend? Alone? Of course. Julianna told me she was tempted to hold her off until after Commencement (to which, as department Chair, she was committed), but there seemed something urgent in the voice, so she said, "Fine." I agreed. "Look, I'm not that busy; it's good you didn't put her off. She's got something on her mind. I'll do the baby sitting," I said laughing, and Julianna heaved an enormous sigh. And so Miranda arrived on a shuttle midday Friday. I picked her up at Logan.

19

The academic year ended as it began, with the death of a colleague. On the Saturday of Commencement, the Concord Police, alerted by a canoeist, recovered a body from the Concord river near the Great Meadows. Not far from where they discovered it leaning into shore, they found an overturned canoe. It did not take long to identify the drowned man, for though he wore no life preserver, his wallet was in his pant pocket. The name was not immediately released, but I was later told it had reached the campus, unofficially, just about the time Commencement was winding down and Miranda and I were circling Walden Pond.

For I had happily foregone Commencement and took Miranda on a sentimental journey to Walden Pond. Usually we had done this as a family in the fall, when the leaves were at their best—red, orange, gold, yellow. But spring, I suggested, was not a bad time, and she was eager to go. Even though it was a fine Sunday, the parking lot was not yet full. We had come early. "Everyone's at Commencement," Miranda teased. "Don't you feel guilty?" Miranda had cropped her hair as she did every spring, but I preferred it longer. The shorter cut framed her pale face, made it more pronounced. Yes, she was definitely paler.

"Not a whit," I shot back. "By the way, it's mercifully cool, so Mom will have an easy time of it." A pleasant late spring breeze blew from the pond, the sun was lording it, only a few cirrus clouds disturbed the blue of the sky. Olive-green leaves were in their youth of late spring, no longer budding but stretched out. We began our walk slowly with Miranda's arm in mine, just as she had done when she was a little girl.

Miranda had not yet offered much about why she had come. Julianna said a little cryptically it had something to do with Robert, but I had guessed that already. She appeared happy enough, and right now she was talking at a rapid pace about her classes, which were not done yet, of course. Hearing Miranda talk so much was a relief after the laconic phone conversations these past few months. Better not press her. When ready she would say what there was to say. She did ask about her grandfather.

"Dad, was there any particular reason that made you decide not to have a family thing? I know cremation is different, but—well, I mean a family get-together?"

I reviewed this silently. All the children had called and asked why we were not gathering, and at the time I made excuses. After all, I knew they were all busy, cremation was not a ceremony, Grandfather had given strict instruction there was to be no memorial service, and there would be the event at Yale, and yes, then, everybody would naturally be there. But I knew that although all true, there had been other reasons.

"It might sound almost indifferent, or something, but you know Miranda, relationships with Grandfather were—well, not sort of Norman Rockwell?"

"I know that, Dad. It's not exactly a family secret. But you know me, I'm a ceremony freak. I mean I'm not second-guessing, but he *was* your father, our grandfather, and I just thought some—"

This distressed me. Father was threatening to spoil this outing, and I would not let him.

"Miranda, let it go. Uncle Paul could not come—or would not, who knows which? And I was doing my own thing. I said kaddish for a week and sat in my study, read and contemplated. It was my way. As for the rest of you—you know, it wouldn't have been meaningful, would it? That may be sad, but it's also the truth. We'll do it when they have that Yale thing."

Miranda nodded, took my hand and squeezed it. "Fine."

The talk turned to Seth. Was he coping? Were *we* coping? It was difficult, wasn't it? I could be honest with her. Well, I was being honest. Seth was Seth. Yes, Seth seemed to be coping very well, relieved now that all the family knew. Were we coping? Well, there was little choice, was there? Mom sometimes turned melancholy and I, too, had my regrets. Mom worried mostly about potential threats to health. She sometimes seemed to be waiting for a call, "Hi, Mom. I have some bad news. I tested HIV"—or worse. But you couldn't be stupid and tell him to be careful. He would never stand for that. Besides, I was sure he *was* being careful. "As for me," I said, "at times I'm also a bit low. Well, yes, I do still think of it as a loss, not my name and all that, that doesn't matter, but just that the so-called normal expectations won't bear fruit, and that's hard at times." Also, I confessed, we didn't yet know how to act. If we sounded too cheerful, Seth would smell hypocrisy; if we sounded down, he would be crushed. So it's a bit of a tightrope, but it will sort itself out. And, yes, sometimes we clung silently to the possibility that this might be a "phase," but we knew that was delusional. No, we had not thought of joining a support group.

We were about a third of the way around the pond and sat on one of the benches to rest and take in the water and the trees. Then we walked very close to the shore line, which was quiet, the pond twinkling in the sun. I wandered to the edge, rolled up my khakis and removed one shoe and sock. I turned to Miranda with a grin, "I grow old … I grow old …/I shall wear the bottoms of my trousers rolled."

"Oh, I know those lines." Miranda sounded delighted with herself. But then she said, in a slightly lecturing tone, "You know what they say, Dad, 'You're as old as you feel!'"

I looked at my daughter with a comically serious face. "Cold. Prufrock wouldn't have liked this," as I stuck a toe into the pond. Pausing, standing bare-foot and relaxed now, my trousers rolled, facing the water, I turned serious. "As for what 'they' say, you know who the 'they' are? Young doctors and—and phys-ical therapists," and I made a pathetic attempt to skip a stone across the water. It plopped straight down within a few feet of where I stood, creating more of a splash and more concentric circles than its weight warranted. Gazing across the pond, I calculated we had walked nearly halfway of the circle. "Truth is, you're as old as you *are*." Ask Medicare! I added silently.

"Well, seems to me Eliot was very young when he wrote those lines, yes?" Now she had a teasing lilt to her words.

"Yes. Right. You've proved my point. He had it all reversed, because he was born old and felt it, and not until late in life, when he remarried, did he grow young. Felt that too." I placed my arms akimbo. "Q.E.D."

Miranda playfully wagged her forefinger toward me. "Oh, no, Dad. That's a trick answer. He *felt* old when he *was* young. You've proved *my* point. Q.E.D.," and just as I had, she placed her arms on her hips and stuck out her solid chin in a gesture of triumph.

I ran my hand through my thinning hair, laughing. "Well, we're playing the way we used to, when you were in high school. Only then it wasn't always play-ing. Glad you're not in my classes! But seriously, I'm feeling older and getting older. And lately those two lines have been like merging parallels. But enough."

She placed her hand on my shoulder. "Dad, I'm sorry. It'll pass. Let's enjoy this day?"

"Absolutely." I patted her on the back, having moved away from the water. "And what a day! You know Thoreau surely had some days like this? All this quiet makes me think of the chapter in *Walden,* on 'Solitude,' where he raves about the virtues of the solitary, but then, just for a few sentences, he pulls back and says maybe he misses human companionship after all. And then he dismisses his own doubts as foolish. I've always been touched by that. I think he was more in conflict than he let on, what do you think? Anyway, I'm glad to be walking with you, not alone."

She looked demurely thankful. "Me too. About Thoreau? Probably, probably. But also, I think my father is projecting a little?" A mischievous face: "Honestly, Dad, I think you're not cut out for solitude, are you?"

"Well, you may be right. But that's not the point. I was thinking of poor Henry David. The fellow was protesting too much about the great virtues of soli-tude, then allowed himself that moment of doubt and suddenly took it back. Lest it ruin his book?"

"Cynical! But you must be a great teacher, Dad. You never allowed any of us to sit in. Why?"

"So you wouldn't discover the truth about me."

"False modesty," and Miranda waved her forefinger. Again. I shook my head.

"Change of subject, Dad. Mom's going to be sixty, and at Thanksgiving I mentioned the idea for a party, or a family get-together. She made 'tut-tut,' but I got the feeling she wanted it. Then last night, when I mentioned it, she almost got angry. 'No, thanks. I need nothing to celebrate getting older. Nice dinner with Dad. Finito.' What's up?"

Of course, I knew at once what was up. Julianna would do everything she could to create distance between her aging and mine. Use all her energy to push back the tide. Useless. Oh, indeed, she wanted no reminders of ending yet another decade.

"Miranda, I'm seriously debating something. Well, I may retire at the end of next year. Did Mom mention it?" I had not particularly thought of saying any-thing just yet, but the mention of a party for Julianna, and her reaction, pushed the news forward. It wanted out. She was clearly surprised, and jerked her head upward. No, she didn't know. Why? Why now? I could stay forever.

"Well, that's exactly the point. I mean staying forever is just letting life rule you. Letting the clock run out. And I decided to interrupt that helpless flow. Decided to take charge of my life, interfere with that clock, and make a decision against that 'forever.' Make any sense?"

"I'm not sure. Maybe. It isn't that false story spread about you? Mom told us. My God, sexual assault!"

"Oh? What did she call you together in a safe house and tell all while I was teaching?"

Miranda shook her head. "No, Mom called me and told me the gist. Then I called Helen and Seth, but he said he already knew something. Played it close to the chest. Mom told us to back off, so that's why you didn't hear any reactions. We were damned upset."

"Well, sorry about that. So was I! Yes, Seth found out by way of a friend who showed him the student newspaper. Seth came to see me at the office, a while ago. He was frightened."

"I can imagine. Poor Seth. He would be afraid."

I had the feeling that my eyes were literally being forced open. Of course, Seth would be frightened by anything about sex now. I hadn't fully understood that the day he arrived at my door. It must have been very threatening. Sitting on a rock, I patted my wet foot with one end of my handkerchief. Then I put my sock on and was lacing my walking boot. "Anyway, no Miranda, it's nothing to do with that. That whole business had a short life," I lied. "There just comes a time when you begin to sense things. It's not that I feel burned out. For a while I did. But now I just feel relief. And you know, I look forward to resting my spirit. Time to write a little. I've always wanted to try my hand at doing something without footnotes. I've come to detest them!" I grimaced, as if in pain. She laughed. "But I haven't signed on the dotted line. I have till July 1. About a month."

Miranda waited and then, "I guess you know. Who am I to say? What about Mom?"

"Oh, well, that's another story. Mom has unlimited energy. She just keeps going. I think retirement hasn't even entered her thoughts. She's peaking! And that's all right. You know she's five years younger. Her time will come. And she'll know it. In the meantime—"

Miranda again took my hand. We got up and resumed walking. It was warmer now. The breeze was gone. She removed her cotton sweater and tied it around her waist by its sleeves. A few cumulus clouds began to build over the pond.

"Well, I'm a little shocked," Miranda said. "Helen and Seth know you're that close?"

"No, not yet. But it's not an illness or something. They'll survive my retirement, yes?"

"Yes, of course. Just asking. But you do have that month."

"Yes. I do. Now Miranda, I've come clean. What's with you?"

To my surprise, she was quick and blunt with her answer.

"Robert and I have split."

I stopped in my tracks. "You've told Mom?"

"Yes. Look—I mean—it's not earthshaking?"

"Five years—?"

"More like four, Dad. Anyway, that's not all."

"What else? And why? Did Seth—I mean did that—"

"God, no! You're being unfair. Robert is no bigot. No, Seth had nothing to do with it."

"Anything special, then? Did you tell him bout my entanglement with that charge?"

"No, as a matter of fact. But it had nothing to do with outside stuff. Frankly, I think it was going to happen, I mean it started happening, long ago, even before—."

We were walking more briskly now. Miranda was swinging her arms, and I found it hard to keep pace. I told her to slow down, but she hardly did.

"'Before' you said?"

"I was pregnant. I lost the baby. It was just what they call 'fetal waste,'" she said with bitterness, "maybe six weeks." Now she was leaning against a tree, and tears came in a torrent. "Oh, Dad, I know this hurts you a lot. And Mom," and as she spoke I gave her my folded white handkerchief, one end of which was a little moist from wiping my foot, and I surrounded her body with my arms and kissed her on the forehead. "Lousy luck, Miranda, lousy luck. Did the thought of a child—"

"Yes and no. Robert wasn't exactly thrilled when I told him I was pregnant. But he was kind, thoughtful, even protective. Just not enthusiastic. Then once I had the miscarriage—I don't want to sound like one of those thirty-something TV shows, but, yes, I think he was frightened at the thought of a permanent relationship. Abortion was never an option for me, so he knew marriage would be the next step. I just think the idea of an instant family terrified him."

"When did this all happen? Why didn't you tell us?"

"Early April. I didn't want to burden you people with more. You had Seth, Grandfather had died. Mom told me about that bogus sex charge. Your back—there was a lot of stuff, that's all. And I had to get used to losing the baby and losing Robert."

April, I growled to myself. Cruellest of months, after all. Beginning of April. Time of the blizzard. "Losing? He initiated it?"

"Sort of. He was very good about the miscarriage. Rushed me to the hospital, stayed with me every moment, held my hand. But afterwards, he just seemed more and more remote, and I sort of knew. We both did. So we parted. I moved out a couple of weeks ago. We're still friends. You mustn't blame him. It happens."

"Yes," I said, "I know. It happens." We had begun to walk again and were within sight of the end. Or the beginning.

"Mom hinted something might be up with Robert, but not the other thing. I take it she knows about the miscarriage?"

"Yes. She said she'd let me tell you. I asked her to let me tell. You aren't angry?"

"No, no," I shook my head. "Angry? Sad—sad for you," and I embraced her again. For the remainder of our walk we were mostly silent. It took longer to reach the end than I thought, but perhaps the quiet made it seem that way. I felt that words would only make things worse. Talk was not wanted. But I was crushed. My Miranda, my dear, dear Miranda, and now how abandoned she looked. Her lover lost, the fruit of their loving lost. What now?

By the time we came home, Miranda had recovered and remarked that Mom would come soon, and we could all go out to dinner. "I'm starved. You cheapskate, you didn't even buy me an ice cream! Some father!" And I loved her even more just then, loved her way of making me feel better, Miranda the child who always worried about others. Miranda, our brave new world. What now?

As we ate dinner at Spanelli's (most of the other restaurants were booked with Commencement families), the Concord Police and Massachusetts State Police identified the body in the Concord river as Professor David Kominsky, "who had taught at the university and served for some time as its Dean of Faculty." When we came home from dinner there were two messages. Edith Sellers and Stanley Habers. Both delivered the news. True, I hadn't known Kominsky the way I had known Leon Adler, but we had just talked. Canoeing? Somehow it was difficult to imagine Kominsky in a canoe. The eleven o'clock news featured the death in its lead.

> "At this time the police conclude this was an accidental drowning. They tell us there was no sign of foul play. The dean at the university, where Kominsky had been teaching for nearly thirty-five years, and was himself Dean of Faculty some years ago, issued the following statement: 'Professor Kominsky was a valuable member of this university community. He had distinguished himself in his field and in service to the university when he was Dean of Faculty. This is a great loss for all of us, and he will be sorely missed.'"

We would need to make a condolence call to his wife, whom we knew only slightly. There were no children. Meanwhile, we still had to deal with bereft Miranda. Dinner was too silent, but we talked about her troubles. Miranda was remarkably together, faltering only when she said, "I'm thirty-one next birthday.

Even these days, it's getting late, no?" We reassured her that thirty, or well, thirty-one, was hardly the end of the line, and nowadays there were people in their fifties having children. "I'm not interested in some freak in Brazil, or wherever," she had said with a touch of temper, "and I'm not fifty, I'm thirty! Besides, I wasn't talking about children but about—I think it's time for nesting." But that was the only rough moment of the night. What we had said was dumb; adversity invites stupidity.

Sunday morning a few calls came in about the "Tragedy on the Concord River," as the Sunday *Globe* headlined it in the "City & Region" section. Old friends from other departments called, and we exchanged fond memories of our lost colleague. Yes, we all agreed, it was terrible. Why wasn't he wearing a life jacket? They hand them to you at the boat house and ask you to put them on! Did he have any experience canoeing? Why alone? Inevitably as people called back and forth, a rumor surfaced: *Was* it an accident? Some claimed to have seen Kominsky depressed of late, more down than usual. His health was frail. He was distressed by the appointment of the new dean. None of this made much sense to me. Appearances can lie, and besides I had just seen David Kominsky within the past week or so, and there was nothing unusual. Most likely, he simply took a silly step into an area he knew little about, a protest against routine. Canoes are notorious for flipping, and as for not wearing a life jacket, that was not hard to understand since he was ignorant of the dangers and was too impatient to follow instructions. The reports said the life jacket was found near the canoe. Most likely he had no clue how to put it on properly and just gave up on it, never realizing the possible consequences. Depressed, maybe. But suicide was not David's style. Too stubborn for that. But whatever reasons I offered to squelch the rumor it only gained momentum in the days that followed, and it was to grieve his widow when even the papers speculated about it, quoting "certain faculty members who did not wish their names to be used." Poor Kominsky! Even in death they haunted him.

Miranda did not speak much of her ordeal, though some of the details of the miscarriage she told Julianna, who later told me. It was a little worse than Miranda had revealed to me on Walden Pond. There had been a lot of bleeding and some anxious moments. But, no, there was no danger for future child-bearing, thank God for that. Miranda was never one to feel sorry for herself. She came home to tell us and to feel close to family. You don't e-mail or fax or even phone that kind of news.

"Don't you worry about me. I have a job I truly love, and I guess I'm not yet ancient. And while I'm not Helen—by the way is she still with that English T.A.?—I'm not closed to new relationships. I agree, four years is a long time, but not enough to despair, all right?" Her voice was steady, calm. "But you know, I'm tired. As I said, I want to nest." And she stood there in tears and took in our embraces like a child.

Still, we were touched by her quest for steadiness. She had carried it off—almost. Yes, she had come for comfort and some old-fashioned family-loving, but she was also aware that once that was achieved, just by being here, she had to reverse roles and be, if not the parent, the oldest child, which meant reassuring her parents. To my relief my possible retirement never came up.

Julianna drove Miranda to Logan late Sunday afternoon, and when she came back she looked as she felt—miserable.

"Darling," I said, "she's strong. She'll revive. I believe that, honestly. Is there more? Something I'm in the dark about?"

"No. It just seems that too many things are piling up, all in a single year. I can't wait for us to get away somewhere, and we haven't even made any plans."

I pondered. "You're right. It's been a helluva year, hasn't it? And you know what? We're still upright. I'm not making light of it, understand that, but in the scheme of things—"

"Optimist Jack?" she said—a little mockingly. "Well, yes, 'consider the alternative.'" She agreed, but still, "You know Jack, I'm weary to the bone. All that vaunted energy you always talk about? I'm tired—in mind, soul, and heart. What have I left out?"

"Body."

"Oh, yes, body. Of course, body. But," she added with a smirk, "don't get any ideas. I'm not joining you in blessed retirement just yet, if that's where it's ending up."

"Hope not! Two of us would double the fatigue. You have every right to be exhausted. It's the end of the year, and we always feel that way, but in addition, there's all the stuff that's hit the fan. Let yourself go."

She looked at me a little quizzically. "Whatever do you mean, 'let yourself go'? What do you have in mind? Well, you know what? I'm going to get my endorphins started on the treadmill. I notice you haven't been on it that much lately."

"Right after you," I assured her, but I knew I wouldn't keep that promise.

Monday morning. I am on the way to the office by eight-thirty. Two late papers from non-seniors are yet to come. The campus has a strange look about it, the reverse of September. Everywhere cars are lined up on the side of the three campus roads and the smaller one-ways that lead to some remote dorms. Parents and their children, sometimes students only, are packing up. The sidewalks are lined with stereos, computers, lamps, clothes, boom boxes, all the debris of a year. Seniors mostly, clearing out forever. And they would leave enough behind to keep the clean-up crew busy at least for a month or more. Most of the blossoming trees are in that in-between state, blossoms dead or dying, green leaves birthing, as if some painter were uncertain whether to create spring or summer. For a few days the campus will be empty, and then the summer session people would come in, a smaller crowd, but still a presence. And again cars and some baggage will line the roads, though many summer students lived off-campus.

I have not yet picked up my evaluations and so I slip into Angel's office and take the large manila envelope. Angel gives me that "Don't take them seriously" look, and I just nod. Back at the office, I decide to take three evaluations at random and read the essay part, which many of them have left blank. Finally I find three. Under the heading: "Below Please Write A Brief Summary Statement Of The Course And The Instructor" are the "essays," usually a few sentences.

The first:

> I liked this course. But the work was too much. There were too many books and the professor talked more and should have let the students talk more. But he's a nice guy.

I take the second and lay it on the desk. It is unusually long:

> While I do not have any specific criticisms of Professor Morris as a person—he is quite amiable—the course was far too low a level for an upper class elective. Assignments were too simple, and the number of books seemed to me to be on the short side. Surely we could have done more. Although Professor Morris is quite knowledgeable, he chose to allow students to talk endlessly, even when they were saying either nothing or were plain out of the loop. Also there was a good deal of repetitious explaining, which I suppose was deliberately aimed at those many students who did not seem to have a clue. In short, I felt I was being talked down to. Professor Morris might have tried to raise the level of others rather than sacrifice those who were eager to learn and ready for more sophistication.

This one I ponder. So well written. Who *is* this? Then I just feel awful for letting her down. Is it a "she"? The writing seems to be feminine, but that Julianna would have said is a silly litmus test for gender. Well, it doesn't matter. I hold the third and final evaluation in my hand, and it is very brief:

> I learned nothing from this class. The professor is a bore. I couldn't stand the reading. Ye gads!!!! He should call it quits!!!

Well, nothing much to cheer me up. Perhaps I will find a few more encouraging ones in the rest of the pack, but for now, thank you, I have seen enough. But almost without thinking, I retrieve a fourth. Its bold printed capital letters hit my eyes:

> PROF DIDDLER WILL GET HIS SOME DAY. HE'S A REAL BUM PRAYING ON ALL THOSE YOUNG STUDENTS! GOD SAVE HIS SOUL!

So at last! In my own class? But *who*? I closed my eyes and summoned up my students. Was it that sour looking fellow in the back row, Alan Scowcroft? Or that C-joke, Philip Bernstein? Why a male? Could be that gal who never had any expression on her face, Bianca Klamm? Or even a graduate student? What hits me is that it's someone who truly believes all this, someone devout, for that "PRAYING" was perhaps not a spelling error after all? Much as I concentrate nothing comes up. Folding the evaluations I put them in my briefcase. Actually, as my deep sigh signals, I feel relief. It is over. (Hadn't I said that once or twice before?)

Little is left but to clean the office of a year's pile-up of now useless paper. This will take a day or two, and I begin this familiar routine with the efficiency of an old hand, thinking meanwhile of Miranda's sudden loneliness, of Seth's recent silences, of Julianna's edginess, of David Kominsky's body in the Concord river.

Knock and entry simultaneously. Stan Habers at the door. He closes it and sits down.

"Six!" he says, and his face is ashen. What? His PSA, it's six! "For God's sake haven't you had any test?" I am surprised by the quick invasion and think quickly and realize Habers is referring to that ritual most men over fifty now undergo once a year, the prostate exam, once limited to the offending forefinger now accompanied by a blood test. Sure I had. Every year. Well, then I knew that six is no good. It's supposed to be two or less! What's mine? I don't know. I'm not sure. (Shades of my cholesterol!) My doctor sends me this sheet and mostly checks off things. So if he checks the PSA, I assume it's within range. Assume? His own doctor may be one of those who thinks you're going to die from something else. There's this school of thought, you know, that prostate cancer can grow slowly, so why interfere with an old guy, it can make things worse—

"Hold, it, Stan, hold it. Did your man say it was cancer?"

"No."

He was letting him make a decision whether to take a biopsy. Didn't make a fuss. All well and good; he looked as if he just started shaving. They all look young, I remember Julianna saying, "But what exactly did your doctor say?"

"Not much! No big deal, six."

Anyway, if he couldn't screw anymore—did I know that was one of the side effects, impotence—and incontinence—God, and Habers literally wrings his hands. I have never seen him in such a state.

"Calm down, Stan, calm down. Get a second opinion. I've read about all the controversies. Why rush into a biopsy?"

"To be honest, he didn't suggest it. But I pressed him, and he said, well that was up to me."

"But he didn't think it necessary?"

"No. But as I said, to him I'm just an old bastard who probably can't get it up any more, so he can be cool about it."

"You know what? Julianna's cousin is a urologist at Mass General. I'll get you his name."

"You don't know his name? He's related, no?"

"Well, I do know his name. Herbert Grossman. I just thought I'd get his number and all that."

Habers is poised, pencil in hand, and he takes a slip of paper from my desk. He bends over. "I can get the damned number myself. Herbert Crossman. An uncle of Julianna's?"

"Grossman. With a 'G'—no, a cousin. Second or third, but we're in touch. Say you're a colleague."

"A neurologist?"

"No, I said a *u*rologist."

"Oh, great! I'll call him. Jack, sex may not be all, but I'm not ready for diapers and only kissing."

"Stop jumping to conclusions. Call Grossman. Make an appointment. And you'll see, it's probably just a benign enlargement. We're getting older, fellow, live with it!"

Habers frowns. "I don't want to!" Placing the piece of paper in his shirt pocket he turns to me: "Do you get up in the middle of the night?" I think a moment and shake my head. No, not routinely. Habers looks disappointed. Then he shrugs, and he gets up and leaves as quickly as he has come.

As soon as he is gone, I call Dr. Hoffman to check on my PSA. Hazel promises to have him call back, but it would be after four. She, of course, cannot give out such information. I understand. For the rest of the day I make an effort to forget my PSA.

Everyone seems to know that I'm thinking of retiring. It has "been out there" and I don't care. On the way to the office I pick up my mail and among the junk of ads and fliers I see an envelope whose shape I recognize. It simply has my name on it and placing the junk mail on a table I open it. Ah! Famous Quotations Ltd., Inc. Again.

> For solitude sometimes is best society,
>
> And short retirement urges sweet return.
>
> —John Milton

The card is signed—as the one like it once before, M. Golden. But I note its cost: $6.00. Wasn't the first one $5.00? Inflation in so short a time? No, maybe more words. That greedy Golden, I say under my breath, tongue's hanging out to take up my modern poetry and fiction courses! But, if I do go, there won't be any "sweet return," Golden. Would my obituary card sent to Julianna quote a quatrain and cost $8.00? No, I don't bear grudges, but right now I don't much like M. Golden. In truth, never have.

By the time I settle down, it is nearly four and the phone rings. It's Dr. Hoffman. What brings on this sudden worry about my PSA? Any problems? Stream steady? Yes, fine. I explain a bit casually about a colleague. Well, the last PSA was 1.0—well within normal, even below, he'd say. I thank him for his prompt call. Nothing to it. Was I feeling okay otherwise? How was the back? Not bad, end of semester. Stress? Better. Good. Happy semester's over, yes? Yes, time to recoup. Well, have a nice summer. Keep in touch. Thanks, I will. Bye. Bye. And I blow out a mighty breath. All right, that's good, I don't need that to worry about on top of everything else.

After returning some library books, I'm back to the office to draft next year's syllabi. I stretch myself and walk to the water fountain. It's hot outside, my mouth is dry, I gulp the cool, refreshing water for a long time. A short distance away I hear the relentless, regular thump-beat of the Xerox machine, which occupies a small cubicle next to Angel's office. But I do not look to see who is there.

Julianna and I made our courtesy call to David Kominsky's widow. They were Russian Orthodox, but religion seemed to play no role in their lives. Word was that visits would be welcomed on given dates. The modest house appeared in genteel disrepair, the living room clean but cluttered. Knick-knacks sprouted on shelves and in a cabinet, the rug was worn, and no pictures interrupted the dull, yellow walls. Most of the furniture was old oak, and the couch and easy chairs were covered dark brown. Platters of food stood on plastic place mats on the dining room table; next to these some soft drinks in a bowl of ice and an oversized coffee urn. Julianna and Mary Kominsky embraced briefly; I offered my hand first, but she embraced me as well. A little heavy for her size, her gray hair was neatly tied in a bun. She wore a plain dark dress. Thanking us both for coming, she offered food, which we declined politely. She sat down in an easy chair and introduced David's sister from Montreal and a cousin from Iowa. A colleague from Chemistry and his wife had preceded us; no one else. I recognized the face, but we all pretended to know one another better than we did as we shook hands.

Mary Kominsky then said, very quietly, that David's death was not what some people thought, David was not the type. After all, a wife would know. He had told her people encouraged him to get some sun, he looked so pale, so he planned a walk in the Great Meadow. Never heard anything about canoes. If she had known she'd have stopped him. He couldn't even swim. And he was happy when he left. It was an adventure. For years he had hated Commencement and loved the idea of playing hooky. To be honest, he hadn't gone often, not since that dean business. David never liked crowds.

When I heard the reference to people telling him to get sun, I gave a start. Hadn't I told David to do just that? My God, I shrank, I'm responsible! After about twenty-five minutes we left. More brief embraces. More thank-yous. More encouraging words. Once in the car, I turned to Julianna, "I was one of those who told him to get some sun. Who would think he would go canoeing, and without a life jacket!" Julianna touched my arm. After all, she was sure others had told him to get some sun—it was just good advice. "Good heavens, Jack," she said, "it's not your fault." But for days after I clung to my guilt.

Natasha and the children had come home, at least for a while, and she looked rested and calm. The children had done well in Grosse Point, and even at their age, grandparent indulgence was plentiful and welcomed, especially by Rachel and Benjamin who were, of course, still teenagers. Natasha said she had not made up her mind to sell the house, but she was thinking of moving to a smaller one. But what happens when the kids marry and have children? She would want to have a house big enough to put up everybody. Leon would have wanted that. We advised her not to make any hasty decisions. But another winter here in this big house? With two children going off to college soon? Yes, that was a problem, we agreed. Had she ever thought of renting for a while? No, she didn't want anyone messing with her stuff, she just felt it was an invasion. We understood. Well, then, we said, wait and see, and she agreed that she would wait.

Epilogue

And so the summer begins; the semester is really at an end. I have one more visit to make to the office. Jane Wheaton is coming to chat about her written proposal that had so impressed me when she talked about it at lunch that day of the blizzard.

As I approach my office, still almost a hallway's length away, I am certain I see a figure standing close to my door. First I stop, then I begin to walk briskly when the figure, hearing me approach, abruptly turns. A woman. For an instant our eyes meet; then she steps rapidly toward the other end of the hallway, heels (or so it sounds) hitting the floor, past Habers' office, toward the staircase. At first I'm totally unable to place the face, I have only had a glimpse, and that in shadows. As I stand in front of the door, key in hand, I see a large maroon poster taped to it, and on it in bold black Magic Marker letters: PROF DIDDLER. From my depths I mutter "'psychogenic deep structures'? I'll be damned!" Was it that older graduate student, who had dropped my fall seminar and had stared into the air when I didn't satisfy her questions? She of the red fingernails and the Mont Blanc pen? *This* was the culprit? How could this be? An adult? She hated me that much? And what of the male voices on the phone? Recruited? A conspiracy ... And the class evaluation? Well, those were easy to hand in late, "Oops, forgot to give this to the monitor, Professor Morris' class," and how would Angel know all the faces in my class? What possible motive to go that far? Oh, as has been famously said by Habers' "man"—"motiveless malignancy." How awful! How very awful! But soon I wonder. Am I being paranoid? May not even have been her at all. Sighting was too brief, too sketchy. Besides, why would *she* care? And anyway, I never saw her place anything on the door.

Tearing the sheet from the door I have opened, I stare at the paper in my hand, crumple it, then straighten it and tear it into small pieces, which find a home in the wastepaper basket. Has anyone seen it? Doubtful, this early in the morning. But was it really her? Have I seen the enemy? A fleeting glance, it makes little sense. Perhaps I will never know. I believe I'm in the wrong office, for a large black tower and a sizeable black screen (like Dr. Golumb's) have taken residence on my computer table. So Sir Walter does not joke. Longingly I look for my old box that has perhaps saved me from perdition, but it's gone.

It occurs to me I have not looked up the word "diddle" in a regular dictionary, only in a dictionary of slang where, among other obscene meanings, I had puzzled over "child molester." During our confrontation in the Board Room, I called Milicent L. Jacobs a child. Something distant about a dream and a little girl, but that memory evaporates. I look at the expanded dictionary in the departmental office: "To cheat, or swindle, or victimize." Ah, but to use the word that way would be the work of a very sophisticated mind, in keeping with my suspect. But conviction gives way to doubt, and once more I'm in the dark. I will need to give this more thought. Later.

But later will not do. Dimly I recall something by Poe. Is it called "The Diddler"? Is it an essay, a tale? *The Complete Works of Edgar Allan Poe* are soon found on the bottom shelf of the furthest bookcase from the desk. Bound in distinctive blue, I picked them up at a flea market in Vermont. The pages of the ten volumes are brittle and dusty, but the print is large. Under "Essays and Criticism," nothing. There are no indexes. But under "Tales" I hit the mark. "Diddling"—a brief piece, and I read eagerly. Poe begins straight off: "Diddling is somewhat difficult to define." But soon he offers a list of characteristics that profile the diddler: minuteness, interest, perseverance, ingenuity, nonchalance, originality, impertinence, and—italicized—*grin*. Grin? I turn the page. "Your *true* diddler winds up all with a grin. But this nobody sees but himself. He grins ... when his allotted labors are accomplished...." Placing the volume on my lap, I stare into space, then nod. A nerve has been prodded, I can't say why. I close and replace the volume. Like one of those sidewalk artists, I sketch my face into a strange grimace intoning in a high voice and louder than I mean to, "High diddle diddle,/The cat and the fiddle," this the epigraph to Poe's piece. And now the dream unfolds in more detail.

Jane Wheaton arrives to the minute. Today she is dressed informally in white, slacks and jersey, no makeup, her hair even shorter. Whether it is end of the year fatigue or a natural letdown, I'm less impressed with the written work (which I quickly scan) than by the words she had spoken at that lunch. Still, it's a good enough job. If I left would I want to direct her dissertation beyond retirement? That's not unusual. But would she want *me*? No, probably Habers.

When she leaves, I see the road obstructed now by large, mushrooming trees. For the first time since I've made my tentative decision, a tsunami of doubts threatens. Am I on the brink of doing something foolish? Am I allowing fatigue to drive me to a hasty retreat (as Julianna had hinted)? What if, after a summer's rest, I feel rejuvenated and return in the fall to regret it all? I retrieve the Xerox copy of the retirement papers from my drawer and hold them, staring at the small print—again.

Yet the unease that had coursed through me like a disease since September is now absent. After all, hadn't Dr. Golomb said doubts were only natural? I'm sitting upright, rigid, my back like a slab. Hoffman would be proud of me. It is not tension but resolve. *I* am making the decision, either way, and that itself is good. I slap my palm on the desk. Yes, it feels right. I have banged hard, but the pain brings pleasure, like recognizing for the first time in a long stretch the solidity of my body. I have regained a sense of my self. With purpose, with lucidity, yes, I will choose my future rather than being its victim. Whatever I do, I am the engineer. And again—although this time more gently—I slap the desk.

Out of my window I glimpse a group of summer session students, men and women in shorts, jerseys, tank-tops and T-shirts. They appear to be lounging and laughing happily. Too far to see faces, but their arms are flailing carelessly in every which direction. The ageless students, who come and go and come. Oh, yes, I would miss them. The young in one another's arms—but no longer in mine?

For what seems longer than it is, I sit and reflect, a little scared, not so certain as I was just moments ago. Spatial distance again, as on "Hill 4" that late afternoon when I bore witness to the sun vanishing into Boston harbor. Visions of me sitting home alone, watching Julianna briskly move out the door, waving cheerily, staring out the window at the bird feeder, sighting Betsy on the lawn, irrigating (or worse). My spirits howl. Gradually I reassure myself that my choice must not be hasty, that I must continue to carefully place all the plus and minus points side by side. I have a whole month.

Glancing at the syllabi for the fall, slowly I am aware of an absence: the surge of excitement at the prospect of teaching this or that book. Gradually, I reclaim a certainty that I should sign my name and be done with it, and my breathing is rapid as if I have been chasing that certainty in a run. I know. Or do I? I do not sign and return the documents to their safekeeping in my desk: in any case they are only Xeroxes. But I'm pretty sure of my decision, so I act on it. I eye those grade books I have so recently searched out. No, these I will keep. Infanticide I cannot commit, since I have always considered my students my other children. Teaching is a form of parenting. Slowly I nod in agreement with myself. Ah, these other children: some have been wondrous; most middling; a few hopeless. But even some of the hopeless ones tried. Yes, even you, Milicent L. Jacobs. God, how hard you must have tried!

My class notes, neatly placed in stacks of folders marked by class number or course name—they, on the other hand, will have to go. It's a start. For the one semester that might remain next year, I will extemporize. If my teaching life would die, then so too must the incarnate version of the spirit that held that life together. They are my talisman and deserve a ceremony. A bonfire in the back-yard is impractical. Shredding them in Angel's large shredder suggests violence, and there is no resentment in my heart. Recently the university has begun a recy-cling program, and on each floor a very large recycling bin stands ready to receive. If nothing else I need this cleansing; the dust has settled on these mementos too long.

When they died, the Anglo-Saxon kings, their bodies surrounded with trea-sures, were placed into coffin-boats and pushed out to sea. Some cultures prefer flames. Some hide the dead under earth. And my treasures? Into a recycling can? But then perhaps they will not die but be reincarnated, become blank pages for someone else's notes? It's an amusing thought. Recycled notes—that's probably what some of my students think! One by one I begin removing pages from the folders (the folders I turn inside out and spare, I'm not sure why) and build piles on my desk. For large lecture classes, notes were typed, though I never read, always spoke mostly from what I memorized, not word for word but in glacial patterns. Now I read an occasional page and hesitate—should I save it for future use? What future? If I change my mind, I won't need these relics. Later sheets merely have phrases, page numbers, key words, key concepts. In the last few years only note cards. Well, they would all be consigned to their respective pile, all of them, sheets and cards.

At first I remove paper clips when I find them, but soon I have to tug at them, old and rusty as they are, and I decide to hell with them, let them all go as they are, keep the shroud intact. It is tedious work, and after nearly two hours I have amassed three piles, each about two feet high, on my desk. They look like the skyscrapers of my empire. I hear Yeats:

> All things fall and are built again,
>
> And those that build them again are gay.

In a separate pile, the note cards, by comparison, appear small. Now I need to fill my trash can with as much as I dare to carry.

Stealthily I walk down the hall to the recycling bin, my shoes on the linoleum floors hardly audible, as I take long steps. I have the impression I have murdered and dismembered someone and am discarding the parts. Well, one could see it that way, but I prefer not to. To my delight, at this time of day, the bin is almost empty. As I turn my trash can upside down, most of the time the pages sink into the large receptacle with a plump, but occasionally a few pages flutter upward as if in protest against their unceremonious dispatch. But what did papers know of ceremony? Once, in my haste, I drop some pages to the floor and quickly crouch in a knee bend scrambling to pick them up with both hands and deposit them into their grave. After many trips between office and recycling can, I'm exhausted, and when I'm finally done, I slump into my chair and listen to my heart beat. Sweat runs down my face, and I'm wet under my armpits. A sharp pain in my back sends greetings; the knee bend has done me no good. As usual the air conditioning is not working or still hasn't been turned on yet, and the day has depressed itself into a humid, hazy vapor.

For yet another time I walk to my little wooden table and return all the books I have used for the year into my bookcases, including the Eliot. I also add the Yeats volume, because I now have two copies and want one close by next fall. So this is it. But Eliot has written in the very *Four Quartets* I have taught in the fall that "There is no end, but addition …" Is this true? Everything adds up and gathers moss. So they say. Not quite right, but never mind. In this life, surely, there are no endings, only temporary pauses when one draws deep breaths before setting out again. Leaving here wouldn't change that either. More than thirty years I have come and gone to this office, and now? As I am about to place the Yeats into the shelf, I open the volume and search for a line and find it. "Around me the images of thirty years …," and a little forlorn, I think of the accumulation of friendships, past and present, the students, so many of them fine and generous, and my eyes fall on the last line of the poem, "And say my glory was I had such friends." *Had*. With that I close the book, push it between Thomas Hardy and Eliot (I have long ago undone my alphabetical order), and I am ready to leave, overcome with a strange feeling that the cleaning has prepared a beginning rather than an end.

On the way out in the hall, I feel a tug from behind. "Jack, have a moment? In my office." It is Stan Habers. Once in his office, Habers shuts the door. Walking over to the large picture window he stares longingly at the group of summer students I have noticed earlier. Before turning to face me, I catch his eyes in profile, wide open, nothing lecherous in them, not at all. But they home in on what he sees with joy and relief, as if he needs all this to continue. My eyes have been wistful; Habers' are still *there*. Yes, I am now on the way to the other side of "there"—almost. Habers appears to have put on weight, looks a bit pudgy in the middle. Perhaps the summer garb, T-shirt, no sweater, no jacket, makes the bulges more visible.

"You know, Jack, in the summer the students look more inviting. Especially the women!" We are both looking at the same students congregated below. Their shouting and laughter penetrates the closed windows.

"Some cousin that wife of yours has!" I'm puzzled, I have forgotten. Habers has called the urologist I recommended? What did he say? Well, it took forever to get him. But he said reassuring things, like for your age, what do you want? He said "something like, hey, that's within range, a bit high. If the count gets to 8 or 9 and keeps climbing call me back. Meantime, relax and have yourself a nice summer." That's it. "What did you want?" I ask. "Sounds great to me." Habers looks hurt. "I'm not complaining," comes the reply.

"Well, the way you started, it sounded as if he suggested penile amputation."

"Hey, Jack, wise guy in your old age," and he gives me a very healthy slap on the back. (I remember what he said when I nearly broke his nose.) Off for the summer? Yes, off for the summer.

Habers says he can't believe I might be packing it in after next year. Why? I'm irritated. "Why?" Why does everybody ask me that? "Your man," I say, "wrote, 'That time of year thou mayst in me behold …,'" and Habers continues, "'When yellow leaves, or few, or none, do hang …'"—God, Jack, *you* autumnal! These days, we all live longer. Wasn't I more like late summer? I say "no." Then: "Why does Shakespeare say 'or none, or few'? Logically, the sequence should be 'or few, or none'?" Habers offers a sly smile. He knows why. The poet has moved from early autumn too quickly to the onset of winter—"none"—so "few" resolves it. It's middle to late autumn. A reprieve. End of story. So where does *Jack Morris* see himself, eh? "Well," I say, pursing my lips and nodding in agreement with Habers' take on the line, "to me it feels like middle autumn—some yellow leaves, perhaps a few, no, not yet none." Habers winces. He hates that kind of talk. "So? A few leaves left?" In any case, I suggest, my man was more direct, and I hear the words,

> That is no country for old men. The young
>
> In one another's arms …

I look at the circle of young people under the window. A woman in tank top and shorts and a bare-chested man are throwing a Frisbee that neither can catch very often. Others seem to be singing and rocking, arms across their neighbor's shoulders.

"Anyway, I haven't decided. I have a month, but I'm pretty sure." Habers looks glum. Not him, he shakes his head, he'll look down there at those young ones forever. "Oh," I say, "you're younger. See you in five!" With nonchalance, he shrugs his shoulders. Well, if you have to, you have to. But did I know retirement can be deadly? The old body and mind stop being stimulated. That's why so many people drop dead so soon after retirement. I own I'm not aware of that statistic. But Habers persists. He read somewhere about 30% within two years. I must get a hobby or two. Habers knows one guy from BU—he retired early and he lost weight, started losing his hair, had teeth problems, had to swallow Viagra every time he—. But I have heard enough. I'd be okay. Let's not go that direction. Please, no more anecdotes, no more statistics.

Habers' face squirms into the hurt look again. Do I know he's thinking of going back to his "man"? Going to write *the* book on *Hamlet*. Starting this summer. Has he got a title? Sort of. How about *Hamlet: The Last Words*? Do I like it? He's grinning. It has a goddamned good double entendre, no? Great title, I agree. Go for it! He promises me first dibs if he has a book sale. Do I know how many books he has from the stuff he'd been crapping around with? I shrug. No, no idea. How many? Well, to sell or give away? Both. Grand total, two hundred and twenty—give or take. I raise my eyebrows. Really? I want to leave now but marvel at this man of numbers. No doubt he has counted them precisely. Then he asks me to guess who persuaded him to go back to Shakespeare, and I venture Bentwick, but Habers laughs. No, Carol Gunderson. At first, Habers says, he thinks it is all too "retro." Anyway, Carol says "retro" is in, look at some of the new cars, and anyway she encourages him *after* she knows of her tenure, so she isn't trying to butter him up. No, I agree, she likes you. *Me?* The "patriarchal tyrant," or whatever she called me. I laugh. Detecting a blush on his cheeks, I say ideology is always trumped by more personal things. Habers' face droops with annoyance. What's *that* supposed to mean? Nothing, nothing, I protest, and I realize he has slept with her. "Anyway," he says to me, "have a nice summer, my best to the better half." We both want to shut this conversation down now, and I'm grateful because I've become entangled, thinking about the giggles Edith Sellers thought she heard behind Habers' office door. I will hand off the regards to Julianna. And I wish Habers a nice summer, too, and salute with my hand, open the door and leave him standing by the window gazing again at the students below. But I, too, steal a last glance.

Smiling, I shake my head. Stanley Habers looking at summer-clad girls, relieved that his machinery is intact. And he will write that book on *Hamlet*, and it will be outrageously good, like all his work. And I'm a little sad that I might not be around when, several years from now, he would have marched into my office to say, "1258, the first three months," or some such figure, referring to the number of copies of *Hamlet: The Last Words* sold. Ah, yes, I would miss Stan Habers. For all his quirks, he is at the core a good man. And if it comes to it, he will literally give you the shirt off his back, grumbling in the process.

I make my way down the hallway and am about to turn to the stairs when I notice Leon Adler's door. I stop as if a hand is pushing me back. The door opens with a turn of the knob, and I place one foot into the office. Then the other. Empty. It has barely been touched since I visited it a few days after the memorial, except the computer has been shut down; the book is closed; the coffee mug cleaned. Obviously Natasha has made no effort to retrieve anything, and the department, out of respect or neglect, has not interfered. September. It seems so much longer! Yes, I have become more used to Leon's absence now, or is it per-haps only an inner ache I'm still reluctant to give recognition? Oh, I have missed Leon, but after my monologue on Hill 4, I have seen him through a different lens. For a long time his absence was his presence, painful. Denial. Now, no con-versations were left. Leon was gone. Summer may change all that, for the summer was a time we hung out together as families: trips to the Cape; the Adlers came up to visit us in Vermont; lots of fun searching for new restaurants, sharing and judging dinners. No, we would never have friends like that again, too late, too old. And Natasha, I guess, will eventually move to Grosse Point. As I shut the door almost tenderly, as if on tiptoes so as not to disturb, I move toward the stairs and then walk slowly down. What is it I'm so afraid to disturb, as much now as on that earlier visit?

Now taking deliberate steps, I hear a distant birdsong and the sounds of the summer students, happy and in full throat. In their beginning is my end. At last my year has come full stop. As I pass my building, my eyes roam and then fix on that lively crowd (the same that Habers had eyed so longingly), dominated by a cigarette-smoking woman with punk-red hair, a gold earring hanging from one of her eyebrows, sitting on the top stone stair of my home away from home. She looks vaguely familiar. I strain to catch her full face as she holds court, laughing and smoking and talking, all in turns. From the top part of my bifocals, shielding myself from the sun, I am finally able to take in her whole face, and there can be no mistake, not this time. No mirage in the snow. Not a dream. This is Milicent L. Jacobs. Consumed with compassionate forgiveness, and chastened never to repeat a mistake, I walk over to the group and raise my hand.

"Hi, Milicent!"

The woman never turns. She averts my eyes and keeps talking, laughing, inhaling from a long cigarette hanging from the side of her mouth and exhaling puffs upwards toward a nearly cloudless sky. Now she is trying to blow circles. I have no choice but to keep walking, and as I do I begin to grin, grin like a *true* diddler, my allotted labors accomplished. She has paid me back in full! This time, unlike Sisyphus, no rock looms in front of me. Now I hear the birds clearly, chatty and eager, not silent like the yellow warbler on that sultry day last August. I recall M. Golden's "Famous Quotations" condolence card that had cost $5.00: "I can't go on, I'll go on."

And why not?

Maybe.

978-0-595-42299-9
0-595-42299-3

Printed in the United States
75181LV00004B/43-90